Ashes

V.J. Gage

TABLE OF CONTENTS

CHAPTER ONE

J ade pulled back the faded floral curtain of her second-story bedroom window and took one final look through the dreary, rain-spattered day. Her head was still pounding from the torrent of warm tears she had shed during the police investigation that morning. Until now, Jade had been unable to find even a second to absorb the full repercussions of what happened. She thought of her mother's body, cold and lifeless at the bottom of the basement steps. She was gone for good, and however bad things may have been before the accident, Jade knew they were about to become worse.

She heard the wail of the ambulance sirens as they took her mother away. Even the closed window couldn't muffle the sounds of official voices as people on the driveway below discussed the tragic events. Jade could see several of the police officers shaking their heads as they continued to take notes. Neighbors stood on the sidewalk, hoping for a snippet of information they could share with one another.

"Jade, what will we do now? I'm scared." Crystal whispered as she looked to Jade for comfort. "This is the worst thing that could have happened to us. Dad might be passed out in his chair now, but what will happen when he wakes up? You have to do something!"

I'll think of something," Jade promised, trying to keep her voice even, not wanting to alarm her youngest sister Amber, who lay rocking on the other side of the bed with her legs curled under her tiny body.

Jade thought of their mother's body, cold and lifeless at the bottom of the basement steps. She was gone for good. And however, bad things may have been before the accident; Jade knew they were about to become worse. She turned away from the window. The sun was just beginning to pierce through the dense, gray clouds. A beam of light shone through the window encircling Crystal and Amber, giving them both an angelic look. As if from nowhere, a song Jade's mother used to sing came to her mind.

"Don't worry, be happy!"

Her mother, Jewell, had loved that song from the first moment she had heard it in the eighties. It had become Jewell's theme song, like a lifeline through the hellish days of her life with Sam. Amber, the youngest, now eleven, held her baby blanket tightly in her small hand while she stroked her face with the other. She rocked back and forth in her usual way. It was at times like this that Jade was glad Amber was so different. Amber seemed untouched by the outside world. Her inability to attach herself to anything real sheltered her from its harsh realities. Jade knew Amber would never be able to cry over their mother's death. But Amber would be able to sense her two older sisters' mood, and today's events would only make her draw further into herself. Jade could never remember Amber making as much as a sound, even as a baby. Amber's eyes could fixate on an object while she rocked and stared for hours, an action that made her father go ballistic. Now that their mother was gone, she and Crystal would have to make sure Sam kept his hands to himself.

Their father treated Amber like a freak. Even her musical gift didn't soften his hatred. However, when Amber played the piano, the heavens would open up, and angels would whisper in Ambers's ear. Jade thought that if anyone were listening, they would be transported to a place only in their dreams. That was when Jade knew her sister was perfect and that there is hope even in a moment of despair.

Jade walked over to her bed. Crystal made room for her, turning slightly so that she could face Jade while still gaining comfort from Amber's rocking motion, who wiggled her bottom so that she would still have a connection to Crystal. Once Jade was curled up beside Crystal's warm body, they both pulled the worn old comforter up around their slim necks, making sure Amber was covered in the process. The room was warm with the window closed, but as was often the case, the comforter was more reassuring than real warmth. It helped to soothe the gripping chill deep in the pits of their stomach.

Crystal finally said what Jade was afraid to say. "You know, with mom gone, we will never be able to live with dad and survive?"

To live with Sam, you needed all the skills and guts you could muster. It was always Crystal, the realistic one, who would meet the challenge head-on. Her fifteen years spent with their brutal father made her the one sister most likely to prevent Sam from doing the unimaginable. They say middle children are like that, and Crystal certainly fits the mold. Once she got a hold of something, she seldom let go or backed down.

"I don't see how we can survive without mom. We will suffer a lot more than we already have." Crystal said.

She didn't say more. She didn't have to. It was the nightmare that Jade had been living since she had gone through puberty. It was bad enough that Jade always had to be careful never to be alone with her father. Still, she also worried about the possibility of future abuse when Crystal started to blossom into a pretty young woman. And then there was Amber. Jade knew Crystal sensed the danger their dad posed and had done everything to be as unattractive as possible. It was her way of hiding the fact that she was maturing. Sensing her father's sick looks made Jade shudder, and she knew Crystal would do anything not to fall prey to his evil taunts and unholy touch.

"I know, but don't worry, I promise I won't let anything happen to you or Amber."

Jade squeezed her sister's hand. She hoped it would never come to this, but now she knew that Crystal was right. They would have to deal with their father, but how? Jade put her trembling hand under her head and rested on her elbow.

"Try and get some sleep because we will need all of our strength," Jade said, pushing back her tears.

Crystal would have been an outgoing, demanding child in a different environment, but with Samuel Walker as a father, Crystal was sullen and angry. The way she dressed said it all, black, black, and blacker.

Sam simply scowled at Crystal and moved away from her as much as possible. He was always afraid of the things he didn't understand.

After a while, Jade moved away from Crystal, who had finally fallen asleep. She pulled the comforter further up under her chin. She loved the smooth feeling of the worn old comforter. It smelled clean and fresh the way laundry did for the first few hours after a wash. It was one of the last things her mother had touched before the accident, and Jade was sure she could smell her mother's clean, floral scent on the comforter. Her thoughts of her mother brought a new rush of warm tears to her face. Her dear sweet mother, Jade, had never heard Jewell speak a harsh word toward anyone, not even Sam.

Jewell had stopped loving Sam years ago, but she bore the burden of Sam with grace. Jewell tried to leave once. The imprint of the violence she endured was still visible on her hand. Leaving wasn't an option; Sam took no prisoners. Jewell had learned to squeeze what joy she could out of each day. Jade knew it was Jewell's fear of what Sam would do to the girls if she were to step out of line that kept her with him. Now Jewell was gone, and Jade would decide for her and her sister's futures. She was the oldest, and the care of her sisters would be her burden.

Jade tried to hold back the stream of tears that ran down the side of her face into her ear while a few drops found their way to her pillow, which would soon be soaked. They would join the thousands of other tears Jade had cried during her seventeen years.

What was she going to do?

Jewell had done all she could to protect them. In the end, even she didn't survive. Jade took one final ragged breath and hoped that the evening would bring her some peace. Thank God detective Dennis kortovich had arrived first. It had made what had happened to Jewell and the horror of the moment so much easier.

CHAPTER TWO

Detective Dennis Kortovich sat back in his old but comfortable swivel chair behind a large, functional desk. He had spent the last few hours updating his current file. His next-door neighbor had an accident, and after falling down the stairs and breaking her neck, Dennis knew things next door would get rough. Sam was a very dangerous man, and now that Jewell was gone, Dennis feared something horrible could happen. He would have to keep an eye on the girls and make sure they were safe.

Dennis looked at the pictures above his desk, a slow smile crossing his face. He and his partner, Chuck O'Brien, dressed in full uniform, were shaking hands with the Mayor; big Cheshire grins spread on their faces. Their first award together. Many more had followed, but this had been their first case and the beginning of a great friendship. With his off-the-wall sense of humor, Chuck had made the past several years more enjoyable. Dennis heard someone approach, and he knew who it was even before he appeared in the doorway. Partnerships were like marriages; after a while, you got used to each other. Once in a while, you become so in tune, you could finish each other's sentences.

"What's up?" Chuck sat down across from Dennis, trying unsuccessfully to cross his short, chubby legs. Chuck had a donut in one hand and a coffee in the other.

Dennis turned to the new case at hand. The Superintendent has given an immediate assignment. Judge Switzer's daughter. She's gone missing." Dennis indicated a file that sat in front of Chuck. "He has asked for us. The Superintendent agreed to assign us to this case at the judge's request. We're to be at his home in less than an hour." Dennis grabbed his jacket from the back of his chair while he continued to fill Chuck in on the case's details.

Chuck and Dennis were usually involved in homicide cases known as heaters, the kind of cases that which the 'press' or the' higher-ups' put unusual pressure on the police department. The latest case involved a serial killer, and there had been more slayings in six months than at any other -time. The press had been all over it, and Dennis and Chuck had become mini-celebrities. With a case as high profile as Judge Switzer's missing daughter, once again, it meant the heat was on.

Judge Switzer was one of the most respected Judges on the bench. For those lucky enough to have him rule on a case, they were assured fair and impartial treatment.

"Judge Switzer's kid can't be more than fourteen or fifteen. He's nuts about her," Chuck said.

Dennis remembered meeting the Judge's daughter at a birthday party the Judge had thrown for his wife's fiftieth birthday. She was the youngest of four children, the only daughter. All of the boys were at least twenty, and Mandy, his only girl, was the apple of her daddy's eye.

"How long has she been missing?" Chuck began to gulp down his coffee and make short work of his donut.

"Just overnight, but the family is bedside themselves," Dennis responded.

"Whatever happened to the twenty-four-hour policy before we become involved?" Chuck stood, throwing his empty cup into the wastebasket beside Dennis's desk.

"Policy is like an old pair of shorts. They get changed whenever things get too uncomfortable or start to stink. If the Judge's daughter doesn't show up in the next twenty-four hours, her disappearance will make headlines, and all hell will break loose. Let's hope she just has a boyfriend somewhere and spent the night out gazing at the stars." Dennis ran his hand over his mustache, something he always did when he was puzzled over a case.

He looked up at the" Dick Tracy" clock on his office wall, a gift from his daughters for his fiftieth birthday. Dennis felt a shiver run down his spine at the thought of anything happening to one of his daughters.

"You know if anything goes wrong with this case, it will be our asses on the line," Chuck stated. "I hate anything political, and this has all the signs of a suicide mission."

Dennis gave Chuck a nod of agreement as he wiped the crumbs from his desk, the remnants of Chuck's donut.

"This is what happens when you're good." Dennis smiled.

"Is there anything you need us to know before we get there?"

"Only that you need to get this solved before the press finds out; I'm counting on you to get the job done."

After a few more instructions, Dennis hung up the phone, a look of angst on his face. He hated the job's politics and having to solve a case on a short timeline made him feel a tightening in his chest, and all a man could do was his best. Would his best be good enough? A young girl's life counted on it.

The drive to the Switzer home gave both men a chance to mull the case over. The Judge lived in an upscale neighborhood called Oak Park; Frank Lloyd Wright had designed many of the homes, and the area had become a tourist destination. It was still a great place to go for a Sunday drive. Dennis maneuvered his car through the elegant entrance of the estates. This was an affluent area, and most of the homes were situated on a full acre of a well-manicured lawn. The Judge lived in the largest house in the historic landmark section, an example of Wright's classic Prairie style. Dominant limestone window sills and overhanging rooflines, along with the horizontal layout, exemplified Wright's quest to reflect America's Midwest. As they walked up to the front door, Dennis noted the inscription, "Truth and Honor," a befitting motto for a Judge who was known to live by those two simple words.

With a quick knock on the ornate door, they were met by a tall thin woman, well past seventy. She was once a great beauty and carried herself with a regal bearing. Her expensive Chanel suit was a soft pearl white, with contrasting gold and black braid running along its edge. Her slim legs were in nylons, and considering how hot the day was, her attire was very formal. But they knew that this breed of woman wouldn't be caught dead with bare legs, no matter how hot the day. The family was old money that demanded refinement and good manners.

"Detective Kortovich and Detective O'Brien" She held out her well-manicured hand as she spoke. "Come in; we've been expecting you."

Dennis and Chuck were ushered into a large elegant entranceway. Dark oak paneling encompassed the foyer with white wainscoting, adding to the richness of the wood. The décor matched the nature of the owner, warm and tasteful. The tall woman slowed before she ushered them into the judges' study.

"I'm Marsha Phillip, Lena Switzer's mother. I came over as soon as I heard Mandy was missing." Marsha lowered her voice and turned her beautiful eyes towards the detectives.

"We're all beside ourselves with worry. I've heard from the Superintendent that you two are the best. Please help us. Mandy is our world, and she would never stay out all night."

She turned and opened the door to the library once she finished her plea for help. Superintendent Tom Holland greeted Dennis and Chuck. He was a tall man in his late fifties; his thick head of dark, wavy hair framed an intelligent face that showed little of what he felt or thought. There was a time that both Dennis and Chuck had respected Tom Holland, but lately, it seemed Tom was more a politician than a cop. Most of the other officers felt he was no longer watching their backs. Maybe that was the way it was when you got to the top. You forget where you came from and how you got there. Dennis was aware that some of the more senior officers were suffering from a bad taste in their mouths from the sour grapes they kept feeding on. It had become a divisive issue in the department, but Dennis and Chuck preferred to keep their opinions to themselves.

Tom Holland was an old friend of the Judge, so when Mandy didn't come home last night, Judge Switzer called him, knowing that he could be trusted to keep things quiet and try his very best to find Mandy.

As soon as Chuck and Dennis were seated, Dennis asked. "Judge, can you give us some of the details?"

Judge Switzer spoke with a cool detachment, but Dennis could tell from the pain on his face and the fear in his eyes that it was taking all he had to give the coolly delivered report. "Mandy spent the early part of the evening at a rave with several friends. The rave was just off of Clark Street, a part of town you wouldn't expect to find a proper young woman, but we trusted Mandy's judgment. At well, after one a.m., when we still hadn't heard from her, we began calling her friends. No one had seen her since midnight. One of her friends, a young man, said he thought she had gone out of the club alone to get some fresh air. He hasn't seen her later at the rave. I'm afraid I have a few other details at this point. We thought it was best to call in expert help before we let too much time pass." Judge Switzer's voice remained steady. "I apologize for the political maneuvering, but I'm sure you understand why I want you two, and the Superintendent to handle this situation." Judge Switzer finished, thrusting his hand forward.

Judge Switzer was a tall, elegant man who wore his wealth and position with a simple acceptance of his position. Dennis always thought Phillip Switzer looked like the James Bond type, minus the English accent. He was tall, slim, and dark. Phillip Switzer's bright blue eyes seemed to see all of life, finding what he saw most amusing. The Judge was known to be obsessed with finding the truth and relating the facts to the law. His obsession could drive a legal mind crazy, especially if a lawyer ever decided to argue a case with Judge Switzer without doing a ton of research first. He had a way of tying his opponent into a mental knot, but you had to respect his mind and his search for the truth.

Judge Switzer stood to introduce his wife Lena, sitting by the window in an oversized, winged-back chair. She got her looks from her mother. Tall, at least five foot eleven inches, fashionably thin and graceful, her fine-featured face was surrounded by an abundance of luxurious shiny auburn hair. Her dark, piercing blue eyes, framed by dark lashes, were red-rimmed from crying.

Lena gave a brief smile and pushed a list towards Dennis. "You will need this; she whispered as she gave Dennis a list of all of Mandy's friends as well as a recent photo.

. "I hope you can understand what it's like to have a teenage daughter. I hear so much about crime and drug abuse; my first instinct was not to let her out until she was twenty-one. But that wouldn't teach her how to handle the choices she will have to make in the kind of world we live in.

"I have two daughters. They're now in their twenties, but it was hard for me too when they were in their teens," Dennis assured her.

"We were to pick her up at six this morning, but she wasn't there. She has a cell phone if she wants to go sooner, and she knew we would be only too willing to pick her up if she wanted to leave at any time. When we didn't get a call from her, we went to the prearranged spot; she wasn't there. However, often we tried her cell; there was no answer. I asked whoever was lingering behind if they had seen her. There was only one boy who remembered seeing her somewhere around midnight. After that, he said he never saw her again. His name is Jackson Page. I took his cell number and home address. He said he would ask around and see if anyone could remember seeing Mandy." Lena handed a piece of paper over to Chuck, who seemed uncomfortable in the deep, leather chair.

"I've made a list of all of Mandy's friends, both in school and out. We belong to the Shore-Side Country Club, and I've also made a list of everyone she knows there too." Lena gave Chuck a second list and handed Dennis a picture.

Dennis looked down at the 8"x10" picture of Mandy. The girl in the photo was a pretty young woman with bright blue eyes and a sweet smile. Long, soft copper curls surrounded an oval face that held the same intelligent look of her father and her mother's beauty, Lena Switzer said as she indicated the information. "She takes after my maternal grandmother when it comes to stature, not me," Lena answered wistfully. "She's not very tall, something she laments regularly.

She is five feet, two inches, and weighs about one hundred ten pounds. She was wearing 'hip hugger' jeans and a tank top with spaghetti straps, in coral and green. She wore sandals. I know it sounds like she is dressed scantly, but it's the way girls dress nowadays." Lena looked sheepish. "I assure you she hasn't any tattoos or piercings. We say no to most things. But going to the raves, meeting up with her friends, and dancing all night is the one thing we relented on. She loves to dance. Now I feel like it's my fault." Lena suddenly started to cry.

Judge Switzer was standing next to Lena when she started to weep, tears welling up in his eyes as well. "Don't say that, sweetheart. Mandy is a responsible girl. We can't protect her from the world. She has to have a chance to be with her friends. We can't blame ourselves." He put his arms around his wife.

Dennis dreaded having to ask the next questions. And although he believed the Judge about how responsible Mandy was, it was still his duty to ask all of the questions, even the tough ones.

"Could anyone talk Mandy into leaving?" Dennis asked, looking the Judge in the eye.

The Judge responded, "I know you must hear this all of the time, but Mandy knows that all of her privileges depend on her doing what she says she will do. She would never take off with a boy. The only thing that concerns Lena and me is that maybe someone slipped something into her coke. We told her never to leave her to drink unattended because of the date rape drugs. She promised that she would drink a fresh coke if she felt someone else might have access to it."

"Is Mandy happy at home?" Dennis asked.

"I can understand you having to ask these kinds of questions." Phillip Switzer said as he stood, his wife standing next to him.

"Let us take you to Mandy's room. She has a diary. I've never read it, but at times like this, we need you to see what kind of girl she is; if there is anything that you have to know about our family and Mandy's feeling about us, it will be there."

Lena Switzer led Dennis to Mandy's room, Phillip Switzer following close behind. Chuck stayed with the Superintendent to go over the procedures he would like Dennis and Chuck to follow.

"This is her room. I'll leave you alone. It's hard for me to be here, not knowing what has happened to my daughter."

Judge Switzer kissed his wife tenderly as she passed. Lena gave him a tearful hug and quickly left the men standing in Mandy's room.

Judge Switzer went over to Mandy's room›s south wall, where a series of pictures hung on expensive frames, taking one from the wall, holding it tenderly in his hands. "She is very special. Our lives would be intolerable without her. Find her for us." Judge Switzer replaced the picture on the wall and turned on his heels, leaving the room without another word.

Mandy's room was tastefully decorated in yellow and mauve, playful but not too young. In the center of the room, a queen-size bed with a grape-colored canopy dominated the space. Matching lamps sat on the top of each bed table with a clock radio on one side and a gilded framed picture on the other. Lena, Phillip, Mandy, and three strapping young men, her brothers, looked like a happy, well-adjusted family. But as Dennis knew, a good investigator must consider all family members as potential suspects. Mandy's diary would give him a better impression, one way or the other. He pulled the white, leather-bound book from the desk drawer.

As he read through it, he began to laugh. Many of the entries reminded him of his youngest daughter Katrina. Katrina was the spunky, quick-tempered one in his family. She had an opinion on everything, as only the young can, but as his wife was finding out, Trina was very wise and profound beyond her years. The problem between his wife and his daughter was that they both wanted control.

Mandy seemed to be cut from the same cloth. "So and so is stupid," "this one thinks too much of herself," "that teacher is an ass," "this boy is a jerk," another might be all right if he "dressed differently and had better shoes" and so on and so on. Mandy had a few crushes; she liked to keep her options open. Most of the entries about her parents seemed to be nothing more than the usual notations about them not being hip enough. Mandy felt that if her mother were ever to wear jeans or a T-shirt, like some of the other mothers, she would faint.

If the only complaints a teenager had about her parents were the way they dressed, that wouldn't be a motive to run away. Dennis put away the diary. It didn't reveal any conflict or discontent.

Dennis decided he would start with the list her parents had given him. Good old-fashioned detective work. He and Chuck would begin with the friends that had seen her at the Rave and hope for a lead from there. Dennis came out of Mandy's room just as Marsha Phillip; Lena's mother came into Many's rooms.

"I was just coming to find you, Detective," she said. "We are just having some coffee and warm croissants and wondered if you would like to join us."

"No, thank you, I'll wait until lunch."

As Dennis returned to the library, Chuck was gulping down the last of his coffee, a half-eaten croissant still in his chubby hand. Chuck had a sheepish look on his round face. Dennis knew he had enjoyed a donut for breakfast and that the croissant would only add to Chuck's weight problem. He gave his partner a big smile. Chuck didn't see it as a problem, but Shelley, Chuck's wife, would give him hell if she found out. As Chuck stood, whipping whipped cream from the corner of his mouth, he held out his hand for one last farewell; Dennis joined in the handshaking, letting Chuck close out the meeting.

"We will be on this case with as much discretion as we can, but if we need to, we may have to put a task force together. If we do, we won't be able to keep it from the press.

So we will handle this first list and see what we come up with. Depending on the time that Mandy has gone missing, every hour that passes puts more pressure on the case. That is when we can decide on other Detectives helping on the case.

We may even have to appeal to the public." Chuck said softly, wanting the family and Judge to know the steps taken to get Mandy back.

After providing assurances and promises, Dennis and Chuck made their way to the car. From the front window, Lena Switzer stared out at the detectives. The strained look on her face told Dennis of the pain that would come if Mandy wasn't found soon.

* * *

CHAPTER THREE

ennis had finished work for the day. It was time to shut down the computer that sat on his desk and bid farewell to the other officers. He and Chuck had spent the rest of the morning following up with Mandy's friends that attended the Rave. Not one of them could remember seeing Mandy after midnight, just as Phillip had told them. Dennis and Chuck spent the afternoon at the country club, asking other friends and acquaintances if they had seen or heard from Mandy. None had. So far, they were at a dead end. Dennis decided to look into all unsolved cases involving missing teen girls in the area, going back at least seven years. Was Mandy's disappearance an isolated case, or had there been others? Dennis would get the report later that night. For now, a few hours at home would be a welcome diversion. As usual, he cleared his desk and put everything in its proper place.

Even the paper clips had a special place and arrangement, 'an orderly desk, an orderly mind.' The small cubed office held twenty years of memorabilia and awards. He got a great deal of comfort from the familiar surroundings, the Dick Tracy clock on the wall, the plaques, and pictures of his family. A few inspirational words etched into wood to give him that 'edge,' a gift from his ever-helpful wife, Veronica. Even the rough sounds and tangy smells from the other officers in the 'pit,' a common area where the detectives had their desks, gave Dennis a feeling of stability and order. In a work world where anything could happen, Dennis's office was a touchstone of stability, and he loved it. Even though it was more of a glassed-in cubical, it still gave him privacy. And having a wall where he could put what was important to him mattered.

Although it was late in the afternoon, the August sun still hadn't been able to break through the thick layer of clouds. A thunderstorm had broken the hot afternoon, pelting blobs of rain onto the streets below, while a slightly cooler wind blew in off the lake, making the day smell fresh, as only a summer storm can. If the storm passed soon, he could still accomplish a few more things around the yard before the day was over.

Dennis' station was in Area 3, on Belmont and Westlen, about twenty minutes from home. The brief drive to and from work allowed Dennis to clear his head and be present, whether at work or home. As a Chicago cop for over twenty years, Dennis held his job as something almost sacred. He couldn't imagine doing anything else.

Looking back at his roots, in the early days of Chicago, many Eastern Europeans settled into a neighborhood known as the Ukrainian Village, where Dennis had lived all of his life. As the years passed, families from other cultures and origins had moved into this district, giving the neighborhood a vibrant 'Bohemian style' that many artistic types gravitate toward. Veronica, Dennis's wife, loved the colorful characters and ethnic diversity of the area and the new creative atmosphere to define the change. She considered the Ukrainian Village to be the best place to raise a family, and she wouldn't consider moving to the suburbs. Veronica owned a beauty salon that she operated out of their wagon house in the backyard. Dennis had converted it to be a home-based business, and her clients were as diverse and as interesting as the neighborhood.

When Dennis thought of Chicago, a city of over six million, his thoughts were of a town with a dramatic history. With bigger-than-life personalities like Al Capone, as well as many other shady characters on both sides of the law, Chicago was a city made for drama. Movies of real-life characters that seemed to define Chicago were a part of the city's personality and reputation, not always in a favorable light. Throughout history, many headlines of the Chicago Tribune were of scandals, often involving those who should be beyond reproach. It seemed the press had always plagued the brotherhood of cops.

There had been more than one scandal involving members of the Police Force or the Justice Department. But for the most part, Dennis believed he could be proud of his fellow officers. Dennis grew up with stories of Elliot Ness and other great cops. Now, at fifty, he knew nothing was black or white. Everyone, the good guys and the bad guys, we're just trying to get by. Dennis had never regretted any decision he had ever made as a member of the force. He had always been guided by the values instilled in him by his Slavic grandparents.

When solving a case, Dennis followed logic and common sense, using whatever information he had at the moment. There were times when Dennis and Chuck's lives depended on it. The last case kept popping into his head. It was the worst case involving a serial killer. What bothered Dennis was that he liked the guy who turned out to be the killer. He felt that he understood what made the killer slaughter over twenty innocent people, which was a little creepy. That realization made him believe that given the right circumstances, anyone could kill. Dennis believed that very few people were born evil. The motivations for their crimes could be as simple as the desperate cries of a child, left without the resources to handle their pain and rage. Dennis wondered what invisible scars he may have left on his daughters, Natasha and Katrina. And although he doubted they would ever resort to murder as a cry for help, anything could happen.

Dennis deliberately pushed the thoughts of his daughters from his mind. He had too many of his own demons to face, and right now, he had a difficult case to solve. Family life had only recently returned to normal, and Dennis hated to think about some of the sins he had committed. He thought back to a moment in his life when self-doubt and personal frustration led to misgivings about his marriage and life with Veronica. These feelings almost led Dennis to make a catastrophic mistake that could have ended his marriage. The shame he felt at his momentary lapse in judgment had been replaced with a renewed commitment and love for his wife and family. He would do anything to protect the peace he now felt.

The drive home allowed Dennis time to take in the familiar sights and sounds of the city. As usual, a brisk wind was coming off Lake Michigan, bringing a clean, fresh smell to the dusty concrete smell of the city. The late afternoon was still hot, and Dennis felt he would have plenty of time to do a few things around the yard, even with a storm moving in before he would have to go back to work later in the evening. Traffic still hadn't reached its bone-crushing tide of homeward-bound travelers.

He was thankful for small mercies. As he pulled his car around the corner of the quiet, tree-lined street near his home on Wood Street, he heard the call over the police radio. It involved a family less than two houses from his home, Walker's residence. Dennis was directly in front of his cozy, brownstone home when he saw Veronica coming down the steps. The sight of his wife brought back strong feelings of love and appreciation. Her tall form was a sight of majestic beauty. Her bright face, big, green eyes, and red hair made her stand out in a crowd, but her shapely body would have been a competition, even for Queen Latifa. Veronica ran to the side of Dennis's Crown Victoria, putting her head into the open side window.

"Veronica, there's a 911 from the Walker residence. I'm going to stop there first and see if I can help."

Veronica answered, concern evident in her voice, "I'm on my way to the market. If the girls need me, call my cell. I hope Sam hasn't given Jewell another beating. When will she learn that she has friends that she can reach out to when he gets out of hand?"

Dennis gave Veronica an appreciative kiss on the lips. "There's nothing you can do if this is a police matter. But I will call you if the girls need a safe place to go."

As she withdrew, she gave him a concerned wave.

Dennis knew his wife had a great deal of difficulty not putting her pretty nose in the Walker's business. But over the years, Jewell had stopped calling the police for help when Sam got out of hand. She repeatedly refused to admit to anyone that her husband caused many bruises, wounds, and broken bones. Veronica had asked Jewell to drop by many times for coffee, but Jewell never came. Whenever Veronica baked, she always took some fresh baking over to the Walker household to keep tabs on the family, using the treats as an excuse. Dennis liked that Veronica tried to keep an eye on the family, especially now that Jewell refused to get help.

The old man Walker was as mean as a man could be and then some, even though he tried to be charming whenever the police came by, but Dennis knew it was a façade, and when the cops left, there would be an even louder cry's coming from the Walker home. Dennis hoped that Jewell and the girls were all-right. The call said there was an accident. The details were scarce. He could only hope Jewell did not take matters into her own hands, as abused wives sometimes do. From what Dennis knew of Sam, no one would ever want to convict Jewell even if she did kill the son of a bitch. Most likely, Sam had gone off again and hurt Jewell. Dennis parked his car and walked to Sam's house in only a second.

As a Metro City cop assigned to Area Three, Berwyn, Dennis's home district, was outside his immediate jurisdiction. As such, he really couldn't do much in an official way. However, as a friend, he could at least give some comfort and secure the accident scene until the area officers arrived. Dennis was the first to arrive at the Walker home. The main door was open; only the screen door stood in the way of Dennis accessing the house. Dennis had no idea what he would find, but he still needed to follow official procedures as an officer.

"Hello, anyone home. It's Detective Kortovich. May I come in?" Dennis called from the front step using his formal title.

"Yes, hurry." A soft, feminine voice answered.

Dennis entered through the front screen door. The living room was empty, and he could tell from the sounds of soft crying that the girls were in the back of the house in the kitchen. As he passed through the living room, Dennis noted the austere surroundings. Few knick-knacks were sitting on the coffee or end tables that flanked the simple but worn couch. Compared to his home, where Veronica kept flower arrangements, crystals, angels, along with a unique selection of candles, and every other popular home decoration, occupying every available space, the Walker home seemed stark and cold. The worn carpet had been vacuumed recently as the streaks made from the vacuum head could be seen in the short pile as it crisscrossed the living room. The smell in the home was of pine-sol and furniture polish. Everything was sparkling, clean, and neat. There was minimal color, most of the furniture being beige and tan. Only a subtle hint of moss green broke up the monotonous, flat tones that seemed to permeate the room. It was as if the room was trying to blend into the background, unseen, much like Jewell and the girls.

Samuel Walker was knockdown drunk when Dennis walked into the kitchen, which also seemed to express little other than a tired, but clean mood. The faded floor had been scrubbed clean. Its dull, white background gives little contrast to the beige and green. The beige stove and fridge blended with the patterned floral wallpaper of yellow and green, once popular in the eighties. Everything was spotless but sterile. Knowing how tense things were in this house, Dennis knew that Jewell would be reluctant to do little more than keep her home clean. Jewell's home was just a place to live, for very little love, other than the love for her children, could exist within these walls. Dennis could hear the soft hiccupping sobs of someone crying. As he walked toward the basement door, his heart sunk to his stomach.

Crystal, the middle child of three girls, sat at the top of the stairs, her knees pulled up close around her small pointed chin, blue eyes as dark as midnight stared up at Dennis as he walked toward the basement. Crystal's eyes were red-rimmed from tears that even now flowed steadily, and the black mascara ran in rivulets down her cheeks. Blotches of red on her nose and cheeks made her skin look ghostly white by comparison. Soft sobs slowly replaced the loud ones as Dennis approached her from the kitchen door. Dennis was chilled by the sound of a voice coming up behind him.

"She's down there," Sam said to Dennis as he walked to the fridge, trying to stay steady on his feet to get another beer.

Sam was only in his late forties, but his leathery skin had more folds than a basset hound. His jowls hung from his long face while his slack smile had a perpetual sneer, making him appear dark and menacing. Dennis noted that Sam's checkered shirt had snaps rather than buttons, a real benefit if you're a drunk.

Sam's red tag blue jeans hung limply on his skinny hips, threatening to fall off if he moved too fast. Sam held a beer in his sun-speckled hand; his eyes were glazed; obviously, this beer wasn't his first.

"Stupid woman can't even bring up a load of laundry without falling and killing herself." Samuel's words were flat and emotionless.

Dennis was sure Samuel was one of the soulless beings whose only feelings were of anger or indifference. Dennis had often heard his loud ranting from his home. Foul, bitter, ravings, which seldom went unnoticed by the neighborhood. But after years of trying to help, Dennis, Veronica, and other neighbors could only pray that Jewell would come to her senses and seek out professional help one day. Dennis looked down the basement steps to see Jade, the oldest girl, holding her mother's bleeding head in her lap. She held the cordless phone so tightly to her ear as she pleaded for help from the 911 operator; it seemed to melt into the copper curls of her long hair.

"Stay with me, Jade, the police are on their way, and it should only take a few more minutes." The steady voice on the other end of the phone assured Jade, who had yet to see Dennis at the top of the stairs.

Jewel's legs were sprawled recklessly off to the side in an ugly, twisted manner, making her look like a discarded doll. Laundry was strewn all over the stairs, and the plastic basket lay off to one side with a few items still tucked neatly inside. Jewell's eyes were wide open; their usual deep blue seemed dull and faded, her skin was pale, her naturally curly hair, which usually hung to her shoulder in soft waves, was matted with blood.

Dennis could tell, even from the top of the stairs, that the fall had been fatal. The basement stairs were steep, and Jewell had taken a fatal fall, hitting her head on the second stair from the bottom. A final crack of her skull had occurred as she hit the cold concrete floor below. Or did Sam have a hand in it? An investigation would reveal the truth.

"Jade, are you all right? I came as soon as I heard the call on my radio. The police should be here any second, and I think you should just stay where you are." Dennis said reassuringly as he began descending the stairs.

Jade stared up at Dennis with the same blue eyes as her sisters and mother. All of the girls were petite, with small, delicate, even features. They reminded Dennis of Dresden dolls, the kind his mother collected. The girls had a look of a time long past when women had a delicate refinement, and the young men wanted to protect and care for such beauties. The girls' copper-colored hair was a color you seldom saw unless it came from a bottle, and even then, you couldn't match its richness. Whenever the girls went out, which was rarely, all eyes turned toward their striking beauty. Now, the crown Jewell lay dead at the bottom of the stairs. Dennis sat beside Jade, gently reaching over to Jewell's cold hand to feel for a pulse, nothing.

"I want you to know that you have friends who care what happens to you; just know that Veronica and I will be here for you and your sisters" he tried to sound reassuring. "Everything will be alright."

Dennis knew he was lying. From the look of Jewell, nothing would be all right, and he could hardly look at the pain-filled, blue eyes that stared up at him in disbelief.

"I'm going to be fine, but you've got to get some help for mom." Jade pleaded with Dennis.

Dennis put a reassuring arm around Jade's tiny shoulder. It seemed to help.

Jade noted that Dennis always looked fresh, crisp, and reassuring, and he smelled good too. She could tell that Dennis must have come from work; his navy suit was cut perfectly, accenting his broad shoulders and trim waist. His light blue shirt had a contrasting red and navy tie that looked expensive and well thought out. He always looked like an executive rather than a cop. Jade knew that Dennis was someone important in the police department and handled some of Chicago's most prominent murder cases. Reporters were always interviewing him, and he was often on the news.

Somehow Jade felt close to him. She blushed a little, thinking of the times she had pretended Dennis was her dad, someone she could be proud of and loved. Many times on her way home, as she reached the Kortovich house, she would pretend that she lived there. She would fantasize about how things would be when she went through the side door and was greeted by Dennis and Veronica.

They would ask how her day was and then insist that she do her homework while Dennis helped. He would be the father she had always wanted, someone who would give a damn about her and would make her feel safe and loved. Each day as she passed Dennis's home, getting closer to her own, a feeling of dread would engulf her. Jade always hoped her mom was safe. At least Sam would be drunk and passed out in his usual chair. Her worst fear had always been that something would happen to her mom or baby sister while she was at school. Jade was jolted from her thoughts by the 911 operator.

"Honey, are you still there? Stay on the line; the police are nearly there."

Jade could hear a siren from a distance, faintly at first, then slowly getting louder as they neared her home. A few minutes seemed to take forever.

Dennis stretched his long legs that were beginning to cramp under him. He didn't want to move Jade or the body. As a good cop, he knew not to disturb anything. He also knew that Jewell was dead. If he touched anything at this point, the evidence could be compromised and unable to reveal what happened. Dennis has learned that often, even first-hand accounts by eyewitnesses were not always accurate. Evidence gathered at the scene, as well as crime-scene photos, could help back up or discredit any story told. It was essential to keep the girls calm and Samuel semi- sober until the investigation was underway. Keeping Samuel sober was going to be the tricky part.

"Lazy, bitch, never was good for nothing. Crap, what am I going to do now? Shit! I can't take care of this fucking family. Nothin but a bunch of useless, stupid broads, and then that slut of a wife has to give birth to a fucking retard. She doesn't even talk." Samuel waved a bottle of half-finished beer in the direction of a petite, curly-haired little girl rocking in the corner. "I have a good mind to take all the money and run. Who needs to take care of a bunch of stupid girls?"

Dennis could hear the sound of tiny tones. It was Amber with her toy phone. As beautiful as the older girls were, the youngest, Amber, was as close to perfection as any human being could be. Her copper hair framed an oval face of pink complexion. Her blue eyes held a blank look, alerting anyone to the fact that she was autistic. Her petite body rocked rapidly back and forth. She sat playing with the numbers on a toy phone. Dennis doubted Amber knew what happened, but he was sure she could pick up on the sounds of her sister's cries. The commotion had worked her into an agitated state. She stared up at some unseen object, continuing her unbroken rocking motion, all the while her tiny fingers were hitting a series of numbers on her play phone, creating her own tune.

Dennis decided he should phone Veronica and let her know what he had found. She would be worried until she heard from him. As soon as he dialed the number, he realized that Amber had imitated him, hitting the same number that he had called. She could hear the tones of the phone as he dialed his wife on his cell; he was amazed at Amber's gift. There was no answer. It was typical of Veronica to take her phone but not to have it on. He would try again later. Dennis noted Sam's look of disgust as he passed by his youngest daughter, muttering to himself as he went from the kitchen into the living room.

"Fucking little retard."

A worn recliner accepted his scrawny form, his weather-beaten face slack forming an ugly scowl. Given enough time, a violent outburst was sure to follow. Dennis hoped for the sake of the girls, Samuel would pass out, but he also needed him to stay sober and awake to give a statement to the police. Dennis thought it was too bad it wasn't Sam at the bottom of the stairs, but as luck would have it, it was not the case. Now there would be little to protect the girls from this depraved, little man.

Dennis yelled up the stairs, "Stay with me, Sam. You can't pass out on me now. The police will need your statement."

Dennis could hear the beer bottle crash to the floor.

"Wake up, you bastard." Dennis's deep baritone-voiced sliced through the air, startling Sam.

"Fuck you, Kortovich, and fuck her too!" Sam's face screwed into a red hot scowl.

Dennis could hear sirens coming down the road as the police and ambulance drew closer; they would be here in seconds.

The girls only needed to answer the police questions once. Dennis would wait with the girls while they told the police their stories. He was a friend, and they would need a strong shoulder to lean on. When Dennis looked at Crystal, she had stopped crying, and with her head resting on her knees, she was rocking back and forth, her arms hugging her legs.

"Now what?" she asked flatly without looking up.

"We simply tell the truth and let the police take care of everything." Dennis tried to reassure her.

When Dennis looked down the stairs, the despair he saw on her face was that of someone who had lived a dozen lifetimes, not a fifteen-year-old. He thought of his two daughters, Natasha, twenty-five, and Katrina, twenty-two. Their minds were still open and innocent, less aware of the world's bitter twists.

"The police," Crystal's tone sounded angry and full of contempt, "what good are they? We've never been able to count on them. We tried and looked where that got us." Crystal finished resuming her position, her head once again resting on her knees.

Crystal's small shoulders slumped forward, discouraged, hopeless. Her bare white legs and arms only made her seem more fragile and helpless. Dressed in black denim shorts and a torn black T-shirt, she looked like a poor orphaned child rather than a young girl about to blossom into a beautiful woman. What remained of her poorly applied makeup, now only a few streaks of black mascara under her blue eyes, fading black lipstick on her trembling lips, strands of her hair still held a hint of faded black dye, a poor attempt to cover her copper curls. Jade could feel her mother's body beginning to lose its warmth as she held on tight. She knew her mother was dead. She could hear the exchange between Dennis and Crystal but felt too drained of emotion to respond. Crystal was right! The cops had failed them. Not once, but many times. She recalled the first time Jewell had tried to run away from Sam. She was very young, but somehow even years later, the memories seemed sharp and clear in her mind.

CHAPTER FOUR

They had never planned to run away; it just happened one dreadful night. Amber wasn't born yet, and Jade and Crystal were still very young, only six and four. It wasn't like they understood what was happening. When you're that young, you never do. How could you know at six that what goes on in your home isn't happening everywhere else? How do you know that slaps, foul words, and threats aren't acceptable behavior? How do you understand that the tears, bruises, and broken bones are more mendable than a broken heart and loss of freedom and dreams? How could you possibly understand a mother's fears as she imagines the gruesome, lifeless bodies of her children murdered at the hands of her husband? The man she swore to love, honor, and cherish. Or worse yet! See her babies left motherless only to be abused by their father. Protecting her most precious possessions, her children had always been Jewell's number one concern.

Jade may have been young, but she understood that her family was different in ways beyond that of a child. As her thoughts drifted back to past events, Jade knew that if they had been able to get away, her mother, Jewell, would not be lying at the bottom of the stairs. Sam still worked back in those days; it was great. With dad gone, the days were peaceful and full of love and joy. After he drove away in the old Chevy, the dark mood would suddenly lift for the rest of the day. Her mother would change from a quiet, sad woman into a delightful playmate that seemed determined to make the next few hours full of fun and laughter.

They would bake cookies or fresh bread in the morning; then, lunch would be a tasty treat of their efforts. Their favorite game was making up funny songs that made no sense, but the game always made them laugh. Naptime was full of soft smells and gentle touches.

Jewells gathered her children tenderly into her open arms, holding them close, and for a while, they were able to lay their fears and bodies to rest. After their nap, playtime focused on books, games, and puzzles, anything that allowed their imaginations to run freely and go into unexplored areas of the wild and wonderful. As the afternoon wore on, Jewell began to watch the clock. The atmosphere would never transform in an obvious way to an outside observer; it was less tangible than that. They could feel the energy begin to change; it was a subtle thing, and they slowly turned from this small happy trio into cowering creatures. If you looked around, everything was still where it always was, but the transformation was as real as if the house was transported to another place or time. You could almost imagine an invisible hand painting the house black, black with fear, black with pain, black with desolation, and isolation. As the clock ticked closer and closer toward five, Jewell began to withdraw and turn inward.

Jade and Crystal would pick up the games and put them away out of sight. They didn't want their father to find their stuff and put his dark, evil stroke on all the things that gave them joy. At the final tick-tock of the clock and the mark of five, they scrambled to their bedroom, where they would stay until their mother would coax them down the stairs to supper. Children were not to be heard, and if Jade and Crystal could have it their way, they would gladly have chosen not to be seen as well. They would slip into their seats at the table, hoping that their dad would focus on his food and TV and not even notice that they were there.

"Where's my superwoman?" Sam would yell.

Jewell never answered; it wasn't necessary. She put a hot meal on the table and sat quietly, waiting for Sam to give the cue. If he wanted conversation, he would ask a direct question to whomever he wanted the answer.

If not, the girls knew to say nothing. It took Jade a few rough lessons to find out all of the unspoken rules. Once when Jade was excited about her first report card, she jumped into an excited chatter about how much fun kindergarten was and how much she loved her teacher.

"Did you like school, daddy? Who was your first teacher? Could you do the whole alphabet? Miss Lane thinks I can read almost as good as a grade one." Jade said excitedly.

Without a glance in Jade's direction, Sam swung his open hand across her face. "If I wanted to come home and listen to the useless chatter of children, I would have signed up to work at a school cafeteria. Don't ever speak to me unless I ask you a direct question." Sam spat, never once looking at Jade to see the shock, humiliation, and fear on her small face. Without a second glance, Sam dug into his food and continued to watch TV.

The kitchen was just off to the side of the living room, and Sam's kitchen chair could be turned so he could enjoy his meal at the table and still focus his attention on the television. Thank God for that small box that blared out the scores and exploits of men who ran around a field or soared across the ice. Sam shouted swear words at the screen and would shake his knife and fork at some athlete he deemed stupid or unworthy. Sam could go on and on about a score, completely forgetting his family. That was when the girls knew they could quietly sneak out of their seats and slip into their room to play until bedtime.

Jewell would stay with Sam, making sure he had his beer and that the remote control was close enough at hand, not allowing him to notice that she was still within slapping range, although the shouts and curses still managed to hit their marks. There were the times when the news or the score made Sam mad, and words turned to beatings, leaving Jewell a quivering mass of tears and blood. It was on one such night Jewell decided to flee. Jade now figured it must have been the breaking point before her mother's spirit was entirely shattered. The mood that night was unusually dark; Sam's day had not gone well. Everyone could sense the danger as he walked through the door. Halfway through the meal, Jewell forgot to ask for the butter. She reached past Sam's plate to pull the butter toward her. In a split second, Sam's hand came down on Jewells, his knife slicing through her skin like a spoon through Jell-O, leaving her hand impaled onto the wooden table.

"You fucking bitch, if you wanted the goddamn butter, you could have asked!" Sam roared.

Jade saw the look of shock on her mother's face, noting that Jewell never moved a muscle; her blue eyes transfixed on her hand. Little blood flowed from the wound; the knife was jammed so far down into her flesh. Jewel's face was ashen, and Jade saw her double over, grabbing her stomach as she tried not to vomit from the pain. Would Daddy stab Mommy again? Jade could feel her legs go weak. She had seen Sam hit her mother many times but never had she witnessed anything like this. Crystal sat across from Jade, her eyes wide, not daring to move.

For a few minutes, Sam seemed to be frozen in time, a strange smile on his lips. Then he slowly pulled the knife from Jewel's throbbing hand, twisting it side-ways as he struggled to dislodge it from the table. He tossed the knife casually onto the table, taking his plate to his favorite chair, and plunked his bony body into its worn frame, his attention once again focused on the TV. At the same time, he mentally dismissed the pain and horror he just caused his family.

Jewell moved like a ghost to the sink to wrap her wounded hand, now bleeding profusely. The tea towel could hardly absorb the blood; most of it was staining the front of her white dress. Jewell doubled over again as she grabbed the sink to steady herself. Jade could tell that she was in a great deal of pain; she was so pale. She had seen a ghost on TV once before, and she wondered if her mother was now a ghost. All of the blood made Jade think that maybe her mother was going to die. Jewell motioned for the two girls to come to her; it took only a second for them to cling to her blood-soaked dress.

The three of them moved to the back door, took their sweaters off the hooks, put on their shoes, and moved silently out of the door. They began to run. They ran and ran and ran until they thought they could run no more. Jade tried to urge Crystal on, her tiny legs unable to keep up the frantic pace. Jewell finally picked up Crystal, pulling her close to her chest, still running. Jade could feel her legs starting to turn weak. She had to keep up. The late spring night quickly engulfed them. Jade followed closely, uncomplaining. The blood continued to gush from the wound. Jewell tried to hold on to Crystal with her good arm. Jewell took a deep breath of the cold spring air.

"Oh God, your father's after us; we are all as good as dead." Jewell cried.

When Sam was in a rage, there was no predicting what he would do. Jewell pulled the girls across the street, paying little attention to the red light that would keep them stuck on the corner, with Sam less than a few blocks away. Jade could hear him racing towards his escaping family.

"You fucking bitch, stay where you are, or I'll punch your face to smithereens," Sam screamed from a distance.

There was no mistaking his tone; Sam was deadly serious. Now that Jewell and the girls were on the other side of the street, Jade thought frantically, where would they hide? Finally, they came to an intersection that led to an alley behind stores so old, and they too looked like ghosts. It was a Monday night, and all of the businesses were closed. No one was around to witness the event that was about to unfold. The alley was deserted except for the petite, copper-haired woman, with two tiny girls clinging to the edges of her blood-soaked dress. With stars as the only witnesses to the terrifying night, they stood for what seemed to be an eternity. Jade could feel the pounding of her heart. It was beating so fast. Her lungs felt as if they would explode. What did it matter? Daddy would find them and hurt them like always. Jade could tell by the look on her mother's face that tonight was different. It was going to be much worse than all of the other times.

"Mommy, Daddy's coming! Run!" Jade screamed.

The tiny, anguished voice of Jade jolted Jewell into action; she started to run, Crystal still in her arms. Jade tried to keep up, doing double time, sweat breaking out on her upper lip and forehead. Jade could feel the warm blood of her mother on her hands. Whipping some of the blood on the front of her navy tank top, it seemed to soak into her skin, making her feel sticky.

Her mother stopped suddenly; they were behind the strip mall. Large, metal garbage bins were the only thing Jade could see. Where could they hide? From the corner of her eye, Jade saw an old wooden boat that was tipped upside down. Jewell saw it too. There was no time to consider how good this small offering would be. Jade could hear Sam's violent expletives as he roared out a string of foul words. His now taxed body was slowing down as he crossed the street. Running to catch up with his fleeing family had taken its toll on his skinny, out-of-shape form. The sound of his cowboy boots could be heard in the distance. Jewell pulled Jade over to the small rowboat, still clinging to Crystal, who was now whimpering softly.

"Hush, Crystal, don't make a sound." Jewell pleaded.

All three of them squeezed under the boat only seconds before Sam rounded the corner. The girls knew that even one sound would mean Daddy could find them. As they scrambled under the old rotting boat, a sliver jammed into Jade's upper shoulder. Her first instinct was to scream in pain, but her fear of Sam overpowered her; not a peep escaped her trembling mouth. As they lay down on the cold tarmac, Jade could hear the clunk, clunk, clunk of Sam's cowboy boots before she could see the scuffed worn toes from under the raised edge of the boat. Sam knew where they were. He walked straight over to the boat. The silence dangled in the air like cheap perfume in a small elevator. It was heavy enough to choke the life from even the heartiest soul. Suddenly a blast rang out into the night. It took Jade a couple of seconds before she realized it was the sound of a bullet. She had gone target shooting with Sam twice before, so she knew the sound. Once again, bang, bang, bang as three quick blasts exploded. This time the bullets found their way into the upper ridge of the bottom of the boat. A whooshing sound made her flinch as the bullet whizzed past her head. No one made a sound, but Jade's fear caused her to wet her pants. The warm liquid ran down her bent legs, spilling and splashing onto the asphalt parking lot as it seeped out from beneath the small boat.

Sam said nothing, and the silence was worse than any tirade. The sound of his boots clunking on the tarmac as he slowly walked around the boat made Jade feel as if her heart would burst. Any second, a bullet would find its way into her mother. Jade could imagine her red blood spilling onto the ground, seeping under the edge of the boat. It could be days or even weeks before anyone would move the abandoned rowboat and find them. Jade felt as if she would burst from the pain in her shoulder. Her panties were now feeling cold, and a sudden itch made her want to scratch. But how could she? She had to be brave.

"I know you're under there. I'll give you less than a second to get out, or I'll start shooting. If you think I won't, then just test me. Neither you nor your brats will get out alive." Sam's voice was ice-cold as he stated the obvious.

Jewell slowly lifted the boat several inches, allowing them to emerge from under its cover. Sam stood there in front of Jewell and the girls, his face a twisted mask of rage. The hate he felt was barely contained. It took two strides for Sam to reach Jewell, slamming his fist into her face. Just as her knees buckled, he grabbed her by the hair, spun her around, forcing her body to fall back against the boat. Jewel's bloody hand slammed behind her back, making the raw wound gush a fresh flow of blood. Sam pressed his body up against hers, his face only a few inches from her cold, clammy cheeks; his breath barely contained his murderous rage. Suddenly the barrel of his gun was thrust down into Jewell's dry, swollen throat, choking off her air, ragged breaths finding their way out of her flared nostrils.

"Never, ever try to leave me, you fucking bitch, or I'll make your brats watch you die. No one will help you!" Sam's statement was final and deadly.

Just then, the sound of a siren blasting could be heard behind Sam. He quickly shoved the gun into the front of his pants. As he turned around, he was careful to conceal Jewell as she crouched next to the boat. The young police officer got out of his car. Sam pulled both girls forward, placing a loving hand on their shoulders, giving the officer a display of fatherly protectiveness.

"Having any problem here?"

The officer walked forward, trying to get a closer look at the family.

"No, officer, we were just out for a walk. We saw this old rowboat and wanted to take a better look."

The officer looked back at his partner, still sitting in the cruiser. He gave him an all's well signal then started to turn on his heel to leave. Suddenly he stopped and turned back to face Sam. He strained to see who or what was hiding behind him. He then directed his question to Sam, "Who's behind you, sir? Maybe I ought to hear from her." The officer waited for a few seconds; no one made a move or said a thing.

"I said. Who's behind you?"

"Just my wife, and as you can see, my daughters, we're all out on a walk. Do you have a problem with that?" Sam's tone was tense.

Jewell stepped out of the shadows, and Jade hoped the police would see the blood on her mother's hand. They would take them away and keep them safe. The officer looked Jewell straight in the eye. He was good-looking in a slick, arrogant way. He had his hand on his gun as if to say, "Don't fuck with me."

The officer then looked at the two small children standing with their father. Silence hung in the air for what seemed to be forever. Suddenly he turned back on his heels, muttering a final statement to Sam as he retreated.

"Well, don't hang around for too long. We don't like anyone behind the shopping mall after hours. Have a good night." With those final words, he got into the cruiser and backed the car up.

Sam gave a cocky smile and said, "You see what I told you. You're just too much paperwork. Unless someone calls in a complaint, the cops hate to get into a domestic fight between a husband and his wife. I'm still the king of my castle, and no fucking cop is going to get involved in rescuing a bitch like you!

* * *

Jade remembered her dad's words, and he was right; many times, the cops had come to their home and only given Sam talking to and a warning. Jewell had never made those 911 calls; it was always her word over strangers and nosy neighbors' complaints. If they had known the extent of the violence, they would have arrested and charged Sam. Then the nightmare would be over. Sam's idea of over was death. At that moment, Jade didn't know there would be another time. It was only later that she found out that Jewell planned their escape down to the smallest detail. When Jewell finally ran again, she would have a plan, and she would make sure Sam could never find them. The lives of her children depended on it.

CHAPTER FIVE

T hat was the beginning of secrets, and for the next year, Jewell made elaborate plans for a final escape. She never expected Sam to find out what she was up to. Jewell was careful to tell no one, especially not the girls. They only knew there were many times that their mother told them she would answer their questions about the secret calls later, but later never came. The less they knew, the less likely Sam would find out. The one thing Jewell never planned on was that evil has a way of finding its way and nothing is foolproof.

Jade was only seven, and it was the spring of her second year of school. She had loved going to school from the very beginning. The laughter and fun in the class made her forget the fear at home. The school was wonderful. The school halls had a feeling all their own, as though the energy of the children had been soaked into the brick and mortar, giving the walls a feeling of life that seemed to embrace Jade each day as she journeyed down the halls. Miss Dreger, her grade two teachers, was awesome, and she remembered the first time Miss Dreger bent down beside her to help her solve a problem she was having. She caught a whiff of something so breathtaking she burst out with a wondrous, "Miss Dreger, you smell!"

At first, her teacher's face seemed stern. Then she broke out into a soft but surprised smile. "Jade, haven't you ever smelled perfume before?" Then Miss Dreger looked at her with all the amusement a teacher could, making sure she did not embarrass her small ward.

"No…. I don't think so." Jade seemed to search her memory for anything as wonderful as the smell.

Miss Dreger said, "Well, I'm wearing perfume, and it is something you spray on so that people will notice you when you pass them and think that you are special."

After that, all Jade could think about was how she could get ahold of some perfume. She had asked her mother, but Jewell said Daddy didn't like it, and when Daddy didn't like something, you never did it, or you paid with your hide. When her mom told her that she would not be going to school, Jade was broken-hearted and didn't understand. Jewell explained that they would be leaving that morning and not coming back. Sam had gone off to work, and they would need the whole day to get as far away as they could. Sam had never allowed them to own any suitcases, but Jewell had managed to save some large paper shopping bags, big enough for them to take a few of their favorite things. Once packed, they quietly left the house, hoping never to return.

"Mommy, where are we going? Why can't I go to school? Can't we live here anymore?" Crystal asked

At seven, Jade was the only one to understand what the shopping bags meant. She saw the look on her mother's face and knew that this was taking all the courage she could manage.

"It's all right, Mommy, I'll help you. I have all my stuff in the bag, and I'll carry Crystal's stuff too. Don't cry. We can do this."

Jade took her mother's face in her tiny hands and looked straight into her worried eyes. At that moment, she was more like the adult and Jewell the child. It was a glimpse into her future and the rest of her life. She was to take care of her sisters, a job that was impossible for a small child.

They arrived at the bus station at ten that morning. Jewell had been careful to take the local bus to a shopping center and then call a cab. She was hoping Sam would never be able to track her from a crowded shopping center. She even bought their tickets with cash. They were going to Gage-town, New Mexico. They had picked the location by rolling dice on a map. Wherever the dice landed was to be their new home. This was going to be a long trip, so Jewell bought lots of treats and games. It was only minutes before they were about to board the bus when Jade looked up at her mother, just to see a look of terror cross her face, while all of the blood left her pink cheeks, making her look once again like a ghost.

Jewell would rather have died than to have the day play out as it did. She would not be so lucky, although later that night, the screams that echoed from the little house on Wood Street did sound as if someone was being killed.

Jade turned to see what had caused her mother such alarm. She was terrified when she saw Sam and the triumphant look on his face. Sam calmly came up to Jewell, put his hand under her elbow, and escorted her to the parking lot where his car was waiting to take them back home. Jade found out years later from her mom that all the planning in the world couldn't outwit Murphy's Law. Anything that could go wrong will go wrong.

Six months earlier Jewell had found out that her parents had died. She hadn't seen them over the past two years. Sam had made it difficult for her to see her parents, who lived in Boston. They had stopped visiting, sensing how difficult life must be for their only daughter once they left. Jewell's mother had begged her daughter to leave.

"Jewell, your father and I are worried sick about you and the girls. Leave Sam and come to live with us. We have plenty of room, and you could go back to school. We would take care of everything."

"No, mother, I can't and won't leave Sam. There is nothing to discuss. He's my husband." Jewell tried to sound firm.

"You can't possibly want to stay with a man like Sam. You come from so much better, and I know he hits you."

Jewell wanted to cry out to her mother for help more than anything in the world. To be able to move to Boston, away from Sam, would be a dream come true. But she knew that the dream would turn into a nightmare; Sam would hunt them down and kill them all, her mother, father, and precious babies. No, she would have to stay with Sam until she could find a way to leave him so that he would never find her. The answer came with her parent's death.

51

They left her the financial resources to leave. Her parent's lawyer was able to get in touch with Jewell without Sam finding out. It was a provision of the will. Together they were able to handle the estate's details and plan for Jewell and the girl's eventual disappearance and a change of name. Everything was handled down to the last detail. It was the perfect plan, except for one thing. The one call that came when she least expected it. The call that Sam answered, the one that let him figure everything out in an instant. All he had to do was be patient until the day she decided to bolt. The rest was easy. Just follow along and show up just as they were just about to board that train, boat, car, or plane to freedom.

The call that let the cat out of the bag came from the lawyer's secretary, who was somehow kept out of the loop. Everyone knows a good secretary does all of the work and always handles the details like that fateful day when there was going to be a late release of money from the estate to the bank.

Because she was out of the loop, the secretary did what she always did and called the client to inform her that the transaction would be delayed.

"Hello, is Mrs. Walker there?" The voice on the other end of the phone asked, sounding official.

It was unusual that Sam would be home at this hour, but a raging headache made it impossible to work. It was just as he came through the door that the phone rang. As usual, Jewell was downstairs doing laundry. She had to be the cleanest bitch in the neighborhood. He couldn't stand to hear the phone ring, so he answered it with a gruff "Hello!" waiting for the caller to continue. It was for Jewell, not that she got many calls, but there were far more for her than he ever got, not that he cared.

"No, I'm sorry she's not." Sam didn't want to shout down the stairs for Jewell to come up; his head hurt too badly.

"May I ask to whom I am speaking?" the voice sounded official.

"I'm her husband, Samuel Walker."

"Are you sure you can't find Mrs. Walker? It is very important?"

"No, she won't be able to talk until late this evening."

"May I leave a message?

"Sure, shoot." He kept his response short. It was easier on his head that way.

"Would you tell her that the money from her parent's estate will be delayed on the transfer by one day? Also, tell her I'm sorry to hear about both of her parents dying so suddenly; it must have been a shock for you and Mrs. Walker."

Now it was Sam's turn to be shocked. You bet your fucking ass; he was shocked. That was an understatement. This call put a whole new light on all of the past few months' happenings, especially Jewel's attitude. No wonder she seemed less stressed. There was a bounce in her step he hadn't seen in years, and upon occasion, Sam would see a faraway look in her eye. At one point, he thought she might even have a lover, but a few weeks of spying uncovered nothing.

"Hello! Mr. Walker, are you there?" The secretary thought she lost the connection. There had been no response for so long.

"Yes, yes, I'm still here. I just had to have time to gather up my emotions; it's been such a sad event for us all." Sam tried to sound sincere and hide the rage that was gathering just under the surface of his voice.

"The money will be sent to the First National Bank of New Mexico and will be in the bank when she gets there tomorrow. Well, be sure to pass the information on to Mrs. Walker, as well as my condolences." The voice on the other end was gone while Sam still held the receiver.

He was still holding the phone minutes later when he heard Jewell coming up the stairs, humming an old 60s ballad. He hadn't heard her sing in years. Did she think she was about to get away with leaving him? Sam hung up the receiver quickly and took up a relaxed position in his favorite chair. He would wait and bide his time. He would never let her leave him unless it was in a coffin. He was glad to see her shocked face the next day at the bus station. Sam would never forget that look of distress and surprise on her face as he walked up the platform. You would have thought the

Devil was at her heels instead of the man she married. Sam laughed to himself.

"Where do you think you're going?" Sam asked calmly as he approached her and the children.

Jewell said nothing. It would only make things worse. She looked around at the crowded platform. Families were boarding the many busses, heading in the hundreds of directions throughout the U.S.

"Don't even think of calling out for help. I'll knock you out cold and carry you out of here if I have to, and not one of these do-gooders will even give you, or you're fucking brats a second look." Sam said his voice deadly calm.

Jewell let go of Jade's hand. She tried to hold the two big paper bags while still hanging onto Crystal's tiny hand. Jewell walked silently behind Sam, her head lowered. Jade looked up at her mother's face; tears were spilling from her eyes. Jade had seen her mother look afraid before, but she had never seen the look on her mother's face as she did on that day. It was as if Jewell's determination to leave had been sealed into a new resolution to stay. Her face was like stone, and only her tears betrayed the fear she felt. Jade fell in step alongside her mother and sister, knowing that life would be even darker from this day forward. That is how Jade thought; feelings had colors. Black! So far, there had been a few pink and purple days in her life. Colors that she could never wear or enjoy in her limited life.

CHAPTER SIX

fter Jewell's failed attempt to leave, she never again had that faraway look of hope in her eyes. When Sam beat her, she simply coped. If the beating was severe enough to put her in the hospital, she lied to the cops and doctors about what happened. Jewell kept the windows closed and doors shut. And never again did she let anyone know what was happening in her little house of horrors. Jade grew up trusting no one, especially not the cops. It was just like Sam said. Women and children weren't important. A man's home was his castle, and he could do anything he wanted within the closed doors of his house. Years later, Jade learned only too well just how unimportant kids were to the cops, especially teenagers. Jade had been going through a tough transition both at home and at school. Her best friend, Charlotte Kennedy, had disappeared, and Jade knew something awful had happened to her.

Charlotte had become her only real connection to the outside world.   She had made Jade feel safe and accepted. Charlotte was a part of the 'in-crowd, and she had taken to Jade at the beginning of grade ten at Lincoln Park High, a school of over three thousand students. Jade had been shocked when the tall, athletic brunette showed an interest in her. Charlotte was always full of fun and laughter. She had good grades in school and was the star player on the high school basketball team. The thing Jade liked best about

Charlotte was her relationship with her family. She envied them the seemingly happy, easy-going fun they seemed to have whenever they picked Charlotte up from school or attended one of her basketball games. Jade was at Charlotte's house on a Friday night, a rare event for Jade.

She had never witnessed a family that was so full of love and respect for each other, except on TV. Even then, Jade suspected it wasn't real, just a bunch of Hollywood crap. Charlotte's mom worked part-time at the school library, and her dad was an accountant. Each parent took turns cleaning the house, cooking, and driving the kids to sporting events and lessons. The result was a loving, close family where everyone was very much in tune with each other. The conversations around the supper table were full of genuine interest in what was happening for each family member, school, friend, and neighbor. Jade marveled at the total absence of fear within the family. It both saddened and impressed her. Everyone laughed and teased each other in a way that made her feel even more isolated and alone.

"Hey Charlotte, don't think just because you have a friend over for supper that you get out of cleaning the kitchen." Billy, Charlotte's older brother, said as he grabbed a platter of chicken, taking a second helping.

"You're not my boss. Mom, tell Billy to mind his own business."

"If you two don't stop this nonsense, I'll tan both of your hides and don't think you are too old for a good old-fashioned spanking." Mrs. Kennedy said.

"By the way, how did your basketball game go?" Ken Kennedy asked, a smile spreading across his face.

"We won. I was the one with the most points, forty-two. It was the most points I've ever scored in a game." Charlotte responded to her father's question.

"That's because Jacob Smith was at the game, and she wanted to impress him. Charlotte has a crush." Billy said, trying to bait his sister again.

Soon everyone was joining in on the conversation, filling Mr. and Mrs. Kennedy in on the details of their day. After supper, Jade and Charlotte sat on the front step of their wrap-around verandah and talked. Jade's mood shifted into low gear, and Charlotte finally asked the one question very few had ever had.

"Jade, why are you so afraid and sad. What's happening to make you so withdrawn?" Charlotte's larger hand had grabbed Jade's small cold hand as she looked Jade in the eye for an answer.

Jade couldn't give her an answer. She had never trusted anyone before and couldn't find a way out of the dark, emotionless pit of fear to feel safe enough to confide in Charlotte. As tears welled up in her eye her only answer was fearful, "I'm just shy."

"That's okay; I'm not," Charlotte responded. Together they enjoyed the rest of the evening, not knowing it would be their last.

Charlotte was one of the dozens of girls who had disappeared over the past few years. Jade knew her friend was most likely dead because she would never have run away. The cops had given up; they said it was just another missing teen. They had failed Charlotte, as they had so often failed Jade, Crystal, Amber, and her mother. The cops had said her mothers' death was an accident. They would never accept that it was their dads' fault. He had abused their mother so severely over the years that a recent bout with the flu had left her weak, unable to recover fully. Jewell hadn't been allowed to rest long enough to get well, her need to protect the girls from Sam's barbaric outbursts and physical abuse had made it impossible to stay in bed and get the much-needed rest. The result was a deadly tumble down the stairs.   Jade couldn't count the times the police had failed her, and she would never trust them in the future. The next time she would take matters into her own hands.

Jade abandoned her contemplation of the past as the loud wail of a siren could be heard.

Dennis could concentrate on the girls and their emotional well-being, taking the time to observe the scene of the accident a little closer. He wanted to see if Sam's cruel hands may have been involved, as he had always anticipated.

"What's going on, Kortovich?" The familiar voice of Sergeant Tilley, the first officer to arrive at the home, was a welcome sound to Dennis.

Dennis had known Ken Tilley for several years. He was a nice-looking man in his late forties with flaming red hair and golden-colored skin, which reminded Dennis of Robert Redford, a pale watered-down version. Many of the women in the force took a second glance whenever he walked by. The police community was close, and Dennis and Ken had attended many local events over the years. Their common profession had drawn the two of them together, and Dennis had come to respect Ken's dedication and sense of fair play. Dennis tried to some things up, knowing Ken would have to follow every angle. "It's an accident from the looks of it, although I suspect the husband isn't above tossing her down the stairs."

The paramedics were right behind officer Tilley. As they descended the stairs, it quickly became obvious that the pretty woman lying on the cold concrete was very, very dead. After a quick check of her pulse and other vital signs, they stood back, knowing they were unable to do anything. As the other officers and Crime Scene Investigators began arriving, Dennis stood back as the investigative team began taking photos and prints while gathering as much information as they could from the scene. It was unusual for the special C. S. I. unit to be called in before the local police requested their presence, but with so many calls from the Walker house, the dispatcher had gone through channels to recommend that the unit be called, just in case.

"What do you think of the situation?" Tilley asked Kortovich.

"I think it's a damn shame that's it's not Sam Walker at the bottom of the stairs." Dennis's response was flat but summed up his feelings.

Dennis knew the girls would feel safer if he stayed, and maybe he could give them some comfort before a new day would begin. As Dennis thought about the girls' futures, he knew that it would be even more terrifying living with Sam now that Jewell was gone. The girls would depend on him and Veronica, and he vowed he would not let them down. This may not be his case, but he sure as hell could keep an eye on things as a good neighbor. If Sam thought he had full reign over the girls, he could think again. Dennis would make sure Sam never got too comfortable with his status as a single dad.

CHAPTER SEVEN

T he girls awoke to the usual sound of Sam's screaming. "Jade, you whore, where the fuck are your sisters? What the hell happened yesterday? I remember cops coming. Where the hell is your useless mother?"

Sam was up, and a new chapter in their lives would now begin. Without their mother, it would have to be a short time. They would have to deal with Dad. They couldn't run away. But who would take care of Amber? If the two girls didn't come up with a permanent plan for Sam, they would never survive the added abuse. Could they frame him for a crime and send him to jail? They would have to think hard. The plan to deal with Sam couldn't surround domestic abuse; they knew from experience the charges would never stick.

"Someone, get up and feed me." Sam leaned against the doorway frame, trying to keep from falling. "I asked you what the fuck happened yesterday."

"Mother is dead." Crystal said. "The cops will be by sometime today to question you because you were unavailable yesterday." Crystal's sarcastic remark didn't miss its mark, and the scowl on Samuel's face let her know she was walking a thin line.

"Screw the cop; she did it on purpose. She never was any good for nothing." Sam spit out his angry words. "She never did an honest day's work." Sam spit out his angry words. "Now she's gone and got herself killed just to spite me, so it's up to you girls to keep me happy now get up; I want something to eat now!" He turned and staggered down the hall. A new day had begun.

* * *

Crystal pulled the covers over her head. The thought of getting up and going downstairs to serve her father made her want to throw up. She knew her mother had always been there to make sure that she and her sisters could spend as little time around Sam as possible. "How could you leave us with him?" Crystal felt the familiar feeling of anger once again taking over her whole body. She had never expressed her feeling towards her father for fear of the physical retribution that was sure to follow. She had always harbored a great deal of anger towards Jewell. She felt her mother was a coward. Jewell was too afraid to leave and too afraid to do something drastic. Not that she knew what her mother should do. If she had her way, she would have pushed Sam down the stairs. Since becoming a teenager, she had restrained herself from running away or screaming at her father. She would have loved to slap someone, anyone when things got tough at home. But all she could do was to stand by silently and listen to the abuse. The only solace she could find was to retreat to her room with Amber, lie in bed, turn on her stereo, and rock back and forth, blocking out the sounds below. One day Crystal asked her mother what had drawn her to a man like Sam. A confused look crossed Jewell's face. "He wasn't always this bad, and I thought I could change him, be his rescuer."

For a moment, Jewel's beautiful face lit up as she remembered back to a time when a girl from the right side of the tracks met and fell in love with a boy from the wrong side of the tracks. He had been a James Dean look-alike. She recalled her first date with Sam and the few good months that followed.

"How come a pretty little gal like you can stand to be with a dirt poor guy like me?" Sam would ask.

It was Jewell and Sam's first date, and he was dressed in clean blue jeans and a white shirt that looked crisp and smelled as good as the first day of spring, clean, bright, and fresh.

Sam's full head of hair hung below his collar, the sun catching the soft, golden highlights in his hair. His face was fresh and young. She thought he was the most handsome boy she had ever seen.

"I don't care if you're family hasn't any money. I'm not like that, nor are my parents. They would never judge you just because they have money, and your family has hit hard times" Jewell lovingly looked up at Sam.

Sam said venomously, "My family never hit hard times; it would mean they would have to have worked to have good times. They are lazy, no good drunks, every one of them. They're not worth the two cents; they don't have to rub together."

"You're not your family. You can be anything you want." Jewell tried to comfort Sam, who seemed to be growing angrier with each passing moment.

"I come from trash. That's all my family has ever been, white, trailer-trash. That's what I am. You should get away while you can. My family is a bunch of mean drunks." Sam shouted. "I'll probably end up just like them. It's in our blood."

Sam pushed her away and started to walk to the car. Jewell's heart broke when she saw how angry and dejected he seemed to be. Jewell thought if Sam was loved and understood enough, she could change him. She was wrong. The only thing that would change was that all the hopes and dreams of a young girl would be destroyed by the fear and isolation that Sam would create. After the birth of Amber, Crystal knew from conversations with her mother that she felt there was no way out. That is until she had tried to run that one desperate night when Sam stabbed her in the hand, then came the second time. Crystal couldn't remember much about either of Jewell's runaway attempts. But she knew of the stories from Jade. The beating that followed the second attempt left Jewell with a broken jaw. But it was what happened after the beating that broke Jewel's spirit. The rape had been brief but brutal. Nine months later, Amber made her appearance into the world. It was only after Jewell discovered that Amber was mentally challenged that she gave up all hope of ever leaving Sam.

Jewel's parents were older and had moved from Chicago to Boston, leaving Jewell even more isolated. After many frantic phone calls and visits, they finally gave up trying to convince her to leave. After a few years, she had become so reclusive that her parents were seldom allowed within the walls of her tiny home, a home that her parents helped them to purchase.

At the time, Sam was working with a Ukrainian immigrant, John Wakulchuck, whose hard work and quick mind allowed him to make a small fortune in scrap metal. He had been a blacksmith in the old country and had figured out a way to smelter down old scraps of iron into small and medium-sized iron balls, selling them back to the iron companies at a healthy profit. Sam was lazy, but John knew how important the money was to his family. John fell in love with Jewell and her daughters' kind and gentle spirit and wanted to protect them, feelings that others would experience after meeting the girls and getting to know Sam. For the years that Sam worked with John, things at home were at least bearable. But eventually, Sam's drinking got more and more out of hand until he was fired. Sam no longer worked, and for Jewell and her daughter's having him home all the time made life almost unbearable. It was a small inheritance that Jewell had received from her grandmother that kept a steady paycheck coming into the family. But, it was never enough to allow Jewell to do more than the basics and the girls often went without extras that so many of their friends took for granted.

As they grew older, Jewell's parents seldom saw their granddaughters. Still, letters and presents conveyed their love. With their time running out, they came up with a plan on how to leave their only child or their grand-daughters the family fortune without letting Sam get his hands on the large sum of money, stock, and property.

Crystal stretched and snuggled her pillow one more time. There was nothing to be gained by blaming her mother for their situation; she had done the best she could. It would now be up to herself and Jade to find a way out of their deadly circumstances. Crystal thought it would be easier if she could just stay in bed forever and never face what was waiting downstairs.

*   *   *

Jade moved off the bed into the bathroom to take a shower. She grabbed her housecoat, covering up her nightgown. As she passed the mirror attached to her dresser, she noticed how dark the circles under her eyes were. She had little sleep and dreams of her mother sailing down the stairs hitting her head had replayed through most of the night. She felt the weight of the world sat on her shoulders.

"Crystal, get up and get Dad something to eat until I get downstairs, and whatever you do, hold your temper in check and don't provoke him. You know what he's capable of."

Crystal nodded thoughtfully, letting Jade know she had no intention of making things worse.

Jade locked the door to the bathroom and, as usual, but the white wooden chair under the doorknob as a precaution when she was only twelve when she found Sam in the bathroom watching her. Her body was starting to develop, and his newfound attention toward her made her feel dirty and ashamed.

At first, Jade didn't know why she was so creeped out, but as she found out more about boys and girls, she knew he was capable of sexual assault without a doubt. No wonder Crystal had started to dress in a gothic style. Jade knew her sister attempted to keep her father away from her. She remembered when Crystal first expressed the desire to dye her hair and change her looks. It was during a visit to Veronica Kortovich's salon for a haircut.

* * *

"What would you girls like me to do with your hair? Just a trim or a new look?" Veronica asked.

"I want to dye my hair black." Crystal said.

"You and your sisters have the most beautiful hair color in the world. Why would you want to change it?"

"I'm too young-looking. Everyone thinks I'm weak and can't take care of myself. I want a new look, and I was thinking of gothic. People stay clear of you if they think you're strange." Crystal said, her voice gaining strength.

Veronica seemed to consider Crystal's request.

"Look, I won't dye your hair completely black, but I will foil a few pieces. I'll use a washout dye, and if you like it, I'll sell you the product and show you how to maintain it yourself. If you like, I'll even show you how to do your make-up in a gothic style. But only if you'll promise me that you won't take things too far. No piercing or tattoos." Veronica's warm, hearty laugh let Crystal know she understood.

Crystal loved her black foils even though they hid amongst her copper curls. She wore more makeup at home than she did at school, and Jade knew why. It bugged Sam. Still, somehow he sensed that Crystal's choice in fashion and makeup was directed at him. He only gave Crystal a hard time once, and then he left her alone.

"What the fuck do you think you're doing with your hair and that black crap you're wearing on your face. Your clothes look like you got them out of the garbage can. You look like a little witch rather than the little bitch you are." Sam yelled at Crystal.

Crystal stood her ground as she gripped the kitchen chair, thinking how much she would love it if her hands were around her father's skinny throat.

"Don't be too sure I'm not a witch and that I won't make a poison potion. One day your beer might just have a funny taste. You wouldn't want to get alcohol poisoning." She said, daring Sam to do something, her small chin jutting out defiantly.

Sam got up from his chair, his right hand in the air, ready to strike Crystal. She stood her ground and moved closer, staring him down.

"Go ahead. You could hit my mother all you want, but if you hit me, I'll make sure that all of us kids get taken away from you. Child welfare would love to find out what happens in this house." Crystal screamed. "If you ever touch me, I'll tell anyone who will listen, and I promise you, I am not my mother."

Jade stood, taking Amber from the kitchen table, fearing that Sam would turn his anger on her youngest. Sam stood with his hand in the air for a few seconds. As he lowered his arm, the look on his face was such a twisted mask of hate; Jade knew her gut was right; without mom, dad would have to go. No one knew what Sam was thinking. The moment was so tense you could almost feel the air turn deadly cold. Sam left the table, picked up his remote, and sat in his chair with a cold beer in his hand, dismissing the moment as if it had never happened. Crystal had won a small victory, and she was determined to push things as often as possible.

* * *

Jade took Amber upstairs to her room to get ready for school. Each day, she was picked up by a bus that would take her to a special needs school for the mornings. There weren't many things that Amber responded to except certain sounds. If someone dialed a phone number that Amber could hear, she could instantly repeat the numbers on her toy phone, dialing the numbers backward and forward continuously with a radiant smile on her face. But it was Amber's musical gift that made her special, and everyone except Samuel made sure she explored it as much as possible. Amber never spoke or made any sounds at all. Often she would become engrossed in repetitive motions or would rock for hours. She never cried, but if touched, even as a baby, she would whimper and pull away. Jewell had purchased a padded jumper in which Amber found a place of safety and joy, where she could rock for hours. Sam rarely directed his anger towards Amber, seeming to dismiss her. Jade remembered when Amber was very little and would be in her jolly jumper. This was before anyone knew for sure that Amber was 'special.' Sam would lean over her small body and pull on the rubber tubing, flinging Amber higher than her little legs could handle. After a few very harsh thumps on her head, Sam would growl. "Fucking retarded frog."

Once or twice, he even kicked her, sending her partway across the kitchen floor before the jolly jumper rubber brought her back to her original spot, along with a few bounces along the way.

Sam would thrust his face into Jewells. "I can't understand why you bothered having another kid. Two was enough. You can't do anything right. I don't know why I married a little mouse like you. It's your fault! I needed a real woman. Now all I have are too many mouths to feed and a life that looks like shit. You can't do anything but a bit of housework. Even your cooking is slop. To top it all off, you give birth to a kid that's a retard." Sam, as usual, went to the fridge and got another beer. Along the way, he tugged on the bungee-jumper, again giving Amber a couple of thumps on the head.

Rather than cry, Amber would hold her breath until Jewels' calming voice could lull her back into a dull, unaware state. "Hush, my baby; momma's here to take care of you." Jewell would coo. Soon the movement of Ambers's little body moving back and forth put her back into a world that only she occupied. Jade was glad that Amber would be unable to feel the terror and pain that she and Crystal felt at their mother's loss. Hot tears streamed down her now rosy cheeks, mingling with the cleansing water of the shower. She would dress and face the day as bravely as she could.

CHAPTER EIGHT

Tonight, Jade thought, she and Crystal would have to come up with a serious plan on how to deal with Sam. For now, she would have to get him drunk enough to pass out before any harm could come to her or her sisters. She would have to go to the kitchen and make sure Sam had a few extra beers close at hand. Jade cleaned the kitchen, taking as much time as she could. It was important to keep Sam sitting in his chair. Making sure she had a beer to give him when he ran out, it was her mother's mission, keeping Sam in his chair watching T.V., and now it was her morning mission. As she handed him his fourth beer, Sam slipped his hands down Jade's blouse, cupping her tiny breasts in his skinny, cold hand. His foul breath assaulted her nostrils as he jokingly pretended to show an interest in her social life. Jade lost her balance, spilling the beer as she moved away from him.

"Well, Jade baby, anyone fuck you yet?" Samuel's tone was light but menacing. "You'll make some young buck happy, just like Jewell made me happy all these years. Now, who am I going to get to fuck me?" Sam slobbered in her ears, trying to drag her back towards his emaciated body.

Sam could see the disgust on her face as she pulled herself away from him.

"Go get me another beer." He snarled, dismissing her.

Jade quickly sidestepped him getting another beer. This time she put it on the coffee table in front of Sam rather than hand it to him directly. She vowed he would never touch her again. Crystal and Amber were in their bedrooms, trying to avoid any contact with Sam. Jade was going to have to try to get her father to understand that they would have to attend to their mother's funeral arrangements. But all Sam wanted was another drink.

Jade had to try to keep the fear from her voice. If Sam found out she was afraid of him, he would use that fear to keep her close, and being close to Sam was never good. She would have to talk to him, but with a taunt, angry voice, hoping he would not see how upset she was at his assault.

"Dad, we are going to have to prepare for the burial arrangements for mom." Jade tried not to break down and cry. "When the Coroner releases her body, you will have to call one of the funeral homes and decide what to do."

"Why should I bother with any of the fucking details? With your mother dead, all the money belongs to you girls anyway, except for Amber, now I will be her guardian, and I can do anything I want with her and the money. I have a good mind to live off the land. That little`fuck head` of a sister of yours won`t even know the difference. Besides, she can`t talk much, so she won`t be able to say no. And a man needs caring for and she ant good for much. Maybe she can keep me happy, know what I mean. " Sam slobbered at Jade, knowing she understood his meaning.

"I don't have any money until I turn eighteen, and I don't think I'm old enough to handle the arrangements. You are the head of this household. It's up to you." Jade's voice sounded as if it would break.

"I ain't got nothing. Your mother's fucking parents tried to fuck me over, but I got my lawyer to make sure Amber stays with me forever; as her trustee, I will have control of her money. If she dies, I'll get all of her money. The fucking little retard isn't any good for nothing anyway. Who would even miss a little retard like that? So you see, if you stay or go, it's of no concern to me; either way, I've got control of enough money to make me happy till the day I die. Not too stupid for an old man with a few burnt-out brain cells." Sam laughed, giving Jade an evil snarl while he slumped into his recliner.

"Dad, how can you talk like that?" Jade cried out.

"Because it's like I told your mother before she married me. I'm a no-good, rotten bastard. It's all her fault. She should have listened to me when she had a chance and stayed with her snotty parents."

Jade stared at the recliner, thinking how much it was like her father, small, dirty, and worn. It looked like it belonged in the dump, like a discarded piece of shit, foul and worthless. It had absorbed so much of Sam's energy that even when he wasn't slumped in it watching television, it still seemed like an evil thing. No one ever touched his chair. Not out of respect but because it was a vile object.

"You girl handle the funeral arrangements. You turn eighteen at the end of the month, so you'll get access to a fucking fortune." Sam's eyes blazed at Jade. "Then you'll be 'Miss Big Shot.' So you might as well start learning how to face life now. I won't be around to protect and take care of you like always, but Amber will always be mine."

Sam stared her down for what seemed like forever but was less than a few seconds. Jade could not mistake his intention. He was telling her the same thing he told her mother, but in a different way. The girls would not be safe if Jade left, so she would have to stay and protect them. They would never be free as long as Sam lived.

"I've taken care of this family long enough. It's time you decided what you are going to do when you turn eighteen. Either move out or stay and take care of your sisters. I've done my share." Sam reached over for the beer turned the T.V. up, dismissing her.

Jade thought, "Talk about blind; Sam did think he helped and was needed in some way. If he saw himself the way others did, he might put a gun to his head and end it all, but that would be a dream come true, and Jade had yet to see even one of her aspirations come to pass. It was always everyone else's fault, and Sam was the victim. The world was out to get him, and as usual, he wouldn't go down without a fight. Too bad he didn't know there was no one left in his world even to care one way or the other if he lived or died. He had isolated himself for so long no one would even miss him. Jade was grateful for that little fact. Once she was back in her room, a plan was beginning to form in her mind.

CHAPTER NINE

Detective Ken Tilley stood outside the Walker home's front door thinking about yesterday's events and the heartbreaking accident that had taken place just twenty-four hours earlier. He was glad Kortovich had been there; it made his job a little less clinical. Now it was his distasteful duty to question Sam. Sam answered the door, still unshaven and dressed in his dirty, stained jogging outfit. Tilley almost wanted to slap the look of indifference off his skinny face.

"You can come in, but I don't have much to say about the bitch. She fell down the fucking stairs bringing up the stupid laundry, and now she's dead. The stupid woman probably did it on purpose so she wouldn't have to take care of the girls and me". He left the front door open, indicating that Tilley should follow. "She always was just a rich spoiled brat and never did understand the hardships of a working man."

Sam staggered through the living room into the kitchen. Tilley followed, hoping Sam would be sober enough to answer his questions hoping to conclude this case one way or the other.

"Well, Mr. Walker, I have to get some background from you about the day and find out what factors may have played a role in the accident."

Tilley wanted to drag Sam to the edge of the stairs and give him a good shove. Even if Sam didn't do anything directly to cause the accident, He knew that Sam had inflicted many beatings on his wife, and it was a miracle that she had not been killed before.

"What do you remember of the morning before Jewell fell down the stairs?"

"I don't remember; all I know is I was sitting in my chair; she was coming up the stairs with the laundry, like always. I was watching the White Sox play Toronto when I heard her scream. Jade was in the kitchen, and she was the first one down the stairs. I never go into the basement. There's nothing down there but a washer and dryer. You'd think there was gold downstairs the way Jewell spent all her time doing the laundry. She was the cleanest woman I ever met. If she wasn't so obsessed with the laundry, she might have been doing something else and would still be alive."

"I must tell you that it seems suspicious that Jewell fell down the stairs. You know that the police have been called out to your house many times over the past fifteen years. You have a record of abuse, and I am inclined to wonder if you pushed your wife." Tilley said.

Ken Tilley watched Sam's face hoping he would give him a clue one way or the other as to his involvement in Jewell's deadly tumble. Sam began to shout.

"No one has arrested me in years. Jewell never pressed any charges against me, and if you ask any of my daughters, except the retarded one, they'll tell you Jewell was always hurting herself. It was never me!"   Sam was right, Jewell had always protected him from the police after each beating, and no one in the family ever spoke up about the abuse. Tilley could tell they were scared to death of Sam, and now death was the final victor. In a way, he couldn't blame the girls for not trusting the system and the cops. The newspapers told story after story of women who their lovers or spouse had hunted down. Many were brutally murdered even after they had sought out protection by the police and the courts. If a man wanted to kill someone, a restraining order couldn't stop him. The police were unable to protect all the women who needed safekeeping. Ken knew thousands of women were like Jewell; feeling they have no way out, they learn to cope.

"Jade, get your ass down here!" Sam yelled up the stairs.

Ken Tilley heard the sound of footsteps coming slowly down the stairs. Jade went into the kitchen dressed in denim shorts and a red T-shirt. Her feet were bare, and her hair was still wet.

"What?" Jade asked, her face showing little emotion.

"Tell this fucking cop that I had nothing to do with your mother's accident," Sam shouted.

"I told Detective Tilley everything I knew yesterday," Jade answered.

"Well, you must have said something to make this bastard think I pushed your mother down the stairs. What did you say?" Sam moved closer to Jade, trying to control his temper in front of Detective Tilley, but the tightly balled fist held by his side gave away the barely controllable rage that always ran just beneath the surface

"Look, Mr. Walker. Jade told me it was an accident, but it's my job to ensure that the truth is known. Family members have been known to lie for one another." Ken Tilley moved forward to stand between Sam and Jade, fearing Sam's temper.

"Well, she told you the truth. I never laid a hand on Jewell. If the little bitch could blame me, she would. Then she and her sisters would be rid of me." Sam scowled.

Ken Tilley could tell the conversation was over. Sam moved from the kitchen back to his chair. Sam picked up the remote turned on the TV; an afternoon baseball game blared so loudly Ken knew talking to Sam was useless. It was time for Ken to do a once-over of the accident scene, draw his conclusions, and then make a report.

Ken was just about to go down to the basement when he heard someone coming up the front steps. As he looked up, the door was open; the serious face of Detective Dennis Kortovich greeted him. Kortovich was a bit of a hero within the department, and many of his peers said he is the finest officer they had ever worked with. Tilley welcomed his arrival, and even though this was not Dennis' case, Tilley figured two heads were better than one.

"Come on in, I just finished questioning the master of the house and was going to have a look in the basement; want to come?"

"Thanks, I'd like that."

Once they were down the stairs and out of earshot of Sam, Dennis leaned closer to Ken.

"I've found myself doing nothing but worrying about the girls since this thing happened. Anything I can do will at least make me feel like I'm accomplishing something to make things better, although I doubt they will be very safe without Jewell".

As they turned the corner at the bottom of the stairs, both officers were in shock. Just past the make-shift rumpus room was the laundry room, and what a surprise! It was a magical room of absolute delight. The walls were covered in a thick layer of foam and soft fabric. The color of the material was mostly white with a delicate rose floral pattern making it seem romantic. Along the wall were white wooden bookshelves that were neatly filled with what appeared to be romance novels.

An old stereo lined a second wall, and hundreds of records were piled neatly beside the unit. Dennis walked over and lifted the lid. Inside, a record still sat on the old turntable. He bent over and read the faded label, Tom Jones; a sensation of the seventies was waiting to be spun for a romantic interlude. Along the ceiling were small indoor twinkle lights that cast an idyllic glow inside the white lace that hung in delicate swags.

The washer and dryer were stacked on top of one another, and beside them were white wicker laundry baskets now empty and clean. In the far corner away from the appliances and closer to the stereo was a great, overstuffed rocking chair covered in a deep rose floral pattern. It was the only real color in the whole fanciful room and gave the appearance of a huge bouquet of roses, making it look even more inviting.

"The human spirit finds a way to make life more bearable in many unique ways, and this room is probably what kept Jewell sane while she endured her life with Sam." Dennis offered as he continued to look around the room and admire the many little special items that adorned it making it look like a treasure chest of feminine delights.

"I agree. It must have been a needed sanctuary for Jewell and the girls. From the looks and the size of the chair, all four of the little beauties could easily fit into that rocker and feel safe." Tilley commented with a wistful tone.

"Sam must never come down here. I bet he's usually too drunk to maneuver the steep stairs. It has to have been a blessing for Jewell and the girls to have had this room." Dennis said.

Tilley looked over at Dennis, and without speaking, they both decided to leave the room, sensing that their presence was invasive to Jewell's gentle spirit, whose presence seemed close at hand.

"The problem is that there isn't anything here that will help us, and most likely, she did just fall down the stairs. Jade said she was weak from her bout with the flu." Ken offered.

"Knowing that asshole husband of hers, the poor woman was worked to the bone. Her death will have to be ruled as an accident, and that shit-faced excuse for a man will be all there is to take care of those innocent little girls." Tilley's summation of the situation was simple, and he could tell by Dennis' scowl that he didn't like it either.

Once back up the stairs, Ken hoped he and Dennis could finish the final few questions. But Sam was passed out in his chair, and the girls were nowhere to be seen.

"I think I have enough to conclude that Jewell's death was an accident. The coroner's

The report will be finished Monday. If everything is alright, we can release the body." Ken said.

"I agree. It was an accident." Dennis said, moving towards the back door with Ken.

Dennis's wife Veronica dropped by just as Tilley was leaving.

"Hi, Ken." Veronica greeted him with her warm, inviting style. "I hope I'm not going to interfere with your investigation, but I wanted to make sure the girls had some good food for the next few days."

"You're just in time. We've done all that we can for the day. I'll have to go over things with the coroner and make sure that it all fits together. I'm sure it's an accident, and there's nothing more that can be done." Tilley gave Veronica a thankful smile.

"Thanks for letting me go over things with you today. It makes me feel as if I'm doing something to help the girls, although for now, I don't know what." Dennis shook Ken's hand at the door.

85

CHAPTER TEN

Veronica had cooked several casseroles and a pumpkin cake, a specialty of her sister-in-law Diane. She had also contributed cabbage rolls and perogies, a Slavic dish she learned from her baba. "Are the girls around?" Veronica asked.

She had no sooner asked the question when the girls came down the stairs with Amber in tow.

Jade and Crystal were thankful for the food. Neither of them could cook very well. Their mother had never been a good cook. Sam never seemed to enjoy eating. Jewell had never been able to teach her young children the fine art of food preparation. As a young woman of wealth, Jewell had only visited the kitchen to be fed by the chef or steal some wonderful tidbit when no one was around. It had never really mattered much over the years. Sam's eating habits were erratic, and because of that, he remained very skinny, albeit a small belly could be detected whenever he wore a T-shirt. Still, Sam looked half-starved. Jewell tried to cook for the girls but had always kept it simple. However, her baking was passable, and the girls loved to help in the morning and enjoy their treats for lunch. Once Sam was home, the kitchen was no longer safe.

Jewell had made a special world of her own within the laundry room. She would spend her time waiting for a load to dry with a good book on the go to help pass the time. For some reason, Samuel never complained when Jewell was downstairs. He knew nothing of how laundry was done and never descended the steep stairs to the concrete landing. All he knew was Jewell went down with a big load of dirty clothes in tow, and a few hours later, she came up with clean clothes.

The girls knew they had the cleanest, freshest laundry in the world. Sheets were changed every second day just to allow Jewell enough dirty laundry so that she could have a least two hours of peace each day while the girls were at school. On weekends they all took their time cleaning and grocery shopping, trying to stay out of Sam's way.

"Hi girls, how are you doing?" Veronica inquired as they continued their descent from the upstairs to the kitchen.

"OK, considering what happened to Mom." Crystal replied first, sounding a little sarcastic.

"Mrs. Kortovich, thank you for asking; we're just fine." Jade's response was added to Crystal's with a little more warmth and appreciation.

They both thanked Veronica for the huge box of food. Often it was Jade who commented on her friendly way. Over the years, they had gone for a few haircuts at her salon, even though it was infrequent. Their curly hair never seemed to grow as fast as most people's. Whenever they did go for haircuts, Veronica always seemed incredibly kind, constantly commenting on their looks.

"You girls will learn to appreciate your curl and hair color more as you grow older and realize just how special and pretty you are," Veronica said each time they came to her salon.

The girls could tell she was sincere, and it always made them feel special. Just knowing that someone like Veronica, who was in the beauty business, would single them out to tell them how special they are seemed to boost their confidence just a little. And she somehow seemed to understand Crystal's need to look different.

* * *

For the rest of the afternoon, all Jade could remember was a blur of small talk. She hoped neither Veronica nor Dennis would be able to tell that she was preoccupied. She and Crystal hoped Sam would just stay drunk and passed out on his chair for yet another night. Eventually, the girls were alone in Jade's bedroom.

"Jade, answer me! What's our plan?" Crystal's voice brought Jade back to the present and to the plan that was yet unformed.

"First, we have to bury Mom." Jade assessed the situation. "Then we can figure out what to do with Dad. I don't know how we will be able to get away from Dad; Mom never could. Maybe we could lock him up in a room and never let him out. We could just keep him in the basement."

Jade was hoping for a plan of any kind that would keep Sam away from them.

"It's a good thing Dad's family are all dead, and no one can tell the police if he goes missing." Crystal must have read Jade's thoughts.

Sam's family has been gone for a long time, and the girls barely remembered them. Both their parents and his younger brother were killed in a car accident. Sam's father was a drunk driver. He missed a sharp bend on a country road and went full speed into a half-frozen pond. They didn't stand a chance. The pond was less than six feet deep, but everyone was so drunk they couldn't figure up from down. Good riddance! They were just as mean and no good as their son; even Sam's mother was a fall-down drunk. Who knows? Maybe it was the only way she could cope. Jade was glad she never had to find out, and at this point, she certainly didn't care. Whoever and whatever Sam's parents were, they had produced a man like Sam, and the girls were not interested in finding out what had made him so mean. There was no excuse and the girls wouldn't give the memories of their grandparents any more thought.

"Money will never be a problem. I get my one-third of our grandparent's estate and full access to the interest of yours and Amber's." Jade looked at Crystal. "Dad doesn't know any of that yet, and if we're lucky, he never will. He'd have a shit fit, and we'll all be dead if he finds out. Mom told me that once I become of age if she's not around, control of the money will go directly to me, so Dad will be penniless without me. He thinks he can have access to Amber's share as her guardian, but he doesn't know that when I turn eighteen,

I become her official guardian as well as yours. If we die, everything goes to Dad, and I think he's capable of anything! I will never feel safe if he finds out I have control of all the money.   When he does, we're all in danger." Jade finished.

Jade never doubted Sam would become dangerous if he felt he would lose the income from her grandparent's money. If she and her sisters were to die, Sam would get it all. That was at least a million reasons Jade needed a plan, and now!

"But how are we going get rid of Dad? I sure don't want to keep the ass hole in the basement; I'd rather bury him in the backyard. But then again, I've watched too many movies, when the bones turn up, someone discovers the body."

Jade's big blue eyes reflected her added concern about getting caught if they locked Sam up or killed him; either way, they couldn't afford to get caught. Who would care for Amber if anything happened to the two of them? Murder was not out of the question, but how would they be able to find a foolproof way of getting rid of the body.

"The details will have to wait; we've got to handle Mom's burial. Dad says he doesn't give a damn, so it's up to us. We're all she ever had, and she stayed to protect us. Mom took his threats seriously, and I know killing us would be easy if he thought we would leave him or if he finds out the details of the will."

Jade moved toward the dressing table that sat off to the side of the bedroom window. The window was still closed, and although the day was much cooler than yesterday, it was still a little stuffy. Jade would open the window later after her dad was asleep. It was one thing to think of running away, but murder? Could they do something deadly to their dad? Jade didn't think they could. That meant they would have to come up with another plan to run away, but what about Amber? How would they take care of her? Even with money, it would be unlikely if they were on the run.

CHAPTER
ELEVEN

Dennis and Veronica sat at their kitchen table. It was a beautiful warm August morning. It had only been yesterday that Dennis and Veronica had been over to the Walker house to help out the girls. Late Sunday evening Detective Tilley had called to say that the Coroner ruled that the death was accidental and the case was closed. But not for the girls who lived in the now motherless home; nor for the two concerned friends who sat and drank their morning coffee only a few doors down the street. Veronica was visibly upset, her large, slightly plump body trembling with anger.

"I don't care what anyone says!" Veronica's rich voice carried throughout the kitchen. "He killed her. He might as well have pushed her down the stairs himself. She was so frail and underweight." Veronica continued as she got up for a second cup of coffee. "If she was sick with the flu, the girls said, then his negligence caused it. Either way, he should be charged. He's the meanest man I've ever met." Veronica's voice was getting louder. "I've often thought we would hear of some disaster at that house. It was only a matter of time." Veronica sat back down, taking a sip of coffee, nudging Dennis for a response.

Dennis was always slow to voice his thoughts. It drove Veronica crazy, waiting for his slow, deliberate answer. But there was a part of him that was always amused by his overly dramatic wife as she waited impatiently for his response. But today, he nodded his assent quickly.

"I know. There's been so little I could do over the years." Dennis held his coffee cup in a tight grip. "I've stayed in touch with other officers who have had to respond to calls of violence at the Walkers over the years, and no matter how often she was hospitalized, Jewell never let us charge Sam. She was so scared that the charges would not hold, putting Sam in a murderous rage that might end her life. And who would protect her babies? She just put up with the beatings, the lesser of two evils."

Dennis stroked his mustache, a familiar habit whenever he was deep in thought. "Who can blame her? We fail a lot of women who are abused by their lovers or husbands, and things usually get worse. It's the hardest part about being a cop knowing that you can't always keep people safe."

Veronica stared at her husband for a moment, noting his square jaw flexing back and forth. His grey-blue eyes were fixed at a spot on the table somewhere in front of him, his toast untouched. It was another sign of his involvement in this case. Veronica knew it was because of his paternal feelings toward the girls. The love for his own two daughters, Natasha and Katrina, made him especially vulnerable whenever kids were involved. Both girls were now grown, each happy with fulfilling careers. Katrina had just started Real Estate with Re/Max while Natasha built a successful clientele at the shop. Tasha had completed an

Honors degree in Slavic language, which she had hoped would be her career. With the fall of the "Wall" in East Berlin and the dismantling of communism. The murder of foreign businessmen and the crime spree that followed did not make going to Russia as a business attaché appealing. Both girls were dating brothers, Carlin and Steve, both kind, intelligent boys that came from a great family. Steve's father was a Doctor, while his wife raised all four children and followed her passion for photography. It was hard to picture what it would feel like if either girl had married someone like Sam Walker.

"Let's make them something more to eat. The girls must be out of the food we took yesterday. No one should cook at a time like this." Veronica slid out of her chair and went over to the fridge. "I have several casseroles that are fresh, some pies and fresh bread. At least this will help a little." Veronica's solution for many of life's problems was solved with good food.

"Good, it will give me an excuse to go over and check in on the girls," Dennis added.

He picked up his empty coffee cup and untouched toast, slipped it off the plate into the garbage, and put the dishes in the dishwasher.

"I don't like the thought of the girls being alone with Sam. I don't trust him in more ways than one. I guess I've just seen too much."

Veronica thought of the years Dennis had spent on the force and knew that in a city like Chicago, you saw or heard it all. Murder, robberies, and drug-related crimes were taken in stride, but when it came to rape, domestic violence, or the abuse of a child, it made Dennis fume. Veronica knew that as a cop, it was always hard to deal with these types of crimes, but as a father, Dennis was never sure what side of the law he would end up on—added to the worry about the Walker girls and the Judge's missing daughter. This new case was going to prove difficult, but Dennis knew he would stay involved in the Walker case; it was his obligation as a father as well as a cop.

* * *

Veronica showered first; it always took her longer to get ready. Once in the master bedroom, she looked around. The green and wine colors of the comforter and drapes were both masculine and feminine; it was her favorite room. A huge king-sized bed dominated the room. It looked like a picture out of House Beautiful; several floral images were arranged on the wall above the bed, along with a huge floral bow done in wines, pinks, and several shades of green. On either side of the bed, hanging floral baskets drew attention to a headboard that supported various matching pillows and cushions, making the bed look like something out of the movies. A large TV sat along the wall opposite the bed with a high back chair sitting in one corner.

The bedroom was the place Dennis would go to watch his favorite programs whenever Veronica was working in the salon. He found that the women got so loud the only way he could hear his favorite shows was when he was at the back of the house in his bedroom. Large patio doors opened onto a deck where an oversized hot tub sat overlooking a spectacular backyard.

Hotubbing was one of Dennis and Veronica's favorite things to do any time of the day whenever they wanted to relax. The hot tub was a great place to get together at the end of a long day, share a glass of wine, and discuss the day's events. Once out of the tub, they would inevitably find themselves in bed for a round of lovemaking. Veronica took a good look at her ample body in the bedroom mirror and sighed. It would be nice if she could take off a few extra pounds, but after a thousand diets with no results, she had given up and accepted the fact that not everyone is meant to be skinny.

Dennis had never once commented on her weight. He always seemed to love her just the way she was. Only once in all of the years that they were married did Veronica ever feel as if he had stopped loving her. As it turned out, things were bad.

Dennis had gotten himself involved with another woman, a good friend of both Dennis and Veronica's. It had taken a great deal of love and patience to work things out. After thirty years of marriage and two daughters, throwing all of that away seemed stupid to the strong-minded Veronica. After a year of counseling, things were better than they had ever been, and Veronica was determined never to take life for granted again.

Veronica went into the closet and took out an Easy-Wear outfit of bright blue cotton. The day would be hot once again, and Veronica loved the lightweight fabric's fit and feel. Besides, it had a Velcro wristband that would allow her to find just the right comfort level. Her hair was easy to do; just wash and style and let dry naturally. Veronica would do her makeup while Dennis showered.

With the cleanup finished and Veronica almost ready, Dennis went to his bedroom to change out of his housecoat. A quick shower, and he would take less than twenty minutes to get ready.

Dennis picked a new gray suit from his closet and a freshly dry-cleaned crisp white shirt and a black and red striped tie. Dennis' black loafers shone like the new leather seats in a Lexus, and he smelled almost as good. Everything Dennis wore looked like money. Once dressed, he thought about his day. First, he would check in on the Walker girls, and then he would meet Chuck and continue with the search for Mandy, the judge's daughter.

Dennis felt a strong need to protect the girls. They would have to handle everything with Jewell gone. Sam was useless, and Dennis was sure he wouldn't lift a finger to help them with their mother's funeral. Maybe there was something he and Veronica could do to help. As they walked over to the Walker house, they were silent. Nothing more could be said about the incident, and now they would have to try to keep the girls safe.

Dennis knocked on the back door of the Walker home. Dennis knew that the family was usually gathered at the back of the house.

"Do you think the girls are home?" Veronica asked after waiting for a few minutes with no results.

"I can't imagine that they have anywhere to go. Jewell has always stayed close to home to protect the girls. I'm sure Jade and Crystal have taken it upon themselves to protect Amber."

Veronica knew her husband was right. Jewell seldom left the house, and even when she went for groceries, she would have Amber in tow. Dennis knocked again, this time with a great deal more force.

"What the hell is all the fuss about?" Sam came to the door, still in his underwear and an old stained T-shirt.

"We came by to see how you and the girls are," Dennis answered, still standing on the back step landing, Veronica at his side. "We thought you might like some baking and casseroles."

"Come on in. I could use some food. The girls can't cook worth shit; then again, neither could Jewell. What you got there?"

"I have a casserole and some homemade bread. I also have a pan of brownies and an apple pie.

The pie is frozen, but I could show Jade how to cook it." Veronica stepped past Sam and put the food on the kitchen counter.

"Jade's not here; she had to go and see to Jewell's funeral. The coroner released her body this morning, and it was shipped over to Greenhill's. It's the closest funeral home." Sam said.

"I would have thought that you would have wanted to handle the arrangements of Jewell's funeral; after all, she was your wife," Dennis said sarcastically.

Sam gave Dennis a dirty look. A few years ago, he might even have taken Dennis on in a fight, knowing Dennis's remark was a put-down. He knew he couldn't beat Dennis, who was at least fifty pounds heavier and seven inches taller. So he backed off, giving Veronica a dirty look instead.

"Why should I handle the arrangements? She never loved me, just the girls. She was their mother. Jade will be eighteen next month, so she might as well get used to making grown-up decisions." Sam walked past Veronica and plopped down in his recliner.

"I'll be sure to let the girls know you dropped by," Sam said, dismissing Veronica and Dennis by turning up the TV to a blaring level.

They exchanged looks and let themselves out through the back door. As they walked back to their home, Veronica was bristling. As soon as she was out of earshot, she launched into a tirade.

"I can't believe Jade has to handle the arrangements of her mother's funeral. She's just a baby. These girls have already endured too much, and now this. I could just slap that man. If I could, I would call welfare and have the girls taken away. But I know they would be separated, and I just couldn't do that to Jade; she loves her sisters."

Veronica was shouting, and Dennis had to give her a look that said, 'keep it down."

"All we can do is keep an eye on the girls. This won't be the last visit, and maybe I can use some of my contacts to see if I can get the girls out of there. If Jade is about to turn eighteen, we might get her as a guardian for the girls. Don't say anything to them until I check things out. They must feel desperate knowing that they are trapped alone with Sam. I hope they don't think about doing something rash like running away."

"I hope Jade can handle making the arrangements for Jewell's funeral. We will have to make sure we're there for her." Veronica said.

Dennis's thoughts turned to his schedule for the afternoon and what he had to do with his new case. All of the footwork needed to find Mandy. He knew that it had already been well over twenty-four hours, the mandatory window for an official disappearance report. Chuck, Dennis, and six other officers had divided up the names. The club manager had also given a list of the kids at the Rave. They had to give their names, address, and parent's phone number because they were all underage. They had worked the case all of Saturday, and it was now mid-Sunday morning, and if she weren't found, he would be hard-pressed to find time to go to Jewell's funeral.

CHAPTER TWELVE

Jewel's funeral service was as depressing as her life had been. The only ones who attended were Dennis and Veronica Kortovich and their daughters, Natasha and Katrina, as well as Dennis' partner Chuck and his wife, Shelley. Not one other person was present, making Dennis even more aware of how alone and dangerous it would be now for the girls without their mother. It was early Tuesday morning, and four days had passed since Jewell's fall.

Jade, Crystal, and Amber were all dressed in black skirts. Crystal, however, had traded in her black locks and grizzly makeup for a fresh, clean look. The light tops they wore, given the heat of the day, were as conservative as possible. It was a hot morning and the day promised to be another scorcher. The two older girls looked drawn and tired while Amber was fresh and as beautiful as a Dresden doll; she could neither feel her mother's loss nor appreciate the pain her sisters felt.

Natasha and Katrina both had wanted to come to the funeral when they heard about Jewell's accident. Although they were both a lot older than the Walker girls, each felt a great deal of sympathy toward them. They had watched Jade,

Crystal, and Amber grow up over the years, and even though the girls had only spoken to each other once in a while, they were at least on casual terms. Natasha had always felt they were the prettiest little girls she had ever seen. Katrina could remember wanting to babysit her younger neighbors, but even though she offered, Jewell never accepted. Veronica had to make sure that Katrina didn't take it personally. Jewell never had anyone babysit her girls, and after a while, everyone knew the reason.

Jade looked around at those who gathered at the funeral home to pay tribute to Jewell. They were outside in a large Gazebo for the service. It would have held at least a hundred mourners, but today the gathering was very small. If Jade had been able to, she would have had only herself and her sisters. She smiled at Crystal and tightly held Amber's hand. Amber rocked gently in time with an unheard beat somewhere in the dark maze of her brain. Her eyes were fixed on an invisible presence.

Jade wondered if she saw an angel from another dimension. It was as if her body was on this physical plane while her eyes and ears beheld an invisible realm unheard or unseen by others. She smiled a radiant smile, eyes wide, her face a vision of beauty. Jade hoped it was Jewell's face she was smiling at. Sam was absent from the funeral. He was at home, falling drunk, rambling on about Jewel's dying on purpose, too angry to attend.

Dennis and Veronica had offered the girls a ride, but Jade insisted that she wanted to go with her sisters in the family van. They would stay a little longer at the funeral home. It was another sunny hot August day, and when the funeral was over, the girls would stay at the pavilion before placing Jewell's ashes to rest in a niche. They were not anxious to let her go nor to return home to the abuses of their father. Jade decided they would spend the afternoon in the sun with Jewell's ashes and remember her sweet strength and all that she had endured for them. This would be her and her sister's private moments and personal farewells. Greenhill's was a beautiful place to spend the last moment with a loved one.

* * *

"I can't believe that there are so few people attending the funeral," Veronica commented quietly to Dennis, not wanting anyone to hear.

"I know," Dennis said, keeping his voice low, nodding in agreement. "It seems strange that there is no one else there. I never saw a notice in the paper, but I assumed that I had missed it." Dennis whispered his explanation for the lack of mourners. "It shows how truly isolated the girls are."

There was no minister to officiate at the funeral, only the senior mortician, Derek Hanson. Dennis thought Derek looked like Ichabod Crane from the Disney cartoon 'Sleepy Hollow.' Tall, very thin, pale, and bony, he looked like a walking cadaver. His face was long, almost horse-like and his buckteeth emphasized the horsy quality. His hands were unusually large for such a slight-looking man. His fingers were long and tapered, while the nails were short and well-groomed. Derek's hair was pulled back into a small ponytail, a leftover look from the '80s. If he thought it was cool, he was certainly out of touch.

The only thing that saved him from being a caricature was his sparkling white shirt and a well-tailored suit that fit to perfection. If you stood closely, he emitted a slight smell of formaldehyde mixed with his fragrance, Drakkar. The nasal quality of his mono-pitched voice sounded flat and mournful. The words of comfort that should have made everyone in the little group feel better only sounded shallow and too rehearsed.

"May she rest in peace!" Derek finished, closing his prayer book, and stood off to the side.

As his final words were spoken, Dennis looked over at the Walker girls; their small faces were drawn and tired. There was a look of determination in the girl's eyes that made him feel as if he were looking at two young soldiers on their final mission. Dennis hoped their youthful resolve would pull them through whatever lay ahead, and they would do what was necessary to survive. Dennis would have killed the bastard if it were him; Samuel was the kind of guy few would notice missing. He quickly pushed the thought from his mind and went over to give one final hug to the girls. Veronica gripped his hand as if reading his mind. He felt a slight blush creep up his already colorful cheeks. She always could read him.

"Are you sure you won't come back with us?" Both girls shook their heads back and forth. No.

"Well, if there is anything you need, let me know. I'll drop in from time to time and make sure you are alright." Dennis said.

"That goes for me too," Veronica added. "I'll make sure you have a few good meals until you are on your feet. If you need any help in the kitchen, you can come over or call."

Crystal was the first to respond with a small smile and stood up to give a gentle hug to Veronica. "Thanks, but we'll be just fine. We have appreciated all that you have done so far, but we will manage on our own."

"Yes," Jade added. "We're all right. Dad will probably stay drunk. We know how to stay out of his way, and I can cook a few good things. If you come by, it will only make things worse for us. So please call first. If anything bad happens, I promise I'll come and get you." Jade said, giving Veronica an assuring look.

"You promise?" Dennis looked both girls in the eye, seemingly checking back and forth to make sure they understood he was there for them.

"Absolutely!" was the answer given in unison from both girls?

A look passed between the girls that Dennis couldn't quite read. He sure the hell hoped they would be all right.

"Okay, but you have to be sure to call if you need us." was Dennis's final response.

As he walked off with Veronica, leaving the girls at the funeral home's outdoor pavilion, Dennis had a gut feeling something bad was about to happen, and he knew his gut was always right. Would he be able to use his skills to keep the girls safe? He put the thought to the back of his mind he still had to find Mandy, Judge Switzer's daughter.

CHAPTER THIRTEEN

Crystal and Jade watched everyone leave. Dennis gathered his family on either side of him, his arms enfolding his wife on one side while Katrina nestled into one arm, holding her sister's hand in the other. It was a sight that made her feel sad and lonely. Why couldn't Sam be like Dennis? It was a question that seemed to have no answer.

"Do you think Dennis will call before he comes over? Crystal asked.

"I hope so. If he comes over at the wrong time, it will be the worst thing that could happen. With what we have planned for dad, we will need to make sure no one comes around for a long time." Jade answered.

"Do you think everyone thought it was strange that no one attended the funeral?"

Jade had been adamant that the funeral home didn't put a notice in the paper. She remembered the argument she had with Derek Hanson.

* * *

"Miss Walker, it would be highly irregular not to have a notice in the paper. You will never be able to contact your family and friends by phone. A notice lets everyone know the funeral details without you having to go over it again and again. It will save you a great deal of pain and grief." Derek Hanson said.

Jade tried to move back a few inches as Derek approached her, but the carpet on the floor prevented the chair from moving back with ease. Derek sat on the edge of the desk directly in front of her, putting little distance between the two of them. Although Derek was impeccably dressed, she still got a creepy feeling from him. As he leaned forward to make his point, he put his cold, clammy hand on her knee. A shiver ran up Jade's spine, and as Derek moved closer, Jade got a whiff of his cologne. The fragrance was familiar, but on Derek, it had a slightly 'off' smell. There was a strong chemical order about him that made her stomach churn. Was it the smell or something more? Jade wanted to get the arrangements of the funeral over and get away from the overly helpful mortician.

"Look, Mr. Hanson. We have no living relatives on either side and as far as friends go, my parents kept to themselves and had few friends. I don't think anyone would even know who my mother even was even if they see the announcement in the paper."

Jade tried to sound assertive as she leaned in, trying to make things seem more intimate and friendly.

"The last thing my sisters and I need is a bunch of do-gooders that come by just because they feel sorry for us.

Please, Mr. Hanson, we don't want anyone other than a few friends to contact us. You know what it's like, a bunch of strangers all gawking around hugging and kissing us, saying they're so sorry. We just can't take it. Please respect the fact that this is how we want it." Jade hoped she was giving him her most assertive look.

A slow smile crossed Derek's long, bony face. His lips slipped past his yellow teeth, spittle forming in the corners of his mouth as he spoke

"I understand completely. I lost my parents several years ago. All I had left was my baby sister, and now she too is gone."

Derek turned around and pointed at a picture of a lovely young girl hanging on the wall behind him. The girl was no more than twelve or thirteen. Her copper, blond hair and blue eyes shone with promise and life. Jade felt a momentary connection; her face seemed familiar. Suddenly a chill passed through her body; she shook it off, concentrating on the details at hand. Jade didn't know why, but she didn't feel safe around Derek Hanson. There was one quiet moment when Derek stared at her with his pale, cold, blue eyes, and she thought she saw a look that was much the same as a wolf when it's sizing up its prey to see if it will be an easy victim. It made her blood run cold. She almost wanted to say, "A penny for your thoughts." but at that moment, she felt she would be paying too much. Whatever he was thinking, she probably was better off not knowing. The way he smelled, walked and talked was almost like a comic book figure, not someone of flesh and blood. Jade could see him stalking some poor girl who was dumb enough to be nice to him. You always knew the mentally unbalanced types.

"I will respect your wish and let you handle it the way you want. Just remember, I'm here for you if you need anything, and I mean anything." His hands lingered on Jade's bare knee.

Jade had to make the trip alone, leaving Crystal to care for Amber. They had never trusted Sam, and their little sister would be unable to protect herself should he decide to try something. After the usual formalities, Derek took Jade on a tour.

"Greenhill's is a state-of-the-art funeral home. Whether you want to bury or cremate your mother is up to you. We have several affordable packages either way." Derek said as he walked Jade through a room full of caskets.

"I would rather cremate my mother." Jade choked out her choice, trying to keep her emotions under control.

"I must confess I'm partial to cremation. It seems degrading to allow a loved one to decay in the ground. Ashes seem to hold the essence of the person. Once they find a beautiful new home in one of our designer urns, the relatives seem so much happier. I think it adds a sense of beauty to the death of a loved one."

Jade suddenly felt a chill run through her spine. The thought of this man touching her beloved mother was more than she could handle, but it was too late to turn back now. The coroner had shipped the body to Greenhill's that morning at Jade's request.

Greenhill's was new, with every amenity needed to help console those who faced the loss of their loved ones. The colors on the walls were soft pastel green, the carpets an understated floral of yellow, rose, and mint, giving the room a feeling of spring, a time of renewal and new beginnings. When Derek first entered the waiting room and introduced himself, Jade had to hide what must have been a look of shock. His face was too long, almost like a mule, skinny, bony, pale, and very creepy. She had the impression he would be happier in a dark, damp cell somewhere in an old castle rather than this modern, bright building.

At the moment, she had a difficult task ahead of her, so she brushed off her unkind thoughts and got to the business at hand. All she had was her dad's credit card. If Sam had his way, he would put Jewell in a box in the backyard, the way you'd bury a pet; cheap and out of sight. Derek remained courteous but calm throughout their dealings.

"I hope credit is alright. It's my dad's. But like I said, he couldn't be here." Jade didn't want to explain why and she left it up to Derek to presume he was too distraught to help with the arrangements.

"A credit card will be fine. I can understand how your father must be feeling. Losing someone you love can do terrible things to a man. I know from personal experience."

She was unable to read anything into Derek's statement, but she presumed he was referring once again to his sister, the pretty girl in the picture. Jade was able to pay a portion if she wanted and wait for the final bill. After assessing the modest needs of Jade's request, Derek was sure she would need very little beyond the basic package. With the business and money details handled, Jade went on a tour of the establishment. She had to pick out an urn and see the mausoleum where Jewell's ashes would be kept. The first stop was to see the crematorium, a free-standing chamber that delighted Derek.

"Here she is," Derek said, a sloppy grin on his face.

The crematorium stood sleek and cold in the middle of the room, not the usual square, recessed ovens that she had seen on television. It reminded her of a huge time capsule, all shiny stainless steel, with black cast iron molded bindings at the ends and the middle of the sleek chamber. This 'dark duchess of death' stood on an independently raised concrete pad in the middle of a beautiful room. The carpet surrounding the concrete base was plush with a heavy pattern of large rosebuds, complementing the leaf green walls and heavily draped windows. Straight ahead, at the front of the room, a small nook was visible. It was draped on either side by a heavy, brocaded material that matched the carpet. Within the nook sat a small ornate desk with chairs on either side. The occupant could close the drapes for privacy or leave them pulled back on either side, making a picture-like frame for the delicate little room. Jade liked the look. It offered privacy, allowing the occupant to stay out of immediate sight.

"This is where we will cremate your mother's body," Derek said, watching Jade's face to see if there was any reaction.

Jade almost cringed. It wasn't the words but rather the sound of Derek's voice that grated on her already overly stressed nerves. It held a tone of evil, making the high-pitched nasal sound of his voice send shivers down her spine.

"To operate the crematorium is simple."

Derek stepped to the front of the crematorium, obvious pride on his face.

"We turn two dials in opposite directions after we place the body directly in the center. Then secure the doorway with an airtight seal."

His bony hands pulled the cast iron handle down.

"There must be nothing in the way to break the seal, or the master switch will refuse to engage. This is the only free-standing unit in the world, and I invented it. Its double coils don't allow for any smoke to escape into the atmosphere. It is environmentally friendly, and it would go undetected anywhere because you don't need a smokestack. It is foolproof, and any child could operate it."

Derek seemed pleased, like a kid with a new toy.

"The contents are reduced to a few ounces of ashes; they are then retrieved after the cooling process, after which we put them in a standard box and later transferred to the urn of your choice."

Once again, Derek watched Jade's face in a way that made her feel like she was under a microscope. It was as if he was trying to figure out something about her that seemed to have him puzzled. Jade was sure Derek didn't handle all of his clients like this. He was a creep. If she could have prevented her mother from being cremated by this man, she would have. But life must move forward, and she was there to make her mother's funeral arrangements with as little attention from the outside world as possible. There was no time to shop around for a different funeral home.

Derek went over to the chamber and demonstrated how to open the door. Next, he went over to the double dials off to the side of the large oval opening. He turned one dial counter-clockwise the other clockwise.

"In less than an hour, it's all finished. The oven heats to over twenty-four hundred degrees like I said child's play."

The final comment caught Jade for the second time. In a flash, she knew this might be a perfect way to deal with her 'problem'. If she were somehow able to have Sam cremated, it would be the perfect way to get rid of a body. Nobody, no evidence, no crime! Jade refused to mull over the tiny seed of an idea any further. After all, she hadn't completely decided how to deal with dad. As of now, she didn't have a crematorium hanging around the backyard just for a time like this.

"You are the last appointment of my day." Derek came over and placed a hand on her shoulder. "With all of the details handled, I think we can safely say we have covered just about everything. I'll just get my coat and see you to your car."

Jade would have loved to say no; she could see herself out, but she had no time. Derek was already a step ahead of her, reaching for his black trench coat. "Thank you." was all she was able to say.

Once outside the large, white, double doors of the funeral home, Derek paused in front of an electronic keypad.

"You'll have to stand a little to the side, please. We lock up with a punch code number, and I would prefer if you didn't watch." Derek said with a self-important air.

Jade moved a few steps to the left of the huge double doors.

"It's not personal, but for security only you understand."

As his finger reached out to press the numbers, Jade could hear the audible tones as each number was pressed. Each key gave off a different musical tone, each perfectly pitched. It was at that exact moment that Jade knew she could get away with murder, and no one would ever find out. It would be her little sister Amber, whose gift would hold the key.

CHAPTER FOURTEEN

Sam's head hurt as it had never hurt before. It wasn't the dull ache that came most mornings before his usual beer. No, this pain was searing and hot. It came from a place in the back of his skull. The kind of pain you would feel if someone smacked you over the head with a baseball bat. He tried to move; he wanted to gather his bearings. He felt strangely disorientated. "What the fuck" he thought. He couldn't move. His arms were bound tightly behind his back; his shoulders restrained as well. When he looked down at his chest, he saw the gray duct tape wound tightly around his chest›s upper portion; his legs were also restrained. When he tried to lean forward for a better look, he almost choked. He could feel the rough fibers of a rope as they dug into his throat. Sam was able to lean back a little and gaze up. As he tilted back slightly, he recognized the black rubber tubing of an infant's jolly jumper. The hook secured tightly into the doorway frame, leading downstairs into the basement.

The chair Sam was sitting on was the old, white chair that was usually in the bathroom. He had to blink a few times to clear his vision. For a moment, he felt as if he would blackout. He was startled by the sensation that he was about to fall backward. It was then that he realized his tenuous predicament. He had a noose around his neck, his feet and hands bound tightly, while he sat on an old rickety chair that was precariously balanced on two legs, and any sudden movement could send him crashing down the steep basement stairs. He found out only too quickly that if he leaned too far forward, the noose around his neck would tighten, causing him to choke and gag. "There must be a robbery taking place, and the bastards must have tied me up." Samuel thought aloud. His memory escaped him; he couldn't remember a thing. It all seemed very professional. He was totally at someone's mercy, although at this point, he couldn't see or hear a soul. At the exact moment, he heard the front door open. The voices he heard were not strangers, "Thank goodness!" Sam thought, relief spreading over his tired, sore body.

"Girls, "Sam shouted. "Get over here; I need help!" Sam had to make sure he didn't move too far forward or back. "Where are you? Fuck! Get me outta here."

Jade looked at Crystal, her heart racing. The thumping in her chest felt like someone was punching her from the inside. Crystal's face looked pinched, full of determination. Jade knew that once Crystal made her mind up, there would be no turning back. There was a part of Jade that still held a small hope that their dad could somehow redeem himself. Maybe he could still say something to help her understand his deplorable behavior. With Sam tied up, it gave the girls a sense of security. Crystal was the one who came up with the idea of the jolly jumper and putting the chair at the top of the basement stairs, the place where her mother had fallen to her death. As they rounded the corner, they were surprised to see the look of excitement and hope on their father's face.

117

Neither girl could remember him ever having more than an evil scowl or being in a twisted temper tantrum, causing his face to distort.

"Thank God you're here. Hurry, untie me before they come back."

"Who?" Jade asked, not understanding what her dad was saying.

"The guys who tied me up stupid!" Sam looked at Jade as if she were missing a few brain cells.

It was at that second that Jade figured it out. Sam thought someone had broken into the house and tied him up. Boy, was he in for a big surprise!

"There are no guys Dad, it was us. We tied you up." Jade's statement was said such a matter of fact that Sam still didn't get it.

"You tied me up?" He repeated.

"Yes." Crystal answered.

"What the fuck for?" he shouted, "Let me go, for fucks sake!" He struggled in the chair, but once again, he began to choke.

"We can't do that, Dad." Jade's reply was soft.

"You sluts untie me now, or when I get out of this chair, you won't be able to walk for a week; I'll beat you so bad."

Sam began to spit as he screamed at them, his face getting redder as he tried to shuffle in the chair without falling back.

Crystal's exploded. "You stupid, mean old man! Do you think you're going to get out of that chair and ever lay a hand on us again, not ever, ever, ever!"

Sam shut up, but only for a moment. "You can't keep me tied up like this; I'm your father. So stop this shit and let me go." Sam leaned a little too far forward after this speech and started to choke once again.

"Don't worry, Dad. We don't intend to keep you tied up for long. We're going to kill you. You haven't given us any other choice. It's you or us. Amber needs us, so it's got to be you."

At this point, Jade was glad that Amber was upstairs in her rocking chair. She wouldn't leave her chair until one of the girls came to get her.

"Why? What have I ever done to hurt you?" Sam's face was pale. You could tell by his small, sneaky eyes that he was trying to figure out what to do next.

"What have you ever done to us?" Crystal repeated the question in a voice that sounded like fingernails across a blackboard.

"Where should I begin?" Crystal shouted, shaking her hands in the air in exasperation. "Let's start with you beating our mother for the past twenty years. Or maybe you're foul-mouthed ranting and raving. The slaps and punches across the head every day. The kicks and shoves if we didn't move out of your way fast enough. Or maybe the dirty little remarks made towards us and the inappropriate touching." Crystal started to choke. "Maybe it's just because you're a no-good sack of shit! Don't look at me that way; I learned all the foul-mouthed stuff from you." Crystal's face was now only inches away from Sam's.

Sam's inability to move only fueled his anger. So when he spit in Crystal's face, she was shocked. She slammed her fist into Sam's mouth as hard as she could, the full weight of her small body put into the punch. Sam's chair tilted precariously at the top of the stairs. The rope suspended from the rubber cord tightened around his neck; the choking sounds weren't wasted on the girls.

"Just remember, you're in no position to push us around or piss us off any more than we are already." Crystal spat back in Sam's face, wiping some of the dribbles from her chin. Sam's spit was already smeared into her copper curls.

Jade moved forward. It was time to get things over. If anyone came to the door, Sam would be able to shout out for help. Jade lowered her face to her father's, putting her hand over his mouth. "Don't!" Jade said, "Or I'll kick you down these stairs."

When Jade removed her hand, Sam gathered as much spit as possible in his mouth and spewed it out in full force. After the warm wad landed on Jade's face, he shouted out with all the hatred he felt. It wasn't personal; he hated everyone.

"You little slut, I'll kill you when I get free. I'll slit your fucking throat!" Once again, he almost choked, forgetting his precarious perch as he leaned a little too far forward.

"That was it." Jade thought, "It's time to end it all."

She kicked at the chair›s legs as hard as she could, breaking one of the spindly legs at the halfway point. The chair started to buckle, pitching back. Sam tried to stop the chair from falling down the stairs by putting his total weight forward, allowing the rope that was attached to the rubber tube to tighten around his throat. With his eyes wide, he teetered at the top of the stairs for a few seconds. It looked like he would be able to steady himself; he sat holding his breath, choking back tears of pain and fear. The chair balanced precariously on its three legs. It was a very old chair, cheap and worn. Even on its best day, it was never really strong. Suddenly a second leg cracked. Time seemed to slow down as the leg buckled. The chair crashed completely under Sam's weight, and although he wasn't a big man, his full weight caused the rope that was suspended by the jolly jumper to tighten completely around his skinny neck. Jade and Crystal instinctively moved toward each other. It was something they always did when things started to go wrong between Sam and their mother. This was different, though. Their hearts beat together in an "off-beat" rhythm that kept pace with the sound of Sam's thrashing as he tried to find some ground to steady himself. It was impossible.

With the chair still taped to Sam's body, he struggled fiercely at his awkward position, twisting as hard as he could, hoping the tape would break. His ankles were secured to the two remaining legs of the chair. As his body arched awkwardly forward, the rope from the jolly jumper cut into his flesh, and as the weight of his body pulled him down, his head bounced a little from the elasticity of the cord. He fought back the choking feeling as he instinctively pulled back. That final movement was all that was needed to break the last two legs of the rickety old chair. Sam now hung entirely by his neck. He was not a big man, only 5 feet 2 inches and about one hundred and thirty pounds, but even so, his weight was too much. The door jamb suddenly gave way, causing Sam to tumble backward with a force so intense he flew over the first few stairs, tumbling heavily down the remaining steps.

The girls watched, still holding each other tightly as Sam tumbled head over heels down the basement stairs, landing on the cold concrete floor where Jewel had landed, almost precisely a week before.

Sam's body didn't look nearly as twisted as their mothers had after the accident and both Jade and Crystal stood transfixed at the top of the stairs, not knowing what to do next. It seemed like forever before anyone spoke, but as usual, it was Crystal who made the first move.

"Now what?" was all Crystal could whisper. The fact that they had done it was just sinking in. "Do you think we killed him?" she continued.

"I can't tell. It's so dark at the bottom of the stairs, and I'm almost afraid to turn the lights on." Jade quivered, still holding Crystal tightly.

Crystal was trembling as she pried Jade's fingers from her upper arm. Crystal's fingers awkwardly found the light switch. Sam lay perfectly still at the bottom of the steps. The only sound they could hear was the beating of their hearts and the ragged-offbeat sound of breathing. They couldn't tell if Sam was contributing to the soft swish of their breaths. They would have to descend the stairs to the basement below to find out if Sam was indeed dead. Jade seemed unable to move, so Crystal took the first tentative steps toward their father.

He now lay at the bottom of the stairs, the rubber cord still hanging awkwardly around his neck. Crystal could tell from her view at the top of the stairs that Sam's face was a twisted mask of hate. Slowly, step-by-step, Crystal put each tiny foot firmly on each descending stair. She hesitated for a few seconds as she continued, trying to make sure her footing was secure. Crystal felt a wave of nausea hit her in the pit of her stomach and her knees felt weak. After what seemed to take forever, she finally stopped two steps away from her father. 'Daddy Dearest!' What was that movie she had watched? Some movie star was mean to her kids; she didn't even compare to her dad. Funny how at a time like this, you would think of some stupid old movie? Crystal noticed that the handrail had been broken by Sam's fall.

Her hand found a small portion of the railing still loosely attached to the crumbling drywall. She instinctively latched on to it, pulling it from the wall. She was now only one step away from the cold cement floor where Sam lay unceremoniously. She lifted the broken portion of the ragged wood high over her head and brought it down on Sam's head. She could hear the crack of the deadly tool as it connected with his skull "one more time for luck." she thought as she went for a second whack. A small trickle of blood had formed under Sam's skull. Crystal was pretty sure he was dead.

"That's for the movies!" Crystal said.

Her voice sounded confidant, even a little smug. As Crystal marched up the stairs, she looked up at Jade, who stood on the landing, looking stunned.

"What did you think?" an annoyed Crystal declared. "That I haven't seen a few movies where the guy isn't dead. I always thought it was stupid when the girl just stepped over or around him, and then he grabs her. I only did what anyone with a few brains would have done. Made sure he was dead." She looked back over her shoulder at Sam's broken body. "He won't be getting up for a second round!" Crystal's fears had been entirely overcome by that final, personal act of liberation.

Jade smiled weakly at her younger sibling. God help anyone who messed with Crystal. Tears welled up in her eyes. Too bad Jewell wouldn't be there to join in. Suddenly a feeling of great calm descended over Jade.

When she looked over at her sister's determined face, she could tell Crystal felt something too. Maybe their mother was there. Tonight they would set an extra plate and celebrate their freedom. The spirit of Jewell would always be with them. They had finally done what their mother had dreamed of for years. Sam would no longer be able to terrorize them. They would now be able to live the life she had prayed for, but only if they could get away with murder.

CHAPTER
FIFTEEN

Dennis was staring at a stack of files. Faces of young girls that had gone missing over the past seven years and had yet to be found. Many girls had gone missing over the past ten years, similar to Mandy Switzer. Dennis's request for more information on missing teen girls had yielded dozens more, but these particular girls were different. They were all honor students with many friends and good families. Dennis hoped that he and Chuck could come up with something that might link Mandy's disappearance with one of them, thus providing them a lead. It took both Dennis and Chuck the better part of a week to get profiles on all of the missing girls to narrow the list down into profiles similar to Mandy. The girls who remained on the list appeared to be well-adjusted teens that had only gone out for a night of fun.

Chuck and Dennis had followed every available lead that could help establish what might have happened to Mandy. No one had seen or heard from her since the night of the Rave, and with each passing hour, Dennis knew Mandy's chance of being found was growing dim. It was now Wednesday, and Mandy had been missing since Friday. The time-lapse was too big to ignore; the chances of Mandy being found alive were now very slim. Judge Switzer was calling morning, noon, and night, and who could blame him. His only daughter seemed to have disappeared into thin air. Dennis knew that the total disappearance of a young woman usually meant foul play. Whoever was responsible for taking Mandy the night of the Rave would likely not have any ties to her. Dennis had no idea if they would get a lead that could help them to find Mandy safe and sound. Hard work and determination were all he had to offer at this point.

Dennis had gone to the office to pick up the files on the girls. Chuck and his new wife Shelley McPherson, a Medical Examiner for Cook County, would be joining him and Veronica for supper tonight. He wanted to take the files home to review them again and see if Shelley and Veronica could help shed some light on the investigation. Sometimes, a fresh set of eyes could see things that may have been overlooked.

Shelley was brilliant; she had a way of interpreting information in a file that is both analytical and precise. Veronica, on the other hand, offered a more unconventional view. It's as if, right out of thin air, she comes up with some idea that at first may seem a little off the wall. Veronica's weird way of looking at things could often deliver a small gem of an idea that led Dennis and Chuck to a new twist in an investigation. Several times over the past many years, difficult cases had been solved after Veronica gave her assessment of the case. Her flashes of brilliance often came from listening to her early morning radio shows that covered everything from aliens, the Bilderbergers, government cover-ups, past lives, and every conspiracy theory and a strange plot that involves secret societies.

Veronica's many talents made her quite the attraction at cocktail parties. Dennis was grateful that her humor and charm could get her through the raised eyebrows and condescending smiles. Good solid detective work always laid the foundation of any case, but inspiration, although only one percent, is often the catalyst needed to bring an investigation to an end. When it came to inspiration, Veronica had her share of it, and then some. Her ability to think "outside the box" often made her helpful. Veronica never thought 'inside the box.'

Chuck had yet to see the many files that Dennis had reviewed. He and the other detectives had been busy all week doing follow up with Mandy's circle of friends. Whenever Dennis thought of Chuck, he'd send up a silent prayer of thanks for his partner and friend. Dennis was grateful to have found a partner with just as much personality as brains. That made his job a lot more exciting than it would be if he hadn't been lucky enough to find a guy like Chuck. Chuck was a lot different than the analytical Dennis, who liked to follow the rules. Chuck would be willing to bend a rule or two, and his cockeyed way of looking at the world had yielded some interesting results on the many cases in which he had been involved. Dennis had decided that when Chuck had a hunch, if he had to open a locked door or tell a white lie to get a confession, then so be it, Dennis would let him take the lead. Bend, don't break.

Although the same age as Dennis, Chuck had many years of seniority in areas that Dennis had yet to experience. After a decade on Gang Crimes and five years in Intelligence and then Narcotics, Chuck was one of the most experienced detectives assigned to Area Three. Now with homicide, Dennis was the lucky guy who got Chuck as a partner.

Chuck knew everyone; personally, a career in the Chicago P.D. still seemed to be traditionally Irish, although not as much as the turn of the century. Being an Irish cop in Chicago meant that the word 'brotherhood' had roots a lot deeper than it would for a guy like Dennis, with almost no roots to speak of. Many of Chuck's family, both past and present, had grown up as members of Chicago's finest throughout the years. Dennis felt closer to the other officers because of Chuck. The thing that made the partnership work was that together they created balance. Chuck was the kind of cop to rush in where 'devil's fear to trod' although he didn't look like a daredevil with his innocent face. Often Chuck would want to take action, while Dennis always looked ahead and noticed every tiny detail in seconds, summing up the situation before making a move. Chuck's real name was 'Charles Patrick O'Brien the Third.' At a young age, his favorite show was 'The Rifleman,' and the name of the star was Chuck. From then on, he wouldn't let anyone call him Charles or Charlie, only Chuck. And when it came to loading a gun and taking a quick shot, Chuck was the best. "Lock and load" was his mantra. The last case was unforgettable, and Dennis, Chuck, and Shelley were glad it was over, but it was Veronica who accidentally came up with the idea that inspired Dennis, thus solving the case. It was while working to solve that killing spree that initially brought Chuck and Shelley together. They often had supper at Dennis's home, but just as friends. Shelley's work as a Medical Examiner also put them together professionally. It was Shelley's lack of luck with men that finally brought them together on a personal level. After several really bad dates, to say the least, one with a stalker, another with the serial killer, made Shelly realize that a nice guy like Chuck would make for a better, more solid partner. Dennis smiled, thinking of how much he loved the two of them. They were perfect for each other.

Dennis put the files of the missing girls into a large briefcase. A little brainstorming wouldn't hurt. Dennis laughed at the thought of the interesting evening that lay ahead as he walked through the pit, where three other officers were sitting at their desks working on cases of their own. As Dennis walked by, one of the officers looked up from his desk and gave Dennis a smirk. He turned his swivel chair toward Dennis and spread his long legs out in front of him, preventing Dennis from passing.

"How are things going with the Switzer case?' Juan Sosa asked, his Spanish accent still heavy, even though he had lived in Chicago for over thirty years.

Juan was the kind of cop that made you think of Heraldo Rivera. He always seemed to be looking for an angle or a way to sensationalize any case he seemed to be working on that might catch the media's attention. Dennis had become the media's darling. His ability to speak to the press and seemingly give his cooperation without compromising a case made the upper brass sit up and take notice. Over the years, he and Chuck had been assigned the cases known to draw media attention, making Dennis and Chuck police celebrities, something that seemed to tick Sosa'.

"No real leads so far," Dennis answered curtly.

"It's almost been a week. By now, I figured you would have tied this case up. Maybe you're slipping. If you need help, you can always ask me. Don't be shy. You're not the only one who can pull a trump card out of his ass, even though the Superintendent thinks you walk on water."

"I'll keep that in mind the next time I'm in hot water, and I feel that I need your help. Mind you, if that stack of files on your desk is any indication of how well you solve your cases, I would think you might need my help." Dennis nodded toward the huge pile of files on Sosa's desk. Dennis knew only too well that the number of cases you solved compared to how many you were assigned sets your reputation amongst the other detectives and police personnel in one's yearly review. Dennis and Chuck's rate of solved cases was the highest on the force, while Sosa lagged far behind. Dennis knew the remark would hit home. Dennis stood in silence for a few seconds while Sosa scowled at him, unable to think of a response. Sosa turned back to his desk and grabbed a file from the top of the large pile, indicating that the conversation was over.

On the drive home, Dennis wondered if Sosa was correct. Would he be able to find Mandy in time? He doubted he would; a week was much too long. If he didn't get a break soon, he would be willing to ask the devil himself for help. Dennis smiled at the thought. He held no such belief in a Devil or a God. Strange how at times in his life, when he felt his back was to the wall, he was willing to pray to some unknown entity and bargain his way out of trouble.

CHAPTER SIXTEEN

As Dennis approached the driveway of his home on Wood Street, he noticed that Chuck's S.U.V was already parked out front of his house.

"Shit."Dennis thought as he looked at the time on his car clock. "I'm late, oh well!" It wouldn't be the first time, and Veronica was a great hostess.

"Hey, everyone!" Dennis shouted as he entered the back door that led to the family room. "I'm home."

"In here, sweetheart!" replied Veronica from the kitchen. "We were about to start without you. We're starving."

Dennis chuckled. The one thing Chuck and Veronica would never do was to starve. Both were food-obsessed, and it showed. Chuck was a solidly built guy with a big round face that, given a little time, would begin to look like a Santa Claus stand-in. His full head of hair was already beginning to show signs of graying at the temples. Chuck's bright red complexion shone out under a full beard that would one day turn silver. Once gravity got a hold of his chest and sunk it below his belt, he would make a fine St. Nick. His nature was jovial, upbeat, and full of laughter, which only added to his overall impression. At fifty, he was a solid guy who was the best partner Dennis ever had.

Then there was Veronica. Still beautiful, but as always, fighting an ever-losing weight problem, one she was destined never to win. The extra pounds only added to her sense of power and presence. Ever the entertainer, she seldom missed the chance to be the center of attention. Her wit, charm, and intelligence made her a star at any gathering, small or large. No, Dennis decided. Neither would starve.

"I don't think you two will waste away just yet, and besides, I'm only twenty minutes late, so no guilt!" Dennis hugged Veronica and slapped Chuck on the back as he came into the kitchen.

Shelley, Chuck's wife's, smiled up at him as she seemingly read his thoughts, giving him a conspiratorial wink, one neither Chuck nor Veronica witnessed.

Shelley was one of those girls whose figure didn't look any different twenty years and one child later. Her freckled face and turned-up nose made her look perpetually young. Shelley would never get fat or grow old. A fact that made most of her friends curse her great genetics.

"I hope that after we eat a quick supper, especially so that you two don't waste away to nothing, I can get some insight from the great minds that are gathered at my humble table," Dennis said with a laugh. "But seriously, we need some help with Mandy's case and quick. I think the time has run out, and I can't bear the thought of telling Judge Switzer that we've hit another dead end."

Being a cop in Chicago, a city of color and with a diverse reputation, meant everyone had a different opinion of the police, some good, most bad, depending on who you asked. From the city's beginnings, Chicago's association with organized crime and the likes of Al Capone types. This left many of its good citizens feeling that city officials and the cops and legal system were often in bed with the very disreputable but colorful citizens that they were supposed to be putting behind bars. This distrust continued to be a significant stumbling block to the Police Department. Even with many attempts to dispel those fears, it was still a hard sell. Especially with the many scandals, the city had to endure.

One scandal in particular that got Dennis's attention was the Dianne Masters murder in 1982, around the time that he had joined the force. Although it was a case that took place outside of the city proper, it still intrigued Dennis.

Dianne was a stunning blonde whose disappearance kept the press and public speculating for years whether or not her husband, a successful attorney with known police and underworld connections, was guilty of her murder. The most bizarre part of the case was just how deep the police and legal system's corruption went and who was in bed with whom.

By the time her body was found, in an underwater dumping ground that was well known to many as a dirty cop, and the years of investigation followed, political blood flowed freely through the streets. Many of suburban Chicago's cops' reputation was under a light that showed just how raw the city's underbelly was. With all the Grand Jury Investigations in Chicago during the early to mid-eighties, it was widely believed that the monkeys in the city's Zoo could do a better job than the cops. At least the monkeys could be paid off with bunches of bananas rather than the wads of cash that were needed to pay off dirty cops.

It was rumored that if you wanted a criminal case to go away, all you had to do was hire Allan Masters, pay enough cash, and 'presto,' Allen could get anything to disappear. The problem was he had to pay everyone along the way, all the way to the top. Depending on the charge, you had to pay cops, clerks, attorneys, and judges. No one was exempt from the graft. It was rumored that the local police 'helped' many of the clubs involved in prostitution simply by turning a blind eye and collecting a few bucks for doing so. Allan Masters had a hand in many of those operations. During the first few years after Dianne's body was found, the question on everyone's mind was whether or not Allan could make a person disappear by himself or did he have help.

It was during this time Dennis joined the force, the fulfillment of a boyhood dream. During this time, Dennis got a good look at the world of good cop, bad cop. When kids played cops and robbers in Chicago, it was difficult to tell the good guys from the bad. Very often, in real life, the cops were the robbers. Many good cops found it hard to face the negative press coverage that seemed to permeate the entire force in the early eighties. A few of the police indicted over the next several years were friends of Dennis and close to many of the officers. The cops that managed to stay clean felt tainted and betrayed by the corrupt high-profile cases, especially the Master's Murder.

One cop, in particular, Sgt. John Reed stood out at the time for Dennis and his partner. He turned out to be a good cop, the sort of police officer that can give a profession back its pride and reputation. Homicide detectives Sgt. John Reed and Paul Sabin, under the direction of Thomas Scorza, a federal prosecutor, were assigned to the Master's case. It was now 1986, four years after Dianne's body was pulled up from her watery grave. The case seemed to have gone cold, primarily due to what seemed like sloppy police work. John Reed's reputation as one of the best in the Chicago Suburbs. Like most of the players in the Master's case, John grew up on the south side and knew all of the people involved on all sides of the law. Reed's involvement was unofficial, and he did most of the investigation on his own time. It took thousands of hours, patience, and good solid police work, but eventually, the case was cracked. Allen Masters was put behind bars for a very long time, and a few others were identified.

Reed was a guy Dennis could relate to, and everything about him made Dennis want to follow in his footsteps. At seventeen, Reed almost became a priest. Lessons learned from childhood became the cornerstones of Reed's principles. As an Irish Catholic and former Marine serving under the Chaplin, Reed knew his duty to God and Country. It made him a great cop. Dennis liked his professionalism, every inch a cop, even in street clothes.

Reed was able to set an example for other officers without even knowing it. He and Sabin cracked the case even at the expense of many police officers' reputations that were either directly involved in the Master's case or had helped stall many areas of the investigation. They won the admiration of the rest of the force. Over the next twenty years, Dennis tried to model himself after officers like

Reed. Dennis enjoyed a similar reputation, and many young rookies watched Dennis, hoping to be like him one day.

* * *

The meal Veronica served was one of her best. Her pork ribs could rival any southern BBQ King. Slow-cooked for several hours with brown sugar, garlic, chili, and a tangy hot sauce, the meat fell off the bone. The special sauce made from a tangy hickory smoke and several secret ingredients that Veronica refused to share made for a mouth-watering but rather messy meal that all four friends seemed intent on finishing to the last rib. Corn on the cob, potato salad, and fresh apple crisp from the tree's apples in the back yard completed the feast. When all was said and done, the topic on everyone's mind was served up with hot gourmet coffee.

"Here's what we have so far," Dennis began, with little formality. "There have been over two dozen girls that have gone missing over the past seven years. They seem to have no reason for leaving; they were good students. Their parents and no problems with them, nor did they have any boys in their lives, no drug or alcohol problems. Many of the girls had part-time jobs or volunteered for local community groups. Here are the dates they went missing." Dennis said as he handed Veronica and Shelley a computer list. Chuck was sitting next to Dennis, and he took the original list from Dennis to give it a look over. Chuck hadn't seen this part of the information yet.

"Wow! It seems that several of the girls went missing on one of two dates. One date is May the 11th and the other November 24th the last girl went missing November 24th and Mandy on the 11th of this month, August." Chuck said simply as he went over the printout.

"Let me see that list again," Dennis said excitedly as he laid the files that had the same date, twelve in all. "Shit, your right. And Mandy went missing last week, August 12th, as did five other girls. It's six for six. The odds are against this many girls going missing on the same two dates is improbable. I should have noticed right away, but I was in a hurry to get home." Dennis smiled at Veronica. "You're cooking is a great motivator for not staying at the office."

"I agree there is little chance that this is a coincidence," Shelley added.

"Let's pull the files of the girls that went missing on these two dates and see if there is anything else they have in common," Chuck said to Dennis.

Dennis pulled the large briefcase out from under the kitchen table. Within a few minutes, he had the files spread out on the table, placing the pictures of the girls' faces up on the top of each file. By the time Dennis laid out the last file, the room had gone deadly silent. Finally, Veronica stood up and pulled several of the files closer to her, lining them up vertically with only the pictures showing.

"Do I have to paint a picture, or do you see what I see." She said softly.

Chuck went pale, a rare feat considering his high coloring and rosy cheeks. The familiar lock of unruly hair that never seemed to find its place fell over one bushy eyebrow.

"Each one of these girls looks alike, and they could all pass for Mandy's sister, except for this one," Chuck said as he pulled one file from the rest.

The picture of the girl was a large-boned, good-looking brunette.

"Look at the other eleven. They all have blue eyes, copper, naturally curly hair, and are no more than fifteen. Shit, three of them were only thirteen. " Chuck looked up at Dennis with a grim look on his face.

"This isn't a coincidence. All of these girls were abducted, just like Mandy. We may not have any conclusive proof, but it doesn't take a rocket scientist to figure out that these girls represent something to their abductor." Dennis finished.

"What makes you think that they were abducted? Maybe they went willingly." Veronica asked.

"If anyone of them went willingly, then there should be a common link for all of them. No one just walks away with a stranger, not this many times. Either they were taken against their will, or if they knew this person, he would have to be in their circle of friends or acquaintances. Chuck, we will have to interview the families of these girls starting first thing in the morning."

"I agree. I'll take the list and make appointments from home, and then I'll come and pick you up." Chuck added.

"This means you two boys may have another serial killer," Shelley said as she slid her slim hand down the files over the lovely young faces of the girls.

"How do you know they're dead?" Veronica asked.

"It's been six years according to the date of the first abduction. If any of these girls were alive, someone would have heard from one of them by now. If these girls didn't run away, and that's what it looks like, someone took them. Few girls are abducted and not sexually assaulted. If so, they are likely dead, and dead girls don't tell. Or the killer may have had a more sinister motive than sex. Our killer has some psychosis around, young, blue-eyed, copper-haired girls with all of the girls looking alike. Maybe it's an obsession? Who knows what drives a man mad. I don't see how the brunette fits in. It may just be a coincidence that she was taken on one of the dates. Either way, this is the file we will start on. What makes her a part of this group? " Dennis said as he pulled the file from the other eleven.

Mandy's file made an even dozen. The brunette was the only file that didn't add up, and Dennis knew in his gut that this was the place to start. He looked over at Veronica's wide eyes; he could see the wheels in her head-turning, so it was no surprise when she blurted out her final comment.

"If some bastard tried to take either Natasha, or Katrina heaven help him. I'd hunt him to the end of the earth, and there wouldn't be a punishment in the world harsh enough to satisfy me. I'd flay him alive. How must it be for the families of these girls not to know what has happened to their precious daughters." Veronica lowered her face into her hands, tears slipping down her clear, smooth skin onto the files.

Dennis moved the files and took one of Veronica's well-manicured hands into his, kissing her on the forehead before spoke. "The families are the hardest parts of our job. It's never easy. It's only when we solve a case that a family gets closure. Although I don't think there is closure when it comes to a loved one."

Veronica smiled back at Dennis and kissed his hand tenderly before she removed it from her face. "I think I will get busy doing dishes while you go over the files."

It wasn't that the girls felt it was their duty as women to clean up; Dennis and Chuck had done their fair share of dishes over the years; instead, they wanted to give the men the time to go over the files make a plan for the next day.

"Can you imagine anything happening to Tiffany?" Veronica asked Shelley.

"There have been times over the years as a Medical Examiner that I have had to see girls that looked just like Tiffany laid out on a stainless steel table with horrible wounds inflicted by some madman during a rape or domestic beating. It has brought me to my knees. The only way that I've been able to stay sane is to divorce my feelings at work from my life at home. The boys have learned to do the same thing. It's hard for you because it's not a part of your daily life, but it's a reality for us." Shelley whispered, trying not to think of her eighteen-year-old daughter, who was currently at home making a new dress for an end-of-summer party.

"I think I'll stick to cutting hair. It's a good job. At least all of the heads I see are still attached to their owners. I'm sure you've seen a few headless customers." Veronica turned her big green eyes on Shelley, who started to laugh.

"Veronica, you have a strange way of looking at things. I wouldn't call the people I see on the job customers. They're dead by the time I have to deal with them, and I usually refer to them by a number. Remember last winter when we had so many corpses with their throats cut? I was beginning to think I was in the middle of a bad grade B slasher movie with Freddie Kruger as the star. As it turned out, I was." Shelley said as she remembered the case of the Vampire Killings.

CHAPTER SEVENTEEN

The phone rang, and Dennis turned to Veronica with his usual look, even though he sat right next to the telephone.

"I don't know why you don't pick it up," Veronica said as she leaned across his chest and picked up the phone, giving him a nasty look.

"It's never for me," Dennis responded defensively.

The call was from Katrina, who was checking in to share the day's happenings and to say she loved them. Soon the conversation was over, and Veronica hung up with a contented smile on her face.

"It's true what they say. 'A daughter is a daughter all of her life; a son is a son until he takes a wife.' I'm sure glad we have girls." Veronica laughed. "Speaking of the girls, have you checked in with the Walker girls lately?"

"I stopped by once." Dennis looked a bit guilty.

He had promised the girls he would be there for them.

"Sam answered the door. He was just about ready to pass out from drinking. Jade signaled behind his back that everything was okay, but I'm not too sure. Maybe we should go over tonight and check."

Dennis looked at his wife, knowing full well she would not think that the past effort was good enough.

"It's not too late. Do you think we could take some dessert?

"It's the neighborly thing to do. I'm sure it's not too late. It's summer, and who goes to bed before nine in the summer?" Dennis answered, trying to make up for not seeing the girls more.

The evening was warm, the stars in the sky barely visible above the city lights. Even so, you could still see some of the major constellations and enjoy the breeze and the magical smells of the August night.

"Dennis?" Veronica asked as she looped her arms through his on their way over. "Don't you sometimes want to take justice into your own hands and just get rid of a guy like Sam?"

"You don't know how often I've wished it was Sam who lay at the bottom of the stair, not Jewell, but it's not the way things went."

Dennis put his hand to his mustache, a gesture he always made when he thought deeply.

"Every day, I see good people suffer at the hands or actions of pieces of filth like Sam." Dennis looked up at the sky, trying not to break the mood. "It's at those times I wonder if there is a God or if this whole world is just full of crap that will never make any sense to me?"

Dennis's neck began to stiffen as he continued. He hated getting into things this deeply, but he was driven by something unexplored inside, and the need pushed him on.

"But then I think of all the pain and hurt that usually goes into making these creeps, and I try to find a little compassion. It's hard, but if I don't, then the one part of me that can love and forgive would die. Then what would I be able to bring home to you and my girls." He looked down at Veronica and squeezed her hand. "No. I try not to think about these kinds of criminals, and when I do, I try to see them as little kids."

Dennis once again stroked his mustache, a sign that he was puzzled.

"Few of us are born evil. Some are unlucky enough to have parents who have lost their way to survive and shut off the part that makes them feel. If I judge and hate, then I'm one of them. I've got to be able to hurt." Dennis felt like he needed a real cleansing of the heart, and sharing his feelings with his wife seemed to help.

"When I'm in the middle of an investigation, I need to stay focused, but later, by myself, then I hurt for everyone, the Sam's, Crystals, Ambers and Jades of the world, everybody. Often as the result of bad family life, victims become victimizers." Dennis blushed at his little sermon.

Veronica beamed up at Dennis feeling privileged at receiving a rare insight into her husband's thinking. She leaned her head on his shoulder. Veronica loved him more now than ever. It was hard to believe that love could continue to grow. Hers certainly had. It wasn't that they didn't have their share of problems because they had. But at some point, you begin to let go of the little things and concentrate on the things that matter.

You begin to have faith that your relationship can endure anything, and that love's light won't be extinguished, even if you don't agree with everything.

* * **

The three girls were sitting at the kitchen table when they heard the first knock. A wave of fear quickly engulfed both of them while Amber sat oblivious to her surrounding, still able to enjoy her favorite food, macaroni, and cheese. Jade was up first, her thoughts quickly reverting to the events earlier and of their father's dead body, still lying at the bottom of the stairs. As Jade rose, she quickly tried to close the door to the basement. During Sam's twisting and struggle, the frame was pulled away before his fall, preventing the door from closing. The second knock got Crystal to her feet as well. She tried to help Jade secure the door, but it was impossible. No matter how hard they tried, it simply would not shut. It drifted completely open. It was difficult to see down to the black recess below with the light off in the basement. All the girls could do, was answer the door and pray everything would be all right. If ever their prayers would need to be answered, it would be now. They looked into each other's identical, blue eyes, squeezed each other's hands, and crossed their fingers in silent prayer. When she opened the door, her heart almost stopped. Standing there was Detective Dennis Kortovich and his wife, Veronica. What the hell should she do now? Hadn't she asked them to call first? She stood still, saying nothing, only looking at them with what she felt must be the guiltiest look in the world."

Hi, Jade. Sorry, we never came sooner, but the last time we came over, Sam answered the door and didn't exactly welcome us with open arms, so we thought we would try again."

Veronica spoke first, thinking maybe the reason Jade stood there so silently was her fear of Sam. Jade looked so small and frightened. Veronica wanted to reach out and enfold her into her motherly chest.

"Are you girls all right?" Veronica asked. "Here, I thought you might enjoy this lemon pie."

Jade knew she looked a little strange just standing there, but at this moment, she could hardly think of a thing to say, and if she invited them in, it would all be over for her and her sisters.

"I'm grateful, and yes, we would enjoy the pie, thanks." Jade still stood in the doorway, not wanting to move.

Crystal came up behind Jade, hoping that if the Kortovichs saw that they both were all right, they would leave.

"May we come in for a moment? We won't stay long; we just want to make sure you are all right," Asked Dennis.

This time Crystal jumped in, trying to prevent the couple from entering the house. The door to the basement was directly across from the back door, and one step forward would allow anyone to see down to the bottom of the stairs.

"Dad's in the basement, and he's all tied up. If we upset him, it won't go well for us." Crystal tried to think of a way to send Dennis and Veronica away.

Suddenly a brilliant idea hit Crystal. "Can I walk you back home? It will give me time to tell you how we are away from Dad."

Crystal pushed past Jade, took the pie from Veronica, and gave it to a surprised but thankful Jade, meanwhile starting down the back steps, hoping their uninvited guests would follow.

Dennis could tell the girls were scared. That bastard Sam had done a number on them. He and Veronica had no choice but to follow Crystal and hope they could be of some help.

"How are you girls holding up without your mother?" Veronica asked in her usual straightforward manner. "Is there anything we can do for you?

Crystal's mind was working overtime. She needed to get Dennis and Veronica to stop worrying. If they came over again before tomorrow when they got rid of Sam, they might not be so lucky. Then what would happen to Amber? Crystal answered hesitantly, at first trying to find just the right words.

"Dad seems to be going off the deep end without mom."

Crystal's mind was keen, and she had a slight idea starting to form, one that just might help them explain their father's future absence.

"I think he's overwhelmed by all of this. I'm sure he'd like just to give up. He always talked about leaving us. He says we're just no damn good. I always felt he talked like that to make mom feel bad, but now I think he's just had it. It wouldn't surprise me if he just took off on us." Crystal looked over at Dennis and Veronica to see if they believed her.

* * *

Dennis got a strange feeling something was up. The tone in Crystal's voice was the same as his daughter Katrina's when she wanted something or was about to confess to some minor sin and wanted to set him up for it.

"Don't worry. If anything happens, we'll be here for you," Veronica responded, her motherly instinct kicking in.

Veronica always took things at face value. She never held anything back while Dennis listened for the things that were and weren't being said. Dennis had an instinct for being set up or if anyone was lying. Something was up with Jade and Crystal. He would have to follow his hunch over the next few days and make sure they didn't need him.

*   *   *

As Crystal walked back to her home, she was suddenly overwhelmed by what was ahead. If they were to get away with killing their father, they would have to be very careful. Dennis and Veronica were well-meaning, but it would be very difficult to hide it from Dennis. It was his job to catch people who did what she and Jade had done. But really, they had no choice. It was either them or their dad, and after this afternoon's events, Sam had lost. She found it amazing that the picture of Sam dead and sprawled at the bottom of the stairs caused her to feel carefree and relaxed for the first time in her life. She felt absolutely no remorse. Maybe she was evil, just like daddy said, 'no good for nothing!' Crystal dismissed her thoughts as she opened the back door after saying good-buy to Veronica and Dennis. Tomorrow would be a long day.

She and Jade needed a good rest if they were going to pull it off. She would have to try and figure life out at another time. For now, she was just too tired.

CHAPTER EIGHTEEN

Jade rose to an unusually hot day. Clear, blue skies spread out over the city of Chicago as far as one could see. The air was still hot from the day before when the usually cool evenings of late summer had taken a vacation as everyone else did in August. Even the breeze that came off Lake Michigan seemed to have deserted those who were forced to stay within the city limits. It would be stifling by noon, but if a cold front moved in later on in the day, a severe thunderstorm was sure to brew up. It was Monday, and today the girls would have to face the gruesome task of pulling Sam's body up the basement stairs and loading him in the old, blue van. They would make sure all of his belongings were taken with him as well. This would be his final journey. If there were an afterlife, Sam would likely be in hell. Destroying everything that had ever meant anything to Sam along with his body somehow seemed appropriate, especially after the miserable life Jewell had to endure. Jade and Crystal felt a kind of justice when Sam died on the same spot as Jewel. The girls had made him feel some of the fear that their mother had felt all of her married life.

The look on his face as he tumbled back over the edge of the steps down to the cold basement floor was one they would never forget. Sam had never shown any fear, and it came as a shock and surprise to see his face twist in fear and horror as the chair tipped backward. The sound of the chair legs crushing and buckling under his weight was all that could be heard just before Sam's cry of despair as he tumbled backward. The girls could finally take control, and no one would ever hurt or abuse them again. It was a promise they made to their mother.

"Jade, how are we going to get daddy up the stairs?" Crystal asked.

Jade looked over at her sister. Crystal stood before the bedroom mirror, raking her long copper curls with her fingers, a frown on her face. Amber, already dressed for the day, sat in her rocking chair, moving back and forth at a leisurely pace starring at the back of the wall at nothing in particular. Jade had always wondered what made each human being so different. She had been given the soft, giving nature of her mother while Crystal was more pragmatic and sensible, seeing everything exactly like it was, not as she hoped it would be.

On the other hand, Dad was mean and nasty, so you just stayed out of his way. You didn't try to make things better. You just took care of yourself and survived the best you could. Amber, however, was not even present until she heard music. Then she did what no one thought possible. She played what she heard note for note with sheer perfection. The old piano that had belonged to their mother's family was never used. It wasn't until Amber was five that anyone knew she had the gift. One day Jewell accidentally turned the radio on to a classical station. A piano concerto by some famous dead guy was playing. For some reason, Jewell didn't switch the station. She let it finish. Jewell was impressed by the piece and went over to the piano and played the scale, something she hadn't done since she left home. For the first time, Amber seemed to focus, really focus. She turned to the sound coming from the radio, listening intently.

When Jewell went to the piano, she moved toward her mother and watched her fingers as they danced across the keys, performing the basic scales. Never before had anyone ever witnessed Amber acting as if she was aware. When Jewells' fingers left the piano keys, Amber sat down beside her. Then Amber's fingers touched the keys. It was shocking. Everyone, including Sam, sat down in total disbelief. Amber played the scales note for note, just like her mother. Then she played the song she heard on the radio, note for note. Later, they discovered Amber could not only play anything she heard note for note but that the numbers on the telephone could also provide a diversion for her.

Soon Amber was trying to use the phone all the time. If they dialed out when she was close enough to hear the musical tones of the numbers, she would rock back and forth until she could reproduce each tone on the phone for herself. Finally, they bought her a special toy phone that could match the actual telephone, tone for tone. It made life much easier and kept Amber happy. The piano and phone became the only objects that ever connected her to the real world. Without them, she simply stared off into the distance and rocked.

They were all very different girls, Jade, the pleaser, Crystal, who pleased herself, and Amber, who would never really know pleasure at all, except with her music. And now Amber's gift would save them, but only if they could get Sam in the van and waylay Derek Hanson at the funeral home before he locked up.

The girls sat outside the Greenhills funeral home for at least half an hour before they saw the big double white doors open. Jade was out of the van instantly, the gift in hand. Crystal pulled Amber close behind, following Jade up the large stairs that circled the front of the impressive building.

"Mr. Hanson," Jade called up before Derek could hit the seven-digit key code. "We would like to thank you for all the help you gave us."

Derek Hanson's gaze rested on the girls, but it was Jade who got the full force of his icy stare, his pale, blue eyes resting on her face in a way that sent shivers down her spine. For one moment, it was as if all the evil that once embodied her father now belonged to this stranger. Jade couldn't get this encounter over fast enough.

"There is no need to thank me, girls, I was only doing my job, but I appreciate your gesture." Derek's voice was unnerving, a sinister tone creeping into his nasal flat-pitched voice.

"You were very professional, and we sure needed the support." Jade thrust the gift she held in her hand forward, indicating to Derek that it was for him.

"You didn't need to do this. As I said, it was my job." Derek's voice took on an added tone of disbelief, even a little suspicion. It was as if he doubted their sincerity.

"It's not much, and we hope you like it. It belonged to my grandfather." Jade's heart started to pound.

She hoped he didn't become suspicious about their reason for being here or wonder about the gift's insincerity. Jade gave herself a scolding. "Get a grip!" she thought. "He can't know anything! He's just a very weird guy." She hoped that her thoughts didn't show on her face.

Derek began to open the gift. It wasn't very big, so he was able to unwrap it quickly. Inside the small case was an antique boy-scout knife. It was the only thing the girls could find to wrap up and give to Derek as an excuse to catch him before he closed the morgue. The knife didn't belong to their grandfather. However, it did belong to their Sam, so giving it away was no problem.

Everything personal Sam had was in the van. Soon it would go up in smoke along with his scrawny body. The wind could be felt on the girls' faces as the sky in the distance started to darken.

The wind was a welcome relief from the still heat of the day. It was coming in from the northwest, and from the look of things, a violent summer storm would soon be upon them.

Derek looked up at the sky, his long bony face screwing up as a few large drops found their way to the top of his head. His ponytail, tied tightly to the nape of his neck, stuck out from the back of his collar like a directional sign. He put his bony hand on top of this greasy head.

"Looks like a big one coming this way," Derek said, referring to the impending storm. "You girls should get going now; I have to lock up."

"Okay." Jade's brain pounded. She wanted to scream out. "Just hit the keypad!" willing Derek to get on with it.

"No time to argue with such beautiful young girls." Derek looked deliberately at Jade as he spoke.

A chill ran down her spine as Derek's pale eyes met hers. Jade seemed to sense the danger as she looked away from Derek's intense gaze.

"Let me lock up, and we'll get out of here before we get drenched." Derek turned to the security pad outside of the doors.

As he hit the numbers and the individual tones rang out, Crystal moved Amber a little closer, making sure she could hear each key as it was being pressed. This was their song of freedom, and as Derek's bony fingers hit each number, Amber's face became focused and alive. When the sequence was finished, she began to rock. Crystal quickly grabbed Amber's hand, pulling her towards the van.

"We'll let you walk Mr. Hanson to his car, and I'll get Amber settled before it begins to rain any harder." Crystal looked up at the sky as she spoke, noting the giant thunderheads that had gathered overhead.

While Jade walked the creepy mortician to his car for final thanks, Crystal pulled Amber into the van. It was difficult. Amber wanted to go back to the keypad and repeat the sequence. She would continue to obsess about the numbers until she could complete them. Until then, Amber would rock quietly and move her fingers in a continuous motion mimicking the numbers' sequence.

When Jade returned to the van, her pale face and taut features spoke silently of the revulsion she felt towards Derek Hanson. "Boy, he gives me the creeps!"

"Yes, he's almost as scary as a dad."

"We better drive away from the funeral home and make it look like we've left, or old creepy face might become suspicious," Jade said, in reference to Derek.

The girls followed Derek as he left the funeral home and cemetery grounds. When Derek turned right, they took a slow and deliberate left, checking their rearview mirror as they continued a short way down the road. At the lights, Derek took another right and was out of sight within a few seconds. Jade braked suddenly, heaving both girls forward.

"Ouch!" Crystal shouted as she placed her hands on the dash, preventing her tiny body from being flung onto the hard plastic. "Next time, warn me!"

"If you both had buckled up, you wouldn't have hurt yourself," Jade snapped back, checking her rearview mirror to make sure Amber was all right.

Amber was oblivious to everything except the notes that played in her head. Even the short plunge forward into the back of the front seat did little to stop her small fingers from their continuous motion as she repeated the pattern in the air. She would not stop until she was able to touch each number in a perfect repetition.

Jade backed up into the short driveway of one of the homes along the road. Once she had turned the van around, she traveled the short distance to the front of the funeral home. Crystal was out of the Van first. As she pulled back the seat, Amber jumped forward. Her focus was on the large double front doors, and she seemed oblivious to her sister. Her tiny feet carried her quickly up the stairs, her fine copper curls bouncing as she quickly moved toward the keypad at the left side of the door. A radiant smile spread across her face as her hand moved over the numbers in rapid succession. The girls were unable to tell if she had hit all seven digits. They wouldn't wonder for long. A loud clicking sound made both girls turn wide eyes towards one another.

"Oh my God, this is it. We've done it! We're in!" Jade spoke first.

"I'm scared!" Crystal grabbed Jade's and Amber's hands, trying to gain a little extra strength from their touch.

"You're never scared, well, at least not much" Jade's reassuring squeeze was intended to let Crystal know how much she admired her younger sister's outer bravado.

Jade dropped Crystal's hand and quickly moved toward the door. "We'll have to get this over with quickly. I'll go in and open the back-loading gate. Can you drive the van around the back?"

Crystal nodded.

"We can pull Dad onto the dock. There's an electric ramp that the caskets are loaded on. They take the bodies to the embalming room, so we'll only have to roll Dad a little way after we put him on the gurney. It'll be easy." Jade said.

"Okay, but hurry, the weather is getting worse." Crystal grabbed Amber's hand and pulled her back towards the van. Once inside, they drove around to the back and waited for Jade.

Jade moved quickly towards the back of the funeral home where the morgue was located. The halls were dark except for a soft red glow that came from security lights that lined the halls. Once down the hall, she entered into a small well-decorated waiting room, the place immediate families went to view the bodies and say a final farewell. A second door at the back of the room allowed Jade to enter the crematorium area that led directly to a loading bay. The bodies were brought here from the various hospitals or Medical Examiner's office, usually loaded in body bags. Double doors led to a large cooler where the bodies were kept until they were embalmed, then buried or cremated. Large sliding doors were the focal point of the room, encompassing most of the back outer wall. Jade quickly ran over to the wall looking for a switch that would allow her to open the large loading door. She quickly found it and stood back anxiously waiting for the heavy doors to lift, hoping Crystal and Amber were waiting outside. As the door rose, Jade could hear loud cracks of thunder as the impending storm drew closer. Large drops of rain began to pelt outside the building, making a sharp 'pitter-patter' sound on the roof.

Soon the storm would engulf them, and few people would venture out on a night like this, making their detection less likely. The smell of the rain, along with the flash of the lightning as it streaked across the sky, was accompanied by loud cracks of thunder, rumbling across the black night. It was a fitting farewell.

Sam would soon be gone forever, except for the memories. The memories that each of the girls would have to deal with, each in her way. Crystal got out of the van when she saw the door to the loading bay begin to open. She then settled Amber safely inside the loading area before she and Crystal struggled with their dad's body. Once Sam was settled at the top of the loading dock, the girls stood hand in hand looking out at the storm-filled horizon. Jade hoped the tempest wasn't a sign of something more sinister for the future. With Sam gone, what could hurt them now?

CHAPTER NINETEEN

Jade looked at the crematorium as it began its final cool-down cycle. She thought how glad she would be when it was finally over, and she and her sisters could get out of this place. They had struggled with Sam's body, especially getting him out of the van. Sam was a small man, well under a hundred and thirty pounds, but the girls were small as well. Sam's dead weight proved to be a workout as they tried getting him up the stairs to the loading dock. Now they were victorious. Sam, his clothes, and a few other personal belongings were just a few dying embers.

"Do you think we can get away with this?" Crystal asked Jade.

"I hope so. We'll have to get our stories straight. Dennis and Veronica will most likely be over to the house." Jade paused for a few minutes to think things through.

"Dennis is smart, but I think he would have killed dad himself if he could. We can only hope he believes our story. We'll have to wait and see which part of him wins out, the detective or the father. Let's hope it's the father."

Jade prayed that Dennis wouldn't be too interested in finding out what happened to Sam and accept their story at face value. Amber stood off to the side of the crematorium, staring off into the distance. The hum of the silver chamber lulled her into her usual continuous motion, her fingers playing some song heard only by her. Suddenly, the sound of a loud click that preceded the front door's opening could be heard; both girls turned toward each other. They knew someone was entering the building, and they would be discovered if they didn't move fast. Jade grabbed Amber's hand while Crystal took one glance around, making sure nothing of Sam's was left. "Shit," Jade thought. "They'll hear the crematorium."

The crematorium was still on, and the timer said it would be off in less than four seconds. Would it stop its humming in time? There was no time to stand around and find out! They would have to hide fast and pray they wouldn't be discovered. The small nook with a carved desk and tick curtains draped the enclosure framing the nook, leaving a little room behind each drape. Jade dashed behind one panel while Crystal pulled Amber close to her and ducked behind the second. Just as the door to the crematorium room opened, the oven shut down. Not a sound was made as the tall, thin man entered the room. It was the mortician, Derek Hanson

Derek stood in the doorway, surveying the room for a few seconds. Something was strange. He just couldn't put his finger on it. The storm outside diverted his attention as another round of thunder boomed overhead, the pelting rain, driven hard by the wind as it howled. Derek shook his coat, making several drops of water scattered across the lush carpet. Everything seemed fine. It must just be the storm. He moved over to the wall just off to the left of the crematorium, where a security pad, hidden just inside a light switch, felt the light touch of his fingers. The tones from the number pad rang sweetly out into the empty room. There was no need to put on any lights. The red gleam of the security lights gave the room enough light. Derek finished punching in the security code known only to him.

The staff at the morgue was never allowed to run his precious crematorium. Suddenly the sleek chamber began to move forward, gliding smoothly over its hidden track. No one knew of the secret room below, and no one ever would. It held his treasure, his great passion. Derek descended into the chamber below. Once again, a red glow lit up the tiny room, spreading a fiery light around the room. At the bottom of the chamber, Derek went over to a stainless steel table that stood in the middle of the room.

"There you are, my little princess. It's me, your older brother and lover. I've missed you so much, but our time together is almost over. You'll have to spend just a little more time here before you retire to your fiery bed. Sleep, my princess. It's almost over."

Derek bent over the table and looked into the face of a fair-haired angel. The young woman who lay on the table was no more than fifteen, a wisp of a girl. Derek put his cold blue lips on the tiny mouth of the pale girl.

"Just a few more hours, and we can make your cold little body heat up with a passion only you can feel for me." Derek ran his finger over the sweet, oval face of his young victim.

"You know you love me, and I'll always love you." Derek took the tiny hand into his large bony one, the long, skinny fingers, finding their way to her ring finger.

"I just need this for a few hours."

Derek slipped the ring from her finger. It was her school ring, and he would need it, but only for a while. Derek had been lax, not handling the ring sooner. He stood up, still having to keep his head bent. The room was small, and Derek's tall, lanky form could not stand at his full height without banging his head on the ceiling, only inches above the sliding track. As Derek started to go up the stairs, he turned back once more to give a silent farewell to the young girl who lay on the cold, stainless steel table. Derek only had a few more things to do before he finished his precious ritual with his new love. He would take the ring back home and make a permanent mold of it. Then the ring would be added to his collection that hung along the wall of the tiny room. The room smelled like embalming fluid, but he loved it. It was the smell of death. He never got tired of its pungent smell, and it clung to him like a damp mist on a foggy night, soft but pervasive. Once out of the room, Derek hit the keypad again. As he looked around the room once more, something seemed amiss. It was more a feeling than anything he could see, but after looking around again, everything seemed fine. He shook off the impression and went back out the way he came.

The girls could see each other from behind the thick curtains. Crystal made sure Amber kept her rocking to a minimum; both girls kept their breathing shallow. Derek seemed to take forever before he came up from the room under the crematorium. All the girls could do was wait and hope Derek didn't need anything from the tiny desk behind the curtain where they hid. When they heard the final click of the front doors, they let out a double sigh. They let go of Amber's hand. Without waiting for her sister to catch up, Amber knew where she had to go. She quickly moved out from behind the curtain and sped over to the keypad. Instantly her fast, deft fingers found the exact sequence of numbers needed to open the chamber below. Again, the furnace slid back, only this time, Amber went down the steep stairs into the scarlet glow below.

Jade and Crystal quickly followed, hoping Amber wouldn't touch anything she shouldn't. Amber went over to the corner of the room, where the red light spread its cinnamon glow. Amber's only interest was watching the shadows she created as she moved her hands back and forth across the light. Jade and Crystal came to an abrupt stop as they saw a sight that left them speechless. Before them lay the body of a young girl dressed in a bridal gown. She was strapped to a steel table. Her lifeless body reflected a soft, pink glow as the light shone onto her fair hair. Both girls slowly went over to the table. The face that stared up at them was tiny and delicate. Her mouth partly opened, her lips smeared with a deep, red lipstick. She looked dead, and Crystal was the first to shake her bare arms; they were cold to the touch.

She was limp, lifeless. It was then that Jade noticed the large bruises that ran along the girl's tiny arms. There were small round burns on the back of her hands, and Jade and Crystal knew what had caused them, cigarettes. Both of them had known their fair share of burns, a gift from their father. It was something they were all too familiar with. Jade lifted the hem of the wedding gown over the young girl's legs. It was ghastly. The extent of the bruises and burns was horrific. Never had the girls seen anything like this. It was brutal beyond belief. There were tiny, precise cuts all along the inside of her legs. Only her face was untouched. The girls didn't need to see beneath the gown's bodice to know that her small breasts would also be mutilated.

Jade and Crystal looked up at each other; neither could speak. Suddenly Jade let out a shocked "Shit" as she looked at the walls behind Crystal. Crystal was confused by what could cause her sister more shock than the young woman who lay in front of them? She followed Jade's eyes as she turned slowly; the hair on the back of her neck stood straight up as a chill ran down her spine. When Crystal turned around, fully facing the wall, she too let out the only expletive she could.

"Oh fuck, what the hell are these?"

Over a dozen clippings with colorful, grotesque pictures were stuck to the wall. Beneath each photo was an object, necklaces, rings, earrings, and broaches, all personal items belonging to the young girls in the pictures. The girl lying on the table looked eerily similar to the girls in those pictures; tiny, perfect females, each wearing the same wedding dress. One of the photos stood out. The girl in the photo was a tall, dark brunette, her body completely naked.

Her breasts had been obliterated, while her face was mutilated with cigarette burns. She alone was different. A large X had been carved at the top of each thigh. Beneath the picture were several more X's, running along its border. It wasn't until Jade looked at the locket that hung below the picture and newspaper clipping that she felt her legs begin to buckle beneath her.

"Shit, shit, shit, it can't be! Look at the picture again, Crystal, and tell me who you see. It just can't be here! I think I'm going to be sick."

Jade held on to the edge of the table, lowering her head, trying to keep the ground beneath her feet from rising and hitting her in the face.

"Oh, Jade, it's Charlotte!" Crystal's voice revealed all the pain anyone could feel when faced with something as horrible as the picture revealed.

Charlotte's last moments were beyond belief, even for Crystal and Jade, who until now thought they had seen and experienced it all.

"It just doesn't make sense. She's the only one that's different. All of the other girls look like… well, they all look like us. Each of the other girls could almost be our sister. Some of them may have a little more red in their hair, but Charlotte is a brunette and so much bigger than any of these girls."

Jade was overwhelmed by fear and grief, but even so, she knew Charlotte didn't belong with the rest of the tiny young victims.

"We've got to get out of here before that freak comes back" Crystal began to feel a sense of panic.

The girl's attention had been diverted to the wall when they heard the soft moan. They stood motionless for a few seconds, unsure of what they had heard. When a second sound broke through the lips of the small girl on the table, Jade and Crystal returned their attention to the young captive.

"Crystal, she's still alive. We have to get her out of here."

"We can't. We'll get caught! What will we do with her? Shit Jade, this is a real problem!"

"I know, I know. When we came up with this plan to get rid of Dad, how did I know we'd find this?" Jade looked at Crystal with all of the confusion and fear she felt. For one second, Jade thought she should just grab both sisters and run, but she knew she could never leave the girl.

If the stranger was alive, they had to get her out, now! Time was something they were running out of; Derek would likely be back soon. Another moan came from the girl, only this time much louder. Jade bent over her face and shook her shoulder.

"Hello, hello, wake up. What's your name?"

The girl's eyes suddenly opened. Jade gazed into two perfect, blue eyes that were the same color as hers and Crystals. The only difference was that these eyes were crazed with fear. She started to scream.

"Shush… You're all right" Jade laid a small, cold hand across her forehead. "We're going to get you out of here." The girl nodded.

"Let's sit her up and see if we can hold onto her and get her up the stairs."

Jade started to pull the small girl forward while Crystal took the cue and slipped her arms under the small of her back. Suddenly she began to choke.

"She's going to vomit. Quick, lean her over."

Jade moved her over the table with one swift movement, supporting her by her shoulders, allowing her head to fall between her legs. The long layers of the wedding gown caught the chunky, foul-smelling, amber-colored vomit.

"Ugh!"

Crystal screwed up her nose while she tried to prevent the girl from falling backward. "That's a real funny smell, almost like ammonia or medication. She's been poisoned or something. Do you think she'll die?"

Crystal tried to hold the girl, but she wasn't much bigger than the stranger herself, so it was difficult. The balancing act between all three girls was almost comical if things weren't so tragic.

"She's been drugged with something. We've got to get her out of this dress. We'll never be able to manage her with it twisting around her legs."

Jade started to undo the tiny buttons on the back of the dress. She could tell from the worn fabric that it was old and had been used many times and, judging by the number of pictures on the wall, more often than she cared to think about.

Suddenly the young girl went limp, falling back onto the table. Jade and Crystal struggled for what seemed like forever to slip the gown over the girl's shoulders, past her waist, and over her hips. With a final hard pull, they yanked the gown over her slim legs and tiny feet, tossing it to the floor. Together they pulled the unconscious girl up and off the table in one swift move. Both girls put all of the strength they had into the upward motion. It was a little too much, and all three went sprawling forward. Together Jade and Crystal regained their balance, holding the girl between them.

"If we could get dad up the stairs, we can get her up," Jade said, more to herself than anyone else.

"Ya, but it took forever to get him up to the top of the stairs, and it was a good thing he was dead because I couldn't count how many times we dropped him. This is different; not only do we have to be more careful, but we need to hurry in case that creep Derek decides to come back.

"Call Amber; she'll follow if we start to leave." Jade reminded Crystal.

Amber responded to Crystal's voice without hesitation. Something only Crystal could do. Suppose it was anyone else; it could take a while. In the dim red light of the secret room, the trio of girls struggled up the stairs with one little girl following, oblivious to the events that had just occurred. Finally, all four were up the stairs out of the small chamber.

"Wait. I've got to go back down. I've got to get something." Jade said.

Jade gave Crystal a no-nonsense look, ensuring that Crystal wouldn't argue with her. She then went back down the stairs quickly, not bothering to wait for a response from her sister, who now struggled to keep the young stranger's naked body from falling face forward onto the carpeted floor.

Jade wasn't sure what drove her back; she only knew she had to go and rescue what was left. These small tokens were all that was left of the missing girls, and somehow Jade felt she had to save them from the cold fiend who had snuffed out these young women's lives. Jade had difficulty finding enough room in her blue jean pockets; Jade shoved a few of the items into her bra. She also decided to take the photos. She wasn't sure what she would do with the pictures and items; she just knew she had to take them. It gave her a warm feeling of satisfaction, knowing Derek Hanson would never touch these precious items again. Jade knew he would become crazed when he found these items missing and his secret chamber disturbed. Derek could go fuck himself and rot in hell. Jade bent down, picked up the crumpled wedding dress, and with all the strength she could muster, she ripped the gown in two and tossed it back onto the floor.

"No one will wear that gown again, you bastard," Jade whispered to herself and the image of the pale evil mortician.

Within moments she was up the stairs, her arms around the strange girl, urging her sisters forward toward the door that would lead to the loading bay and freedom.

"Who would have thought?" Jade whispered to Crystal. "That we would bring in a body and take out a body." Jade giggled over the irony of the moment. The humor made the moment all the more surreal. Life was like a roller coaster. You never knew what was around the bend, but boy, what a wild ride so far!

The door was just beginning to close when the girls heard a loud click from the front doors once again. They knew it was Derek returning to claim his prize. Shit, they only had a couple of dozen steps to go, and they would be out of this hellish place. Could they make it? The van was just outside the back door of the loading gate with the keys in the ignition. Jade and Crystal doubled their pace, rushing through the door. Any second now, Derek was going to enter the room that had once held the treasures that he had gathered at such great expense. They stumbled down the stairs with the copper-haired girl pulling her into the van. Amber followed like a well-trained terrier, happy to follow. Jade slipped into the driver's seat, checking to make sure her three passengers were at least safe inside, all the doors shut and locked.

"No lights. Let's just get the hell out of here!" Crystal said.

Jade accidentally stepped on the accelerator, causing the engine to make a roar, heard even above the storm.

Derek was entering the crematorium room when he heard the sound of an engine roaring at the rear of the building. Someone was leaving. Had they been in the building? Did they know of his prize? As he walked toward the back loading area, he noticed the inner door was open. His heart picked up a beat. Once in the loading area, he became even more confused. The double loading doors were wide open. As Derek ran to the door, he saw the taillights of a van speed off into the darkness. He glanced around only once before he ran back into the main room. The stainless steel machine was rolled back, exposing the hidden staircase leading to the space below. His long legs propelled him forward in seconds; once he stumbled to the bottom of the stairs, he screamed a long, blood-curdling howl of disbelief.

Gone! His bride, his love!

One more look around, another scream ripped from his lungs. His head felt like it was going to explode. As he looked around the small underground chamber in disbelief, the realization that his world had been torn apart set in. Gone! Everything that meant more to him than life itself was gone. The newspaper articles, photos, and souvenirs, all of it! The photos he had taken of each of his brides just before consummation of their marital rites. The pale, lifeless, angelic faces that usually stared out at him from the collage' along the walls were now gone, leaving only outlines of glue and tape.

He felt inconsolable. Those rings and trinkets held each girl's life essence, and without them, he couldn't feel or touch their spirits. They had been ripped from his heart, leaving him feeling sick to his stomach. His throat choked, threatening to close off his air preventing it from reaching his lungs. He breathed deeply through his nostrils, sucking the lingering smell of his bride deep into his lungs.

A third primeval roar ripped from his chest, finding its release. At the same time, the sound of his scream assaulted his ears; he dropped to his knees, feeling the loss even more than he thought possible.

"Fuck, fuck, fucking shit, fuck!" Derek screamed. "This can't be happening!" He could hear the pulsing of his blood as it pumped through his veins. The pounding only added to the intense pain that engulfed his head. He bent over, grabbing the sides of his skull while applying pressure, trying to keep his head from exploding. That's when he saw it, the white shimmering satin dress.   "No! No! It can't be." Derek thought. The wedding gown lay on the floor ripped from the back of his beautiful prize. He let go of his head; the pain was temporarily forgotten as he bent to pick up the crumpled fabric. As he lifted it to his face, he noticed a second piece of shimmering satin. He picked the fabric up. Torn apart, ripped like some unwanted child from its mother's breast. The once beautiful gown hung limply from his large hand. He bent once more to pick up another piece of fabric, gathering it into both hands, pulling it to his face smelling deeply of its scent. The smell of his young bride lingered on the fabric, musky and light, better than a puppy's breath, innocent. Each girl had felt her skin next to this sacred fabric. Now it was torn into pieces. Part of the gown was foul with vomit, ruined. How would he ever find love now? Without the dress, everything was hopeless. Derek felt his legs turn rubbery as he walked over to the stairs that led to the floor above. Once he ascended, he sank quickly before his legs buckled. With his back next to the furnace, he could feel the warmth as the heat penetrated his jacket. "What the fuck?" He thought as he stood up. The knowledge that the furnace had been used recently only added to his already confused state. Derek went over to the door and unlocked the airtight seal, hearing the soft whoosh as he swung it open. The embers were in the last stage of cooling, but he knew that this couldn't be happening. He had cremated the last client early that morning.

There should be nothing in the 'belly of the beast' but before him were ashes, more than he had ever seen before. One person usually left what amounted to the size of a medium cookie jar. His bony hands reached for a ceramic scoop, similar to a cat scoop used for kitty litter, but he was an expensive ceramic scoop, imported from Italy, only the best for his clients. It was used to sift out any bones, buttons, or teeth that the fire might not consume. It didn't happen often, the temperature in the crematorium was as high as eighteen hundred degrees, and little escaped its all-consuming heat. But once in a while, an object would survive the fire.

Whoever had used his machine had also taken his bride and his treasures. The van was familiar, but in the state, he was in presently, he had no clue as to who it could be.

"Clink!" The sound of the ceramic scoop hitting the unexpected object startled Derek. When he pulled the small shovel from the oven, he could still see the glow radiating off the item. He quickly walked through a door off to one side of the furnace to the embalming room. At the back of the room was a sink. He turned the tap on to hot and placed the object at the bottom of the sink. It sizzled as the water hit the thing, sending a column of steam just out of reach of Derek's face. He turned the hot water to warm and finally to cool than cold. Whatever the object was, it would lead him to his enemy. The one who had snatched his prize and treasures away! At the bottom of the sink, a black oval-shaped object lay innocently awaiting Derek's inspection before giving up its secret. He held it in one hand, while in the other hand, he ran his bony fingers over the surface. Grooves could be felt on its now grainy surface. The back of the object had two protrusions equally spaced. He knew instantly what it was. A belt buckle, the kind cowboys wore.

To the side of the sink, he kept several compounds and a special light that could be used to magnify objects. He usually used it to examine photos of loved ones to present them to their families as life-like as possible. Often images that the families brought didn't offer enough detail. The use of the magnifying light helped to clear up the most minor aspect. He dipped the buckle into a special jar with a clear liquid and held it between a set of stainless steel prongs. Once again, the object sizzled as the liquid came into contact with its silver surface. He dipped it a couple more times, making sure its surface was clear. After wiping it with a special cloth, he held it under the light. Much of the surface was worn either by time or the fire, but enough was present for him to make out the stylized letters of S.E.W.

He ran the letters over in his mind; at the moment, he could think of no one whose initials matched those letters. He placed the buckle on a pan next to the sink and washed his hands. Something was rattling around in the recess of his brain. He had seen those letters before recently, but where?

Suddenly he saw it all. Everything was crystal clear. It was the girls this afternoon on the steps. He could hear them thanking him for his help with their mother's funeral and see them giving him a gift, a knife that belonged to their grandfather or someone. He had only glanced at the knife briefly. He had been anxious to go home and prepare a special mold for the ring his bride was wearing. He reached into his coat pocket and pulled out a small white box. He removed the lid, and there lay the knife gleaming up at him with the telltale markings flashing under the glow of the magnifying light. Derek held the knife under the lens. His flash of insight was rewarded when he saw the same stylized initials were the same as the buckle, SWE.

He walked calmly over to an old gray filing cabinet, one of several that stood along the wall. He opened the drawer and found the folder he was looking for. Walker. He flipped through the papers and found the photocopy of the visa slip that Jade had signed for her father, a man Derek had never met. At the bottom of the visa, the slip was a name that would lead him to his enemy, Samuel Elliot Walker. The buckle was Sam's, and so was the knife. The girls had visited him so they could use his furnace. He remembered how fascinated Jade had been over the cremation process. It had to be Samuel's ashes in the belly of his pet. They had somehow figured out the key code and entered the funeral home. Now he knew a secret about them, and he would use it to bargain for what was his.

CHAPTER TWENTY

The storm softened, leaving only a light patter of rain on the windshield. It wasn't until the girls turned onto a road that leads away from the funeral home that they even dared to let out a sigh of relief. As usual, it was Crystal who spoke first.

"Holy shit, now what? We barely escaped with our lives! If Derek had found us, we'd all be Frankenstein's bride by now."

Crystals' dramatic outburst almost made Jade laugh, but not quite.

"Look!" Jade responded. "If we don't calm down and figure something out, we'll get caught."

Once again, a soft moan could be heard from the back seat. It was the young girl, she would need medical attention, and they would have to figure something out. Jade pulled off to a side road, well out of sight of any passing cars. She turned the engine off. The soft sound of the rain made a "pitter-patter" sound on the tin roof of the van. It was a soothing noise that gave them a sense of safety along with the dark sky and swaying trees.

"OK, let's think this through. We just burnt up our dead dad, who we killed, and rescued some girl from a serial killer, who's sure to be pissed off and is likely to kill us if he finds out who we are."

Jade paused for only a second. Her blue eyes were becoming larger as their predicament became clearer.

"We can't go to the police. We don't know who this girl is or what to do with her. Shit! We're fucked, and I'm still a virgin."

Jade's voice was becoming higher and more hysterical as the picture of their predicament became clearer.

"Don't lose it on me now." Crystal broke in. "I'm in this with you, remember. We have a little sister to care for, and we can't just leave this girl." Crystal looked at the young girl in the back seat. Her head was slumped forward, resting on her chest. She was naked from the waist up with only a pair of white sports briefs covering her battered body. Jade gave their young ward a blanket, one they always kept in the van. She wrapped it around her tiny shoulders, trying to stop her uncontrollable trembling. Amber sat next to her, unaware of what was happening. Amber's gentle back and forth motion did little to disturb the tiny victim who drifted in and out of consciousness.

"She needs help, and we can't give it to her. We'll have to drop her off at a hospital or something." Jade said, anxious to be done with things and get on with a new life, which was undoubtedly causing them some further complications.

"Yes, you're right." Crystal said. "She'll be hysterical when she comes to!"

The young woman's bruises and cigarette burns were only a small part of what she had gone through. Whatever she had been drugged with was wearing off, and they would have to dump her soon before she could answer any questions and lead the cops to them.

"The hospital is ten minutes from here. We'll have to take our chances and hope we don't get caught." Jade finished, starting the van once again, backing onto the road.

The emergency drive-in at the hospital was a semi-circle. Jade got out while Crystal stayed in the van checking things out; it was nearly midnight, and so far, things looked quiet. Jade went in through the automatic double doors and found a wheelchair. They would need it. There were security guards stationed at the entrance of the emergency door. They would have to create a diversion.

"I'll need your help Crystal," Jade said as she wheeled the chair close to the van. "There's a security guard just inside the doors. You'll have to create a diversion. There are also cameras, and we have to make sure we don't get caught on film."

"How," Crystal asked. "I don't know what to do?"

"You go in first and act as if you are going to faint. Just get the guard to concentrate on you, not me. I'll wheel the girl in right behind you and hope the guard doesn't notice me. But make sure you put your hoodie up and take her to the left, close to the seats surrounding the intake nurse. I don't think they have a camera on the chairs, only the nurse."

Jade could tell by the look on Crystal's face the last thing she wanted to do was to fall helplessly into the arms of anyone who carried a gun, especially after what had happened during the previous few hours. The darkness and late hour of the evening, along with the storm, gave the evening a spooky feeling.

Crystal got out of the van and made sure Amber was buckled safely in her seat, then helped Jade put the girl into the wheelchair, all without saying a word. Then Crystal pulled back her shoulders and marched up to the double doors where she stood and took several deep breaths. Crystal gave one backward glance at Jade to make sure she was right behind her, with the small victim in the wheelchair. She lowered her shoulders, hung her head low, and went through the doors into the Emergency Room.

Once through, Crystal went over to the guard and grabbed onto his chest, and then she promptly sunk to her knees, still holding onto his shirt, keeping her face hidden. The guard was taken back by the young girl who seemed to require his help; as he bent over to see what was wrong, Jade wheeled the chair past him into the waiting area, right beside the chairs by the intake nurse.

"Are you all right?" The guard asked as he tried to hold onto Crystal, preventing her from falling to the floor.

"I have a terrible headache, and I thought I was going to faint. I knew you wouldn't let me fall." Crystal answered, staring innocently up at the guard with her big, blue eyes.

"Here, let me help you to a chair. I'll get you a glass of water. Then we'll see if we can get someone to look at you." The guard guided Crystal to an empty chair beside a young woman with a baby.

When the guard left to get some water, Crystal looked around to see where Jade was. Jade had already wheeled the girl into their chosen spot. Crystal had hoped they could just park the girl on the inside of the double doors and pray someone would take notice and get her some help. She figured most people who come to emergency this late at night had enough of their own troubles without paying too much attention to anyone else. With Crystal's award-winning performance, Jade was able to slip past the guard unnoticed.

The shift from dark to light caused the girl to moan and shift suddenly as she drifted in and out of her unconscious state. The old blanket that Jade had wrapped around the girl was slipping off her shoulder. Jade pulled the blanket back up around her neck, hoping in the process no one would notice her. She stood away from the wheelchair to see if anyone was paying attention to them. So far, everyone seemed concerned with their troubles. She looked around for Crystal, who was sitting on a chair next to a young woman with a crying baby. Just as she was about to approach Crystal, the guard came over to her with a glass of water. Crystal took the water and gave the guard a thankful smile.

Once he was assured she was all right, he went back to his post at the emergency door.

* * *

Mandy was aware that her surroundings were different. She even felt safer without knowing why. This had begun when she heard the voices of the two girls. Their faces had drifted before her, only a couple of times during the past few hours, although time was distorted, and what had seemed like a few hours may well have been a few days. She could remember the echo of a soft feminine voice telling her she was safe and that "that bastard" wouldn't get at her again. Somehow Mandy knew it was true, and when the angels yanked that vile wedding dress past her hips, she knew her ordeal was over. Mandy allowed herself to sink back into the blissful state of unconsciousness, where she could forget what had happened. A small part of her brain that received the signal to forget let go of it all. She was safe, and she need never relive these events again. Darkness claimed Mandy once again as the face of Ichabod Crane drifted before her mind's eye, and the headless horseman galloped into the night.

* * *

Jade slowly stepped away from the wheelchair leaving her small ward. The blanket that was wrapped around her body slipped once more, revealing one small bare shoulder. Jade wanted to go to her side and pull it back up, but Crystal stopped her, motioning for Jade to sit in the waiting area while Crystal sat beside her. It seemed strange that only half a dozen people were waiting; it was usually a lot busier than this at the Herotin Hospital. But both girls knew if they were to go undetected, they would have to sit and wait. They wanted to make sure someone would claim the girl. So far, no one had even looked up. The clerk that did admissions was busy at the computer helping an elderly couple enter their health care information. The girls suddenly felt anxious.

"What if no one notices her?" Crystal asked.

"Someone's bound to see her. No one with her. She looks awful. If the blanket falls off of her shoulder, someone will see what happened. It's awful. No one could pass and not cringe." Jade answered, looking around the room hopefully.

The TV in the waiting area was the only sound they heard beyond the occasional cough or moan. It was Crystal who squeezed Jade's hand and motioned for her to watch the TV. The newswoman was reading a report about a missing girl, and the picture that was flashed across the screen was their victim. They read the name underneath the picture, Mandy Switzer. Both girls sat silently, intent upon hearing the rest of the news broadcast.

"Mandy Switzer, daughter of Judge Switzer, has now been missing for almost one week. An inside source has linked her disappearance to over one dozen other young girls who have gone missing over the past six years; none have been found. They have all been between the ages of thirteen and fifteen. Foul play is suspected. Family members of the missing girls claim that their daughters would never have run away. They say the police have been reluctant to treat the other missing girls' cases as anything more than 'runaways. We have reliable information that the case has been under investigation for a week, although no leads have been found." The dark-haired newswoman then finished her report. "If anyone has any information, they are asked to call Detective Dennis Kortovich or Chuck O'Brian of the Chicago Police Department."

With the closing remarks, both girls looked at each other once again.

"Shit, she's a judge's daughter!" Jade exclaimed.

"Yes, and Dennis Kortovich is investigating." Crystal said. "What are we going to do?"

"Nothing, no-one knows about us, and Mandy Switzer is in no condition to tell anyone about us either. No one knows about dad. We just get away from here and keep quiet." Jade said.

At that moment, the Admission Clerk noticed the wheelchair with its patient sitting by the chairs unattended. She didn't remember anyone checking in with her, so she got up and went around the counter to see if she could remember if she had seen the young girl before. When the clerk got in front of the wheelchair, she lifted the girl's face up off her chest, and as she did, the blanket fell the rest of the way down her shoulder, exposing her tiny breast. What she saw caused her to scream.

"Oh, may God have mercy! Somebody get me some help! This girl is in real trouble!" The nurse pulled the blanket back up over the girl's battered shoulders.

Soon security guards and other hospital staff started pouring into the waiting room to see what the commotion was about. This was the cue for the girls to leave. The uproar in the entranceway was beginning to look like a scene out of ER, as hospital attendants, nurses, doctors, and other patients gathered around the girl in the wheelchair. What they saw caused them to stare in disbelief and horror. The young woman's body was covered in cuts and bruises, but it was the hundreds of cigarette burns that covered her small breasts and abdomen that made them stare in disbelief. The diversion allowed the girls to slip out unnoticed.

CHAPTER TWENTY ONE

When the call came in, Dennis was fast asleep, trying to catch up on some much-needed rest. The past year had been a tough one, and Dennis found himself unable to sleep as he got older. His dreams had taken a bizarre twist, leaving him drained and shaken. Just when things started to get back to normal, he had begun to worry about Crystal, Jade, and Amber. Now, these missing girls would begin to haunt his nights. With one case solved, another one would start; that's how it was in this business. There was always enough crime to go around. Dennis's observations from the cold files led him to suspect that the girls' were dead and another serial killer was running around. Dennis hung up the phone, and as usual, Veronica, a light sleeper, sat up, wanting to know what was up.

"It's the Switzer girl; she's been found. Someone dropped her off at the hospital, beaten and half dead." Dennis pulled on his pants. "I've got to get there before the Judge does. From the sound of things, she's in real bad shape, and when she sees her parents, she'll fall apart. If I'm going to get anything, I'll need to get there right away."

"I was beginning to lose hope. When this much time has passed, it's usually bad news." Veronica said as she grabbed her robe and got out of bed.

Dennis grabbed his housecoat from the back of the bedroom door and turned to look at his wife. He knew Veronica would head to the kitchen to make a quick coffee and put it in his thermal mug. A bagel would be quickly toasted and put into a bag. Veronica always made sure her family was fed and comfortable. He stood in front of the mirror; he needed a shower and shave, but there was no time; he'd have to go to the hospital first. For now, a quick splash of cold water. He would put on the clothes he had worn that day and hope the case didn't get away.

From the time Dennis and Chuck had left Judge Switzer's home almost a week ago, they had been going over the information in all of the files trying to see if the missing girls' last location could shed light on who might want to abduct them. An 'all points bulletin' had been put out on Mandy along with her photo. Dennis and Chuck had questioned all of her friends, teachers, and country club members. By the time all of the interviews had been finished, there didn't seem to be any one name that stood out as a suspect. Now Mandy was found, and Dennis decided that getting to the hospital first, before the family, was his best chance at conveying important information. He made a call to Chuck during the drive to the hospital.

"I'm sorry to bother you, Shelley, but could you put Chuck on the line," Dennis asked after waking her from a dead sleep.

"What's up, bud?"

"Mandy's been found. She showed up at the hospital wrapped in a blanket and nothing much more. It seems she is in very rough shape. The doctor who called said she had been drugged and tortured. I'm on my way now. Get Chuck to the hospital as fast as you can."

"He is on his way," Shelley said as she hung up.

The drive took less than twenty minutes; there was less traffic at this hour of the night. Lightning lit up the sky, like a knife cutting through a dark, velvet cake. As usual, the rain only made the night seem more ominous.

Dennis was ushered into the waiting room; the nurse said he would need to see the doctor before going in. Mandy was just coming out of a drug-induced blackout, and they were monitoring her vital signs constantly to make sure there were no complications. He had been rehearsing in his mind the questions he would ask Mandy. He wanted to make sure he followed everything by the book. He was startled out of his musing when the doctor came up behind him.

"Not many people get to startle me and tell about it!" Dennis smiled as he held out his hand to the young intern, who quickly gave his back for a thankful shake as he introduced himself.

"I'm Dr. Grout."

His freckled face was solemn. He was no more than thirty, but Dennis felt sure that this skinny, young man could give Mandy the care she deserved.

"I'm so glad you're here; everyone's just sick about what's happened to Mandy Switzer, but she's finally coming around, and I think she can answer some questions now."

Dr. Grout motioned for Dennis to follow him to a private room that was just across the hall from the area where they were standing. Two small fluorescent fixtures that hung over the bed, lit the room. The rest of the room by contrast was dark and quiet. A nurse sat on a chair off to the side of the bed, keeping an eye on the monitors. An I.V. of saline solution was being pumped into Mandy's hand, helping to dilute the unknown drug that had been given to her during her ordeal.

"I've sent blood samples to the lab to test for toxic substances that she may have ingested. We should get the results back soon. I put a STAT order on them. I also took pictures of her body. I've never seen anything like it. She floats in and out of consciousness. She's really out of it. She was able to tell us her name. When we phoned the Judge, he told us to call you as well." Dr. Grout offered.

* * *

Mandy could hear voices somewhere 'out there beyond a world of dreams to reality. She knew that she was no longer in danger, but at this moment, she didn't seem to care to find out exactly where she was or why she was safe. Her small body felt as if it were being 'held down' by a thousand tiny hands. Suddenly she was transported back to that place! Mandy could feel her heartbeat faster while her blood ran cold. Her head was being held tightly to a hard surface by some unseen force that pressed against her face, its hot breath sickenly close. The air felt as if it were being sucked from her lungs. 'A kiss!' She remembered a wet, hard kiss. Words of love had been whispered nearby, but all she could remember feeling was fear. Flashes of pain, now gone, replaced by a dull throb all over her tiny body, she remembered a face that was long, bony, and ugly. Yellow teeth, huge wet lips, the smell of something from the lab at school. The stuff she had used on that stupid frog. She drifted deeper and deeper to some dark corner of her mind, a place where anything could happen.

Suddenly a headless rider thundered down a dark, windy lane, its head tucked somewhere under its dark billowy cape. All of the images swirled around inside her scrambled brain. The fear she had felt was gone, replaced by a drug-induced state of nothingness. She left the world of strange and crazy things, back to a place where only black nothingness and soft voices existed. Suddenly all of the tiny hands were demanding that she sit up. They pulled and prodded her tender flesh. Flesh that had been pinched and burned and would have felt a blissful nothingness if it weren't for the dull ache and those demanding little hands. How could those sweet voices demand that she sit up? Didn't they know she no longer cared? All she wanted to do was sink back into a state of nothingness.

Mandy wanted to forget as she melted into the pounding thump of the music and the dance. There she could abandon all of her youthful energy into the pulsing beat. She remembered drinking some pop and suddenly feeling ill.

She had gone outside of the club that had sponsored the rave to get some fresh air. Mandy bent over feeling faint when a large bony hand suddenly clamped down across her face. She saw no one until it was too late, as she began to sink to her knees. One deep breath and she was out. What happened later was too awful to bring to her conscious thoughts. She would think it out of existence. If that meant she would perish as well, so be it. She would never live with the memory of that face, that mouth, that man.

Mandy sank into blackness for what could have been forever or only a second. Suddenly the upward motion of her body being pulled forward by those tiny hands made her stomach rise from its depths to spill forward, a bitter, acrid liquid with chunks of some forgotten meal. It was the last meal she had eaten. She was a guest to her own bridal supper. She had been dressed in white. The monster had dressed her. He pulled the gown over her tiny breast that bore the physical expression of his love - burns, slashes, and bruises. He said he would stop if she would accept him willingly. He exposed himself to her, thinking she would be impressed with the size of his penis. He placed her cold petite hand on his throbbing member. It made her feel sick. She had never seen, let alone touched one before, except in sex education, and even then, it was rubber and gross, but not like this. The phallus in class was a soft, cold rubber, while Derek's was a hot throbbing mass that felt like it would explode with little provocation. This was even more of a nightmare than she could ever have imagined.

Mandy felt she would rather be dead than accept that thing between her legs. She would never allow him to enter her. None ever had, and now none ever would. She was sure death was only a few minutes away. He had made it clear she had a choice, death or him, all of him. She would choose death. He hurt her for what seemed to be a lifetime just to see if she would change her mind. Finally, he gave up. He said she was like all of the others and that she deserved to die, and he would be only too willing to oblige her. He wrapped her up in a blanket and took her from someplace that you could only believe existed in the movies. A cathedral of death! Mandy could remember the look on his face when he accepted defeat. The look of rage turned from a fiery hot eruption of all of the emotion a human could contain inside without exploding to a cold, dead, dull acceptance of defeat. She was sure he had been in that state before. He would now allow for a final few steps before it would be all over. Mandy was sure death would be her only way out. Once again, she found herself sinking into darkness. Then those pesky hands and soft voices started at her once again. Maybe she was dead, and these beautiful voices and persistent hands belonged to angels.

The hands were soft, tiny, but unrelenting in their insistence that she sits up. But no, you surely couldn't vomit in heaven, and Mandy was sure she had just vomited. Mandy put as much effort as she could to open her eyes. It wasn't as hard as she thought it might be. The light that shone on the three angelic faces bathed them in its soft pink glow. All of the faces looked alike, blue eyes, tiny noses, and soft curls, catching enough light to make their hair shine like jewels of ruby and gold. They were perfect, and somehow they looked just like her. Maybe that's how it was in heaven. Everyone looked like you. So that you could feel better and more at home.

Mandy could suddenly feel the hands pull hard on her dress as she shivered from the cold air as it hit her bare breasts. It made sense. In heaven, you would have to dress like an angel, but these soft hands suddenly became rigid and tore the gown from her body. She was sure she must have died and gone to heaven, not the other way. She was much too young to have committed enough sins for hell, and these lovely faces were full of concern and compassion. She was being pulled up off her cold hard bed of steel and dragged up several steep steps. One of the angels held her against a warm, steel wall and then dragged her out into the cold night. The rain beat down on her for a few minutes, and she knew she couldn't be in heaven or hell for that matter, rain, wind, and cold all around her. A blanket was being wrapped around her tiny shoulders. She was still in the real world. She must forget. Forget it all. It was never real. It couldn't be.

More voices…male…one… no two and a woman, lights overhead, tubes up her nose, in her arm. She could feel the heaviness coming out of her body and could make out a few phrases.

"Where did they park the wheelchair?" A male voice asked softly

"By the intake desk, we didn't see anyone near her." A female answered.

"How drugged is she, and how deep are her burns and cuts." Dennis's voice was husky with concern.

"We started an IV, and as soon as we find out what she has taken, we can take steps to counter-act it. The burns and cuts are on the surface only, but there are so many. I'm sure they'll traumatize her." a female voice replied.

"All in all were making progress." A second male added.

"Can I speak to her?" The first male asked.

"If she comes around, she keeps going in and out."

Mandy's eye's opened once again. Wow! She wasn't in heaven. She wasn't even dead. However, she had seen angels, and she had seen the devil! She knew she had. The angels' hands had placed her near safety, while the devil had marked her: for his own. Mandy couldn't take any more memories. She could hear her name being called from somewhere above, pulling her back up from the abyss. She opened her eyes to see a handsome man with a kind face and a caring look sitting on the edge of the bed. He told her his name and said he had to ask her some questions. It was important. What could she tell him? It was all a hazy dream.

* * *

Dennis sat on the bed, calling Mandy's name softly, her hand resting like a delicate flower in his large one; soon, the young girl's eyes fluttered open. At first, all Dennis could concentrate on was the blue of her eyes. His heart sunk as he noted their vacant stare. He could see the bruising on her neck as well as the marks and cuts along her arms. Dennis could get all of the medical information later. For now, he needed Mandy's best recollections of the past several days.

"Hi Mandy," Dennis's voice was soft and reassuring, "my name is Detective Dennis Kortovich; I'm a good friend of your dad and mom." he paused, noting the moment of clarity and recollection in her eyes. "I'd like to ask you a few questions if you're up to it," Dennis said as he reached into his coat pocket. "I'm going to take notes and tape our conversation. Is that O.K.?" He pulled out his small tape recorder, turned it on, and set it at the head of the bed as he spoke, never taking his eyes from hers. Mandy nodded. From his breast pocket, Dennis pulled out his familiar black notepad and pen. Nodded to the Doctor to stay and asked Mandy once again, "Ready?"

"Yes." Came a weak reply.

"What do you remember?"

"Angels. Two. No three angels."

"What do you mean?"

"They rescued me."

"How?"

"They took me away."

"Away from where?"

"The ground. A man underground somewhere."

"Can you remember the location?"

"No."

"Who was the man?"

"I don't know."

"What did he do to you?"

Mandy squeezed her eyes shut; a tear slid down her cheek.

"I don't remember." She said slowly.

Dennis could tell she was reluctant to go into the details of her kidnapping, so he decided to leave that line of questioning alone.

"O.K. Can you tell me what he looked like?"

"I can't remember."

Dennis could tell from her breathing that the questions were taking their toll. She either could not or would not remember, but he had to press on.

"What things do you remember?" Dennis asked, keeping his voice soft and reassuring.

"A bridal chapel with wedding music and a gown."

"Were you at the wedding?"

"Yes. I was the bride," Mandy's voice began to quiver. "We were the only ones."

"What did he look like?" Dennis asked, once again.

"A headless man, it's like a dream. I see a headless man on a horse riding at night. He has a sword, and he's going to cut me." Mandy's voice was beginning to rise, hysteria just a breath away.

"It's O.K. You're safe." Dennis' tried to calm her, keeping his voice steady.

"What about the angels?" He decided to try a new angle.

"They swore." Mandy gave a small smile.

"What do you mean?"

"The angels swore. Then they said I was safe, and they took off the wedding gown. Then they swore." Mandy said, looking a little more upbeat.

"What did they look like?"

Mandy closed her eyes, trying to draw the image of the angels to her mind. When she opened them, she smiled a brilliant, wonderful smile, like a child does when they know they have the correct answer.

"Like me, they look just like me, but they're angels, especially the youngest one."

"How old is the youngest?"

"Maybe, ten or eleven."

"And the other two?"

"Like I said, just like me."

Slowly, Mandy's eyelids drifted over her glazed, blue eyes. She was out once again. He would have to wait for a-while before he could continue. The doctor came around the bed to Dennis's side and motioned him to follow him back to the waiting room.

"She'll be out for a while." He said quietly. "We can try again later."

Once they were seated in the waiting room across from Mandy, Dennis asked Dr. Grout about the extent of Mandy's wounds.

"She has cuts and bruises all over, but what is even worse is that some sick bastard took a cigarette and put hundreds of small burns all over her chest. It's awful. We've bandaged some of the deeper cuts and put special burn pads all over her chest, making it a little more comfortable. The wounds will heal, but I'm afraid she will still have scars."

"What about sexual abuse?" Dennis was almost afraid to ask, but it was better to get the answer before her parents arrived.

"No. She's still a virgin, but I do not doubt the story she just told about a wedding that she was due to be someone's sex bride. She also has burses on the inside of her legs." Dr. Grout continued. "Whoever got her away from that monster did so just in time. Whatever drugs she was given, we'll know which sent her on a real trip soon enough. It will be a while before she sifts through that angel and headless rider stuff."

"Thanks, Doc; I'll wait here for the judge and his wife. When they get here, can you bring them to me first?"

"Sure thing, just relax. I'll be back soon."

Dennis sat down in a high-back chair, the kind that was made to sleep in. He could picture family members worried over the health of loved ones being able to catch an extra forty winks in a chair this comfortable. Angels and headless riders, were the only clues he had so far. How much was real, how much was fantasy? He sure hoped he would be able to find out soon. Dennis was replaying the tape recorder when he heard the sound of excited voices and purposeful steps coming from the hall. He could tell there were at least five people, four men, one woman. No. One more woman followed behind, trying to catch up.

He stood just as the Superintendent, Judge Switzer, Dennis' partner Chuck, the doctor, and Mrs. Switzer came through the door. Behind by a few steps was Mrs. Switzer's mother, Marsha Stewart. All except the doctor looked relieved.

The Superintendent was the first to speak. "What do you know, Kortovich?

"Yes, how is she?" Judge Switzer spoke next.

"When can I see her?" Mrs. Switzer turned to the Doctor with a pleading look.

"She's asleep again, and I suggest we wait for a while. She drifts in and out." Dr. Grout tried to calm the excited bunch. "Every time she rests, she gains a little more strength. Let's all sit down and go over what we know."

Once they were all seated, the doctor motioned for Dennis to start. He would fill in the medical information after. He was still waiting for a report from the lab.

"So far, she's still pretty groggy. Whatever her abductor gave her was powerful enough to knock her out for a few hours. Whatever his final plans were, he didn't want her to fight back. She was found in a wheelchair in the emergency lobby. Other than panties, she was naked, wrapped in a plain gray blanket. The lab will run tests on the blanket when I leave here. No one saw anyone put Mandy in the lobby, but I was able to ask a few questions before she drifted off. I'll play the tape, and you can hear everything first hand."

Dennis knew a full disclosure would be appreciated, and once again, a different insight into the questions and answers would help. Often crimes were solved by the astute observation of some small, overlooked detail. They just finished listening to the last of the tape when the nurse came into the waiting room and announced Mandy's return to consciousness. Everyone quickly filed into her room. Judge Switzer and his wife Lena were at her side in seconds. Her grandmother stood at the foot of the bed. The Superintendent, Dennis, and Chuck stood back, giving Doctor Grout and Mandy's family room to gather around her bed. Once the hugs and tears were over, Mandy tried to assure her family she was all right. It wasn't too long before everyone could see a wave of sleepiness once again overcome Mandy's tiny face. Her blue eyes began to close as she drifted off to sleep. Mrs. Switzer wanted to continue to stay at her daughter's side, unwilling to let her hand go. She waited while they returned to the waiting room to continue their discussion of the tape and get the final details on Mandy's condition.

"What did she mean by angels and headless horseman, and why was she naked?" It was t Judge Switzer who offered the questions first.

Dennis knew Judge Switzer was a loving, caring man, but at this moment, his face looked like a thundercloud. He wanted answers, and Dennis knew he would go crazy when he found out the condition of Mandy's body. When all of the information had been given to everyone present in the small waiting room, no one was left standing. Everyone sat on the chairs scattered about the room, trying to digest the unfathomable information he had given them.

They tried to make some sense of what, at this point, made no sense at all. All they knew for sure was that Mandy had been lured away from the rave several nights before. She had been beaten, cut up, and sadistically burned over and over in a brutal attempt to accomplish something only the abductor would know. Mandy had been somewhere before, because of her drug-induced state, she thought she was at a wedding, where she was the bride. Three angels who looked just like her had rescued her. A headless rider had chased her, trying to strike her down with a sword. It was going to be Dennis and Chuck's job to sort out fact from fantasy, something that would take time and patience.

Finally, the Doctor got the medical report from the hospital lab. He went over the information with everyone, Mandy had a deadly, mind-altering agent in her system, and he had already ordered an anti-dote. Thank God whoever found her got her to the hospital when they did. It was only the intravenous that had been given to her as soon as she arrived that allowed some of the poison to be diluted enough to gain consciousness. She needed time, and Dr. Grout made sure the family knew they could stay in the waiting room, just in case she woke up again and asked for them. Dennis and Chuck decided to call it a night and return in the morning. Dennis had the old gray blanket in a plastic bag and the hospital report. He would drop the blanket off at the forensic lab before going home and try to get a couple of hours of sleep. It would still be a long night, and Dennis gave the judge his tape recorder with a fresh tape, asking him to record anything Mandy said. Everything or anything could be a clue. Once outside in the cool August evening air, Dennis and Chuck exchanged their personal views.

"Whatever happened to the other girls, almost happened to Mandy tonight," Chuck said.

"I agree, and I'm sure the only reason Mandy's alive is that one or all of the angels are real. They rescued her just in time."

Dennis gave the toxicology report to Chuck. Once he read it through quickly, Chuck gave a low whistle.

"She had enough shit in her blood to kill her if we hadn't got an I.V. into her in time. And whoever moved her got her to vomit, and that alone made a big difference. Moving her also got her heart rate up before she lapsed into a state of unconsciousness. Mandy owes her life to whoever brought her here. It's our job to piece it all together."

Chuck gave the file back to Dennis. "Let's meet in the morning for breakfast and go over it once again before we return to the hospital."

Both men agreed, and as they drove off into what was left of the early morning, they thought about the other girls in the cold case files and could only guess at the horror of their deaths. With no bodies, it was still only guesswork. All of the missing girls fit the same profile except one, Charlotte. Either she wasn't a part of these crimes, or she would be the missing link

Either way, it would be her case that they would start with to see if they could find out why she was the only one different from the other girls and how they all fit together. Both men hoped they could get some much-needed sleep before they would begin the around-the-clock investigation of what was now one hell of a bizarre case. In a city where crime and death sometimes seemed commonplace, both men still found it challenging to understand the kind of man it would take to lure away young, innocent girls from their homes. And then inflict untold pain and horror on their bodies before a brutal end. They never noticed the old station wagon parked just off to the emergency side as they drove away.

* * *

Derek sat inside, his face hidden by the shadow of the building. As the men drove off, Derek pulled forward, turning in the opposite direction. He had seen the news about Mandy and his need to retrieve his prize and finish his task drove him to the hospital in the hopes that he might be able to get Mandy back. It seemed that would now, be impossible. They would likely have a police officer guarding his prize. Oh well! There were other plums to pick.

CHAPTER TWENTY-TWO

Derek Hanson woke up the following day to the sound of birds and bugs shouting out a discordant tune, even though all of the windows and doors of his tiny acreage home were shut tight. The curtains were drawn to keep the morning light out of the dreary little farmhouse. The sound of the birds and bugs singing their morning song fell on deaf ears. The only thing Derek heard was the echo of screams and the sound of profanity from the night before still ringing in his ears. "Fuck you, you freak."

Derek couldn't smell the clear fresh air; all he could smell was the lingering odor of vomit on the torn hem of the wedding gown as he pulled it to his long bony face. An evil smile exposed his yellowed, bucked teeth. Flashes of her young, white body assaulted his senses, making it difficult to sort out what had happened, or better yet, what had gone wrong. Stolen, she had been snatched away from him just before he was about to consummate the wedding night.

Derek slipped into a world of delusion. From the day of Lisa's death, Derek had tried to make his young victims see how much they needed him like he always did on August twenty-fourth. Lisa, his little sister, the love of his life, was gone, and this young woman would take her place.

He had loved his baby sister from the first moment he saw her. The day his parents had been called by social services to come and pick up their new daughter. She was perfect. He had just turned seven, and even then, he had been too tall and thin. His bony features and strange looks caused him to feel isolated and alone. He, too, had been adopted, and often he found himself wondering what kind of unholy union could have made the likes of him. Although at seven, all he could think of was how ugly his birth parents must have been to give birth to a boy as ugly as him? The other children in school tormented him, calling him all sorts of names. The older children who beat and bullied him couldn't understand that his unusual height belied the fact that he was little more than a child. For the first seven years of his life, he felt isolated and alone. Now he would never be by himself, he had a baby sister, and she would never leave him. She would love him forever and ever.

* * *

Derek shook himself out of his review of the past and drew the vomit-stained dress away from his face. He placed it gently on a chair that sat in the corner of a dirty, tiny living room; above the chair hung a picture of Lisa, his sister. The face that smiled down at him was the last one taken, just before his mother and father had died. It was a terrible accident, but one that was bound to happen, given the condition of the old boards around the well. Their deaths left him as the only guardian and family his little sister had. By then, she was twelve, and he was an ugly, gawky nineteen years old. As ugly as he was now, he looked even worse then. His skin was a mess with white pussy pimples that covered his face. The light fuzzy stubble that covered his chin and upper lip made his face appear dirty. He was unable to shave often due to the condition of his skin. He had always worn his hair long in an attempt to cover ears that were so large they protruded through the greasy hair. His buckteeth had a dull, yellow tint, and when he spoke, spittle filled the corners of his mouth. Derek had always known he was adopted, but it becomes even more apparent as his little sister grew into a tiny, delicate beauty.

Lisa's blond hair, with its copper highlights, made the natural curl look like spun gold, framing her tiny, perfect face. Her clear, blue eyes looked out under perfectly arched brows that were framed by lashes that touched their finely featured arches.

When she was very young, Lisa adored him, but as time went on, she noticed that he was different. The more Lisa pulled away from him, the more obsessed he became. At first, he tried to bribe her with treats and presents. But after a while, she rejected the bribes, forcing him to take out his pain and frustrations on small animals and the neighbor's dogs and cats. This behavior started his lifelong obsession with death, which eventually would lead him to his present career as a mortician. Derek found his greatest pleasure came from causing small animals a slow, torturous death. It was the cigarettes that gave him the biggest rush. The smell, the sizzle, the howls of pain from the helpless animals gave him a sense of power that he had never known before. He would often replace the cat's real-life image with the latest bully's face, providing an extra rush to the torturous deed.

Derek took a picture of Lisa down from the wall. As he gazed at the lovely face in the frame, it stared back up at him. He stroked her cheeks and caressed her hair as if she were still a living, warm, being of flesh and blood, rather than a face in a cold, framed picture.

"It's your fault, Lisa. If you had loved me, none of this would have happened."

The sound of Derek's voice was flat and emotionless like the heart that beat in his chest, a heart that kept his body alive but never pumped life into his soul.

"You could never love me, and your betrayal made me do what I had to do. One day I'll find love. She will see what you couldn't. Being loved by me could have made you happy. I would have given you anything, but all you wanted was some pretty boy." Derek's face twisted into an ugly smile.

* * *

He remembered when Lisa was only twelve and had a crush on an older boy who took a fancy to her. The young man's name was Tim something or other; Derek couldn't remember his last name; after all, he meant nothing to him. Tim was only a temporary problem. He rode on the same bus as Lisa and often got off to walk her to the door and talk for a while after school.

Their parents thought it was cute and encouraged the relationship, hoping Derek would let go of Lisa's obsessive hold. Derek tried to tell his parents that Tim wasn't good for Lisa, but they only got angry with him.

"Derek, stay out of Lisa's business. She is old enough to decide who she likes and has as a friend. It's healthy for a young girl to have a crush, and as long as Lisa sees Tim here, at our home, we don't see the harm in the friendship." His father, Elliot, stood close to Derek in a way that said he was willing to take him on if he were to argue any further.

It was late spring, and Derek decided that he would quit arguing and take matters into his own hands. From Hanson's house, the walk to Tim's home was about one mile. It was a shorter distance if you cut through the woods, even if the terrain was rougher. There was one spot where a stream cut across the property, and the only way across was to step on several large stones. The runoff from the snow plus the spring rains made the stream much more difficult to cross in spring. It was here that Derek decided to make sure that Tim never crossed the stream again.

Tim had stayed a little longer than usual talking to Lisa, and the sun was going to set soon. Rather than walk the long way around, he decided he would go through the woods. . Derek kept himself hidden from view as Lisa sat with Tim on the front porch. He held her hand, his face close to hers. Derek felt like taking a run at him and slamming his fist into his pretty-boy face. He held his impulse in check listening to Tim as he wined to Lisa about Derek's dislike just before he headed home.

"Your brother hates me, and I think he would rather hit me than say hello. I don't know how you can stand having him hover over you so much? He never seems to leave you alone." Tim squeezed Lisa's hand, letting her know he was trying to understand the relationship and not judge it too harshly.

"I know Derek seems creepy, but it's because he's lonely, and I'm the only one he's got. He's never made any friends his age, so I'm the only playmate he's ever had. I guess he just can't see that I'm grown up now and need to have friends of my own. He's just afraid I'll get hurt." Lisa said.

Derek watched as Lisa looked up at Tim.

"It's more than being lonely and wanting to keep you to himself, and I sense something evil in him. It's not right the way he looks at you.   It's like he wants to be your boyfriend. Don't you see it?"

"That's not nice to say; Derek is my brother. I don't like him that way. It would make me sick. I'm sure you're wrong." Lisa recoiled away from Tim.

"I still don't like him, and he creeps me out. I have to go." Tim said as he moved away from Lisa. "Just think about what I said."

As Tim ran through the woods, Derek followed close behind, making sure Tim didn't see him. Tim began to pick up speed. Did he see him, Derek thought as he followed close behind? Derek could almost smell Tim's fear as he stumbled through the damp underbrush and long grass, trying to get to the stream. It was early spring, and although the air was still cold, Derek could see sweat break out on Tim's face. Soon he was running ahead to the stream. Tim had to slow his pace to cross safely. The stream was high and rushing in a torrent; one slip and Tim would be pulled under the current. He carefully started to make his way across the stream, watching each step, making sure his footing was steady before advancing. He was halfway across when he looked up, stopping dead in his tracks. Derek stood in front of him, an ugly sneer on his long, bony face.

Derek's eyes were blazing, his breathing short and shallow. Staying ahead of Tim had required Derek to move at full speed. But the adrenaline was pumping into his blood, and Derek felt like a 'Superhero.'

"Well, I guess it's just you and me out here." Derek's voice was low and menacing.

"Look, Derek, I don't want any trouble. I just want to go home. So let me pass, and I won't say anything to Lisa about you following me." Tim said.

"You think you're going to tell Lisa, you little fuck face! You'll never say anything to Lisa ever again. If you think I'm going to let a young bastard like you touch my little sister, you got a lot of thinking to do."

Now Derek was beside himself. Anybody who witnessed his temper would feel as if they were in the presence of someone who was totally out of control. He had used it many times to keep others at bay. When he was younger, it was a defense mechanism to keep bullies from beating him up. But as he grew older, his rage grew deeper and deeper. Soon he knew he was capable of killing. He encountered the bullies many times over the years, and once when they cornered him, he went berzerk, striking out at the small group that had gathered to torture him with taunts and slaps. He went so crazy that all of the young boys ran away in fear. They never bothered him again. And it was the last time Derek was ever afraid of anything.

"Look, just let me pass!" Tim tried to gain access to Derek's larger rock, hoping he could surprise him and knock Derek off and get away as fast as he could.

Derek was tall and lanky, but his upper body's strength and added height were no match for the younger, well-built teen. Derek would have to use intimidation as an advantage. Derek growled low and then howled. It caught his prey off guard, and Derek had him by the throat and shoved him as hard as he could. Tim went down in the frozen water, shock running through his body. Derek could feel the pull of the current and knew he had to get to Tim before he got to his feet. Derek jumped off the rock and stood over Tim's soaked body. Tim's hands were behind him, and he was flailing like a fish trying desperately to get up off the stream's bed.

"Get away from me, you fucking freak!" Tom shouted.

Derek grabbed Tim by his hair, shoving him further back to the point where Tim was almost fully laid out. Then he used all of the strength he had and held Tim's head under the rushing water.

"You cock sucking, little scum bag of shit. Don't you ever think you can threaten me or take what's mine? Lisa will never be yours, and no little prick-faced kid will ever touch her!"

Derek held Tim's head under the freezing stream while he screamed obscenities at the struggling young man. The water was cold, and every movement took all of Derek's strength to hold Tim under. The cold took its toll, and slowly the will to fight drained from Tim's body, and he stopped struggling. It was over. Derek was the victor. Now no one would touch Lisa again.

The next day when they found the body, the police ruled it an accident. They said Tim had slipped off the rock, and his foot had jammed between two large boulders causing him to be pulled under by the rushing current. His winter clothes prevented him from being able to pull himself up and free his stuck foot. Lisa had given Derek a look that said she somehow held him responsible, but she never voiced her suspicions. Even Elliot and Gabrielle Hanson had a twinge of suspicion but quickly brushed the thought aside. Derek was strange and obsessive, but he would never kill someone. At least they hoped not. The police said it was an accident and they decided to leave it at that. It was a decision they would live to regret. As time went on, Derek's obsession with Lisa became even more apparent. Family photos became a nightmare when Derek announced that he would not pose for a photo. He was too ugly. They were already at the studio when he backed out, so they had no option but to do the sitting with only the three of them. Lisa did a separate portrait, one that showed what an outstanding beauty she was. Derek had a huge copy made and hung it over his bed. Elliot and Gabrielle overheard him talking to the picture in loving, obsessive tones more than once. Something would have to be done with Derek, but what?

Derek was no longer afraid of his parent's dilemma of 'what to do with Derek?' They both, unfortunately, met with an 'accidental death.' That left him to make all decisions regarding himself and Lisa. He no longer had to worry about his parents getting in the way, or anyone else for that matter.

* * *

Derek was drawn back to the present, and he focused on the picture of Lisa that he held in his hand. He was reminded of how little consolation it gave him compared to the warmth of her flesh and blood.

"But everyone's not like you, Lisa. Others will see me for what I am, a man of power, power over life or death. I may not look like a God, but I am one, a fucking God!" His voice rose, spittle forming in the corners of his mouth. "No one can stand in my way of getting what I want. Not mom or dad or some young skinny kid who thought you were hot."

Derek began to put the picture back on the wall, pausing for only a second to place his protruding lips on the picture's glass. He closed his eyes, thinking of her white skin, tiny breasts, and perfect face. He would have her still and take his revenge at the same time. "They tried to destroy what we had, but I'll get even. I'll get back my treasures, and this time I will be loved!"

Derek finished hanging the picture on the wall and turned his thoughts to revenge. He knew who the driver was. He had known about the family long before Jade had come up to arrange her mother's funeral. Jade had almost belonged to him. Derek had spotted her just outside of the high school two years ago. She was perfect, and he needed her to belong to him. It was the fourth anniversary date of Lisa's death. A death he regretted, but she had forced him to choose. He could lose Lisa to another in life or keep her to himself through death. There was only one way to keep Lisa forever, but Derek found himself driven to find a different ending, other than the death of his beloved Lisa. That was the beginning of his need to re-enact his last moments with her.

So far, the story was always the same. Each one rejected him. But one day, one of the girls would see him for who he was—a man to be loved and who could love back. The first time Derek ever abducted anyone was on Lisa's birth, the second time on the date of her death.

He had continued the pattern ever since. The girls all resembled his beloved Lisa, and Jade was perfect. Her hair was a little redder than Lisa's, but her eyes, face, and body were perfect. Derek knew she would fit the gown he had bought especially for his bride and that Jade would wear it on the day of his special event.

Two years ago, things had gone wrong. Derek had stalked Jade for months, something he always did. It made him feel close to his victims. He could never love a stranger. Derek knew Jade would be more difficult than the rest. She seldom went anywhere except to school and back home. Then things changed. Jade began to go out and visit a new friend, a tall brunette. This new friendship would make things easier. Jade finally came out at night and would walk home alone. Now he could capture her undetected and make her his bride. Derek knew that after Jade visited her friend, she would stop by the park and sit on the swing, watching the stars. The night he spotted her sitting on the swing set was a cooler than usual evening, even for the end of April. The black coat she wore was pulled up tight around her neck; an oversized hood pulled up over her head, she swung slowly back and forth, unaware of his slow, deliberate approach. The evening was a dark, moonless bed of black. At times it was hard for Derek to see much in front of him. He followed the sound of the swing and the sweet sound of her voice as she hummed an unknown tune. He had a bottle of chloroform. It should be easy.

Jade was small, and only fifteen, the same age as his sweet Lisa was when she rejected him for the last time. Derek came up behind Jade, wrapping one long arm across her chest, grabbing her left hand with his as he leaned over her body. Suddenly she shot up off the swing and tried to run. Derek held fast to her left hand as Jade swung around, falling hard. She started to scream. Derek had counted on the element of surprise to help him silence her with the use of the chloroform. Now she was a wild cat and much stronger than he had anticipated. Derek had to straddle her body and sit on her chest while trying to pin those arms that were now pounding him with all of their strength. Boy, did it hurt, and she packed one hell of a wallop. The screaming got louder, eventually attracting attention from a neighbor nearby who turned on a backyard light, suddenly casting a glow across the park. The hood fell from her face as she stared up at Derek, seeing him fully in the light.

The eyes that stared up at Derek weren't a perfect blue. They were a dark, smoldering brown, and the hair tumbled out from under the hood was a rich, dark brown. She saw him just as he saw her. It was wrong! All wrong and Derek knew what he had to do. He struck her hard across the face. He could hear her jaw crack from the force of the blow. He could feel her go limp as he shoved the dirty chloroformed cloth in her face. Derek was angry. So angry that the fabric he pushed onto her face was delivered with such force that he could feel her nose crumble beneath his large hand.

"Fuck!" he thought. This wasn't Jade. It was that tall bitch she hung around with. The kind that was popular and had always given guys like him the cold shoulder. Derek stood up, pulling her to her feet. She hung limply in his arms. He wasn't sure if she was knocked out from his assault or if he had killed her, but he knew he had to get her out of the park. Derek was tall and skinny, but he possessed an unusual strength few would suspect at first glance. He bent forward, pulling her toward him, and in one swift movement hoisted her quickly over his shoulder. Derek carried her the same way a hunter carried a deer after the kill. However, Derek wasn't after this prey, so he felt none of the hunter's pride, only rage. The kind of rage one feels when the thing you wanted most in life had been taken from you. The type of rage that needed to be vented on the object that circumvented him from fulfilling his needs, she would pay for being here tonight.

Derek didn't know what had gone wrong. How had it been that bitch of a brunette Charlotte and not Jade on the swing? She had ruined everything, and he would skin her the way he had all those cats and small dogs over the years. It was wrong, all wrong, and he would cut her with Xs and cross her out the same way he would any useless, unwanted thing. Derek swung her into the back of his old station wagon and drove off onto the black night. He could hear her breathing. She was still alive. She would regret that the blow to her face didn't end her life, right then and there. What he had planned would be a fate worse than anything he had ever done before. Skinning her alive would give him a great deal of pleasure. Charlotte would represent all of the popular kids that had ever tormented him and caused him so much pain. They were the ones that had made his Lisa see what a loser they thought he was. He would show her just what a loser could do.

Derek had taken Charlotte straight to the funeral home. He would not have her defile his chapel of love. She would not live long enough. Charlotte was laid out on the steel table in the hidden chamber beneath the crematorium.

"What do you plan to do with me?" Charlotte asked once she regained consciousness and realized she had been abducted.

"I never had any plans for you. You just happened to be in the wrong place at the wrong time, and now you've wrecked my plan. You will pay for this." Derek put his face close to Charlottes while he pulled her head back, yanking fiercely on her thick head of hair.

Charlotte spits in Derek's face. "You let go of me or else."

"Or else, what? You're tied up, and it seems as if no one is here to defend you. It's just you and me. If you treat me well, maybe I'll let you go." Derek said, knowing he would never let Charlotte live. Even if she did try to please him, she wasn't what he wanted, and there was no going back. This little game would have to be played out to the end.

"Look. I have brothers, and they'll kick your ass. Now let me go."

"It's time to play a little game. It's called ashes." Derek said as he lit a cigarette, dragging deeply.

"I don't smoke, and you can't make me," Charlotte said, screwing up her nose.

"You think the game is to get you to smoke? Shit, when I'm finished with you, you'll be begging to take a drag. No, my sweet. I have a better use for this cigarette than to suck on it with you." Derek laughed with disbelief.

Charlotte gave Derek a cold stare and tried to pull her head from Derek's grasp. Suddenly Derek stood up, dropping her had hard on the steel table. When he turned around, the cigarette was red hot. He pulled it from his mouth into his bony hand and placed its hot tip on Charlotte's face. She screamed out in surprise and anguish.

"This is just the beginning," Derek said as he touched the cigarette to her face again and again.

The screams that echoed inside the small chamber made Derek feel strong and powerful. It took several hours for Charlotte to finally die. She was a strong, determined young woman. When Derek put the knife to her breasts and started to carve them from her chest, she took her last breath. But not before she made one final statement. "Fuck you. Rot in hell."

Derek went crazy. It was always the same. She would pay for her last insult. Derek carved Charlotte to pieces.

Over the next two years, he had continued to abduct young girls, finding perfect replacements for Lisa. It had been a full six years since Lisa's final rejection, and except for the brunette, he had loved over one dozen perfect girls. Next would be Crystal, not Jade, who would be his new bride. Jade was now unacceptable, while Crystal was perfect. Jade would have to give him back his treasures, and Derek knew Jade would willingly walk into his trap. He would have her sister for 'better or worse.' Derek knew the girl›s secret. Jade would come out of love for her sister and self-preservation. Derek knew what they had done. But first Derek would have to go shopping. His newest bride would need something beautiful to wear, and Crystal would make the perfect bride.

CHAPTER TWENTY-THREE

Dennis and Chuck sat across from each other in Dennis's cubicle at the Area 3 police station. Along the small wall were pictures of Dennis, Chuck, and his other partners. Dennis and Chuck had received many awards of merit. There were pictures of Dennis exchanging handshakes and awards of recognition with the mayor and many other notables, even the President, Bill Clinton. During the past twenty years, he had moved up the ranks, as did his partner. Dennis was the most decorated and respected police officer on the force and his favorite partner, Chuck.

Dennis hadn't joined the force until his late twenties. A former trucker, he had always had a lifelong interest in the Chicago police force, and so his wife Veronica had finally convinced him to try out. His high scores on the written exams and his still youthful physical abilities had proven that age was no barrier. Dennis often beat most of the other men who were much younger. Now fifty, Dennis could still boast a slim, muscular body, a contrast to his dedicated but chubby partner Chuck.

At fifty-five, Chuck was packing around an extra thirty pounds, and although it made him appear heavy, he was still able to pull off a good chase if need be. Chuck's easy nature and keen mind added a new perspective to Dennis's methodical, logical and meticulous police work. They were a great team and even better friends. Chuck had what many envied, a will of steel, with the nature of a saint. Dennis knew Chuck loved his job and woke up most mornings itching to get on with whatever case was at hand. He was still the kind of officer who liked to 'rush in, where fools fear to tread,' and Dennis kept him grounded from his usual Maverick style.

"O.K. Chuck, including Mandy, what do you see when you look at these photos of our missing girls?" Dennis pointed to a string of pictures along a short wall to the side of his desk. The photos were placed in two rows, one image on top of the other, making thirteen photos in all.

Chuck was looking at them all together for the first time. Until now, he had glanced briefly through several of the files noting their ages and addresses, only briefly looking at their pictures.

"It's easy when you see them like this; they all look alike except for the brunette. She's the only one that stands out as different." Chuck stated the obvious.

"Right, and they are all thirteen to fifteen years old as well." Dennis went over to the computer and pulled off a print-out. "Now, here's something else that will seem unusual if these were just a bunch of runaways." Dennis handed the list to Chuck.

"Holy shit, this confirms your suspicion that these girls were abducted." Chuck ran his finger down the list. "All of the girls went missing on either one of two dates, and so far, it's an even seven girls on one date and six on the others. The brunette must have been a mistake. There were two abductions on the same day. Mandy's disappearance was two days ago on August twenty-fourth, the same date as the other five, while the other six were at the end of April, on the twenty-ninth." Chuck put the list on Dennis's desk.

"These girls are probably all dead, and whoever's doing this has done away with the bodies. We've never found even one girl or a single clue."

Dennis picked up the file that had all of the written reports. The one he held was Charlotte's, the only girl that seemed to stand out as different from the others.

"This is the only one that's different." Dennis flipped through the file. "So this is where we're going to start. She might not be connected at all, but we may find out what went wrong." Dennis looked up from the file at Chuck's earnest face. "If we're going to find out anything, we have to either rule her out as having any connection at all or find out why she's a part of this other bunch of girls. She went missing on the same date as six of the others, April twenty-ninth. But she isn't even close to the physical appearance of the others. Let's see if we can find out what went wrong and who the killer was after."

Dennis grabbed his suit jacket off the back of his chair and headed toward the door.

"What makes you think he wasn't after Charlotte?" Chuck was curious about Dennis's conclusion.

"It's just a hunch. But you know I could be wrong." Dennis gave Chuck a friendly slap across the back.

"When have you ever been wrong?"

Chuck followed Dennis out of the office door as they headed toward the staircase leading to the main lobby.

Dennis always took the stairs; it was one way to stay slim. Chuck didn't mind going down but coming back up was a killer, so he often took the elevator, leaving Dennis alone for his trip up the stairs.

Dennis knew Chuck was impressed with his ability to draw conclusions often based on instinct and a gut feeling as well as the cold hard facts. But, if his gut went contrary to the evidence, he used his gut. It was a trait that would usually be foreign to Dennis's factual nature, but over the years, he had learned to trust his intuition. This ability had helped him solve hundreds of cases over the years, giving him an almost mythical reputation on the force. If Dennis' guts said the killer had made a mistake and was after someone else, it was his job to find out whom.

Dennis and Chuck wove their way through the afternoon traffic, heading back to Ukrainian Village, Dennis's neighborhood, and the place where Charlotte was lived. They were going to question Charlotte's mother and father. An appointment had been made for the supper hour. As they tried to find a place to park in front of the reconditioned walk-up, an old brownstone building that had been restored to its original condition, his area known as the 'little Ukraine.' Dennis gave Chuck the list of questions he had prepared, hoping Chuck would see if anything else should be asked. It was a double-check system that would maximize their efforts; after all, two brains were better than one.

Mr. and Mrs. Kennedy were an attractive, middle-aged couple that seemed eager to meet with Chuck and Dennis. The greeting at the door indicated the anticipation of their arrival. Once they were seated, it was Mrs. Kennedy who took up the lead.

"We were so glad to hear from you. When Charlotte went missing, we tried to convince the police that she wasn't a runaway, but they acted like they didn't believe us." Mrs. Kennedy leaned forward, her pretty face showing both concern and relief with Dennis and Chuck's presence.

"What is it you would like to know?" She stated. "How can we help?"

"We would like to start from the beginning, and many of the questions may seem the same. Nonetheless, there might be something that was overlooked. We're hoping to pick up a new clue and follow it."

Dennis wanted to put the couple at ease; he could sense their pain at not having any answers about their daughter's disappearance.

"Sure." Mr. Kennedy spoke up for the first time. "For us, it still seems like yesterday. We'll do anything to help."

"When exactly did you realize Charlotte was missing?" Dennis started on the list.

"By around eleven that evening."

Mrs. Kennedy answered many of the questions; mothers were always aware of their children's comings and goings.

"Where was she going?"

"Nowhere, she had gone out with friends, came home, changed into some casual clothes, and went out for a walk.

"Was that normal?"

"Yes, she liked to unwind by going for a walk; it helped her sleep."

"No worries about being out that late at night?" Dennis looked to see if they would object to any personal reference that they had done something wrong.

"No, after all, this is Berwyn, and we always felt safe." Mrs. Kennedy continued. "When you're fifteen and don't drive, walking home at night or going for a walk isn't unusual."

Dennis continued to jot down notes. She was right, his daughters had walked everywhere at that age, and he and Veronica had never worried.

"Who was she with?"

"Several friends, I think I gave the original officer a list."

Dennis pulled the list from the file and handed it over to Mrs. Kennedy who quickly gave it a once over.

"Yes, these were her closest friends. If they met up with anyone else, I don't know whom. I'm assuming the other officer followed up, but who knows?"

Dennis could sense her disapproval of how the first case was handled.

"Can you think of any reason why Charlotte might run away?" Dennis knew this would hurt, but he had to ask.

"No, as I said to anyone who would listen, she would never run away."

"Can you think of anyone who would hurt her?" Dennis continued.

"Never in a million years! Charlotte was the kind of girl who was very popular. Furthermore, she spoke to and befriended everyone. There were all sorts of kids at school who felt she was a good friend, and they came from all kinds of groups."

As a mother, Mrs. Kennedy was very proud of the spirit that Charlotte possessed. After several more questions, Dennis and Chuck stood to signal their departure. "Before we go, is there anything else that you can add or think of before we go and question her friends?"

"No, I don't think so." Mrs. Kennedy turned to her husband.

"Can I see that list first?" It was the first time Mr. Kennedy had spoken up since they had exchanged their earlier greetings.

"Sure." Chuck handed the list to him.

Mr. Kennedy looked the list over thoughtfully. "Honey, there is one name missing, that new friend of Charlotte's. She was only here a couple of times, but it could be important."

"Who's that sweetheart? I'm sure I included everyone." Mrs. Kennedy took the list from her husband and gave it a worried look, hoping her mistake hadn't interfered with the return of their daughter.

"You know, that pretty little one with the copper, blond curls and blue eyes."

When Mr. Kennedy gave the description, Dennis and Chuck exchanged a knowing but surprised look.

"Yes, yes, you're right, how could I have missed it? She was a new friend, but Charlotte took a real fancy to her." Mrs. Kennedy put her hand to her face in dismay at forgetting the girl. "Her name was Jade, yes, Jade Walker."

Dennis stopped writing on the pad. Blood rushed from his head, past his heart, into his stomach, making him feel sick. In a flash, he knew his guess was correct; the killer was never after Charlotte. He'd been after a perfect little girl with copper, curly hair, and beautiful blue eyes. Jade looked like all of the other girls. She was a perfect match. She could have been a sister to any one of the other dozen girls who had gone missing. The only lucky thing that had ever happened to Jade was that somehow the killer had missed her and, from the information, got Charlotte by mistake. Dennis hoped Jade could offer him some answers.

Chuck and Dennis thanked the couple and excused themselves. They wanted to say out loud to each other what was rushing through their brains. They were onto something, and now this case was beginning to hit close to home.

Dennis wanted to get back to the station. He had a new computer program that could give him a geographic location of the suspect, using the locations of the crimes. Historically, murders committed by serial killers often occur in places familiar to the killer. If you enter enough information into the program, the alga-rhythm could provide a location within a five-kilometer radius where the suspect is likely to live or work. It wasn't a new theory, but coming up with enough data to get an accurate location was often tricky.

"What are you thinking?" Dennis asked Chuck once they were out of the driveway of the Kennedy home.

"I think that technology is wonderful and that we need to put all of the information into the computer and see what we come up with. I don't understand why no one else saw all of the correlations in these cases, the dates, the girls' descriptions, and the locations. I'm sure we'll pin this bastard down soon. They always shit in their backyard, and the stench leads us to them." Chuck answered.

Dennis knew Chuck was right, and he felt that they would have to come up with the location soon. Would he strike again if the killer were unable to complete the abduction and murder of his latest victim? Dennis's gut said yes! He only hoped the killer hadn't found a new victim, and they would have a slight lead time before anyone else was hurt. And then there was Jade. Was she an abduction gone wrong? Dennis felt that she was. The question was. Would she still be safe?

CHAPTER TWENTY-FOUR

J ade, Crystal, and Amber sat around the kitchen table. It was already late in the afternoon. Between last night and this morning, their world had undoubtedly taken a dangerous turn.

"What the hell are we going to do about this mess we're in?" Crystal's tone was more an accusation than a question.

"By 'mess,' do you mean the killing and cremation of dad, or finding out Derek Hanson is a serial killer. Maybe it's the part about that girl being a judge's daughter. Better still, what about Detective Kortovich showing up and asking questions about Charlotte." Jade shot back with a fair amount of sarcasm in her voice, her face looking dark and stormy. "We're somewhere between a rock and a hard place. If we had told the police about what we found, they would have discovered our reason for being in the morgue. Then Derek wouldn't be the only one going to jail." Jade finished, dropping her defensive tone and letting the worry of what lay ahead sound in her high-pitched voice. "But if we shut up, Derek will go on killing. After what we saw, we can't let the bastard get away with it." Jade finished.

"I know." Crystal stood up and started to remove the dishes from the table. As usual, lunch was Kraft dinner, Amber's favorite.

Jade looked at Crystal's drawn face; then at Amber's sweet, unworried one, she envied Amber her exceptional condition. She was able to live in a world where there was no trouble, no reality. All she needed was a bed, food, shelter, and the love of her sisters, and of course, her toy phone; everything else took place in her head, and who could understand what was going on in there.

"We have to find a way to stop him, but how? We're in a real pickle, as mom would say." Crystal looked at Jade, hoping for an answer.

"When Dennis and Chuck arrived at the door, I thought we were under arrest. It took me a while to figure out what he wanted. When he said it was about Charlotte, I was relieved but worried as well." Crystal continued moving around the kitchen while Jade watched.

"The first time the police investigated her disappearance, I was never even questioned, only her old friends. Did you see the way they both stared at us like they were seeing us for the first time?" Jade automatically started helping her sister with the clean-up. It felt good to be doing something normal.

"From the questions, they asked they know nothing about dad, but they are investigating the disappearance of the girls."

Jade drew Amber out of the kitchen into the living room and sat her in a rocker to the TV side. It would keep her calm for hours. She just rocked and stared at whatever was in front of her on the television, often a game show. Crystal followed them into the living room, and soon she and Jade were curled up on the couch trying to come up with a plan to get out of their predicament.

"Somehow, I figure we're tied into this mess beyond our little visit to the morgue." Jade looked into Crystal's blue eyes and saw what Dennis and Chuck must have.

"Did you notice anything about those photos we found as well as the pictures Dennis showed us?"

"No, they're just a bunch of missing girls, and we are the only ones who know they're dead and who killed them." Crystal gave the answer she thought was obvious.

"Look again." Jade drew the pictures out of a shoebox that had been hidden under the couch. Inside were all of the pictures she had torn from the wall of the hidden chamber, as well as the rings, watches, necklaces, and earrings that had belonged to the missing girls. She spread them out in front of Crystal, thirteen in all.

"What do you see?"

"Dead girls in a wedding dress, except for Charlotte and shit, she looks awful." Crystal answered defensively.

"There's more to see than that, Crystal, and we're a part of it. I can see it as plain as the nose on your face."

Crystal picked up each picture slowly, trying to see what Jade saw, feeling stupid and frustrated for missing whatever it was she was trying to point out.

"I give up." Crystal said, throwing the last picture back in the box.

"What is it that you and the cops have figured out that I haven't?" Crystal's voice was rising, her anger mounting.

"They all look like us!" Jade almost shouted, lowering her voice so she would not have Amber move from her chair. "Small, light, reddish hair, fair complexion, curls, and blue eyes, we could all be sisters." Jade knew she was close to an answer.

"Shit!" Crystal picked up a couple of pictures at random, giving them another look. It's time for a new perspective. "We do look like them, but what does that mean?" She was still confused.

"I've been thinking about it ever since Dennis and Chuck left, and I began putting it together by the way they acted and looked at us." Jade changed her position on the couch, sitting back, pulling her legs up under her chin.

"I think that the night Charlotte went missing, Derek was really after me. It wasn't supposed to be her. It was supposed to be me." Jade rested her forehead on her knees, feeling sick about what must have happened.

"I was with her that night; a bunch of us were. I was supposed to stay for supper and then watch a movie, going home somewhere around eleven." Jade reflected on that night, trying not to feel the emotional impact of what was supposed to happen.

"Mom called because dad was going berserk, so I left early. I slipped out the back door and cut through the neighbor's yard, taking a shortcut. I would usually go through the park, but I was worried, so I took my chances cutting through several yards. When I found out the next morning, Charlotte was missing. Her mom said she went for a walk and probably visited the park." Jade turned and looked at her sister again.

"I think Derek must have followed me there and waited. When he saw Charlotte, he must have made a mistake, somehow thinking it was me, but taking her. Or maybe Charlotte surprised Derek while he was lurking outside her house. Somehow I feel she was a mistake, and he wanted me. Look at the pictures. He's put X's all over her body and even cut off her breast and mutilated her. He's angry, but only with her. He may have hurt the others, but look at the way he's laid them out in the wedding gown. They look perfect. He's replacing someone with girls that look just like us, and now we've walked back into his life." Jade looked up for a few seconds before continuing.

"Did you see the way he looked at you during Mom's funeral?" Jade turned fully toward Crystal, dropping her legs, placing her feet on the floor.

"He's after me now, and I sure hope he doesn't know it was us at the morgue last night, or he'll be pissed, and boy, we will be in trouble." Crystal said.

Jade took in what Crystal was saying, and however fantastic it may have sounded, she knew it was true. Two years ago, Derek had meant to kidnap her and somehow got Charlotte. With their mother's death, Jade and Crystal once again came into view of Derek. With the killing of Sam and his cremation, the girls had stumbled onto Derek's secret. Crystal and Jade were now caught between a killer and the police. Jade laughed to herself. It was ironic that they, too, were killers. The difference between them and Derek was survival. If their dad stayed alive, he could have beaten them to death or, at the very least, finally unleashed his unnatural desires on them along with the verbal, mental, and physical abuse. Jade and Crystal had no choice but to kill, and they had killed for their and their sister's survival. Jade wondered what drove Derek to do what he had done. Did he have a choice, or was he driven by some unknown fear or frustration that forced him to unleash his unnatural obsession with young girls that looked just like them? It felt weird trying to find a reason for someone to do what Derek had done. There was no way he could justify his killing of young, innocent girls. It wasn't life or death. It was an evil and unnatural obsession.

"I can't come up with a single idea about what to do; I'm just too tired from all of this. It was only the day before yesterday we killed dad, and yesterday we got rid of him. Now we're in an even bigger mess. I just want to forget it all for a while."

Crystal grabbed the remote and turned on the T.V. It was her way of saying it was over, at least for a while. Jade knew they would have to come up with a plan, but she felt every bit as tired as Crystal, so she too just let things go for a while.

"The return of young Mandy Switzer has the police baffled. Reports from an inside source said that her arrival last night at the Henrotin Hospital is shrouded in mystery. Her rescue is credited to three angels. Our sources so far say there is no lead as to the identity of the so-called angels. We'll bring you more on the story as new details unfold; let's turn to Charles Dunken for a report on the weather." The voice on the T.V. changed as the weatherman took over and gave the latest weather report.

Jade and Crystal turned off the T.V. and slumped over, feeling dejected. They were so drained of emotion, neither spoke, each caught up in the horror of their present situation. Would they now be an obvious target for Derek if he could put things together with the report on the news? For all the girls knew, Derek was already planning his revenge, but tonight they just needed some sleep.

CHAPTER TWENTY-FIVE

Derek awoke to the smell of vomit; the torn gown lay just beneath his long oversized nose while the scent of soured food mingled together to make an unusual aroma. Derek had taken the gown with him to bed. It somehow gave him a sense of comfort. The smell and the feel of satin and lace, along with the importance of the gown, gave Derek some comfort, and he had finally drifted off into an uneasy sleep.

Images of young girls running, tripping. His hands striking them down, his body on theirs, tiny breasts, large hands, the moans and tears along with vile tirades, their language hurtful. Small hands tied to their sides while the smell of flesh burning, along with the scent of his cigarette, gave him that familiar feeling of power, screams, begging to be freed, calling out for their mothers. Their rejections of him, along with his anger, mingled with the smell of fear, again the white dress billowing all around him then splitting into pieces along with the flesh of the young girls, blood everywhere, the white turning to crimson. Once he had regained his senses, the dreams fading, he lay naked beneath the dirty sheets of his bed for a few minutes before putting his feet on the cold, gritty floor.

Derek concentrated on what the day ahead would hold. He needed to get a new dress for his bride. Tonight it would no longer be a hard cold hand in his bed, it would be a copper-haired princess, and this time he vowed he would make her love him, the way he longed to be loved, touched, and admired. He was a man, and he knew if given a chance, he could prove it. Derek looked down, a frustrated look on his face. Damn his manhood. It always betrayed him. One touch, and it went off like a new recruit with a trigger-happy finger, bang, bang, you're dead.

Derek pulled back the sheets and rubbed the creamy white liquid into his stomach. He liked the way it felt beneath his fingers, sticky, hot. Today Crystal would become the new Bride. If she refused, she would feel the total weight of his rage on her body. Alive or dead, he would have her. Derek no longer cared how things played out; he was driven by something dark and unexpressed inside. He would could not look beneath the rage he felt. Death would no longer be an option. She would have no choice but to accept him.

Naked, he walked purposefully. His feet felt the dirt on the floor, but he was used to the filthy condition of his home. The stale smells, the clutter of old newspapers, fast food cartons, beer cans, and unwashed towels, to him, it was home and a part of whom he was. The bathroom was small and dingy, with only a stream of light finding its way through the unwashed window over the tub. The mirror that reflected Derek's long bony face was spattered with years of toothpaste, soap scum, and water stains. He no longer needed to see himself when he shaved, and he liked things that way. Seeing his face in the mirror only made him feel that 'sinking' lonely pain. If he didn't see his face, he could forget just what a cruel joke life had played on him. When he did manage to catch a glimpse of himself, he would curse his unknown parents and wonder again what unholy union had spawned a man, such as himself. It was at times like this that he would feel a seething rage. He never asked for this life. It was the death that he yearned for, and until that welcomed time came, he would visit death daily at the morgue, the only place he'd ever felt safe.

Grieving people were too full of their pain to cause him any with their looks and whispers. At the funeral home, he felt respected and powerful, full of exalted self-importance. More importantly, the dead never judged him. Their lifeless bodies seemed to welcome his ideas and confessions; Derek felt safe confiding his secrets to them; often, their faces would appear to him in his dreams, spectators to his fantasies and guests at his weddings. They smiled their approval with his bride at his side as he stood before the altar, confessing his love to his bride.

Derek dressed in the dark. The shirt he wore was a blinding white, the only clothing item that made him appear professional. The clean navy-blue tie made the shirt appear even brighter. He had one dozen shirts. He had them dry-cleaned to a crisp, perfect look. It made his appearance just passable. Derek used an electric shaver. He hated the feel of water on his face and only showered once a week. He used a strong deodorant. This, along with a clean shirt, got him through the week. He pulled his long, greasy hair into a tight ponytail. He was off to go shopping, then to work and later—well.

* * *

Derek had passed the boutique many times, and he always found himself looking at the elegant window display. Every once in a while, he would see a gown that would almost take his breath away. The little boutique specialized in affordable wedding gowns, and once or twice he was so taken with a dress in the window he found himself pulled into the store. He had to touch the soft fabric of the white designs, and he would fantasize about some young, innocent girl. It was nearly noon when Derek finally left the puzzled and exasperated clerk with his prize under his arm. It was wrapped in a clear, plastic specialty bag so that all of its beauty could be visible through the packaging.

Derek could tell the clerk recognized him from his previous visits into the shop. By now, she figured he was just a looker, and she only glanced at him when he entered the shop. She had already gotten used to his unusual looks. When he finally approached her to see what she had in size two, she was able to keep her face open and pleasant, making him feel relaxed and excited about his purchase. He proved to be a demanding customer. He had a certain style in mind. Just when she had exhausted all of her sales skills, she remembered a gown she had in the back room. It had arrived the first thing that morning, and up until then, she felt she was at a dead end. She thought the gown would be too expensive.

"You know, Mr. Hansen, we had a wonderful gown arrive this morning, and I have a feeling it might just be what you're looking for." The dark-haired clerk's eyes were hopeful.

She returned from the back with a gown that almost stopped Derek's heart from beating. It was what he had always imagined his Lisa deserved. The gown style was very similar to the one that had been torn from Mandy's innocent body only yesterday, but it was also different. This was the real thing, not like the cheap one that now lay on a heap back at his home. Derek could feel his hands go clammy in anticipation.

The straps were thin and small rhinestones were set among the white pearls, where a tasteful sprinkle of the gems was arranged in an intricate pattern that dropped to the bodice. From below the bust line, the dress's waist dipped into a V, dropping to a full skirt that fell to the floor in a cadence of lace and satin. It was a strange combination of innocent style and sophisticated detail. The dress was meant for a princess. Could a prince that looked like a frog win his love's heart? He had to have the gown. Derek never even blinked or missed a beat when he heard the price of the dress, two thousand- eight hundred dollars. He simply took the gown, twirling it around for a full view. Derek's thick lips curled up over his bucked yellow teeth as he smiled a slow, wicked smile with white spittle forming at the corner of his mouth. Derek said nothing as he reached into his pocket and pulled out his wallet, removing his gold bankcard to pay for the gown. After Derek walked out of the store, the clerk let out a suppressed rush of air.

"Poor bride who marries a man like that, I think I'd rather be dead." The clerk thought as she returned to her new inventory getting the gowns ready for display.

It was now noon. Derek was so engrossed in his thoughts and pleasure with the purchase of the gown that he didn't look up until he bumped into a man who was sharing the sidewalk with him.

"So sorry!" came a familiar voice.

Their eyes met at the same time, each unaware of the other until they collided.

"Mr. Hanson, nice to see you; I hope I didn't knock you too hard. I just wasn't watching where I was going."

Dennis held out his hand, noting Derek's hands were full. It took a few seconds for Dennis to realize that what Derek held in his hands was a wedding gown.

"Getting married?"

It was an open question but somehow automatic. Dennis knew Derek was single, and he couldn't picture what type of girl would be attracted to Derek. He shook off the uncharitable thought. The day was already hot, and it continued to be a sweltering, muggy August. You could tell that tonight, another summer storm would brew up from the lake when things cooled down.

The sweat on Derek's brow felt cold, and a sudden chill engulfed his skinny body. Derek knew he had no answer for the detective, but he had to say something.

"No… No… um… it's not...for me. Oh uh...nope...it's... it's for a friend, yes. I'm picking it up for a friend. She's busy.

It's a favor." Derek knew he sounded stupid, but he could not think of anything else to say, so he just stared at Dennis, waiting for him to comment.

"Well, I guess I'd better let you get going. It's pretty hot out here. I'll let you deliver that dress. It looks pretty special." Dennis could see the flash of jewels sparkle through the plastic.

Derek looked down at the gown gave an embarrassed nod, color rising to his pale face. "Ya, I gotta go." His long legs carried him off as fast as they could.

Dennis continued to walk towards his favorite restaurant, and on the way, he passed the bridal shop. He had seldom given the store a second thought. Now he stood in front of the window, wondering what his encounter with Derek was all about. One of two things came to mind: Derek had a sweetheart, and the gown was really for her, or he was a drag queen, and the dress was for him. The mental picture of Derek as a love-struck groom with some young woman standing at his side made Dennis shiver, even on this hot day. Then again, Derek's long, bony body in sparkle, the studded wedding gown, wasn't a pretty sight either. Dennis had to go into the store and solve the mental puzzle. It would drive him crazy if he didn't have the answer. The tall brunette was precisely the kind of woman who worked in a specialty boutique. She was slim, classy and her greeting was warm yet professional.

"Hello, how may I help you?" The rich tones in her voice matched the perfection of her stylish look.

"There was a man in here that just picked up a gown for a friend. What can you tell me about him?" Dennis got right to the point, flashing his detective badge while he asked the question.

"I can tell you the gown wasn't for a friend. I just spent the better part of the morning showing him everything in the store. The one he finally picked was the most expensive one we had."

Her tone of exasperation and surprise was evident from her statement. Her professional demeanor dropped by Dennis's surprise visit.

He was still confused. What could Derek want with a hand-stitched, expensive wedding gown? Who was it for?

"What size was the gown?" Dennis decided to try his second choice of reasons for Derek's interest in a wedding gown.

"Size two, he said it was for a perfect angel. He was adamant that she was very tiny and nothing bigger than a size two would do."

The name on her nametag was Clarisse. Dennis figured it suited her. She was a classy Clarisse.

"What else can you tell me," Dennis pushed further for something that would make sense.

"Other than the fact that the mortician makes an unlikely groom?" her question was rhetorical. She continued without waiting for an answer. "He said she was like a precious jewel. He described her as an angel, with ivory skin and reddish, gold hair that curled in ringlets to the middle of her back." Clarisse looked as though she found it difficult to believe anyone of that description could be willing to marry a man like Derek.

"I always ask for a physical description if someone comes in to look at the gowns without the bride, although it's usually an overly anxious mother." Clarise waited for Dennis to continue.

"Well, can you tell me what he paid for the gown?"

"Sure. It was just a little over three thousand dollars with the tax. Derek never even batted an eyelash, just paid with a credit card."

Dennis was quiet as he took a look around the elegant store with all of the beautiful white gowns encircling the perimeter. It made him think of what the inside of a cloud must look like. White on white or cream on white, soft, beautiful like a dream, he thanked Clarisse for her trouble and left the store, his mind working overtime.

What the hell did Derek want with a wedding gown? He had lied when he said he was picking the dress up for a friend. Dennis then pictured in his mind what his second options were, Derek in drag, what a thought. He almost started to laugh at the mental picture of Derek in a skimpy bridal gown. Derek was an ugly guy, but as a woman, what a scary thought. Ugh! But a size two, never! He was defiantly not the one dressing in drag unless he had a twisted, emotional view of his body.

So what did Derek want with a wedding gown, one that was important to him in some way? There was a nagging thought at the back of Dennis's mind. Mandy! She said she was a bride at a wedding. Was there a fit somehow? Dennis decided he would have to follow the trail to whoever was supposed to be wearing the gown. Whoever it was, they would require a warrant to check Derek's home and office to see if there was a connection. It would be difficult. He had no evidence that Derek was involved with the missing girls in any way, just a hunch. He had no witness, nothing, only Mandy. Then suddenly, the idea of the crematorium flashed before his mind. His heart started to pound. Dennis felt he was on to something as he once again got that 'gut' feeling. A chill shot through his body. Dennis somehow knew he had to push for a warrant. It was as if someone's life depended upon it.

Dennis was about to meet Chuck for lunch and go over the computer-generated data when he ran into Derek. He would keep his suspicions to himself, for a while at least. It would be challenging to convince Chuck that just because a man had a dress fetish, it wouldn't make him a serial killer. The restaurant was just beginning to fill up when Dennis saw Chuck burst through the door. He looked excited and full of purpose.

"What's up? You look like you just figured out who killed Kennedy, and you know the odds on that." It was a running game between the two of them on who was the best detective.

The Kennedy assignation was the ultimate cause, and they had each come up with several unique theories of their own over the years. If they ever discovered who was behind the Kennedy murder, both Dennis and Chuck were sure one of them would go missing.

"So confess, what is it you know, that I don't?" Dennis asked.

"The computer program finally finished compiling the data and came up with relative vicinity for the suspect, and I think you'll agree there are some key points that will help to narrow down our killer," Chuck said excitedly.

"Let's see. You talk. I'll read. It will make things go faster.

Dennis took the printout from Chuck while he settled in at the table. A waitress came to the table with a notepad and a smile.

"What will you have, boys? Why don't you surprise me today and take a look at the menu and live dangerously? Who knows, you might find something different." She was unaware that 'different' in a restaurant was something both men wanted to avoid.

Dennis and Chuck ordered their usual favorites from the waitress, Sherry, a middle-aged widow who was now a good friend. Chuck liked the chicken, a change from steak. After the last case they worked, he would no longer eat beef in a restaurant, only at home, where his wife Shelley assured him it was safe. Dennis was a little braver and could still eat a good steak anywhere, even if he wasn't too sure how it was prepared. Even so, they both still had a lingering fear from that last case.

The burgers at Paddy's Family Restaurant were good, but Dennis felt the best were still at Moody's Pub on North Broadway, another of their favorites. Charcoal-grilled, Moody's Pub always cooked their burgers to perfection. A quarter-pound of beef that could almost make one forget that hamburger was the lesser byproduct of meat. Again, after that last case, beef would never be the same.

"OK, it goes like this." Chuck started his explanation as soon as Sherry left with the order. "All of the girls came from three residential districts, Oak Park, Bowyn, and Elmwood Park. The rave that Mandy attended was smack in the middle of the geographic area in the Newton section. It seems Mandy hung around the area at a few of the clubs and always went to the same place for the rave. So we have a similar geographic area for all of the missing girls. Now we have to look around for either a likely place for the suspect to live or work. We have a large business district as well as the usual community services, like churches and schools". Chuck took a deep breath and continued. "We can rule them out, I think because the girls went to different schools and different churches. That leaves us a commonplace they might all go in the business area—the clubs, eateries, shops, etc. But look at this hot point on the sheet. It's not even near the business section. It's near a fucking graveyard. The computer is pointing to an area that seems unlikely. What do you make of it?"

Dennis couldn't believe his eyes. The printout was done in 3-D, making the most likely point bright red and at the highest elevation. This geographic profile was a computer program that a cop in Canada did, and although it was a helpful tool, it was not infallible. He could feel the hair on his arm stand on end, and goosebumps travel up his arm to his neck, causing his ears to ring. This time he knew the computer was on target. Right in the middle of the hot area was a funeral home, and who worked there? Derek Hanson.

CHAPTER TWENTY-SIX

J ade was the first to feel the warm breeze on her face and hear the early morning sounds burst forth to announce the beginning of a new day. She could smell the sweet scent of freshly cut grass and hear the sounds of a robin's chirp and the jays' awful two-toned screech. It was all very new to her because she had seldom allowed a window to remain open. Over the years, Jade had learned that Sam could turn into a screaming maniac at any time of the day; an open window was out of the question. Whenever the screams could be heard to escalate into physical violence, Dennis would be the first to arrive. Without Jewell charging Sam, there was little that could be done.

Jade could hear the sounds of her siblings in the room next to hers. It was larger than the tiny room that held all of her precious belongings, but Crystal and Amber had always shared the room; now, they could all have a room of their own if they wanted. Crystal had decided to leave things the way they were for a while, even though Jade pointed out the advantage of a room of her own. She just wasn't ready to make any decisions right now. Besides Crystal loved sleeping with Amber, it was the way Amber rocked herself to sleep each night that had helped Crystal put away her worries and drift off to sleep. Amber also felt warm and smelled like baby powder. For now, Crystal just wasn't ready to give up that feeling of comfort. Jade burst into Crystal and Amber's room with a big smile on her face, taking Crystal by surprise. Jade was always very serious, while Crystal was just plain angry. It had become more and more of who they were, and nowhere was Jade with an entirely new look on her face.

"What's with you?" Crystal scowled at her sister. "You'd think you found the winning lotto ticket from the look on your face." Crystal got up out of bed. She needed a bathroom urgently.

"Hey, where ya going? I thought we could all cuddle and talk, it's still early, and we can get up whenever we want." Jade said, sounding hurt.

"If I don't go pee, you'll be laying in a wet bed. So move and let me by." Crystal sounded annoyed.

Jade knew Crystal wasn't annoyed. She would like a morning in bed, just talking and hugging. But when a girl had to go, it was best not to stop her.

"O.K., but hurry, I can't believe we don't have a dad in the house anymore, and with such a beautiful day ahead, I just can't seem to worry about getting caught, even if I should."

Jade jumped into the queen size bed, a gift from her mother to the girls on Crystal's thirteenth birthday. She cuddled into Amber's warm body, now doing her familiar rocking back and forth. Jade put her nose close to her sister's face. She, too, loved the clean, fresh, baby smell of her hair and the feel of her soft skin.

"Move over and make some room for me, you bed hog." Crystal jumped in next to Jade, her personal needs taken care of.

"I can't; Amber's almost in the middle of the bed; besides, this bed is big enough anyway. Wow!" Jade continued. "Can you smell how wonderful the fresh air is?"

Crystal and Amber's bedroom window was also open. "I know. It's just wonderful." Crystal piped in, taking a deep breath.

All three girls lay side by side, saying nothing, just enjoying the sun, the smells, and the feel of their warm, soft bodies as they cuddled. Jade and Crystal's thoughts were drifting back to all of the events of the past week, starting with their beloved mother's death and ending with Mandy's rescue. They had learned almost to read each other's thoughts, especially because, over the years, their survival had depended on this ability.

"So, now that we're alone. What's next?" Crystal always wanted answers.

"We need to do two things," Jade said, becoming serious as she temporarily put aside her early morning mood.

"First, we need a good story about dad, one that we stick to no matter what." Jade sounded confident. "And second, we try to find out if Derek has figured out that it was us at the funeral home. And if so, we'll have to figure something out that won't get us caught but might lead the police to him. Either way, we need to figure out a way to lead the police to Derek."

"So what do we do? Crystal's anxiously asked.

"We can stay near the house and wait for Derek to make a move, or we can follow him and see what he's up to." It was all Jade could come up with.

"If Derek does know it's us, he's going to want that stuff back that we took from the funeral home." Crystal shot back.

Jade had forgotten about the trinkets and photos with her temporary enjoyment of the morning.

"We need to get the pictures and jewelry to the police somehow. Then they'll know the girls are dead, not missing. Maybe there are some clues in the photos that the police could use that might lead them to Derek or the funeral home".

"Alright, so how do you suppose we get the stuff to the police without getting found out, smarty-pants? We can't just drop them off. Someone may recognize us, or maybe they have video surveillance since they are, after all, a police department. We've had so many officers in and out of this house over the years; they are practically like family." Crystal pointed out what Jade was already thinking. We can't risk being identified.

"No problem, we'll mail the stuff," Jade said simply.

"What if they can track us from the package? It's easy for the police to trace things, don't you watch CSI?"

"We'll mail it from downtown. That way, the postmark will be from a different section of town." Jade said.

Sounds good to me, now let's just cuddle and forget all this stuff".

Jade was satisfied with the plan, and for now, she felt safe in her sister's bed, in her own home with the two people she loved most. Jade missed her mother, but at least she would never have to feel the sting of her dad's hands or hear his foul words or have him grope her body. Peace at last.

* * *

It was late afternoon, and Derek was just finishing the final touches to an elaborate plan that would soon unfold and deliver a new young bride into his awaiting, anxious hands. He had the perfect dress. It was even better than the old one, although he would never throw the torn gown away. It held their smell, all of the girls who had been objects of his obsession. He needed it to feel close to them. He thought that the new gown would bring him the luck that so far had evaded him, failing to bring him the love he needed.

* * *

Dennis Kortovich awoke early the following day feeling anxious. He had dreamed a strange but telling dream most of the night. The wind had howled and blown around him. The moon was bright, setting off the hangman's tree that was dead and withered as it reached into a cloudless midnight sky. The headless rider thundered down the windy, moonlit, dirt road, suddenly stopping in front of the knarled old tree. The white, ghostlike horse reared into the air while the unholy rider waved his gleaming sword over his head. During the dream, Dennis was aware that he was dreaming, but it was more than that. It was as if he stood outside of himself, time and space having little meaning in this world of dreams. He could view the dream in much the same way he would have if he were at a movie. However, Dennis was somehow in the dream and out of the dream as well. The headless rider held his severed head under his arm, his cape flapping in the wind. As the rider thundered closer and closer into view, Dennis was suddenly shocked to see the gruesome face of the beheaded man while the rider cushioned the head under his arm. Dennis awoke with a start, his eyes wide open; he knew whom the face belonged to. Dennis had seen the face as a child. The face was on the Disney movie Sleepy Hollow. The cartoon face of Ichabod Crane and the flesh and blood face of Derek Hanson, the mortician.

Was it a hunch, a prophetic dream, or was this Dennis' gut instincts working overtime? He knew the day ahead would give him the needed answer. It was early morning now, but he felt the urgent need to dress and get going for the day. There was an idea that stood at some level in his subconscious brain, like a stalker hiding in the shadows, not willing to reveal himself until just the right moment. Dennis felt the need for a cup of coffee and a fresh doughnut. Somehow the mundane was what was needed to coax that evasive idea into the light of day. He was well on his way to the station, his coffee half gone with the remnants of his doughnut, now only a few crumbs at the bottom of the bag, when the inspiration from the dream hit him. It was something Mandy had said.

Mandy had referred to a headless rider. She, too, had been struck at a subconscious level of how much Derek Hanson looked like the cartoon character of Ichabod Crain. His subconscious was trying to tell him something like it often did. They had a saying in police work, "ninety percent perspiration, and ten percent inspiration." Often it was that ten percent inspiration that made all the difference in a case. Dennis was sure of his interpretation of his dream, as well as this gut feeling that Derek Hanson was somehow involved in the kidnapping of Mandy Switzer and the other girls. He had little or no proof, only two small coincidences that tied Derek to the case.

The first, Mandy's description and his subconscious recognition, was Mandy's insistence that she was the bride at her wedding. Running into Derek with a new wedding gown under his arm, cinched it. It was a perfect size two, the same size as Mandy and the other missing girls. But it was Chuck and the printout that took his hunch and turned it into more than speculation. Whoever was killing these girls lived or worked smack in the middle of the hot zone, and the only business in the area was the Greenhill's cemetery.

Dennis was sure Derek was somehow tied into this case, but all he had to go on was a hunch, a drug-induced dream of a highly traumatized young girl, as well as a new investigative tool that has yet to stand up to scientific scrutiny. It wasn't much, but it was a start. He was sure that if he followed the clues to their conclusion, he would come up with some answers. So far, he had more questions than answers, and he was determined to see exactly if, or how, Derek Hanson fit into the still elusive picture that was beginning to reveal itself. Dennis hoped the revelation would happen before anyone else was hurt or went missing.

CHAPTER TWENTY-SEVEN

Jade, Crystal, and Amber were sitting around the kitchen table, the large cereal box dominating the small table. The carton of milk is half empty and the sugar jar off to one side, completely empty.

"We're going to need grocery money soon if we don't want to starve," Jade said, getting up from the table and going over to the fridge where she began to take stock of what would be needed to feed her family, now that it would be her total responsibility.

"I'll turn eighteen in just a few more days, and then money won't be a problem. I'll get my share of our inheritance, and both of you will have access to the interest of your money until you're eighteen, when you'll both get your share."

Jade wanted to make sure Crystal knew exactly how things would look, now that they were on their own.

"Grandma and Grandpa were smart. They knew we would need the money while we were young so we could get away from dad."

Jade continued her inventory, going through the cupboards and side pantry.

"If they hadn't been willing to give us access to the money until we were older, we would have had to endure dad a lot longer. Without mom around, we'll get mom's share of the estate as well. We are very, very rich young ladies. The only problem is we are just a little bit broke right now."

Jade looked down at the list she had written and realized that they would need at least a hundred dollars for food, as well as some gas for the van.

"I'm sure we have enough beer cans and liquor bottles to cover our immediate needs. After I have seen Mr. Barrett, mom's lawyer, and sign the papers, we should have it easy from then on".

Jade looked over at her two precious but hungry sisters as they devoured the last of the corn flakes as well as the milk. Even without the sugar, they had finished eating everything in the box.

"Crystal, if you help me load the bottles and cans into the van, I'll go cash them in and pick up enough groceries to get through the next few days."

Amber followed the girls outside to what at one time was a carriage house, now a garage of sorts. Inside the family, the van sat next to Sam's old 88 Chevy. It was then that Jade realized they had another small problem. They had been able to get rid of Sam's body and personal things, but what about the car? If Sam had run off like they had planned to tell anyone who asked, and they figured few except Dennis would, then the car would have to go too, but where?

"Shit!" Jade's tone was more irritated than angry, "I forgot about dad's car. Where can we dump it that won't cause any suspicion?"

Crystal looked over at Jade, indicating that the scope of the problem wasn't that big of a deal.

"Why don't we order a plane ticket over the phone in dad's name and just leave the car at the airport." Crystal's solution sounded good to her; she had a satisfied smile on her face.

"That won't work. Once they figure out that he never used the ticket, the police will suspect foul play."

"Well then, the bus depot, anyone can buy a ticket at the last moment, and they don't record the name for most of the destinations. We can buy one for Milwaukee and sign his name. You've perfected his signature, and as a matter of fact, most of the bills are paid by you or mom because he was usually too drunk or just didn't care, so why not the ticket."

"You've got a good idea there," Jade agreed. "but one problem, when I sign it, I'm a girl, not a guy, then what?"

"Look, let's just try it. If they ask any questions, just pay cash."

Crystal seemed annoyed. She hated solving problems. When things got tough, she usually just got mad and started fighting. Crystal was always the tough one, and she seldom cried. For Crystal, problems were usually faced head-on. If you had to, you lied and said whatever was needed to end the problem or make her opponent feel as if they had won. Her usual opponent was her dad. Crystal had gotten very good at being able to look you in the eye, smile, and tell a whopping lie, that even Crystal herself could be surprised at just how quick and fanciful her lies could be. Maybe one day she would write a book; God knew she had a good enough imagination.

"Ok, I'll take the cans in first, then I'll get groceries; after that, I'll take dad's car to the Greyhound bus depot and leave it thereafter I get a ticket. It may not be as hard as I think it is. Dad's card is S.J. Walker, Samuel Jackson Walker. If they ask, I could show them my I.D." Jade said.

Jade's full name was Samantha Jade Walker. She was sure she could pull it off. They could make it look like Sam had enough of them and left for parts unknown. If he went to Milwaukee, then he could go anywhere. Sam was about to become a missing person. It was too sad to think that, in reality, no one would miss him at all. As far as a person of flesh and blood, Sam had become something much less than human years ago.

* * *

Jade was finished with her plans for the day and was now sitting comfortably in the back seat of a cab. She had called the taxi from Dunkin Donuts. She didn't want anyone to trace her to the bus station. It was all effortless. Jade had simply walked up to the wicket and had asked for a one-way ticket to Milwaukee, Wisconsin. The young girl who sat behind the computer barely looked up. When she asked how she wished to pay, Jade said Visa. Next, the girl asked for two pieces of I.D.

Jade decided to be brave and pulled out her driver's license and school I.D. The girl glanced at both, asked what name she wanted on the ticket and the receipt. "Just use my initials, the ones that are on my credit card, please." Jade's voice was smooth and sweet as she handed Sam's credit card over. Once the ticket was purchased, Jade looked down at her receipt and accompanying ticket. S.J. Walker was blazed across the computer-processed ticket. The Visa was a receipt from an electronic machine as well. She had to sign their copy, but the girl never even compared signatures. Jade knew the signature wouldn't be an issue; she has signed her dad's card more than he had, with the same sloppy flair that Sam had developed in his writing.

Dad would soon be gone for good; now, all she had to do was get the ticket to the bus driver. There were three copies. One the clerk had kept, one was for her, and one had to go to the driver to ensure that his copy would get back into the buses' accounting system. It was easier than Jade had expected. The bus lineup was a sell-out, and as the driver began to let everyone board, Jade simply got in the lineup and went on to the bus. Only a few more people to get on Jade left the bus with a couple of women who looked like motherly types. They had assisted their loved ones to their seats and left the bus just before it was due to pull out.

Jade never looked back. The ghost of Sam sat somewhere on the Greyhound Bus, and Jade wouldn't give her father's memory the satisfaction of a backward glance. Gone were all the fear, hate, and evil she and her sisters had been forced to live with. Jade took the extra copy of the ticket and the receipt, pausing for only a second to throw them in the trash. She would cut up the card when she got home. She and her sisters would make a celebration of Sam's final farewell. They would put the cut-up plastic credit card in an ashtray and watch it melt as it burned. Jade was surprised to find herself in front of her home. The cab driver asked her for the fare. She gave him her last twenty-dollar bill. The groceries she had gotten earlier would do for a few days; then she would see the lawyer and have access to all the money they would ever need. Jade smiled. Life was going to be great, and they had just gotten away with murder. She felt no malice, only relief at having survived.

When Jade walked through the front door, everything seemed normal, and then suddenly, she noticed the kitchen chair was turned over onto the floor, and a broken coffee cup lay beside the vinyl chair. The hair suddenly stood up on the back of her neck. Where were Amber and Crystal?!

"Amber" Jade called her name, there was no use, because although she understood her name. Amber could or would not respond. Amber had no verbal skills, and other than a whimper or a soft moan, she was unable to communicate verbally. As Jade moved up the stairs, she could hear the creaking of a rocking chair in Crystal and Amber's room. At least Amber was here, Jade thought. The hall was lit by daylight coming through the open bedroom doors. She looked into Crystal and Amber's room. She could see Amber rocking silently, staring at some unseen force above her head.

Jade quickly checked her room. Everything was exactly how she had left it.

Next, she checked their parent's room. Maybe Crystal had decided to nap in the king-size bed, which she sometimes did when her dad was not home. The room faced north, and it was always a little cooler. The day was still very warm. Nothing! The space was empty. What could have happened to Crystal? Where could she be? Jade had never known Crystal to leave the house if she was caring for Amber. A cold, knowing chill swept over Jade's body. Crystal hadn't left Amber, someone had taken her, and she knew whom. It was more than a hunch. Jade could smell something. It was the same unusual scent that she had detected at the morgue. Derek Hanson had been there. Jade ran back down into the kitchen. When she looked around, she was hoping she would be wrong. Maybe Crystal would walk in from the backyard and lay her fears to rest.

It was when she glanced around the kitchen for the second time that she saw it. The pocket knife they had given Derek as a ruse of gratitude lay neatly in the middle of the table. It was his calling card. Crystal had a date with death. Jade knew she would have to find Crystal somehow and rescue her from a man eviler than they had ever encountered. Even Sam wasn't capable of the evil Derek had committed. Jade's legs became weak and rubbery. She managed to slump to the floor before her legs betrayed her. They could no longer support her frail body. She realized she was no match for a killer like Derek. She had seen pictures of his handy work. All of the girls had been beaten, tortured, burned, and murdered. Now Crystal was in the hands of this madman, and it was all Jade's fault.

She should never have left the girls alone. They were so happy to finally feel safe. It was Jade's fault that they had let down their guards, knowing that a killer may be after them. It was a stupid mistake. Derek did know who they were, and now he had Crystal. How could she call the police? They would find out about Sam. Derek would make sure of it. Jade knew her sisters needed her. If she called the police, she and Crystal would go to jail, and Amber would be taken away. They had killed their father to protect each other, pure and simple survival. Now Crystal was in danger. Jade knew her sister would die at the hands of that madman.

She only had a few hours to get her sister back. Jade took several deep breaths. She had to come up with a plan to rescue Crystal and ensure they don't go to jail. As Jade got up from the floor of the kitchen, a strange calm came over her. She'd be damned if she was going to let a man like Derek hurt her sister, and she'd be damned if she's going to jail for killing a man like Sam. Damn them both! She'd send them all to hell before she'd let any harm come to her family! She had endured enough. It was time to pick herself up and dust herself off and catch a killer. A plan started to take shape in her mind. She knew she didn't have the physical strength to challenge Derek, but she was sure she could outwit him. A madman never saw the world the way it was, only the way he wanted it to be. Jade would use all the survival instincts that she has learned over the years. Living with Sam had given her the resolve to carry her plans through, and Jade knew there was only one man that could help her.

CHAPTER TWENTY-EIGHT

erek had his beautiful prize beside him. She was presently bundled up in an old musty blanket, her arms and feet duct-taped. Crystal's mouth was covered in a large, multi-colored tie, the kind you get at a Disney store with cartoon characters on it. Lisa had given it to him when she was eight and Derek was fifteen. It was his first tie, and Derek had always used it to gag his victims.

Crystal was silent, unmoving. Still out cold from the knockout drops he had put into the pop can that sat on the kitchen table. Derek had waited until he saw the old car pull out of the driveway with Jade behind the wheel, and it was precisely what he had hoped would happen. He had everything ready. He knew he could be much bolder than he had ever been before. The belt buckle from the crematorium proved that the girls were now parentless. There would be no one for the girls to turn to. No mother. No father. They were all alone with each other, and Derek knew first hand they had few friends to speak of. There had been almost no one at the funeral, only that detective, Dennis Kortovich, and his partner Chuck, along with their wives and children. Derek wasn't too sure how close Dennis was to the family, but he had a feeling the relationship was professional, probably due to the investigation of the mother's death. He was pretty sure that the only ones who knew of Sam's death were himself and the murdering little bitches.

Now Derek was about to pay them back for destroying his bridal gown, stealing his treasures, and rescuing his latest bride. He was about to seek revenge, and the three sisters would realize what happens when you mess with him. He was a man who held the power of life and death, a man who knew death intimately. He smelled it, touched it, and drank it in every day. Death was his friend, and they would all have to die. But first, there was to be a wedding.

*　*　*

Crystal could feel her lips as they pressed against her teeth. The taste of blood still lingered on her tongue, now swollen and dry. Her eyes were shut, they were much too heavy to open, but her senses were beginning to return. Her hands and feet had been bound. Her mouth was gagged so tightly that her teeth cut into her lip, drawing blood. She could smell something. It was familiar. Yes, it was that madman! Derek Hanson. Crystal's heart started to beat faster. It only made the pounding in her head hurt more. All she could remember was that she had smelled that same chemical odor before she gulped down half a cola. Awareness that she had smelled that same smell only twice before hit her just as the room started to sway and turn black. Crystal remembered smelling that same distasteful odor on the day they buried her mother. And again, on the day she and Jade had killed and cremated their father. Derek must have been in the house, but awareness came too late; Crystal's knees gave way while blackness engulfed her.

Now she lay beside Derek. Her head rested on his lap. The smell from his clothing made her want to choke. Crystal knew she was in real danger. Derek would be pissed at her and Jade's discovery of his chamber and the rescue of Mandy. She also knew he would want his pictures and treasures back. Crystal prayed Jade would realize that Derek had abducted her and know what to do. She would have to stay calm and trust that fate or God would help her get away from Derek alive. She knew she would have to make Derek think that she was still unconscious until she could assess her surroundings. She felt overwhelmed by the fear of what may lay ahead. She had to choke down the urge to vomit. Quite out of nowhere, Crystal could hear a tune in her head. It was her mother's voice, "Don't worry, be happy." A silly, tuneless song, one Jewel often sang to the girls when they were alone, now repeated in her head. She could feel her mother's arms around her. It was the first time since Jewell's death that Crystal could sense her mother's presence. A warm glow enveloped her, making her feel like she did as a child when she rested her head on her mother's lap. The scent changed from a gross chemical smell to one of fresh laundry. That was when Crystal knew for sure her mother was with her to protect her from harm.

Jewel loved doing the laundry and the scent of it at this time was a sign from heaven. Often the girls would join Jewell in the basement. The best times were spent taking the sheets from the dryer and pressing the warm fabric to their faces and smelling the clean, fresh scent. It was the scent of their mother, and now at the most terrifying and desperate moment of Crystal's life, Jewel was here. She kept her eyes closed, hearing and smelling her mother's message of hope with every fiber of her small being. She would be safe. It was a promise that Jewel was singing in her ear, and even though Jewel couldn't protect her children completely in life, she would protect them in death. Crystal heard that promise and let go of her fears. Crystal wouldn't worry, and she just knew that she and her sisters would be happy one day.

* * *

Derek pulled his old station wagon up in front of his little house in the country. It was isolated, so no one would hear if Crystal woke up and made a fuss. He looked down at Crystal as her face rested on his lap. He liked the way it made him feel protective. Her small face was covered by a mass of golden, red curls that hid the tie that covered her tiny mouth. She was perfect, and Derek knew this one would be different. This small girl would love him and become his bride. He would even invite her family. They had already received his calling card, a knife, so they would be expecting an invitation soon. Derek had sent it along with special instructions. He wanted all of his prizes and pictures. He needed them to relive each event over the past six years.

Each of his weddings was unique and special, and the tokens from each girl held their spirits. They were his brides, and he loved each one as much as the first, his true love, Lisa, his little sister. As Derek looked down at Crystal's face, he could hear and see Lisa when she was small. She had loved him then, but as she grew older, she began to shun him. At first, he had begged her to love him, always trying to please her. As the years went on and Lisa turned into a young teen, she voiced her disapproval of his obsession with her.

* * *

"Leave me alone, Derek, stop following me everywhere. The other kids call you creepy. They say you're a freak. At first, I didn't believe them, but now I think they're right. You follow me everywhere. I catch you staring at me all of the time. And you're always touching me. I don't like it. If you don't stop, I'll tell mom and dad, and they'll make you stop." Lisa put her tiny hands on her hips, trying to look strong. "I even heard dad tell mom he's worried about how you act around me, and he thinks they should send you away. You're close to twenty now. They don't have to let you live here anymore." Lisa sounded triumphant.

Derek could see Lisa's copper curls bob up and down as the fury of her anger and frustration showed on her face. Send him away! Never! Lisa was his! His parent had said so when they brought her home to him when he was only eight. They were both adopted. They belonged to no one, only each other. He wouldn't let them send him away. He would make them understand how much Lisa meant to him. His parents would have to let him have her.

* * *

Derek got out of the car, breaking through the memories of his past. He had to get Crystal to the chapel. All was prepared and waiting for them. Derek picked Crystal up, his long arms engulfing her tiny body. Carrying her, he traveled away from the house toward a heavily wooded area. Once into the woods, he zigzagged through the dense brush in a way that would make it difficult for anyone to follow his footprints. There was no discernible path; Derek only went to his secret place twice a year, once on the date of Lisa's birth and once on the date of her death, each time with a new bride. Never before had he made preparations for extra guests. But this time was special.

Derek held Crystal in one arm as he bent forward and brushed away a few leaves that had fallen; soon, summer would be at an end. Derek hated the thought of another winter. Winter was a lonely time of year. Only late spring and late summer held any joy for him. Once he cleared away the leaves, he bent over and pulled on a large iron ring. A heavy metal door announced their arrival with a loud screech.

Once it was open, Derek descended the concrete steps that lead to a large round door that looked much the same as a door that would lead to a bank vault. No one but Derek's family had ever known about this place, and it was a legacy leftover from the cold war in the late 50s when the threat of nuclear war seemed very real. It was a bomb shelter built by his adoptive grandparents. He had never met them. They had died in the early 60s, leaving his parents the land, home, and this relic.

Derek's parents never told anyone about the shelter. They seemed a bit embarrassed at their parents' fears, especially since at the time of its construction, the cost of the shelter was more than the cost of their modest little home. The shelter was a model to be envied by anyone's standards at the time. The large living quarters and storage area would have met their family's needs if a bomb had ever landed. But none had, nor would it be likely one would. Soon the shelter was forgotten until Derek discovered it when he was ten. He and Lisa had played house in the shelter over the years. It wasn't until the children were much older, Lisa nearly eleven, and

Derek almost twenty, that his parents, Gabrielle and Elliot, discovered that the shelter had become a place to play. They disapproved and insisted they not use it.

* * *

Gabrielle and Elliot had become aware of Derek's anti-social behavior and a few unsavory genetic quirks. Besides being ugly, Derek had a temper that could set off a rage when he didn't get what he wanted. He would rant and move toward his parents. His huge hands were ready to strike. He controlled his rages when he could, but more often than not, he would choose not to, preferring to see the fear on his parent's faces. His parents began to fear for their safety as well as Lisa's. One night when his parents thought they were alone, they discussed the problems of Derek among themselves. The outcome was to send Derek away to a university in another state. They had submitted Derek's application behind his back, and they had just received his acceptance letter.

"Sweetheart, we need to decide how to tell Derek that he has to move out of state." It was Gabrielle who spoke first, the letter from the university in her hand.

"I know, but we need to figure out how to approach the subject so that it won't cause him to go crazy and do something dangerous. I haven't felt safe ever since they found that young friend of Lisa's in the river." Elliot said.

"Somehow, my gut tells me that Derek was involved. Derek hated him, and I could see the rage in his eyes whenever the boy was here. It made my hair stand on end, and now I fear it could be us in danger."

Elliot Hanson looked at his wife in a way that showed just how great his fear was.

"We had better not do it alone. We could call Larry O'Conner. He's a great cop and would be able to handle Derek if he goes off the deep end."

"Perhaps you're right. Derek may behave himself if Larry is here. He's a tough cop, and nobody's going to mess with him." Elliot was sure it would go well if they had some backup.

Now Elliot and Gabrielle would have to tell Derek of the need for him to leave, but their fear of him made them hesitate. The only solution was to have a witness on hand when they broke the news and hoped Derek wouldn't go berserk. Having a friend on the police force might make the unpleasant task safer. They would call Larry in the morning.

Derek's parents would never make that call. Derek was in the house when the discussion was taking place. He had been out earlier, but he sneaked back in a little after Lisa's bedtime. He had slipped in bed beside Lisa, as he had done so often as a child. As a full-grown man, his feelings toward her were no longer those of a boy. As he pressed his large, awkward body next to her tiny perfect form, he looked down at the sleeping face of Lisa. He could see the evidence of the young woman she was turning into. She would be his one day, and no one was going to send him away.

The following morning after Lisa went to school, Derek put his plans in order. His parents worked as freelance writers, so other than research and the occasional trip for seminars, they worked from home. Derek's father, Elliot, had gone out to the small barn to clean out a bunch of junk and get it ready to take to the dump. He never even turned his head as he heard Derek approach, continuing to move a bunch of stuff around, bent over in deep concentration. Elliot wasn't a big man, and he barely struggled as Derek put the lightly chloroformed cloth up to his face, pressing with just enough strength to prevent him from getting away. Derek knew it was important not to bruise the body in a way that would not be consistent with a fall. There was an old abandoned well on the property that was usually fenced in. Derek had asked Lisa to help him remove the light fencing, saying that their parents wanted them to clean the weeds around the well so that it would be visible above the fence line. This way, no one would miss the well and fall in. Later he told Lisa to put the fence back around the well because he wouldn't be able to get to it for a few days. He made sure that Lisa was busy when he told her. She would soon have to catch the bus to school.

"Why do I have to do it? I have to go get ready for school. Why did we take the fencing down if you weren't going to do it today?" Lisa lashed out at Derek, feeling frustrated at having to do it just before the bus picked her up.

"Dad wants me to help him in the barn, and I still have to finish up the cleanup in the garage. It only takes about three minutes to put the fence up, so just do it and get on the bus." Derek hoped he sounded truthful and pressed for time.

"OK. But get out of here so I can get ready. You're always hanging around and getting in the way." Lisa said, turning back to the mirror, dismissing Derek in her usual manner.

Lisa suspected nothing, and as usual, she forgot. That would make her the guilty one. Now his father lay crumpled at his feet. The chloroform was light and would only keep him unconscious for a short while. Derek knew a lot about putting animals under. His interest in death had driven him to make a makeshift morgue in the back of the shelter. He had learned many things about death and how to preserve the bodies of dogs and cats. It would come in useful.

Derek had no time to waste. He had to get to his mother, and the timing would be important. Gabrielle was at the desk when Derek came into the house. She never even looked up as he approached her. Gabrielle was small, and getting her body to the well would be easy. Derek's father was just regaining consciousness as Derek approached him with Gabrielle in his arms. He placed his mother at his father's feet. Elliot was trying to stand up.

"What's happening Derek, I feel sick? What's wrong with your mother, and why are we at the well? Where's the fence?"

"It's OK, Dad. Moms not feeling very well either. Just take her hand and see if we can get her to stand up. Don't worry; I'll help you both." Derek picked up his mother's small form off the ground and placed her hand in his father's.

"This will be perfect, lovers, to the end," Derek said as he assisted his parents to their feet.

"What do you mean?" Elliot was beginning to see just how close to the well he was and how unsteady he and his wife were.

"Walking can be dangerous, and we all know how deep this well is. You will both be together forever like all lovers should." Derek smiled as he spoke to his father.

"Why are you doing this?" Elliot was still too weak to run, but he knew what his son had planned for them.

"Why? You know why! You and your mother were going to betray me and send me away so that you can keep Lisa from me. You said Lisa was mine, and now you are trying to take her from me. I can't let you do that." Derek's voice was calm, belying the anger he felt deep inside.

Derek could see that his father was getting stronger and more alert by the minute, and his mother was beginning to stir as well. There was no more time for talk. He gave both his parents a shove and watched as they descended the deep well. The muffled thud assured him that they would now be spending eternity together.

The police ruled it an accident. When Lisa found out about the fall, she blamed herself for not putting the fence back up. She was inconsolable and suspected nothing. She became so distraught at the funeral that no one found it surprising when Derek told everyone she was depressed due to her parent's death and had a nervous breakdown. Of course, Derek was caring for Lisa as best he could. Soon no one was calling, and even the kids at school forgot about her. Lisa was at Derek's mercy.

* * *

The loud click of the door startled Crystal causing a shock to move through her body. Derek could feel the movement. He was holding her body next to his as he made his way into a large storage chamber at the front of the shelter. There was a massive tank in the center of the room that held water that was pumped from an underground well when needed. It stood empty, filled with dust and mice droppings, having never been attended to over the years. The shelves along the walls were open, except for a few boxes of candles and matches. At least a dozen empty cans of gasoline stood off to one side, the plastic containers a faded red.

Their spouts capped off. A generator large enough to keep several families going for quite a while stood off to the side at the back of the chamber. Next to the generator was another door, much like the first, leading to the shelter's living quarters. Derek laid Crystal down next to the generator. He leaned over her now inert body and slapped her face firmly. Not hard enough to make a mark, but with enough force to shock her into awareness. Her blue eyes opened suddenly, his pale eyes starring back. Derek reached around to the back of Crystal's head and untied the Disney tie from her mouth.

"Don't say a word or scream. No one will hear you." Derek's voice was calm and confident.

This was his world, and she was his guest. Derek stood up, leaving a silent Crystal on the ground gazing up at him with what she hoped was a stunned, unaware gaze. She needed time to get her bearings and see where she was. Derek seemed satisfied that she was still groggy and half out of it before he stepped away from her to move toward the generator.

With Derek's back to her, Crystal could get a complete look around the dimly lit room. A large lantern that dominated the center of the room gave off an eerie candle-lit glow. She saw the tank, empty shelves, gasoline, matches, and a few other boxes of stuff, nothing that allowed her to guess where she was.

Derek started the generator, and soon a low hum could be heard and felt. Suddenly the room lit up brightly as large florescent lights swung overhead lit up, revealing the space in its dirty, decaying form. Derek turned unexpectedly toward Crystal, catching her off guard as she gazed intently about the room.

"I see you've come around, my love, welcome home. You and I have a date with destiny, and soon our guests will arrive. Come, we must get ready."

Derek took one long stride toward her. He bent down, scooped her up into his arms, and moved toward the second vaulted door. Crystal could once again smell the clean, warm scent of fresh laundry as he swung the door open. Jewel was still with her. The knowledge gave her a great deal of comfort and strength, but not enough to prevent the gasp of horror that rushed from her mouth as she saw what lay behind the door, a sight that would shake her faith and weaken the resolve that she would need to get out alive.

CHAPTER TWENTY-NINE

Detective Dennis Kortovich sat at his desk in total disbelief. In front of him were the pictures of over one dozen young girls, all of them wearing a death mask, their faces twisted, white marble, showing the pain and horror of their last moments of life. Each girl lay on a stainless steel table, the same kind used by a medical examiner or at a morgue. The white wedding gown was identical in each picture. All but one of the girls had light, copper, curly hair that surrounded tiny, perfect faces. Only she was different, a beautiful, full-figured brunette. She alone lay marked and naked on the table, her body mutilated by someone who was in a rage. Dennis knew he was right. Charlotte had been taken by mistake. The killer was after her friend, Jade Walker.

Along with the pictures of the girls was a collection of what appeared to be personal items, gold hoop earrings, a diamond-studded watch, a pearl and rhinestone necklace, a snoopy watch, pearl studs, the list itemized thirteen individual pieces of jewelry, each one probably belonging to a different girl. Dennis put his hands over his face and breathed deeply. The package had been left at the front desk. The sergeant in charge said he saw no one when it was delivered. He had gone to the back of the room for a few minutes to retrieve a few more pens for the front. When he returned the large manila envelope with Dennis' name in large, the black print was sitting on the counter. He had looked around to see if anyone was still in the lobby that might have left it, but no one stood out as the person who may have dropped it off. The lobby was full of an odd assortment of people so that it could have been anyone. The sergeant had sent the envelope up to Dennis immediately. It had been marked urgent, and he knew Dennis was working on the abduction of Judge Switzer's daughter as well as the other missing girls.

When Dennis finally pulled his hands away from his face, he stared at the young girls' lifeless forms. The envelope meant only one thing; someone knew who the killer was and whoever it was, he or she was trying to tell him something, but what? And why didn't they just say who the killer was and help him out? Dennis picked up the envelope one more time. Maybe there was something he missed. When he shook the envelope, nothing fell out, empty. One last look, Dennis opened the envelope wide and looked again.

There was something stuck in the seam. He reached inside and pulled out a clipping. The advertisement from the yellow pages cut neatly around the edges, no more than two inches by four inches.

Greenhill's Funeral Home was the feature of the ad, followed by the location and phone number. A picture of Derek Hanson was on the top right-hand corner. It made Dennis feel faint, and all the color drained from his face.

He knew it! Derek was somehow a part of the puzzle, and someone was leading him right to Derek. But why not come in person? What were they afraid of? Dennis stood up, grabbed the photos, and dialed Chuck's cell phone. No time to waste figuring out why. Dennis had to get to Derek right away and see what role he played in the murders of the girls. Chuck agreed to meet Dennis at Greenhill's. Dennis pulled his white Crown Victoria up behind Chuck's SUV just seconds after they both arrived at the funeral home.

"Great timing; thanks for dropping everything and meeting me here without an explanation." Dennis walked toward Chuck as he greeted him.

"You know me, never a day's rest. We work till the job is done." Chuck rolled his eyes, indicating that this job would always be first; the rest would wait. "What the hell's up? You sounded real shocked on the phone, and why were you at the station anyway?" Chuck asked.

"I thought we were going to meet for breakfast and go over our notes to see if we could find a final clue to pull this together. The geographic profile confirmed a suspicion of mine, but I wanted to take the time to see if all of the pieces fit before I accused anyone. When I was at my desk, this was delivered to the station." Dennis said nothing more as he handed the envelope to Chuck.

"Holy fuck, where the hell did you get these? This is fucking unbelievable."

Chuck's already bright face got even redder, his eyes nearly popping out of his head, his face registering total disbelief.

"I have no idea they were left at the front desk. No one saw who left them, and this came along with the package."

Dennis reached into his shirt pocket and pulled out the ad, handing it to Chuck, who now leaned against Dennis's car.

"This is as good as saying Derek did it. What proof do you have?"

Chuck knew it took more than the pictures and an ad to prove anyone, even a creep like Derek, had committed these crimes.

"I already had a hunch. I ran into Derek yesterday just before our lunch. He had just paid a whack of money for a wedding gown, size two. Then there was something Mandy said about a headless horseman. It didn't mean anything until I had this strange dream and then I got this package. What cartoon character does Derek remind you of." Dennis was sure Chuck would see the resemblance.

"Shit if I know!"

Chuck stared at the picture of Derek, drawing a blank. The last thing that he could think of after seeing the mutilated young women in the photographs was anything about cartoons.

"Ok, Sherlock. So who does Derek look like?"

"Remember the Disney movie, 'Sleepy Hollow'?" Dennis asked.

"Holy shit!" Chuck responded. "Ichabod Crain!" "He looks just like him, only uglier."

"Yes, Ichabod Crain and the headless horseman." Dennis's flat response made it sound as if Mandy's statement was obvious. "So far, we have no real evidence, just a prophetic dream, an envelope with photos of dead girls, jewelry, and an ugly guy with a wedding dress. All of the girls are wearing a wedding gown, and I just know it's all tied into Derek."

"Who sent this to you and why?"

Dennis looked at Chuck, his jaw locking as he clenched his teeth and stroked his mustache. "I don't know, Chuck, but whoever sent the envelope wants our help. I only hope no one else has gone missing while we're trying to come up with enough probable cause. Or that some other young girl is wearing that new dress."

CHAPTER
THIRTY

Jade knew she stood no chance of facing Derek alone. She would need help. Dennis was the only one Jade could turn to, but she couldn't go to him in person. Jade knew she would have to develop a plan that would lead Dennis to Derek and allow Jade to find Crystal and rescue her before Derek did her any harm. She was just beginning to formulate a plan when she received a special delivery. It was an invitation to a wedding. The groom was Derek Hanson, the bride Crystal Walker. It would take place that evening, and Jade was instructed to stay put; she would be picked up at seven. Jade was to dress accordingly and bring Amber. The pictures and personal items were to be brought, or Derek would make sure that Sam's ashes and belt buckle would find their way to the police.

Her only hope was Dennis. Jade knew it would be a trap and that she and her sisters may never get out alive. She had no idea where Derek would take her and Amber, but she would have to trust someone for once in her life. Dennis was the only one she believed in. He would find them. Jade only hoped it would be in time and that she would be able to find a way to save herself, Crystal, and Amber without Dennis finding out what had happened to Sam. The idea to send Dennis the photos and items came minutes after she received the invitation. Someone would have to know it was Derek who was killing the young woman. She had no idea why all the girls looked alike or why Derek was driven to this madness. The face of the girl in Derek's office came to mind; that was it. Lisa, Derek's sister, was like her, exact copies. Whatever had happened to Lisa Hansen, Jade was sure she was about to find out. All of them were replacements for Lisa. Would she and her sisters meet the same fate as all of the other girls? If she had put her faith in the right place, it would not be God that rescued them but Dennis Kortovich, the only person Jade felt she could trust. If Jade and her sisters were to survive whatever was to occur tonight, Dennis would have to find them. Jade could only hope that wherever Derek would take them, a trail could be followed by a detective as good as Dennis.

* * *

Dennis and Chuck entered the large, bright foyer of the funeral home. The different shades of green and rose created a feeling of peacefulness and rest. It was a decorative theme that Dennis liked. The office to the funeral home was off to the right, the door was slightly ajar, and Dennis could hear a woman's voice talking softly to someone on the other end of the phone. She assures them that all of the details for an afternoon lunch would go well and there would be plenty of food.

Dennis and Chuck needed to get some answers quickly. Once the woman hung up, Dennis knocked quickly on the door, a sense of urgency resonating from the knock. An older, middle-aged woman, somewhere near sixty, opened the door, a look of calm and serenity on her face. Dennis was sure she had mastered the look over the years. It was good for business. One needed to be calm when it came to matters of a departed loved one.

"Good afternoon; how may I help you?" The sound of her voice was low and soft, again very calming.

Dennis flashed his badge and held out his hand; she extended hers quickly, her grip even and well-practiced.

"My name is Detective Dennis Kortovich, and my partner here is Detective Chuck O'Brien. We're from the Chicago Police Department. We're wondering if we could ask you a few questions about Derek Hanson."

Dennis looked at the woman and knew from the way she held herself that she would find it difficult to answer questions without feeling compromised.

"How may I help you, Detective." She asked, her face remaining unreadable.

"Where is Derek Hansen? Do you know where he lives?" Dennis asked.

"Where he is right now, I really couldn't say? He lives on an old farm about three miles from here, in Elgin. It's about a quarter-mile off the main road. You may have to walk in. Derek doesn't keep the driveway well attended, and you may have to leave your car on the road. It would take quite a beating."

It was the only time Patricia Applegate showed any emotion other than serenity. Dennis and Chuck could detect the disapproval she felt on how Derek kept the driveway.

"I think he keeps the driveway that way so no one will visit him when he's not working. He's very reclusive." Her voice still held the tone of disapproval.

"Could you tell me anything more about Derek, especially these last few days?" Chuck offered this last question.

"Well," Patricia said with a measured tone. "Derek seems to have a rough time of it. Especially right now, late summer. I understand why. His family was killed in a home accident, and his sister Lisa; died around six years ago. He was devoted to her. His office is like a shrine to her, and I think her death unbalanced him a bit. She's all he ever talks about or thinks about." Patricia paused a bit before going on, seemingly unsure whether or not she should share her views on Derek.

"I sometimes think his love and devotion to Lisa is a bit sick. It even scares me at times."

Patricia looked apologetic. It was as if her last observation was a bit on the gossipy side. She was a woman of integrity, and Dennis could tell that it would take a lot for her to make a negative comment about someone.

"May we see Derek's office?" Dennis asked.

"I'm sure it will be all right, it's not locked, so I doubt it will cause a problem." Patricia paused for a moment. "I would prefer, however, that you didn't go through his desk drawers without a warrant. I don't want any trouble. We do have to work together."

"That will not be a problem. We just want to look around." Chuck responded.

As Patricia Applegate swung open the door to Derek's office, Chuck and Dennis had to stifle back an urge to gasp and choke. In the middle of the feature wall was a quilted, framed picture that dominated the wall by its sheer size. The beautiful young woman who stared at them with bright, blue eyes was a dead ringer for all of the missing girls. The girl in the photo was no more than fourteen, her delicate, pale skin surrounded by an abundance of curly copper, red hair. Her lips rosebud pink, while her incredible blue eyes surrounded dark, long lashes, a delicate young beauty. Lisa was also the spitting image of Jade and Crystal.

"Shit!" Dennis was first to break the silence. "We'd better get over to Derek's right away and see what he's up to. Then we'd better check in on the girls and make sure they're all right. I have a feeling Derek's our man, and Jade or Crystal will be next." Dennis said.

"No wonder we've never found the bodies. This guy can just burn them up and any proof they are missing. No trace, no case." Chuck added his thoughts to Dennis, who nodded in agreement.

Both men barely said a formal goodbye to Mrs. Applegate, who followed them out of the double doors at the front of the building. There she waved a final farewell with a look of concern crossing her face, breaking her usual look of controlled serenity.

It only took ten minutes to get to Derek's property line. The driveway was in worse shape than either detective thought it would be. Without a solid suspension, the Crown Vic would have taken a beating. They had left Chuck's SUV at the funeral home so they could drive together and review the evidence they had so far and formulate a game plan.

"Chuck, we have no real proof. All we have is a purchase of a wedding gown, a guy who's ugly and looks like a cartoon character that you dreamed about, and Mandy, who was half-crazed from her ordeal, saw in a vision who's dead sister looks like our missing girls. None of this is probable cause. Even the envelope proves nothing directly about Derek. The ad is only someone's guess that he's our man. Unless we find some evidence stronger than that to get a search warrant, we can't do more than ask a few questions and hope Derek says something we can use to arrest him." Dennis's running dialog was beginning to sound un-plausible even to himself

Dennis and Chuck removed their suit jackets, leaving them in the car. The day was scorching, and the walk to the house would make wearing them much too warm. Without their jackets, their holsters, with their guns, were in plain sight. They were hoping that would be intimidating, just if Derek were so unbalanced that he would attempt to give them a hard time. While walking up the driveway, attempting to avoid the potholes, both men noted the tall grass in the middle of the road was bent over. This meant Derek drove in and out. His car was modified to handle the deep ruts. The weeds along the road gave off a sweet, spicy aroma that was somewhere between nice and too sweet. Still, the sounds and smells of summer made one wish you could take a walk in the country every day. As the men approached the old farm, they both noted how run down all of the buildings were, especially the house. The front porch of the house looked like it would fall off at any moment. Chuck almost decided not to ascend the rickety stairs, fearing that the old porch's worn boards might not support his excess weight. When Dennis and Chuck stood in front of the door, Chuck almost let out a sigh of relief. The porch was stronger than it looked and only gave way a few inches under his weight. The screen door was half off its hinges and bounced slightly, causing quite a racket when Chuck banged his large fist against its paint-peeled frame.

"Looks like no one's home." Chuck surmised after a few minutes of silence.

Dennis and Chuck looked around the yard and noted a patch of grass that was flattened and faded. It was obvious that it was the spot where Derek parked his car. It seemed from the house's silence and the empty space in the yard that no one was home.

"What's the chance that the door's unlocked?" Dennis looks at Chuck, knowing full well unlawful access could cause them problems.

"You know, anything we find inside without a warrant we won't be able to use in a case against Derek," Chuck said.

Dennis knew Chuck wanted to make sure they were on the same page.

"Only if he knows we were here. Touch nothing, open nothing. If we come up with any evidence, it has to be in the wide-open, then we can get a warrant and come back."

Dennis was always by the book, seldom bending the rules. But when Dennis did bend the rules a little right of center, he always made sure he never compromised a case. Cross the t's and dot the i's was a motto to be lived by. When Dennis put together a case, it was solid and rarely fell apart in court. But at this moment, both men were more concerned with the package that was dropped off and what it meant. They were sure that time was of the essence and that whoever had dropped it off was not about to become another victim of Derek Hansen's.

Chuck tried the door. It was locked, but the lock was simple. It would only take a credit card to get in. Both men put on rubber gloves. No prints; they were never here. Once in, they were overcome by filth. The smell of rotten food and dirty clothes made them gag. Other than the smell of a decaying corpse, neither Dennis nor Chuck could remember smelling anything as bad as the small house. Chuck called out from the dining room off the kitchen.

"What is it?" Dennis asked as he approached Chuck.

"Look on the table." Chuck nodded his head in the direction of the evidence.

There on the table, taking up its entire length, were plaster molds. There were thirteen, well-defined indentations and it was pretty easy to identify what kind of objects would leave marks like the ones they were looking at. Dennis pulled the photos and list from his hip pocket.

He then referred to the list of objects, watches, earrings, and necklaces, even a headband: thirteen molds, thirteen items on the list, all a perfect match.

"Wow!" Chuck's face became a bright red, betraying his excitement. "All of these molds match the list of items worn by our missing girls. He might as well have given us the bodies with his fingerprints on them."

"This evidence is enough to help us put him away for life. But first, we had better get out of here and get a search warrant." Dennis left the molds on the table and continued his look around. "Be careful not to touch or move anything. If this creep gets wind of our being here before we get a warrant, this whole case could go up in smoke." Dennis moved toward the back of the house where the bedrooms were.

"Shit, look at this." Dennis motioned for Chuck to follow him into the larger of the two rooms. On the floor was the torn wedding gown, each piece tossed carelessly on an already cluttered bedroom floor.

"What?" Chuck asked as Dennis moved aside to give him a complete view.

"It's the same gown as the one the girls were wearing in the pictures." Dennis's response showed his excitement at having found such conclusive evidence.

"Let's go. We need to get back here as soon as possible, and it's never easy getting a search warrant. We can't even tell anyone what we've seen." Dennis was already down the hall heading towards the front door.

"We're going to have to convince a judge we have more than just a hunch to go on to get a warrant."

"Why don't we ask Judge Switzer first? With Mandy having been involved, wouldn't that be just as simple?" Chuck's logic sounded good to him, but it met with a disapproving look from Dennis.

"The problem with that idea is that Judge Switzer is too close to the case, and his judgment could be questioned, putting the case in jeopardy. We're better off taking a little extra time and getting things right by securing a warrant from an impartial judge rather than risking an unlawful search and blowing the case on a technicality. If we do this, we do it right and get a warrant from an impartial judge, and there can't be any accusation of prejudice in this case."

The thought of having the evidence so close and not being able to touch it or use it without a warrant was frustrating, but Chuck nodded in agreement. This case had to be handled correctly. As they left the house, they ensured the door was locked, and everything looked exactly as it had when they entered. Dennis and Chuck were sure Derek wouldn't know if anything was amiss; the place was so filthy, but rather than take a chance, they did their best to secure the place and make sure all was as it should be.

Once they were in the car and well on their way back to the city, Dennis spoke up first. "We also need to check in on Jade and the girls and make sure they're all right. After what we've seen, I know one of them will be targeted next, either Jade or Crystal."

Dennis turned his vehicle onto the Northwest freeway. In a few more minutes, he would be at his office. Once he got his warrant, he would contact Jade and make sure everyone was O.K.

CHAPTER THIRTY-ONE

J ade got a telephone call from Derek later that afternoon. She was to meet him at his place. Let no one know where she was going, and be sure to bring Amber as well. If she did anything to bring attention to his place or leave any clues about where she was going, Derek would kill Crystal immediately and come after them. If Jade wanted to keep her sister alive, she would have to do precisely as Derek told her.

Jade made a quick review of everything that had happened over the past week, hoping to gain insight to help her face what lay ahead. Although it was an accident, her mother was dead, and their father was as responsible as if he had pushed her himself. Now, he too was killed at the hands of his daughters. Now Crystal was in extreme danger, and Jade was feeling helpless. Their only hope was Detective Dennis Kortovich, and Jade had to make sure he could figure things out and somehow not discover their deadly secret.

Jade knew it was a calculated risk, but without Dennis, she knew there was no hope. The clock on the wall was getting close to seven. The day was nearly over, and she had less than thirty minutes to get to Derek's farm, to face what was to come. She prayed that she and her sisters would be able to get out alive. Jade needed to make one quick call before she and Amber left. Should she call the police station or Dennis's home? Finally, Jade decided to call Dennis' house. Hopefully, Veronica would answer, and she could pass a message onto her husband. Jade dialed the number, her heart pounding. Timing would be everything. She would have to get to Derek before the police and hope that she could come up with a plan to keep her and her sisters safe once they arrived. If not, plan B was in Dennis' hands, and timing would be everything.

"Hello," it was Veronica's deep, warm voice.

"Hi Mrs. Kortovich, it's me, Jade."

"Hello, Jade, nice to hear from you, dear. How are you and the girls doing?" The tone in Veronica's voice went from professional to mother in less than a hear-beat.

Jade hesitated for a moment, hoping what she said next would work.

"We're fine, but I was wondering if Dennis was in?"

"No, but I can get him if you want, or you could page him."

"No…. No, just pass on a message for me".

"O.K. dear, what is it."

The concern in Veronica's voice gave Jade a feeling of hope. She knew that Dennis and Veronica cared for her and her sisters, making Jade feel less alone.

"If he wants more information about Mandy, you know the girl who was kidnapped or my friend Charlotte then I need him to come over to my house in about half an hour. I have something important to show him, but not before 7:30. I won't be home before then, and I have to run out for a while."

Jade hoped Veronica would pass the message on time and that Dennis wouldn't come over seven-thirty. If so, everything might work out.

"Of course, but Jade, this is important. Are you sure I shouldn't come over or at least get Dennis on the phone right away? " Veronica answered.

The tone of Veronica's voice one reminded Jade of her mother, all concern and love. Jade felt terrible that she couldn't just confess everything and cry on her shoulder.

"No.… just tell Mr. Kortovich to meet me a 7:30. And thanks. Thanks for everything. I'll talk to you soon, bye."

"Bye, dear." It was all Jade heard as she put the phone down quickly.

With Veronica living next door, Jade did not want to wait to find out if a concerned Veronica would end up on her door-step. It was time to face the devil and hoped that the flames of hell wouldn't devour her and her sisters. Jade went upstairs to get Amber. They would have to leave right away if they were to arrive on time. Jade left the door wide open, allowing Dennis access to the house. The slightly ajar door wasn't noticeable from the street, and someone would have to come up to the door to see that it wasn't shut, but Jade felt Dennis would know there was a problem with the house wide open and no one home. Once inside, the note on the table would lead Dennis to Derek's house, but not before she and Amber would have a chance to see if they could rescue Crystal. Jade hoped that she or the police could stop Derek before he killed again. The note was simple. It read: **Dennis; Derek Hanson has Crystal, we've gone to rescue her, come and get us, but be careful, or he will kill us all. He's crazy. I think Derek abducted the Judge's daughter Mandy and my friend Charlotte. I'm sure it was me he wanted, not Charlotte. Now he wants Crystal. Be careful. Jade.**

Jade could never admit to all that she knew, or it would implicate her and Crystal in their dad's murder. She couldn't afford to think of what would happen if the police found out about Sam, so she pushed it from her mind as she went out the front door to the van with Amber in tow. The ride over to Derek's place seemed to take forever. While Jade drove, she tried to keep her heart from sinking into her stomach and making her want to vomit. Once she came up to Derek's driveway, Jade turned the van onto the narrow, weed-filled road. She had only driven a few yards when she realized the ruts and grass would make it impossible to continue. She stopped the van and took Amber's hand; the walk would help her gather her strength to face what lay ahead.

Amber looked like a beautiful doll as she bounced happily down the road. Her copper curls catching the evening's setting sun, like spider's silk when its web dances in the breeze, flashing the light of the day through its intricate silk-spun pattern.

The breeze was light and warm. August was in all of its glory, the smells, colors, and clear blue sky. Within the hour, a soft blanket of midnight blue would descend on the little farm that lay just ahead. If a stranger were to view the two perfect young girls walking hand in hand down the rugged country road, it would make a beautiful, innocent picture. However, the girls would never guess what unbelievable horrors lay ahead.

* * *

The afternoon had not gone well so far. Dennis and Chuck had been unable to secure a search warrant. They were at a dead end, and hunches were not enough probable cause to search someone's home. Even the pictures and list weren't enough because Dennis couldn't tell anyone what he and Chuck had found at the Hanson farm.

They were about to play the only card they had left, Judge Switzer. With Judge Switzer, they could at least play upon his involvement. If they did get the judge's warrant, it might compromise the case, but they were at a dead-end, and Dennis felt it might be their only hope.

When the call came in from Veronica, Dennis knew the girls were in trouble. He already suspected that Jade was Derek's real target when he abducted Charlotte; now he knew his hunch was correct. For now, Dennis and Chuck needed to get over to the Walker home. Dennis only hoped Sam wasn't drunk and unruly or that asshole wasn't abusing the girls. Dennis didn't blame Jade for not turning to her father for help. Sam was a useless piece of shit, and she was right to call him and Chuck for help.

Chuck and Dennis arrived a little before 7:30. By the time they reached the front door, their imagination was in full gear. With the front door ajar, there were no answers from their anxious calls as they entered the home.

"Jade, Crystal, where are you?' Chuck was the first to send out a second round of calls.

"Shit, shit, shit, I should have guessed!" Dennis stood over the table, reading the note.

"What is it?" Chuck was at Dennis's side, leaning over his shoulder.

"Wow!" The note took him off guard.

"Where's Sam? Maybe he knows something. He's probably passed out; let's hope we can get something out of him."

Dennis started up the stairs to see if he could find Sam. He was nowhere in sight. The master bedroom was empty, and the closet door stood wide open. "Chuck, what's strange about this room?" Dennis stood off to the side, allowing Chuck a complete view.

Chuck hated being asked these kinds of questions. Dennis was a master at seeing all of the details, and Chuck lagged far behind in quick observation skills.

"No time to guess. What is it?"

"The closet, look and tell me what you see?"

"Clothes in a closet." Chuck's answer was bright, maybe a little too optimistic.

"O.K. I can see you're getting good at this." Dennis responded with the same over-the-top, overly cheerful tone.

"What kind?"

"A woman's." Once again, the sweet, bight tone in Chuck's voice meant he was being sarcastic.

"And?" Dennis played along, adding to the game.

"And, I don't know." Chuck gave Dennis a brilliant smile, and he was done with the game.

"Where are Sam's clothes?" Dennis finished the exchange.

"Wow! What do you think it means?"

"Sam's gone."

"Another thing I noticed in the kitchen, there aren't any bottles of booze lying around," Chuck added, his tone once again professional.

"Well, there's no time to figure out what happened to Sam. We need to get to Derek's. The girls couldn't be lucky enough to have had Sam take off on them. And right now, they're in real danger. Let's hope we can get there in time. They're no match for a man like Derek. We need to get there, now." Dennis said as he headed out the front door with Chuck close behind.

CHAPTER
THIRTY-TWO

Jade stood with Amber in front of the rundown house, wondering what to do next. Derek was nowhere in sight. It was Derek's game, and all Jade could do was wait and hope she could learn the rules fast enough to win; lives would depend on it, theirs. She pushed back the hope that Dennis would rescue them. It may boil down to her, against Derek. A sound came from a bunch of trees alerting Jade to someone's approach. When Jade turned toward the sound, Derek came towards her after emerging from some tall trees and thick bush. Crystal was nowhere in sight.

Welcome to my celebration." Derek smiled, his large lips sliding over his yellow, uneven teeth. "I'm glad all of my little princesses will be with me to celebrate this important day. Come, take my hand; the evening is about to begin."

Derek took Amber's hand; she was only too happy to follow and was unaware of the danger she and her sisters were in. The underbrush was thick and unruly. Derek deliberately kept the farm that way so that no one would suspect that less than three hundred feet from the house were a bunker that had become his cathedral of death.

Jade had no choice but to follow, even though the branches tore at her arms, leaving a few long scratches. She worried that the trees would assault Amber, but Derek was careful to make sure she wasn't hurt. When Derek came to a mound that seemed to rise out of nowhere, Jade realized just how much trouble they were in. How would Dennis find them in the middle of this thickly wooded area? Derek let go of Amber's hand and grabbed a hinge from what seemed to be nothing more than a rise on a mound. Jade was shocked to see that it was a door-way or hatch of some-kind, an entrance to an underground chamber. When Derek swung it open and pulled Amber in, all of Jade's hopes vanished as she followed Derek down several stairs.

Jade was sure it was a bomb shelter. She had heard her father talk about the '50s when everyone was afraid of a nuclear bomb being dropped. Derek shut the hatch, blurring any hope Jade might have of Dennis finding them.

Once inside, Jade could see a large, round storage area shaped like a huge culvert. Empty shelves lined the curved walls, except for a few boxes of matches and candles. A generator sat at one end, running on full, and several empty gas cans were piled carelessly off to the side. A large door stood before them. The fluorescence light in the storage area cast a dim reflection on the door ahead, and Jade had an uncontrollable urge to shout out 'and behind door number one.' It was an automatic impulse to lighten up what was becoming an ever more desperate situation with every step they took.

"You and your sister will be my guests of honor. You're the only ones besides my own family and my other brides to see my cathedral of love." Derek said, giving Jade a toothy smile, swinging the second door open with as much flourish and flair as any magician performing his favorite trick.

Jade was transfixed by what she saw and heard. Before, she was a vast cavern lit by hundreds of candles that stood on a variety of cast iron stands. Dark, red velvet tapestry hung from the walls creating a heady feeling. Pictures of mythical demons and gods, reminiscent of a medieval castle's grand hall, covered the tapestries, making Jade think of a time long past when Knights courted fair maidens. A plush, red, and gold carpet, with designs of a mystical motif, covered the ground. The room's most spectacular feature was the large altar that encompassed the entire rear of the shelter. It featured a vast granite table that stood almost four feet high and at least six feet long. Behind the altar was a large cross adorned with not a sculpture of Jesus, but rather it was adorned with a strange-looking demon. The head was a goat, while the upper body and arms were of a man and the lower body was also that of a goat, its legs crossed with nails driven through its crossed hoofs. Both hands were impaled, and a wreath of thorns adorned its head. When Jade looked into the face of the demon, she was struck by the fact that rather than a look of compassion that was usually depicted on the front of Christ, this impostor stared at her with a look of utter contempt. It was as though all of the hate ever directed at mankind was embodied on the mask of this goat-like monster.

Music assaulted her ears. It was the eerie sound of Monks chanting, the low hum beginning to drone even louder. It seemed as if everything was happening in slow motion. Her senses were so overwhelmed by the unexpectedness of the bunker that she knew her grasp of reality was fading. A flash of white caught Jade's eye, and when she realized who was lying on the altar, all of the blood drained from her face.

"Oh my God!" Jade screamed. "It's Crystal, and she looks dead. You bastard, what have you done to my sister?"

Jade turned to Derek, whose triumphant face said it all.

"No, she's not dead, only drugged," Derek started toward the altar. "a beauty rest. She'll come around soon. I timed it for your arrival."

A soft moan came from Crystal's lips. Derek stood above her. He placed his large hands on her small breast and softly traced her entire body with his hands.

"She's absolutely perfect. They all were." Derek looked up at Jade. "You were perfect, Jade. I almost made you my bride, but I got that foolish brunette instead. She fought me, you know, and it wasn't easy. She was adamant, but I'm tougher, and she wasn't what I wanted."

His eyes narrowed, showing his anger. He moved closer to Crystal, like a protective lover.

"You messed things up for me, and after I kidnapped Charlotte, you were never available to me again. I stalked you for weeks before I finally gave up. Too much time had passed after the anniversary date of my dear sister's death. Then you showed up at the funeral home, but you were too old by then. But Crystal was perfect. Now she'll be my bride." Derek bent his head and put his wet sloppy lips on Crystal's.

Crystal could dimly hear voices, but it was like listening through a fog. The more she tried to move her head, the more her senses seemed to dim. The heavy mist swirled around her, weighing her down. It wasn't until she felt wet lips on hers and felt a hot tongue probing her mouth, making her choke, that she was finally able to become aware of her surroundings. When she turned her head to avoid the invasive tongue, she saw her little sister, Amber, standing silently to one side, fascinated by the flickering candles that surrounded the altar. Crystal was able to look around a little better when the wet mouth left hers. It was then that she spotted Jade.

"Jade!" was all Crystal could whisper from her dry, drug-parched mouth.

"Crystal, don't worry, we're here." Jade could answer back.

Jade had no way of offering Crystal any hope, and she knew the tone in her voice betrayed her.

"Enough talk!" Derek moved away from Crystal, who was already attempting to sit up. "I want to introduce you to my family. I know they'll love you all."

Derek walked toward what looked like church pews, long wooden, high back-benches that stood off to the right, directly in front of the granite altar. As Jade and Crystal's eyes followed Derek, she noticed feet protruding from a blanket of deep purple velvet. Derek flung off the blanket in theatrical style. Screams tore from Jade and Crystal's throats as the mummified faces of the frozen figures were exposed.

The faces of the three mummies were grim masks of horror. The thin, waxy skin stretched across the bones like paper on rocks. The hollow eyes of the trio stared wide-eyed, directly at Crystal. Frozen smiles stretched over decayed teeth. The hairstyles and sizes of the corpses revealed the sexes of the mummified guests. The tallest was a male, the second, sitting in the middle, was a woman, her hair tied back into a ponytail. The third body was tiny, her hair flowing in soft, rivulets of curls still holding onto its copper and red color. Both girls had no idea who they were staring at, but from the way, they were displayed and preserved, they must have meant a lot to Derek. For both Jade and Crystal, the piercing, fixed eyes of the figures brought waves of pure hysteria to their hearts.

CHAPTER THIRTY-THREE

As soon as Dennis and Chuck left to go to the Hansen farm, Dennis called into the main office and talked to the desk sergeant. He told the sergeant to contact the other members of the special task force. Dennis and Chuck had put together a special task force to help investigate the missing girls soon after Mandy Switzer had been found. Hundreds of tips had been called in once the press got a hold of the story. It would take hundreds of hours of extra legwork to follow all of the leads. The detectives he had of the case were also dedicated and talented. They would need all the help they could get. Time was running out, and both detectives felt a sense of urgency and a little fear.

Dennis was able to obtain a search warrant from Judge Heart solely based on Jade's note. The team was to meet Chuck and Dennis just outside of Derek's property. Once they were all assembled and organized, they would storm onto the farm from several different coordinates and surround the small house. Hopefully, Derek would be unaware of their arrival, and they would be able to use the element of surprise to enable them to affect a rescue and an arrest.

By the time the task force had gathered, the wind had picked up considerably. Dennis gave instructions to the men; within minutes, they were down the scruffy road surrounding the house from all sides. Dennis and Chuck were now at the south side of the house, just under the dining room window. The view from the window allowed him to see into the house and down the hall into the bathroom. There was nothing! No sounds, no one was walking around! The kitchen window was too high to peer through. Dennis waited several more seconds before he motioned to the men lying in the tall grass to wait. Finally, he waved everyone forward. If they were to storm the front door, it would have to be fast. The front porch was so run down it would announce their arrival. While Chuck took the rear of the tiny house, along with three other men, Dennis took the front door with two veteran officers he trusted the most. The other four men remained in the fields, just in case Derek was somewhere else. As far as Dennis could tell, all of the outer buildings were empty.

The assault only took a few minutes. After calling out Derek's name and announcing that they were police officers, the task force broke in with full force. Once inside they were puzzled when they found that no one was around. Not the girls, nor Derek.

"Fuck, where are they?" adrenaline-pumped Dennis, approached Chuck from the kitchen.

Chuck and two other men were standing in the dining room, the look on their faces mirroring Dennis' verbal outburst. "Shit! I don't understand it. Jade's van is on the road and Derek's station wagon is outside. They're not here, so where the hell are they? The outbuildings are practically collapsing on the ground so I doubt if Derek and the girls are in any of them."

Dennis looked at Chuck and the two other police officers for an answer. They had none.

"O.K. let's make a thorough sweep of the area to see if we turn up anything." Dennis moved past the men and out onto the porch.

The wind had begun to roar through the trees making a loud swishing sound. Dennis shouted to the officers in the field to go over every inch of grounds on the old farm. After a full thirty minutes, they turned up nothing. Dennis, Chuck, and the other officers gathered on the rickety front porch that rattled with the wind as it tore over the roof, sending the occasional shingle, whizzing through the air.

"They are here somewhere and we don't have a lot of time!" Dennis shouted over the wind to Chuck.

Dennis turned to a young officer who had recently been promoted to a detective.

"Ben, get on the phone and call the station. We need Lucy now! She's the only one who can help us find the girls, and tell Max Grant to hurry. Dennis turned around and went back into the little house that was now shaking and rattling frantically from the wind.

"I hate this damn wind!" Dennis shouted at no one in particular, leaving the rest of the team wondering if they should just stay on the porch or go inside. When a large branch from a tree slammed into the side of the house, shattering the window, the officers went inside.

"Make sure you touch nothing unless you wear gloves. Let's gather and bag as much evidence as we can until Lucy gets here." Chuck said.

With that statement the officers began to get to work, filling the next half hour gathering evidence. Dennis went into the dining room where the plastic molds of the missing items worn by the girls, were found. It wasn't until they had bagged everything that seemed important that Dennis noticed a silver buckle among the leftover clutter. He picked it up, turning it over to inspect the intricate pattern carved into the front. Dennis noticed that the edges were charred as if it had been in a fire. The center of the buckle he could make out the initials. S --W was all he could make out, the middle initial was almost illegible. Suddenly it hit him, he knew who the buckle belonged to, Samuel Walker. Jade, Crystal, and Amber's father! What in hell was the buckle doing here? Dennis looked back down at the table. What else was under the pile of crap that filled the space on the table? A wooden box sat under a cloth. Dennis picked it up and peered inside, ashes, nothing but ashes, but whose? He would have to get these things down to forensics. They could belong to any of the missing girls.

Dennis could hear the barking of a dog. "That was fast!" He thought as he placed the buckle in a bag that sealed the box of ashes. Once out on the porch, everyone could see the uniformed officer running to keep up with a beautiful, German Sheppard who seemed to enjoy being in the wide-open space of the outdoors, even if the wind threatened to blow them both away.

"That was fast." Chuck was the first to greet the officer; he bent to put a gentle hand on the Sheppard's head while the officer held the dog in check, signaling that Chuck was a friend.

"Good girl. We're sure glad to see you, Lucy. We need to find some friends real quick." Chuck scratched Lucy behind the ears, giving the officer a thankful smile.

Dennis was following close behind, he held his hand out to the veteran trainer who was a long-time friend and colleague.

"Max good to see you, there's no time for details; we have to put Lucy to work right away."

Dennis turned back toward the house motioning for Officer Grant to follow, as he neared the porch he handed the buckle and box to another detective.

"Bob, get all of the stuff we've gathered together and secure it in my car. We need to make sure nothing goes missing. Stay in the car so the chain of evidence isn't broken."

Dennis turned to another officer, Terry Mahoney, a veteran officer with over thirty years of experience. "Terry, secure the house. Derek may return without our being aware. We still don't know what we're up against."

Bob, the young officer nodded, took the buckle and box from Dennis as well as several other bagged items, and headed up the road to the car. Terry retreated into the small house while the rest of the officers waited for further instructions. Dennis disappeared into the house, returning in a few seconds with a faded black coat jacket of Derek's.

It was one he had worn many times by the look of the collar and sleeves, which were worn and frayed. The jacket was also faded and in need of a good cleaning. Dennis approached Officer Grant who took the coat from him and placed it under Lucy's nose. Lucy buried her nose in the fabric, then sat down, raised her head, and sneezed, a loud, wet, head-shaking sneeze that caught everyone off guard.

"Boy, that's never happened before!" Max put the jacket back under Lucy's nose. Once again Lucy stood, put her nose deep into the jacket, and once again sat back down, this time giving off two short 'achoos' into the air. Lucy shook her head, lay down, and placed her paws over her nose as if to say "phew!"

"What the hell's on this jacket anyway? I've never seen her act this way. Max brought the jacket close to his nose and quickly held it away. "What's this guy do? The jacket smells like chemicals."

Dennis took the jacket and put his nose close to the sleeve. "It's embalming fluid. The guy's a mortician and obviously a sloppy one."

By now Lucy was standing, her tail straight and her nose in the air. In a few seconds, she was pulling Officer Grant toward a large clump of trees that looked menacing as the wind rattled their tops.

Officer Grant turned to Dennis. "She's off and running. Let's go."

Dennis, Chuck, and the rest of the officers followed Lucy and Officer Max Grant, who was now disappearing into a thick clump of trees. Dennis knew somewhere deep in this wooded area they would find Derek and the girls. But would they be in time?

CHAPTER THIRTY-FOUR

Derek stood next to the grotesque forms of his family, a look of insane pride shining on his face.

"Mother, Father, Lisa, meet my new family, Jade, and of course the little one, Amber."

He pointed to Jade who stood almost directly in front of the mummified forms and Amber who remained transfixed by the flickering glow of the candles. "And most importantly my bride-to-be, Crystal Walker." Derek motioned toward Crystal with a gallant bow.

Crystal was now sitting up, her legs and hands were free, but the effects of the drugs were still evident. Her head hung on her chest. As the fog slowly began to lift from her drug-induced brain, she lifted her head from her chest just long enough to catch Jade's eye and let her know she was all right and getting stronger every moment.

Jade had been staring at Derek who seemed to be absorbed in his introduction of Crystal to his family when she saw Crystal's head lift. Jade could tell Crystal was coming out of her drugged state. This was the first time Jade was able to get a full view of Crystal and when she did a shocked scream escaped from her lips. "Oh, no!"

Crystal's upper body and bare arms were covered with burn marks and tiny bruises. Derek followed Jade's eyes and outburst to its source, Crystal.

"Her condition is a necessary initiation in the art of love. And don't worry, she's still a virgin."

Derek moved toward Crystal, touching her tiny face with his large, bony hand. While he circled behind her, he made sure his hand never left her body. Finally, he settled his hand on her copper, red curls. As Derek slowly stroked Crystal's hair, her eyes found Jade's once more, but now they were completely clear. A grim determined look crossed Crystal's face. It meant only one thing; Crystal was ready for a fight.

Jade knew they only had to find the right moment and hope they could overcome Derek, somehow getting away. Crystal had to stay alert and Jade had to come up with a plan. First Jade needed to know what Derek had planned for them.

"So what now? You have us all here. So how do you think you're going to get away with this?' The steely sound of Jade's voice surprised even her.

"Who's going to stop me? You can't! Not even my parents could prevent me from having what I wanted."

Derek dropped his hand from Crystal's hair and put his long fingers on her throat.

"Lisa was my angel. She was too young to know what she wanted. If I'd only had enough time to show her the real pleasure of love, things would have been different. But she fought me. I had to burn some sense into her. Even then she resisted. Lisa said awful things, hateful things. I had to shut her up. Her neck snapped. I know she could have loved me if only she would have listened." Derek shouted, spittle forming along the edge of his mouth.

Derek tilted Crystal's head back and looked into her deep, blue eyes, his voice menacing. "But you'll listen won't you."

Derek bent his head over Crystal's face and placed his wet, hot lips over hers, once again plunging his tongue deep into the cool wet recess of her mouth. Crystal tried not to choke or pull away. The years spent with her father had taught her not to resist openly when he was in one of his drunken obsessive moods. She knew that the less resistance she gave Derek, the more likely he would be to loosen his grip on her. If she was going to get out of Derek's reach, she needed to have him feel safe and in control. Crystal let her body go limp; her eyes stayed wide open never leaving Jade's face.

Jade knew that Crystal was terrified. But the years with Sam had taught them strong survival skills. Their motto with Sam was, "Say yes, wait, and get out of sight." It would have to be the same motto with Derek. Show no resistance, wait for him to relax his guard and then run like hell.

* * *

Derek liked the feel of Crystal in his arms. He liked the way Crystal melted at his kiss and touch. The others always fought. Crystal was different from the beginning. He had made sure that all of the girls knew he was the boss. Derek gagged them and tied them to the table at first. Then he pinched and burnt his victims repeatedly, letting them know he was the one in control and unafraid to use whatever means necessary to manage them. The others had struggled and made horrifying screams when he burnt their skin with his hot, searing, cigarette or pinched them with his strong fingers, all the while telling them it was hopeless to struggle. They were his. But none of them had ever listened before. They struggled to the end. It was always the same. When he removed the tape from their mouths a foul string of words would follow. When he pressed his lips to theirs they would bite and spit. Derek's efforts to subdue the girls resulted in the same ending. He simply snapped their necks as he had done to the cats and small dogs that resisted him over the years.

Sometimes he would drug the girls and take them back to the funeral home, hoping to give them one more chance to become his. When it became apparent that they were only going to resist, Derek did what he had to do. The 'belly of the beast' was their final resting place, a place where each would burn in hell. But Crystal was different. She welcomed him. She needed him. He could tell by the way her blue eyes stayed steady as he branded and pinched her tiny arms and chest. Never once did she let out a single peep.

When he removed the tape all Crystal wanted to know was where she was and what did he want with her. When he explained the way things were going to be, she seemed calm, accepting. Derek knew Jade and Crystal had discovered Mandy. Derek thought Crystal would be terrified of him. Instead, Crystal seemed resigned to be his. Crystal was the one Derek had waited for all of these years for, a delicate little flower to call his own. Now Crystal lay limply in his arms, welcoming his kiss and his touch. Derek felt an almost hysterical joy as the tears welled up in his eyes and he turned away from Crystal, facing the goat-headed God behind him, one hand still gripping her shoulder tightly.

"You promised me a bride. All I had to do was be patient and you would deliver her to me." Derek's voice rose as he began his prayer of thanks. "Now a new life will begin for me, a life in which I can love and be loved." The sobs began to tear from Derek's chest between his words of thanks, directed at the evil image.

"Never again will I doubt you know that you have delivered my bride to me." The uncontrollable emotions and pent-up feelings overwhelmed Derek, making him drop to his knees.

This was it; Crystal knew it was now or never. She could see Jade had moved over to oblivious Amber, who was still transfixed by the flicker of the candles as they danced across the multi-colored tapestry lining the walls. By the time Derek dropped to his knees, the girls were ready. The door leading out of the storage area was only a few hundred feet away. They would need to run like hell and hope they could run faster than the awkward, but long-legged Derek, and somehow make it out of there.

Once Crystal saw that Jade had Amber's hand she grabbed the bottom of the wedding gown, pulled it up to her waist, jumped from the granite slab, and began to run like hell. Jade was running just a few feet ahead, pulling Amber close behind. They were only halfway to the door when a gut-wrenching scream echoed against the walls, assaulting their ears. Derek was up off his knees moving quickly in their direction. The look of total disbelief on his face for having been stupid and letting his guard down enough to trust them. Derek's long legs allowed him to gain on them quickly. Jade reached the outer door first with Amber still in hand. Just as she began to open the door she could hear Crystal's screams as Derek lunged toward her, grabbing the back of her gown.

Jade could hear the loud rip as the back of the gown was torn away, the heavy fabric of the train preventing it from ripping further. It allowed Derek to hold Crystal in place until he could pull her to the floor with him.

Jade managed to open the heavy chamber door and push Amber through before closing it. Then she turned back to fight Derek off Crystal. At least Amber would be safe for a while Jade thought, as she put all of her strength into a kick at Derek's head. With Derek on the floor trying to subdue Crystal, she was able to get in another two big kicks at his face before his large hand encircled her tiny foot and brought her to the ground. Crystal was tangled up in the volume of the fabric of the gown as she twisted and turned trying to get her feet free. Derek found it difficult to hang on to Crystal as she twisted and turned. He grabbed at the folds of white material as it bunched itself up around Crystal's waist still fending off Jade's kicks and slaps.

"You fucking little bitch, I trusted you! I loved you! I would have protected and cared for you!" Derek spits out the words with all of the frustration and hate he now felt, a sharp contrast to the feelings of thankfulness he felt moments before. "Now you two little whores will die just like the others."

Jade could feel Derek's hand tighten around her foot, dragging her closer to him, his face only a few inches from hers. She stopped struggling for a few seconds, allowing Derek to pull with the same force but with no resistance from her. As he pulled her quickly towards him a look of shock crossed his face just as the feel of her foot caught him a full force on the bridge of his long narrow nose. Jade could hear the crack as the bridge of his nose shattered from the force. Derek let go of Crystal, as a loud scream of pain passed his full, wet lips. The blood gushed from his nose out over his chin as his large hand smeared the blood onto his face. Jade jumped to her feet and grabbed Crystal. The gown had to go. She spun Crystal around and pulled as hard as she could on the lower portion of the gown. It ripped only a couple more inches but it was enough. The straps of the gown were already over Crystal's shoulders; Jade pulled them down over Crystal's arms and continued to pull with all of the strength she could. The gown fell over Crystal's slim hips, crumbling around her feet. Crystal quickly stepped out of the heap of white lace and jewels as Jade pulled her towards the door. Again they were only seconds away from freedom. Jade began to swing the heavy chamber door open when two large bloody hands lunged toward Crystal pulling her back. Jade was almost out when she felt Derek's hand give her back a violent shove. She fell forward, out of the chamber door. She found herself sprawled out on the cold concrete floor of the outer storage area. The heavy door shut behind her, her ears ringing with the final screams of Crystal. "Don't leave m..." before the hollow silence engulfed her.

*   *   *

Dennis was only a few feet away from Lucy and Max Grant. The dog's tail was wagging, her excited bark rising above the howling wind. They were now almost three hundred feet into the dense underbrush. Dennis could tell that the heavily treed path the dog followed was not well traveled, but there was still a path nonetheless.

Lucy was leading them to some unknown destination, she shifted from full gear into a sudden stop, the barking now an excited whining.

"They're here." Max turned toward Dennis letting Chuck and the other detectives catch up and gather around Lucy.

There was a small rise, about three feet up, directly ahead. Dennis knew instantly what it was.

"It's got to be the entrance to a bomb shelter, most likely built in the mid-50s or early 60s." Dennis turned to all of the members of the team.

"The entrance is here somewhere." He turned back to the mound searching for the door. "Chuck, you and a couple of officers come with me. The rest of you stay here. There's no need to announce our-selves by making a grand entrance. We still need the element of surprise. So, quiet everyone. Let's go slow. We don't know what is behind the hatch. Just find it, now!"

Dennis, Chuck, and two other officers felt around the ground on the mound. It was Dennis who found the hard iron of the door's handle beneath his palm. He pulled hard and a metal door gave way, pulling up toward him, still covered in quack grass and a variety of other weeds. The light of the day was quickly fading as they descended the dark passage. After a few yards, they found another entrance that opened into a large storage area. By now their eyes had adjusted to the dim light of the fluorescence bulbs overhead.

Dennis was both shocked and overjoyed at the sight that greeted him. Amber stood in front of him in the middle of the room; just outside of the large door lay Jade in a heap, her feet up behind her and her belly flat on the floor. She looked up as she heard their approach. Her face was distorted with grief and fear.

"Thank God you're here! Help me. Derek has Crystal and I'm sure he'll kill her, hurry!" She screamed. Her voice broke as she regained her footing.

Dennis raced forward, covering the distance in a few long strides. He bent over and pulled Jade up, helping her to steady herself as she pulled away from the door. The room was growing ever darker as the generator ran out of fuel. Chuck was right behind Dennis and he pulled a lighter from his pocket and flicked it open to get some more light in the room.

"Get the girls out of here." Dennis turned to the young officer, the newest and youngest member of the team.

"Get your fucking hands off me." Jade spat at the officer as he started to put his arms around her, attempting to escort her out.

"I'm not going anywhere without Crystal and you'll need me!" Jade shouted in frustration.

Jade's face was now lit by a couple of candles that Chuck had found on the shelves, allowing the eerie glow to show the look of stubborn determination on her face.

"And there's no time to argue. Take Amber, but I'm staying." Jade's chin stuck out in the air, her tiny face fierce with defiance.

"O.K., O.K. No time to argue with anyone as angry as you are." Dennis looked down at Jade's red-rimmed, bright blue eyes.

"Take Amber." Dennis motioned to the confused young officer "And get some more light down here when you come back. There are more candles on the shelves."

Dennis turned his attention once more to Jade. "O.K. Tell me what we're up against. What's behind the door?"

"It's like a church, candles, an altar, pews to the front and three special guests, all dead, Derek's family. I think he stuffed them like they do dead animals. It's almost like they're real." Jade was nearly breathless, her need to be of help overcoming her fear.

"Does he have a gun or a weapon?" Dennis could hear the young officer's return as he asked the question.

"No, none that I saw. I don't think Derek was expecting anyone but us girls and he felt we were no threat."

The room was now much brighter as more candles were lit and lined up along the half-empty shelves.

"Derek doesn't know you alerted us?"

"No, I wasn't sure you'd get my message, so I felt I was on my own," Jade answered back.

"Good, then we still have the element of surprise." Dennis turned to Chuck and the two other officers.

"We need to get in the room without Derek's knowledge. Stand ready to take my lead."

Both men nodded as Chuck replied an audible "Got it".

Dennis turned to Jade. "Do you think you can go back in and get Derek to concentrate on you while we try to get in and take him by surprise?"

"Absolutely" Jade's fear seemed to melt away now that Dennis and the other men were there. "There are tapestries along the wall, hung from the piping. They are about a foot away from the walls; you could slip behind them and make your way fairly close to the altar. That's where he'll have Crystal." Jade stated, sure that Derek would return to his original plan for Crystal.

"O.K. let's go. It's up to you." Dennis put a firm hand on Jade's shoulder to let her know that he would be right behind and he would get them out safely.

Dennis and Chuck pressed close to the wall in the outer chamber just to the side of the door. The other officers stayed just outside, ready to burst in at the first word from Chuck or Dennis. Jade grabbed the handle of the heavy chamber door and gave it a hard tug. It took all the strength she had to pull it fully open. The candles in the outer chamber had been put out, all but the one that Jade held in her hand. She hoped that Derek would concentrate on her and not detect any other movement. As the door swung open, Derek turned towards the sound, not altogether surprised. Jade was a spunky little thing. She wouldn't give up easily. She must have taken Amber out of the shelter Derek thought as he noticed Jade's solo entrance.

Jade stood alone in the doorway, a candlelit up her beautiful face. For a second Derek didn't know whom he wanted more, Crystal or Jade. What the fuck! He would have them both.

Crystal was now lying on the altar, her tiny breast bares with the removal of the gown. She wore lacy white panties and a garter. Her white nylons held up by their tiny clips, her feet shoeless. Crystal held on to her tiny breasts with both hands, hating the feeling of helplessness.

Being half-naked made Crystal feel violated and close to hysterical. When the door shut on Jade, leaving her alone with Derek, Crystal thought she would lose it. All she could do was to pray. Once again Crystal could smell the fresh scent of laundry. She knew she would be safe.

"I'm not leaving without Crystal. So I guess you'll have to have us both." Jade said seductively.

Jade moved steadily toward Derek. He was standing at the altar. Jade kept her eyes on Derek's, willing him to look only at her. Derek's face took on a look of triumph. The way a bully does when he's taken the lunch money from someone smaller and weaker than him.

"So, you've decided to sacrifice yourself for your sister. How noble. So I'll let you. You're both perfect for me." Derek's eyes never left Jade's.

Jade continued to move forward focusing the candle on her face, holding Derek's attention. The music that played in the background continued its hypnotic chant. For a moment Jade forgot that Dennis was somewhere behind the heavy tapestry, making his way toward Derek. Her eyes and ears were focused on the madman in front of her. Derek put his hands-on Crystal's neck, his long fingers pointing down towards her naked breasts.   "The only way you and your sister make it out of here alive is if you both give yourselves to me willingly," Derek commanded.

Derek slid a hand down Crystal's chest and cupped her breast, squeezing her nipples hard. Jade could hear a small cry of pain from Crystal as she turned her head to look at Jade. Behind Derek, Jade could see a small amount of movement from the tapestry. Dennis was now directly behind Derek. All Dennis needed was a diversion. Jade knew it was up to her to get Derek to move away from Crystal before he could hurt her. Jade stopped, standing between Derek, who was only a few feet ahead, and his mummified family who were only a few feet behind.

Jade turned around quickly and moved toward the gruesome forms that sat silently on the pew behind her. She circled and stood next to the figures of his mother and father, just between his sister and obsessive love, Lisa.

"Why not have all three of us. I'm sure Lisa won't mind. Oh, I forgot, she didn't want you any more than Crystal or I do. Maybe once again you'll have no one." Jade hoped Derek would forget Crystal and respond to her taunt.

Derek's eyes narrowed, Jade knew she was close to getting the response she wanted, but Derek's hands never moved from Crystal's body.

"What's the matter? Does the truth hurt? It must be difficult to be such a fucking freak. You want young beautiful girls, but we don't want you. You're just too fucked up to get it."

Jade could smell the embalming fluid and whatever other chemicals were used to mummify Derek's family. Jade was sure they would be highly flammable.

"You shut your foul mouth up or I'll kill your little bitch of a sister and then I'll kill you. When you are both dead I'll take you anyway." Derek sneered.   'Death excites me. Your cold lifeless body under mine is what makes me come, so don't fuck with me little girl, you'll never win."

Dennis had moved out from behind the curtain, he was only a few feet away from Derek. His gun was drawn, he was about to shoot Derek. Dennis noticed that the one hand that held Crystal's breast right above her heart had a small, silver pocketknife in it. If Dennis made the wrong move Derek could plunge it into Crystal's body in a second. He needed to get Derek to move away from the terrified girl. Dennis froze, hoping Derek wouldn't turn around and see him. He would be forced to fire his gun and from the position of Derek's hand over Crystal's breast, he was unsure of the result. Crystal could die if he didn't get Derek to move away from her. Dennis would have to leave it up to Jade and hope her taunting remarks would get Derek to move.

Jade saw Dennis just behind Derek, the look on his face told her that he couldn't make his move on the madman who was bent over her sister. Jade would need to get Derek to move.

The smell of the corpse that Jade stood next to make her look at the candle she held more intensely. As she looked up from the candle to Derek's face Jade could see he knew what was going through her mind.

"Noooo!" Was all she could hear as Jade put the candle to the copper curls of Lisa's hair. Instantly flames leaped and sizzled from the cotton-candy strands. Next, the mother, she too sizzled as flames started to flicker from her stretched skin. The father was next. Jade swung the candle to his clothing, hair, and face. Swoosh the fumes and gasses from the bodies exploded, sending Jade backward onto her ass.

Derek ran from the altar, his knife still in his hand, Crystal now forgotten. Derek's family was swiftly engulfed in flames. He had to do something to put them out. As Derek reached into the family circle to pull Lisa away from the soaring flames, the sleeves on his jacket caught fire instantly. Within seconds Derek's jacket was like a torch, the flames reaching up to his long hair. The look on Derek's face was one of shock and terror. In his attempt to rescue his family he had forgotten that the embalming fluid was formaldehyde and highly flammable. His jacket was always soaked in the chemicals from his work at the funeral home. A scream of anger, contempt, and surprise tore from his lips as his eyes bore into Jade's.

"You Fucking Bitch!" The epitaph attached itself to the end of Derek's gut-wrenching scream.

Derek's face was now a mask of contorted pain. Rather than run from the flames, Derek held Lisa's torched body closer to his. The flames were now rising well above his face. Jade could barely see his skin or hair through the flame's flickering, red fingers. Derek moved closer to Lisa, his beloved sister, and put his melting lips into her now charred undistinguishable face. The air was finally choked from Derek's lungs.

Derek and Lisa fell forward into the bodies of their family. The whole chamber was now lit by the fierce glow of the flames as they consumed the Hansen family. Dark smoke filled the room while the flames spread rapidly.

Dennis could see that the horrible scene in front of Jade had her transfixed. If she didn't move soon the flames would engulf her, making Jade a part of the family's tragic end. With one arm firmly around Crystal's shoulder, Dennis took three giant steps toward Jade, shouting her name as he moved towards her.

"Jade, move!" Dennis shouted.

Jade heard Dennis' command above the crackling roar of the flames that now danced along the walls of the thick tapestry. She looked up and blinked twice. By the time Dennis was at her side, her arms were stretched out toward him. Dennis gathered Jade to his chest and turned toward the chamber door.

Chuck and the other young officers were only steps behind him. Chuck grabbed Crystal from Dennis and gathered her in his arms while Dennis held Jade firmly. Dennis and Chuck could do nothing for Derek and every second was needed if they were to get out of the black, smoke-filled room before all of the air was sucked out by the fire, which now shot flames over everyone's heads, the sparks falling dangerously close as they retreated. They ran to the metal door closing it just in time, Derek's screams fading as the door shut. Dennis, Chuck, and Dennis along with Jade and Crystal fell in a heap as they bolted through the outer storage area. Dennis placed Jade on the dirt floor and turned to Chuck, who still held Crystal. With the loud thud of the closing door, the storage room became strangely quiet as the rest of the cops slumped to the floor, drained. Nothing was said for what seemed like forever until Crystal began to cough, tears streaming down her face partly because of the smoke, but mostly from relief. Dennis noted that Crystal was still half-naked. He nodded toward one of the officers who removed his bulletproof vest and took off his blue shirt, handing it to Dennis.

Crystal looked up at Dennis, never had he seen such a look of relief mixed with confusion and fear. Crystal's eyes turned toward Jade sitting on the other side of Dennis. Dennis noted how Crystal and Jade exchanged a strange look that made him wonder if there was more going on with the girls than a near-death by fire. Dennis felt that he should have seen a look that said it was over and everything would be all right. Instead, the look on their faces was more like their worries were just beginning. Maybe they were concerned about Amber.

"Your sister is all right. She's just outside the bunker." Dennis could see that this did little to lift their mood.

"Come on everyone, let's get going, the smoke is beginning to drift under the door," Chuck said.

Dennis gathered Jade up in his arms, her tiny body light and easy to move as she clung tightly to his neck. Chuck took his cue from Dennis and scooped up Crystal. The whole group made their way out of the storage room into the passageway that led up and out into the black, star-filled night.

Dennis could hear Lucy's excited bark as they drew closer to the outer door, the evening air caressing their faces with its welcome coolness and fresh forestry scent. The wind was now little more than a brisk breeze. As if rehearsed, the group took a deep breath at once, releasing it slowly their lungs welcoming the clear pure air.

"Let's get you girls home. Tomorrow we'll deal with the details." Dennis said.

Dennis gathered the rest of his team around him, giving orders to the men about a de-briefing they would hold at the station after Dennis got the girls home. Dennis asked one young officer to run ahead and bring one of the cars down the rutted bumpy road. The girls would be too tired to make the trek back. The ride would be rough, but it would be better than the walk.

Chuck and Dennis had seen to it personally that the girls had gotten home and were safely put to bed. Veronica came over and rather than give her a blow by blow on how the rescue went he simply asked if she could stay. She nodded in assent.

"Just one more question before we go, where the hell is Sam?" Dennis asked.

A look of fear and confusion spread across Jade's face.

"I honestly don't know. He simply left a few days ago."

Jade looked briefly into Dennis's eyes before quickly lowering hers. There was a moment of silence between them before Crystal quickly interjected.

"You know Dad, he hates us and with mom dead, we were probably too much. He just took off."

The sound of Crystal's voice held just a twinge of hopefulness. Not that Sam was gone, but more the sound of hope that Dennis would believe her. Something was up and Dennis would have to find out what.

* * *

Dennis looked over at his partner. Chuck was leaning back on his office chair, swigging down the final drops of his strong, cold coffee. They had gone over all of the evening's details with the men. Their reports would be required quickly before the press got wind of Derek's death and involvement with the missing and now known dead girls. It was over. Dennis, Chuck, and the team had put an end to an especially cruel and clever, serial killer. So far Dennis hadn't mentioned his thoughts on Sam's disappearance, preferring to keep his unspoken suspicions to himself.

Chuck stood up and ran his fingers over the jewelry molds they had found at Derek's house. Items were once laid into the soft clay, making the imprints of personal things that had once belonged to the young victims. Along-side them was the knife that had been held to Crystal's throat as well as a belt buckle, ashes, pictures, and undeveloped film. All of the items held clues or proof of Derek's horrible crimes.

"Do you want me to take these things to the evidence room?" Chuck asked.

"No, I'll do it. Once they're signed in and tagged they'll never be seen again. With Derek dead and our testimony, none of these items will be needed for evidence. I just want to be the one to put it all away forever. Maybe it's because I'm a father and I know how the families will feel when we tell them it's over." Dennis said.

Dennis ran his hand over his face and stroked his mustache, a familiar move.

"There is no hope that their baby girls will ever be coming home. I know how I would feel if it were one of my girls. I want to show the memories of the victims a little respect and spend a few more minutes getting this stuff ready for lock-up."

Chuck could tell Dennis needed this time alone. The items would soon find their way into some numbered box, never to be seen again. Dennis was right. A little respect was needed before everything was put to rest. He nodded and left Dennis to perform the last rights.

Dennis leaned over the desk and picked up the small knife. Until now he had little opportunity to examine it. As he flipped it over he was startled to see that there was an intricate set of initials carved into its silver body. S.J.W. Dennis reached over and picked up the belt buckle that lay on the desk next to the molds. The same silver initials were carved into the buckle. In an intuitive flash of insight, it suddenly became very clear to Dennis what has gone on in the last few days.

* * *

Jade and Crystal sat on the back step of their home while Amber was swinging on a hammock. Amber would stay on the hammock and swing for hours, only stopping if one of the girls came to get her. They couldn't believe what had happened so far that morning. Both of the girls had been too tired the evening before, so nothing about the past day had been discussed between them. They had hoped to get up early and discuss their story, getting the details straight before the police came to question them. They had only just gotten up when the front doorbell announced Dennis Kortovich's arrival. Both girls exchanged a fearful look before they had to answer the door.

Dennis looked fresh and relaxed, his clothes perfect, making him appear more like a businessman than a detective, his handsome face rosy and happy. His mood caught the girls off guard. They were expecting their crime to be discovered at any moment, knowing they could face a lifetime in jail for Sam's murder. Dennis had a statement with him that he had prepared earlier. It was simple and stated that the girls discovered Derek's involvement with Charlotte's disappearance which led in part to Crystal's subsequent kidnapping. Derek's blackmailing attempt, inducing Jade to join him at the farm and his attempt to kill the girls at the bomb shelter.

It was straightforward and said nothing about Sam and other things Jade was sure he knew, or questions she thought Dennis would ask. What about the knife Derek had? And what about the buckle Dennis found at Derek's home. Most importantly, what about the ashes? Both girls knew the police now had all of the evidence. Would they ask more questions about where their father was? There was no way a detective as good as Dennis would let any of these questions go unanswered. Both girls exchanged uneasy looks waiting for the ax to fall. After each girl signed her statements, Dennis said his fair-wells got up to leave. Jade walked Dennis to the door, still a little shocked at how easy Dennis made closing the case on Derek seem. Dennis said it would soon be over. As he held the door open, looking intently into each of the girls' eyes, he could see two beautiful girls who had lived a cruel and bitter life. Sam was as evil as they came. The Walker girls deserved a life free of fear and harm. They would have that now.

"By the way, I have a little gift for you. Open it after I'm gone." He thrust a small wooden box into Jade's hand. It was wrapped in simple brown paper.

As the morning breeze blew softly across the porch both Jade and Crystal couldn't contain the tears that slowly slid down their smooth, young faces. It was over. They would never have to live in fear again. In the plain wooden box were their future and freedom. Lying in the ash-filled box were two silver items, Sam's buckle, and knife. The morning light glittered off the intricately carved initials. All they could do was smile at each other through their warm tears. Jade was the first to stand, the box rested in her tiny hands. She looked down at Crystal, her voice soft and contented.

"It's over Crystal. Let's go bury dad!"

BLOOD GAMES

CHAPTER ONE

The Chicago wind howled from the north slapping the snow across the open field like a hockey player shooting at the net in a frantic last attempt to score. Detective Dennis Kortovich parked his Crown Victoria away from the howling northern wind, knowing that the vehicle would only give a small amount of cover, his partner Chuck O'Brian followed close behind. A police cruiser had already arrived at the scene and two young officers were questioning a young man in a bright, red hooded jacket who moved back and forth blowing on his hands, trying to keep them from freezing in the sub-zero weather. The January day was as cold as a whore's heart and twice as deadly.

"Put that young man in the back of the cruiser," yelled Kortovich shaking his head at the need to state the obvious. "He will be able to answer the questions if he's not half-frozen."

As the wind whipped around Dennis' ankles trying to find entry into his warm boots, as he moved around to the south side of the cruiser to get a full view of the crime scene, knowing what he would find. The markers made it easy to focus on the bodies of a young couple. The male lay a few feet from the female, his body facing toward the young woman. His arms were stretched toward his partner in an effort to embrace her. She had her arms crossed on her chest seemingly rejecting him, even in death. It was obvious that the killer had posed the couple after he had dumped the bodies in the open field. Dennis looked away from the bodies as a gust of cold wind whistled past his head. The sky was heavy with bleak possibilities of even colder weather coming in from the north. The wind made it difficult to breath; it assaulted Dennis' lungs with its frozen fingers, its grip tight and unforgiving. God, how he hated these freezing Chicago winters, he thought as he moved closer to view the scene. As he stood over the bodies Dennis began pulling off his winter gloves replacing them with latex gloves. If he had to touch anything he wouldn›t compromise the evidence. He pulled his fur-lined hood over his head and bent down over the closest body, the young women. Chuck stood off to the side, his notepad in hand.

"How many of these bodies do we have to find before we get a break?" Dennis said under his breath, his rhetorical question unanswered by Chuck.

Dennis explored the body of the women, Chuck made notes in the familiar black pad. The victim was young, under thirty and pretty, her long dark hair partially covering her face. Her makeup, once artfully done was now a death mask of horror. The winter coat she wore was twisted around her body and looked as though someone had put it on after her death; the buttons were not in their correct holes, she wore a skirt, legs a bluish hue from a night spent in the cold field of snow and ice.

Her wrists had been bound and taped, marks could be seen where Jack Frost had laid his icy fingers. Her ankles also bore the marks of her assault.

"There's something different about this one." Dennis turned to his partner as he looked up from the victim. "What do you make of it?

Dennis could see a twinge of irritation cross his partners face when he asked the question. It wasn't that Chuck didn't know the answer. Chuck was a great cop with well-honed observation skills, but Dennis knew Chuck wished he would just tell him what he saw and let him off the hook. Dennis liked to irritate his partner with his Holmes and Watson antics. It made solving crimes a lot more fun when his good-natured partner was put on the spot. Besides, it was a good way of thinking out loud and getting on the same page, not that they disagreed very often.

"As usual, this isn't where the murders took place; this is just where he dumped the bodies. There are no fluids around the bodies; everything is clean as a whistle. But the victim didn't put the coat on herself. It had to have been put on by her killer. It's the same MO as the others, but it's the first time the killer has gotten sloppy. If we are lucky he might be getting cocky. If so, mistakes will be made, there always are, eventually. Maybe we'll get a break and find a print on one of the buttons. " Chuck referred to the miss-buttoned coat as he looked up at Dennis, the look of irritation still evident on his chubby face.

Dennis nodded in agreement. So far the killer hadn't made a mistake. However, the killer was upping the pace he had dumped more bodies over the past few weeks than he had since the crime spree had begun in early November. Once again the victim's throat had been cut clean by a very sharp object. As often as Dennis had seen death over the last twenty years, this was still a chilling and uncomfortable sight.

Dennis had seen death in all of its insidious shapes and forms, but death was something that he had yet to make peace with. These murders however, were more depraved than the other homicides that Dennis and Chuck had dealt with in the past. Most of them gang and drug related with the occasional spouse offing their partner.

"Look at her ankles. It's the same. You can tell by the severe indentations that she had been hung by her ankles before she was killed. The killer once again slowly slit her throat and drained all of the blood while she was still alive, bleeding her, like cattle at the slaughterhouse." Dennis said trying to keep the disgust from his voice. "It's the same guy and we still haven't enough clues to even come close to one suspect."

Dennis reached over to the side of her coat to see if anything would be in her pockets that might help with the investigation. He pulled out several gum wrappers and a ticket stub from a movie house. The date on the ticket said it was from the night before. They would follow up later in the day to see if anyone at the theatre would remember the couple. A boot lay a few feet from the body; it had fallen off when the killer had dumped her. Her handbag lay at her side. Dennis touched her frozen face; her skin almost seemed translucent, pale beyond imagination. He didn›t have to look at the girl's companion to know that he too had come to the same grizzly end.

"The crime scene investigative team will be here in seconds, they can go over the scene for fibers and prints. All of the other victims have been clean. No evidence that can be traced back to a suspect.

With all of our victims from out of town it's impossible to link them to one common suspect." Dennis said as he walked over to the male. "They look like they had one hell of a scare just before their deaths. I'm sure they were aware of what was happening just before he slit their throat. It would be terrifying to come to this kind of an end."

Chuck stood by Dennis as he bent over the young man and continued his summation. "I'm going to assume that they were drugged just before their deaths. The Coroner said all of the other victims but the first had a dose of halcyon just prior to their murders. It would have knocked them out long enough for our killer to tie them up without a struggle. Still, by the time he slit their throats they would have been fully aware of what was happening to them." Dennis said as he pulled the coat away from the young man's chest reaching inside the jacket pocket pulling out a small bag of soil.

"It's the same killer alright. He's left his calling card once again. What the hell is he trying to say by planting a bag of soil on each of the victims? This is one crazy bastard and we had better catch him soon."

Dennis placed the bag of soil back in the victim's pocket while a team of investigators descended on the area. Dennis stood and greeted the senior member of the team, a woman by the name of Corrine Wilson.

Corrine Wilson was a tall brunette with more curves than the Indianapolis 500. She was close to the same age as Dennis, fifty, but her face was holding up well. Strong features with smooth, wrinkle free skin, made her a shoo-in for a Dove commercial. Corrine's bulky winter coat covered up her abundant chest, an embarrassing divergent for Dennis. He always found himself straining to keep his eyes on her big, baby blues.

"What have you got, Kortovich?" Corrine asked as she drew closer to the scene.

"The same thing we've had for the past four months." Dennis said as he moved closer to Chuck, allowing Corrine to view the two victims now behind them. "More bodies than clues."

Corrine gave Chuck a friendly nod, turning her attention to Dennis. "I'm about as sick of this as you are. It's starting to get embarrassing. My reputation is on the line." Corrine said.

As Corrine moved closer to the male victim the rest of the team started to take photos and scour the scene. She was recently promoted to head investigator of her forensic team. A bright, energetic woman who had been divorced for almost a year, she had earned Dennis's respect. At almost six feet, Corrine could look a man straight in the eye. It made her seem powerful and in charge of her environment, qualities Dennis liked in a woman. He respected her ability and enjoyed working with her in the past. But recently he felt as if her energy had taken a strange shift toward him and he still hadn't been able to figure out what was different.

"Look, let me do my job. It's still early and I'm sure I can get the basics done by the end of the day. If you're up to it, we can meet for a drink and go over the preliminary report." Corrine said in a professional tone. "The medical examiner will need a little more time with the bodies, but I'm sure I can get you photo, print and fiber reports as well as a toxic screen. The soil analysis shouldn't take all day either. We have all of our resources working 24/7 on this one."

Dennis knew she was right and that everything the department had was being diverted to the multiple bodies that had been turning up all over Chicago.

"Call me as soon as you have anything and I'll see where I'm at then. If we have time for a drink, fine. If not, just scan and send me the report on my cell." Dennis said, noting a strange look crossing his partners face.

Dennis would have liked to ask Chuck what the look was about but members of Corrine's team were moving in on the male victim's body. It was time to leave and let the investigators do their stuff, besides Dennis was beginning to feel a little warm, even on subzero winter day. As they moved away from the scene Dennis turned around to take one last look. Corrine was still standing where he had left her, the look on her face intent. Dennis thought maybe a drink would be nice, after all this case had turned into a nightmare and Veronica, his wife, was used to his working around the clock.

Dennis Kortovich was one of Chicago's finest detectives. With nearly 20 years of service, Dennis' reputation for detail had made him irreplaceable when securing a crime scene. It was his ability to see the micro and macro of his surroundings that always amazed his partners. Dennis' notes were meticulous and he seldom forgot a conversation or an interrogation. He could recall hundreds of small details of cases long past, an ability many of his colleagues envied. His first partner, now deceased, used to say. "When in doubt, ask Kortovich," knowing that Dennis always had the details and answers well at hand. But lately he knew he was slipping and this case was beginning to make him doubt his long years of service and the department's recognition for his ability to solve crimes on good solid work and observation skills. He had never been one to hang his reputation on hunches. Give him the facts and only the facts.

«Well what do you think?» Chuck's brisk baritone voice broke into Dennis' thoughts, the strange look still on his partners face.

Dennis decided to ignore the look. Chuck had been Dennis' partner for the past four years and Dennis knew when to just leave things alone. Chuck's square face and evenly placed features gave him a familiar look, everyone felt as if they had met him before and they had, in the imaginations of their youth. His thick hair hung over bushy brows and full rosy cheeks. Dennis figured one day twenty years from now when Chuck hit seventy, he would look into a mirror and realize that if he ever grew a beard he could pass for Santa Claus. His stocky build and barrel chest would eventually succumb to gravity and become a paunch, definitely a Santa Claus stand-in. Dennis smiled. He really liked the guy. So far Chuck was his favorite partner and as such was a frequent guest at his home. Veronica, Dennis' wife of 30 years also had a soft spot for his chubby partner and thought it was a shame that he was single. An extra plate was always set at the table every second Sunday, with an occasional female guest thrown in for flavor. Veronica hated to see a sweet guy like Chuck stay single and she was determined to find him a good wife.

«What I think," responded a frustrated Dennis. «Is that there are too many bloody bodies and it›s starting to make me sick." Dennis removed his latex glove as they moved closer to the Crown Vic.

"These are numbers ten and eleven and the hell of it is we still haven't a bloody clue what the hell is happening. Who? Why? Not even one suspect. It's now the end of January and we›re almost four months into the investigation and we have nothing. Meanwhile the superintendent and mayor are having a shit fit.» Dennis said as he pulled the front door of the Vic open.

Once in the car Dennis pulled his warm gloves back over his frozen hands before pulling away from the scene of the crime, his foot pushed all the way down on the gas causing the car to veer to the right, just missing the police cruiser with the witness. He had instructed the officers to bring the young man to the station. They would need to handle the questioning of the witness themselves. Every 'T' would have to be crossed and 'I' dotted. There was so much heat coming from above they couldn't afford to miss a beat.

Dennis knew that his usual calm was beginning to crumble. This string of murders was just about the biggest and toughest case the city of Chicago had ever seen. A full task force had been pulled together after the fourth and fifth bodies had been found and it was Dennis who had been put in charge. Six more bodies later and he was feeling like a man going down for the third count in a boxing match, KO'd out cold for the match.

"So, what is it we know so far?" Dennis asked Chuck, wanting a brief overview of all that had happened to date.

"The first body was discovered alone, the next two were a young couple found together then numbers four and five, all within two weeks. Except for the first, all of the victims were found in pairs." Chuck flipped through his notes as he spoke. "It was early November when the first body was discovered and it is now three-quarters of the way through February and these two make the body count eleven." Chuck summed up what they both already knew. "Our killer is getting bolder. He is killing at a faster pace. If he starts to get too cocky he may start making mistakes. Till then we are out in the cold." Chuck said looking over at Dennis as he continued. "These latest two victims must be a yuppie couple. Their clothes were expensive, matching mohair dress coats. Rolex watches. The male's suit was Armani. Other than the gash across his throat, I'd say he was a real catch." Chuck rolled his eyes and then gave a small laugh. "Neither of them could be over twenty-five and from the looks of them I'd say they have a hefty paycheck in order to afford to dress the way they do. We will get more information once we run a check on their ID and prints. Before the end of the day we should know everything we can about them." Chuck slapped his notepad shut.

"There hasn't been any forensic evidence to go on so far and the killer seems to have knowledge of police procedures and the way we collect evidence. He or she has the ability to cut a clean, precise incision along the neck much like a butcher or meat cutter. It's hard to say what kind of knife made these incisions. We'll have to get the M.E. to nail that down. All of our victims are thirty or under.

There is also a small bag of soil planted on all of the bodies except the first, an indication that the first killing was done on an impulse while the others seemed planned. All of the victims had the same contents in their stomachs and were killed within hours of their last meal." Chuck finished, without the benefit of his notes. "What do you think the odds are that eleven people could be killed and all of them would have the exact same meal?"

"Slim, to none. But it seems each of them ate their last meal in their hotel room. I think the killer may have sent them the meal. Either they knew the killer, or it was an unexpected gift from a stranger. Never look a gift horse in the mouth. I'm sure the victims ate the meals without ever knowing who sent them." Dennis said, hoping he was right.

"If not, the killer would have to have stalked his victims first, something that seems unlikely given that they were from out of town. What information did you get from the ID in the women's purse?» Dennis asked knowing Chuck had made note of the information once the forensic team had arrived and processed the purse.

«As usual they're from out of town, New York. Pretty soon word is going to get out and no one will want to come to Chicago." Chuck answered, once again referring to his black note pad. "It seems someone wants to kill off our tourists and it isn›t good for business when they turn up dead. This makes visiting Florida look like a walk in the park." Chuck said referring to the car-jacking and murders that had plagued Florida years before. "Whatever else we find out will have to wait until the reports are finished. I'm sure Corrine will be only too happy to fill you in on the rest of the details over a drink." Chuck's tone was solicitous, the strange look returning to his face.

"What the hell do you mean by that?" Dennis asked, irritated by Chuck's tone.

"I think Corrine is going above and beyond the call of duty doing a rush on the reports and then inviting you for a drink. Why not just email you? Information and refreshments seems a little out of line don't you think?" Chuck asked.

"What's out of line? I think this case has us all spooked. Corrine has been the lead CSI in this investigation from the beginning and I for one am grateful that she has been willing to pull all the stops and get us the information back so quickly." Dennis said defensively.

"Why not invite me? I'm on this case as well. Let me assure you she wanted only you to meet her for a drink, I'm not invited." Chuck's tone was sharp. "Hasn't she noticed you are married?"

Dennis knew Chuck was usually easy going and enjoyed a good laugh at anything that would embarrass Dennis but the usual humor was lacking in his tone at the moment. He would likely get a laugh out of seeing Dennis uncomfortable at the thought of having a drink with a female colleague if it meant more than a work related event, especially a female with all of the abundant talent displayed by Corrine. But Dennis was sure it was just the heat of this case that had prompted Corrine to extend the unusual invitation.

"Look, I'm sure she assumed you would come too, after all, were a team. Why would she want to meet me alone? Corrine knows I'm married and she has never been anything but professional."

"Corrine has been divorced for more than a year maybe she's lonely?" .

"There are lots of single guys. I'm not the one to fill her lonely nights." Dennis gripped the steering wheel tightly as he maneuvered through the traffic.

"Are you sure of that." Chuck asked letting his question hang in the air.

Dennis tried to ignore his partner saying nothing in response to Chuck's question. Things had been different lately. He had been wondering about life and hadn't come up with any answer that seemed to make sense of how he was feeling. There was a restlessness that seemed to gnaw away at the pit of his stomach. He loved his wife and he loved his job. But somehow each day seemed a little flat. Maybe it was that each day offered more questions than answers, questions about his personal life and these crazy murders. Dennis had chalked his restlessness up to his inability to solve this case but the fact was he had been feeling this way for a long time.

Veronica, his wife was going through her own change of life. It had forced her to move into the spare room, an arrangement that didn't make intimacy easy. And as usual, she was as busy as ever. It seemed as if they had been drifting apart for the past few years. Often weeks went by before they connected. Dennis knew he loved his wife, but he seemed to be asking the same question lately. "Was this all there is?" He hadn't been able to find the answer.

"Look. Right now all I need is a hot cup of coffee and not a hard time from an old fart like you. I'm not about to get into trouble with Corrine or anyone else on the force." Dennis said bluntly, hoping Chuck believed him.

With an obvious end to the conversation Dennis continued to wind through the late morning traffic his thoughts turning back to the case where it seemed safe. Thoughts of murder were a lot more comfortable than thinking of having a drink with a woman like Corrine. Dennis pushed all thoughts of Corrine from his mind.

This case was getting to everyone and was now considered a 'heater' a high profile case. The press was all over it like gaudy makeup on prepubescent teen and the more murder victims that turned up the more the press piled it on. By now it would take a carving knife to peel away the muck and get to a likely suspect. Because the blood had been drained from the victims every cult and weirdo in the city was on the carpet for the murders. But so far nothing had turned up; the teams of investigators that Dennis had assembled to help solve the case were frantically chasing down every lead they could find. Chicago was a city with a raw underside and if you wanted to find something that suited your fancy from the weird to the wacky you didn't have to go far to find it. And these killings qualified as just about the most bazaar case Dennis and Chuck had ever seen.

After the first three bodies were found it didn't take Dennis and Chuck long to explore many of the satanic cults and devil worshipers in the hope of finding a clue, so far nothing. Now even the sickest members of the night world of Chicago were trying to give the police a helping hand.

The murders were bad for business and many of the after hour clubs had seen a decline in attendance because of the series of shocking murders.

They would have to dig a little deeper into the habits of the many night crawlers of Chicago to find out what the blood might be used for. And it was tough enough dealing with the usual thugs let alone a killer that left his victims looking like they had made a trip to a slaughterhouse.

* * *

It was now bright out; the clouds had disappeared as the sun shot gold beams of light on the frozen marshmallow world. Chuck could see Dennis' reflection in the window as they passed a large grove of trees. At fifty Dennis was what one would consider good-looking. Not great, just good, square jaw, straight nose, gray eyes and medium brown hair. Once it all came together he had an 'All American' look. Dennis' moustache covered a generous mouth and the dimples in his cheeks gave him a slightly 'Magnum' look. His broad shoulders tapered into a narrow waist. Chuck envied him the fact that he never worried about his weight a fact of life for Chuck. One of the most outstanding characteristics about Dennis was how neat he always was. As detectives, they wore their own style of clothing but Dennis seemed to put it together better than anyone else. You couldn›t really say he was a fashion plate but he usually wore his clothes in a way that made everyone else look slightly out of date. Maybe it was because Veronica bought his clothes for him but he managed to make them look better than anyone else. He could have been the CEO of a Fortune 500 company. He looked as if he came from money, but Chuck knew that was far from the truth. He just had good taste and a way of standing out in a crowd. Maybe that was why Corrine had asked Dennis out for a drink. Chuck had a bad feeling about the invitation.

Lately Chuck had seen his partner fall into a slight case of the blue's. It had started right after Dennis fiftieth birthday. Veronica had thrown Dennis a small birthday party with close friends and family. She was usually a great hostess but for some reason the party seemed half done, something out of line for the vivacious Veronica. And neither Dennis nor Veronica seemed to connect. This wasn't the usual loving couple that Chuck had learned to envy. It would be terrible if Dennis were to go through mid-life crises. Chuck decided he would have to keep an eye on his friend and make sure he didn't do anything stupid at this point in his life.

CHAPTER TWO

Once back at the station Dennis and Chuck headed for the conference room that had been converted into 'Command Central' for the special task force assembled for the multiple murder cases. As he swung open the double oak doors he was still impressed with the expensive furnishings in the room, a result of a recent renovation. The Superintendent had been able to twist a few arms to get the quality furniture not the usual cheap crap they were used to. A twenty-foot solid oak table that was rounded at either end gave the illusion that it was oval. Thick padded leather chairs were drawn neatly up to the edge of the table on either side, sixteen in all. Currently there were only eleven detectives assigned to the case, more could be added as needed and often the Superintendent or the Mayor would sit in on updates. Along the south wall directly to the left, was a huge, white board. Written on it in big letters were all the key words that tied this baffling case together. In bold capital letters it read.

TIME OF DEATH: Three to six hours from last meal.

All of the victims ate the same meal, steak, potatoes, salad, along with desert and wine.

METHOD OF DEATH; Hung by heels, throat slit, and blood drained from body, traces of halcyon in stomach.

PROFILE OF VICTIMS; All under the age of thirty. Victims were all from out of town, upper to middle income, first murder single, white, female. Other victims white couples.

OTHER COMMON DENOMINATOR FOR ALL VICTIMS; none apparent so far, may have been random. Killer probable didn't know his victims

B.O.S.F.O.B.

The cryptic code of initials stood for 'bag of soil found on bodies'. It had been agreed upon that no one would speak beyond the confines of their team about the soil for fear of alerting the press to this valuable clue. Pictures of the victims lined the west wall. All were taken post mortem. Pictures of pale human beings all with a different story, except that they all died the same way, but why? Dennis hoped that he and Chuck would find the answers to that question soon. If not, the body count would continue to climb.

* * *

Chuck was ready to go home to bed his report finished, he liked to keep the paper work simple, while Dennis was methodical and meticulous. They had been going around the clock and Chuck could sleep on a dime. Dennis on the other hand, couldn't.

"Go home Chuck. There's nothing to do until today's report is in. I'll head home in a few hours as soon as I'm done here."

"You don't have to ask twice. Call me when you hear something. I'm bushed and can hardly think straight. Half of my nights are spent seeing our victims swinging from their heels with blood gushing from their throats. I sleep better in the daytime."

"Let the ghouls deal with these murders for now I am just going to forget about what kind of sick mind comes up with these kinds of killings." Chuck said grabbing his heavy winter coat as he went out the door.

Just as Dennis was about to call it a day and head home two veteran police officers who had been assigned to the case came into the boardroom. Both were in an animated discussion about another case they were currently working on. They followed calls generated by the press and Dennis' case was their primary investigation while the death of socialite Margaret Mendoza, the wife of lawyer Jackson Mendoza, was their secondary case. At the moment most of his team had several unsolved homicides to deal with in addition to Dennis and Chuck's case.

Margaret was the daughter of Robert Grey one of the richest men in Chicago and great grandson of one of the original Rubber-Barons. Grandfather Grey held the majority of control over the rubber industry that sold raw material to the tire manufacturing companies, making him a very rich man and one of influence. It was a shock to Robert Grey when his only daughter fell in love with the handsome Jackson Mendoza. Mendoza was a third generation, Spanish Columbian who was rumored to have ties with the illegal drug world of the Columbian drug lord, General Zaragoza.

"I don't care what you say. Mrs. Mendoza would never have gone to a Doctor like Clarence Fielding. She's probably never even been on the south side of Chicago let alone gone to the office of that loser." Detective Ferine O' Donnell sounded miffed and irritated at his partner who seemed unwilling to let the discussion end.

"Who knows what these rich socialites will do and maybe it's like the husband said, she didn't want her friends to know that she wasn't feeling well. I can understand that especially in a town that 'tells it all' like Chicago." Detective Patrick Getty shot back.

"Hey, don't you two have something better to do than argue about how the rich get medical treatment?"

Dennis welcomed the diversion. He liked the two officers, who were ten years his junior. Ferine was well over thirty-something a man whose rugged good looks had most of the female staff drooling over the 'Irish Stud' every time they came into contact with him. He was often the butt of many of the other officer's clumsy sex jokes. After all, Ferine was single and could get laid anytime he wanted.

At this point he seemed less interested than he had in the past, the result of a crush on one of the new female rookies who so far wouldn't give him the time of day.

On the other hand, Patrick was bald and a little paunchy the result of a fifteen year marriage to a wife who was rumored to be a gourmet cook. From the look of Patrick's protruding belly Dennis felt the rumor must be true. Patrick was a man of great humor and joy which made him one of the most popular lunch and after hours' drinking partners on the force.

"Hey Dennis, I didn't see you there. I was so busy trying to knock some sense into this lazy partner of mine." Ferine turned toward Patrick and gave his shoulder a friendly punch.

"What are you still doing here? It's OK to go home once in a while you know!" Patrick said as he approached Dennis.

"I was just heading out when you two loud mouths came busting in. By the way, what's the argument about?" Dennis always found it amusing to watch the volatile but loving chemistry of the two partners.

"It's the other case we're working on, the death of Margaret Mendoza. Her husband told us that she had two doctors." Ferine said. "One has been the family doctor for over thirty years but apparently she had a second doctor for the past three months, a Doctor Fielding. But he's a scummy low life who has a major drinking and drug problem and I can't see why a classy dame like Mrs. Mendoza would even go to the south side, let alone to the grubby office of this slime-ball. It just doesn't make any sense yet he was the last one to treat her before she died. My partner here is giving me a rough time and says no one can figure out the rich." Ferine gave Patrick an evil look. "Besides, I think there is something fishy going on and that there is a tie in on our case to the new Doctor. It all just seems too convenient to have a new doctor and then die so suddenly."

"Hey I didn't say I didn't agree with you, I just said who can figure out the rich? They sometimes do some strange things. If this Mrs. Mendoza were anything like what her friends say she was, I agree. She wouldn't go to a man like Dr. Fielding." Patrick said, a wicked smile crossing his face.

"I think I'll let you two boys figure things out on the Mendoza case without me, I have enough on my own plate. By the way how are things going on the phone leads?" Dennis hoped something would have turned up that could lead them to even one suspect.

"Every nutcase in Chicago has us running all over the place. Half of the weirdo's and mental patients have confessed to being the killer, especially the ones with a fascination for blood. They think that they have killed the victims by sucking them dry, but none of them know about the soil so we've had to rule them all out."

Ferine aimed his answer directly at Dennis turning his back on his partner letting him know he didn't appreciate the rough time he had been given in regards to the Mendoza case.

The team of men and women that were assisting Dennis and Chuck with the case had been sworn to keep the information about the soil secret. It was only spoken of among the members. It would be the one thing that would help them to determine if they had the real killer. Often in high profile cases they would have some unbalanced 'son of a bitch' confess to the crime. It was only the small details that could confirm or deny if they were the real killer. The press was often their biggest problem. If too many details were published about the case then the fake confessor could fool the cops into thinking they had the murderer, often letting the real killer go free until he struck again. The result was egg on the face of the investigating officers. The details about the bag of soil were guarded within the investigation circle, and Dennis hoped it would stay that way.

"All right, I have a bunch of other leads on my desk. If you two could follow up on as many as you can we may turn something up."

"No problem. We have a lot of delay time on the Mendoza case. We have to get access to medical records of Mrs. Mendoza and the husband is giving us a rough time. We talked to the original doctor and you could tell he wanted to co-operate with us but he can't unless we get a warrant to get access to his records. We're just waiting to get a request petition before a judge." Ferine said.

"Well good luck but I'm out of here. I'll see you both at tomorrows briefing. Let's hope someone on the team turns something up."

Dennis grabbed his coat and left the two detectives still bantering different theories back and forth. They were a great team and debate seemed to be what held their ten-year partnership together.

* * *

Dennis received a call from Corrine just as he was getting into his car the report was finished and she wanted to go over it with him. Veronica was still working in her salon. She had been a stylist for over thirty years and after selling her salons she went home based and had never been so happy, after all, getting to work was just a step away. As Dennis looked at his watch he figured he had time to meet Corrine at O'Malley's for a drink and still be back for supper with Veronica and his daughters, Natasha and Katrina.

As he walked into the bar he noticed several other officers that he knew. It seemed strange to be meeting Corrine at a bar. It was the first time he had ever met with her outside of the crime lab. Still, it was work and this case was different from all of the others. Everyone needed more than a drink to get through this one. What harm could a few drinks be?

He knew even as he asked the question of himself that he was wading ankle deep in water that was rising fast, and he with-out a lifeboat. Was something about to bite his ass? He hoped not. How far he was willing to go before he was pulled under he still didn't know. Hell, he loved his wife. Corrine was a colleague and he had no idea what she was thinking. All she wanted to do was to give him some information on the case. He was making stuff up in his mind that he had no business thinking. Dennis shook off his thoughts and tried to stay aloof. He had a job to do and it was up to him to stay focused. As he walked up to the table where Corrine was sitting he noticed that under her bulky coat she was wearing a low cut, V necked top, that exposed her abundant chest. The smile that greeted him showed even, white teeth. Dennis hoped he could stay focused. He cursed himself. What was happening? He'd never felt so disconnected.

"What's up Corrine?" Dennis asked as he sat down beside her.

"I wish I could tell you we found something different with these two but I can't. It's all pretty much the same, still no prints or fibers. I even got the toxicology reports back from the lab, Halcyon, like all the others." Corrine said, looking sheepish. "I shouldn't have called you out again tonight. I could have e-mailed you the reports but this case has me so frustrated I needed a drink and I hate to drink alone." Her voice was soft and appolegetic.

Dennis knew how Corrine felt. This case was taking its toll on him as well. Something was different about how he felt about life, his family and his job. He didn't want to look deeper. It would mean making the right decision and right now Dennis didn't feel like doing the right thing.

CHAPTER THREE

The Beef Chateau, one of Chicago's best-known steak houses, was full of the sounds of success that Saturday night back in early in November. Waiters and waitresses were dressed in the famous Red & Gold of the Beefeaters 16th century guard regalia, setting the tone for an authentic glimpse of the past. The eager young men and women hustled to pick up their plates loaded with hot potatoes, salad, mushrooms and thick slabs of homemade bread smothered in sweet garlic butter before they went to the hot sizzling grill to pick up their individual cuts of beef, cooked to perfection.

Back in the kitchen plates clattered and silver resonated with a low-pitched 'clickity-clack' the way heavy cutlery sounds when it's dumped onto cooling trays fresh out of the dishwasher. The atmosphere was up beat and it had a rhythm and pace that was unique.

The owners of The Beef Chateau, Lexy and Bara, had found a surefire recipe for success. Everything was brought in fresh daily except the beef. It was cut and hung in a huge meat locker at the back of the twelve thousand square foot restaurant for a full twenty-eight days of perfect aging. Lexy

Cohen and his wife Bara had lived for well over six decades and for over forty years they had been in the food business. It was only in the last ten years that they had come up with the idea behind the Beef Chateau. The problem with most eateries was that the menu had too many items and spoilage often ate away at profits. The Beef Chateau featured steak, steak and more steak. Everything was streamlined. Their prep chefs had it down to a science.

Every night things came together like a symphony, the movement, flow and rhythm reaching the crescendo around nine when the crowd in the restaurant would hit its peak. The number of out of town guests often rivaled the locals and The Beef Chateau had developed an international reputation. Grade A Prime Cut Beef, the finest in the world. Grain fed it had a taste like no other and the citizens of Chicago loved it. But it was the secret to the special steak marinades prepared by Brian Bentham, their head chef that soon became the most sought after secret recipe in town, a combination few could beat. The Beef Chateau was located off of Columbus Drive not far from the Goodman Memorial Theater. This had added greatly to their success with a large before and after theatre crowd.

Lexy looked around the dining room at the end of the evening feeling a great deal of pride. November was a great month for business and Christmas parties were well underway. The Red and Gold décor seemed to be especially appropriate at this time of year. As a good Jew his reason for loving Christmas was mainly due to the increased dining traffic but some of the sounds and spirit of the season flowed over into his joyful soul, making him especially happy during the holiday season and Hanukah was also his favorite time of year.

Everything about Lexy made you think of circles. His round head, big blue eyes, round button nose, full round lips, round wire rim spectacles, round shoulders, round tummy setting atop short legs, all seemed to add to the impression of a big butterball. Even his temperament was well rounded; always smiling, he seemed to enjoy each minute with just the right level of excitement or dismay.

Most of the staff had been with Lexy from the beginning. And a few had even followed him from his very first venture forty years ago, a specialty deli. His maitre d' André was now a little over sixty and Lexy remembered how young he was back then and still seemed to be now. As he looked back at the many years he had been with Andre, Lexy hoped his old friend would be with him for many more. One more look around. As usual everything seemed perfect. Chairs were tucked neatly under the tables, white tablecloths, stemware, and coffee cups all in their correct place. Everything was clean, crisp and perfect, lights out.

Next Lexy waddled over to the kitchen where his wife Bara was overseeing the final cleanup. Once through the double swinging doors his eyes were assaulted by the bright lights of the kitchen. All was quiet. The dishes were piled neatly in stacks of forty covering a long row directly behind the huge cold and hot preparation area. Stainless steel gleamed from everywhere. When the late morning shift arrived they would fill the huge cooler trays with fresh crisp lettuce, shredded carrots, green onions, bacon bits and all of the other items needed to compliment the steaks. A huge row of deep silver trays ran along the south wall near the prep station, full of over a dozen different dressings. All made fresh by the head chef, Brian Bentham. Secret recipes like the steak marinades, unique to the Beef Château.

«There you are my little dumpling.» Lexy cooed to his wife Bara as she rounded the corner coming from the office at the rear of the restaurant.

«Where did you think I would be? Ten years and every night you find me here checking out the kitchen to make sure everything is clean and put away. Did you lock up the cash and transfer the debit's to the bank?» Bara launched back at Lexy.

«What else? Every night I do the same thing and every night we have this same conversation.»

With that final remark, Lexy kissed Bara on the forehead, slipped his arm through hers and headed for their coats at the back of the restaurant. Like clockwork it was always the same. As they donned coats and gloves, Brian Bentham, the head chef emerged from the meat cutting room.

Lexy knew Brian still had another two or three hours of work left. He had to finish cutting hundreds of steaks, some with the automated processor and dozens more by hand. Only the very best cuts were good enough for their clientele. Next Brian would prepare his special marinade. Most of the steaks would soak in his 'world famous' secret recipe for up to forty-eight hours while they were kept in a special cooler to ensure their freshness. Brian was the best chef the couple had ever had and they had learned to love him like a son. It had taken several years for Brian to open up to the couple and even after a decade of service he still seemed guarded. Lexy and Bara knew Brian was giving them all that he had of himself and they were grateful for him being a part of their business.

«Another great night," Brian said as he came forward to give his customary hug to Bara. "Drive carefully and I›ll see you both tomorrow."

Brian stepped back and gave Bara a loving look. "Are you losing weight? I swear you're at least ten pounds lighter than yesterday. If you don't watch it you'll

melt away to nothing and then how much fun will it be to pull your chest into mine." Brian winked down at Bara.

Hugging Bara was great. At only five foot two inches she was almost as wide as she was tall. With a full, forty-eight inch chest that felt like a soft cushion when you pulled her into your arms for a hug, she was a wonderful pillow of a woman. Bara still had a beautiful face surrounded by thick naturally curly hair, cut above her shoulder and dyed dark. Her hair framed her clear, creamy white skin and made her bright blue eyes seem almost bottomless when her intense gaze fell upon you. Dark brows and long lashes made it difficult to pull your eyes away. Forty years ago she was a real beauty but now she was a bit of a dumpling, although still beautiful.

"Oh you bad boy, you tease me so!" Bara laughed, beaming like a schoolgirl as she looked up into Brian's handsome face.

"You know I love you and think you're the most beautiful woman in the world and I never want you to change. So just stay the same so I can get the best hugs in the world." Brian squeezed a little harder making Bara give out a happy, girlish squeal.

This completed a customary ritual that ended every night just before midnight for the past ten years. Although the evening's custom remained the same, tonight would be an exception. Tonight Brian›s life would change forever.

Once Lexy and Bara left through the back door Brian pulled the dead bolt back, locking the door securely. He usually set all the alarms but tonight was different; he would have to open the front door for a special guest set to arrive very soon so the alarm would be of no use. As Brian walked through the kitchen toward the double swinging doors his thoughts turned to the past, to a day he would never forget, a week before his ninth birthday. The day his life was altered forever, the day his mother left. At least that's what his dad told him but he never believed it. Not then, not later and not now.

He knew with all the heart and might a little boy could possess that his mother would never leave without him. He knew his father's secret and he had learned to hate himself for keeping it. He never told anyone back then and now it was too late.

Brian still remembered that night so long ago when the police showed up to investigate. His dad made his story sound pretty truthful. She had run off with her hairdresser, Max Fielding, who was also missing. All of the stuff in the hairdresser's apartment was gone as well as his mothers, but the lady who owned the salon where Max worked said he would never leave without his paycheck, so she called the police. She told them he had been friends' with Brian's mother and that's when they came to investigate and talk to his dad.

"Mr. Bentham, I'm officer Crain and this is Officer Butler." The taller cop introduced his partner and himself when his father came to the door.

"We have had a complaint about a friend of your wife's who's gone missing and we were wondering if Mrs. Bentham was in and could answer some questions."

Brian stood behind his father when the door was answered. Brian's heart beat faster, waiting for his father to give an explanation.

"Don't hold your breath officers you won't find my wife here or that slimy hairdresser seeing as my wife ran off with him last week. He can have her. She's nothing but a slut. The whore was dicking him for the past year and now she's gone off with the bastard." Joe Bentham's face was a twisted mask of contempt.

"Do you have any idea where she is or if you will hear from her?" This time it was the second cop, Butler, asking the questions.

"I haven't a fucking idea but if you'd like to come back next week who knows? Till then, I've got nothing to say about where she is. She can go to hell for all I care; no good bitch left the kid and me. Now I gotta do everything myself."

"Well, if you hear from her will you have her call us?" Butler said handing a card to Joe.

"If I hear from the bitch I'll pitch her ass onto the sidewalk."

"If we don't hear from you within the week we will have to come back and reinvestigate."

"Fine!" Joe slammed the door in the officer's face as he turned toward his young son slapping him across the head as he passed by heading for the kitchen to get a a beer.

"Don't even think you know anything. Your mother left for a faggot hairdresser she never loved you and she never loved me. They will never find her she's gone for good and no one but the devil knows where she is and the cops will never find her."

But no one asked Brian where his mother was. No one cared what he had to say, the little boy that was left behind, the little boy that knew where his mother's suitcase was and all of her things. The box filled with her jewelry and all of her bathroom stuff. The stuff she would never leave without. And he knew she would never leave without him. No one asked about the secret place in the basement behind the wall. The place only his father was supposed to know about. The place where his father kept 'those' magazines and the video's he would watch late at night.

Brian prayed the officers would ask him a question but they never even looked at him. They came back a couple more times but Brian's father managed to convince them that she was just another runaway wife. And each time they ignored the little boy who stood by his father, his eyes pleading to be asked about the secret place. He couldn't tell and they never asked. He was just too scared to cry out that his dad was a liar.

At night in his dreams he did cry out for his mother's arms. But it was his dad who jerked him from his sleep, shook him hard and told him to stop crying like a baby. It was his dad's fist that slammed into his face and twisted his hair telling him no one cared. Not about him or his 'fucking' mother. Brian could smell the stale whisky on his breath from an evening of drinking. He never forgot the stale smell of his father or the sweet smell of his mother.

* * *

Brian was startled out of his dark glance at the past by a loud rap at the large oak door at the front of the restaurant. As he swung it open, Brian knew he was about to cross a threshold that few ever had and once having done so he could never turn back.

Standing outside the door was a beautiful tall redhead. He had spotted her earlier that night and had asked Sherry, her waitress, if she was from out of town. She dined alone and often that meant a visitor and The Beef Chateau had many. Sherry confirmed his suspicion.

As was his custom he went to her table to welcome her making sure the food was to her liking. While he engaged her in a conversation he felt as if a dark cloud had lifted from his brain and suddenly he knew he had a solution to a problem that was keeping him up after his late night shift. Long nights and little sleep were taking its toll.

Brian had felt a strange surge of power as he approached the woman's table. He knew women found him irresistible and he hoped his charm would hold for the invitation he was about to make. It was in the instant that he introduced himself that he knew that the dark side was about to take over. After all, hadn't his father told him often enough that he was no good?

"Hi, my name is Brian Bentham the head chef. I hope the meal is to your liking." He leaned over to get a whiff of her perfume.

She seemed flustered that he had come to her table and he planned to take advantage of the moment. Brian took her hand after a formal shake refusing to let go. Her hand was cold, his warm, and he could tell she felt a connection in the instant that they touched. Her face went red and she lowered her eyes, unable to keep contact with his piercing baby blues.

"If you're not doing anything later I would love it if you would come back and take a private tour of the restaurant. Please don't think I'm being forward; it's a custom to ask a special guest back each night and share the secrets of the marinades and dressings. And tonight I can't think of anyone more lovely to spend the rest of my evening with." Brian flashed a brilliant smile few could resist.

He didn›t know if anyone would fall for a line like that but she did and now she stood just inside the door. Brian locked the door behind her just before he took her coat and flashed one of his most glorious smiles.

* * *

Gloria couldn›t believe her luck. She was in Chicago for a week staying at one of the better hotels just a few blocks away. She was from New York, working for a promotional company featuring a new computer disk business card. Gloria knew the electronic card would be a great success. She had been pitching the disk to a high-level brokerage firm for the better part of a week. With the sale closed she was ready for a little rest and relaxation. Tonight would be special, an evening she was looking forward to. The Beef Chateau was one of the best restaurants in Chicago and she wouldn't have missed eating here for the world. As it turned out, the food wasn't the only great thing being offered.

When the head Chef came to her table she didn›t know what to expect. His long legs, lean body and broad shoulders were magnificent, but it was his face that made her heart stop. Blue-black hair, dark skin and flashing blue eyes made her heart flop once. Then he smiled and her heart did a second flip-flop. His even white teeth covered by a full sensuous mouth made her feel weak in the knees. He was glorious and he wanted her; she could tell by the way his eyes seemed to devour her. There was a moment when their eyes met that she thought she could see a flash of light. She got a feeling unlike anything she had ever felt before.

It was like he was having a sudden realization, as if a solution to an unanswerable problem had suddenly been solved just by looking into her eyes. It was intoxicating and now here she stood in front of him. Hopefully there would be more than wine and a secret sauce. Hopefully there would be sex. Great sex if the looks this man gave her, were any indication.

* * *

«Welcome Gloria. I wasn›t sure you would take me up on my offer. It›s the first time I›ve ever invited anyone back. It was just a line when I told you I did this every evening. This is really my first time.» Brian took her coat as he guided her into the dimly lit interior of the restaurant.

Brian could tell by the red glow starting to run up from her chest to her pretty face that Gloria was excited and flattered by the attention Brian was showering on her. He knew he had her in the palm of his hand.

«No problem, I was hoping tonight would be something special too." Gloria said, her breath catching in her throat.

«More special than you will ever know.» Brian guided Gloria into the recess of the restaurant knowing tonight would be delicious, simply delicious."

* * *

It was easier than he had ever dreamed. Cattle were more difficult to lead to the slaughter. The rest of the evening had been easy. With the chit chat over he had gone in for the kill. The final drops of blood were now just dripping slowly over her chin. He spun Gloria around once looking objectively at his delectable sacrifice. She hung limply from her ankles, the strong ropes cutting into her flesh. Swinging from the meat hook, her hands dragged along the cold concrete floor still bound by the duct tape. Gloria's red hair dragged softly against its cold surface. Brian had drained all of the blood from her body. He had to hold her head to one side to ensure that the flow of blood would leave as little mess as possible. She had been alive and fully aware when he brought the small automatic blade to her throat. She had struggled for the first few minutes and it wasn't until near the end that she stopped jerking around. As the blood drained into the plastic bucket Brian was excited by the amount he had collected.

He would be able to make a wonderful batch of his secret marinade with this warm, red elixir. When he was finished he poured some of the blood into a new marinade pan. Brian thought it was nice to have the bright, shiny, stainless steel pan used only for this sacrifice. Gloria would never know it but her blood was needed like air. It had become as important as his very breath and Brian knew he could no longer live without it. They say once an animal has a taste for blood, it can no longer go without. Brian now knew it was true. The thirst for blood and the sense of well-being it gave him had driven him to do what he had never thought possible.

* * *

Brian had spent the first hour of the evening sharing a wonderful white wine, Kaiserstuhl 98, with Gloria, asking all sorts of questions. They sat in the front of the restaurant, music softly adding to the sense of romance Brain was trying to create.

Did she have any family in Chicago, friends? When was she due back? Where did she work? Did she have to check in back at the office? He tried to get as much information as he could, after all he knew how important it would be if he wanted to get away with the murder.

Murder, he never imagined that one day he would do to someone what he his dad had done to his mother. Kill. He had imagined the murder of his mother in his head a thousand times. How had she died? Strangled? Stabbed? Shot? Was it an accident? No! When his dad moved the other woman in Brian knew his father had planned it. The bitch was still living in his house years later sleeping in his mother›s bed and he still hated her. But he hated his father even more. «Like father, like son!» No! Never! He just had to do this. It wasn›t personal. He just needed the blood. Everything in his body yearned for the feeling he got from devouring what was forbidden.

When Brian felt he had enough information to complete his plan he invited Gloria to take a tour of the restaurant. When he opened the cooler door he knew she would find the meat processing room fascinating.

"This is where we cut the steaks." Brian said as he welcomed her into the room. "Come over here and I'll show you how everything works."

Brian walked into the middle of the room where a very large wooden block stood. Overhead a rack of knives hung, each on a special tool for the carving of the steaks.

"We cut our steaks here. But it would be much too difficult to cut them all by hand so I have the help of an automated processor." Brian said as he turned around and opened a small door off to the side of the wall. "It's tucked in here and runs on a special arm."

Brian pulled the round saw like apparatus from its small chamber. It looked like a small buzz saw and ran on a pulley that would allow Brian to maneuver it with exact precision. Brian then walked over to a large set of doors that was off the right of the room. He opened it and showed Gloria a room full of trays stacked on dozens of shelves. They were wrapped in layers of what appeared to be cellophane.

"This is a flash freezer. It hits sub zero in seconds. We can freeze our extra steaks and they will still be as fresh as the day they were cut. This process makes it's impossible to tell that the meat was ever frozen once it is thawed." Brian said with pride.

Once out of the flash freezer Brian moved Gloria closer to the middle of the cutting room. On the meat table he had a wooden mallet used to beat and tenderize some of the cheaper cuts of steak. He turned Gloria so that her back was against table in an effort to give Gloria a kiss. She moved in closer, her head turning up to receive his lips. Brian knew he had her.

As he slipped his hands up her skirt to the warm recess of her body he knew he would be able to enjoy her in more ways than one, sex and murder, an intoxicating mix.

* * *

It was finally over. Now he had to make sure that the cleanup and the disposal of the body was meticulous, he knew what to do. After he had enjoyed the warmth of her body Brian's hand closed in around the mallet. Gloria lay face down on the wooden table. As Brian withdrew from her body he had the mallet in his hand. Before she knew what was happening he brought the mallet down upon her pretty, red head. She had no idea what had happened. By the time she came too, Gloria was bound by her ankles with rope, hoisted off the ground by a hook that usually supported a hind of beef, her hands bound by tape. Her mouth was also taped shut, Brian had heard enough from her pretty lips. Why spoil the moment now by listening to her pleading for her life. He preferred to stay aloof. He simply swung Gloria around, bringing the automated blade to her throat. Brian knew how to slaughter his prize and take advantage of the blood her body would provide.

The terror Gloria would feel in the moment would provide a wonderful mix of hormones, a very powerful combination. Once Brian soaked his steaks in the special blend of wine, blood and herbs he knew that the human blood would provide a special kick. He would once again get that unique feeling. But first he would have to make sure he cleaned up. There would be no evidence. Brian knew what to do.

As he lay Gloria out on the floor that he had covered with bubble wrap he stroked he face and kissed her lips once more, cold. He carefully washed her hands with warm soapy water. Finally he brushed her hair with the brush he found in her purse, placing it back in her handbag. He made sure that there would be no fibers or hair from his body found or her. After he hit her with the mallet, he had dressed himself in a full white disposable body suite. He had used them in order to keep the cutting room hygienic, making sure that the beef that was served would never have a human hair, now it would protect him from leaving any clues for the police. . Next he carefully examined her lifeless body to make sure there was nothing on her clothing to tie her to the meat cooler or to him. He ran a large piece of tape over her dress, panties and private parts, making sure he removed any of his hair that might have attached itself to Gloria. Brian had made sure he wore protection when he came inside of Gloria. No DNA. Brian knew that the rope fibers around her ankles were a standard issue, the kind you found at any hardware store, nothing unusual there.

The floor of the cooler was unpainted and washed twice daily with a water-soluble detergent: the kind of soap common to 90% of all commercial buildings, again, a tough lead to follow. The cops could follow the smallest clue and Brian would try to give them as little as possible to go on. He knew that the contents of her stomach would be examined and he would have to be sure that no one would suspect that her last meal would have been at The Beef Chateau. He would be sure to dump the body a few days later, but for now a little hocus-pocus.

He had a sure fire way of confusing the police. If they could pin down the time of death they could trace the murder back to the restaurant but he had a way to baffle the police and he knew he could get away with it. Next he dragged her body into the special freezer. Brian wore his latex gloves, the kind you find anywhere. This would prevent him from contaminating the body and leaving any evidence. As Brian laid the body in the center of the freeze zone and closed the door he turned the dial slowly. She would be frozen in less than 30 seconds.

The process was called 'flash freeze' but in reality it took a little longer. He had removed the bubble wrap before placing Gloria in the freezer. He knew it couldn't stand up to sub zero temperature that was needed to freeze the body quickly. Once done, he re-entered the cooler and gently rolled the body onto the wrap. Frozen, she needed to be handled with care. Again he examined the floor to make sure it was spotless. He didn't want any evidence that the meat freezer might give the CSI team, he knew would investigate.

Brian would have to load the frozen corpse into the back of his van. He would then take the body home with him and put it into his empty deep freeze before dumping it a few days later. He would have to lay out a clear plastic tarp over the van floor to ensure that fibers would not be found in the wrap, nothing that could lead the police back to him. Now all that was left was to load the body into the van, lock it up tightly and return to the restaurant to finish his evening's work. Later he would plant the rest of his evidence to lead the police on a wild goose chase.